P9-BYU-534

Raves for the *Alien* novels:

"For those craving futuristic high-jinks and gripping adventure, Koch is an absolute master!"
—*RT Book Reviews* (top pick)

"Koch still pulls the neat trick of quietly weaving in plot threads that go unrecognized until they start tying together—or snapping. This is a hyperspeed-paced addition to a series that shows no signs of slowing down." —*Publishers Weekly*

"Aliens, danger, and romance make this a fast-paced, wittily-written sf romantic comedy."
—*Library Journal*

"Gini Koch's Kitty Katt series is a great example of the lighter side of science fiction. Told with clever wit and nonstop pacing . . . it blends diplomacy, action and sense of humor into a memorable reading experience." —*Kirkus*

"The action is nonstop, the snark flies fast and furious. . . . Another fantastic addition to an imaginative series!"
—Night Owl Sci-Fi (top pick)

"Ms. Koch has carved a unique niche for herself in the sci-fi-romance category with this series. My only hope is that it lasts for a very long time." —Fresh Fiction

"This delightful romp has many interesting twists and turns as it glances at racism, politics, and religion en route . . . will have fanciers of cinematic sf parodies referencing *Men in Black*, *Ghost Busters*, and *X-Men*."
—*Booklist* (starred review)

"Gini Koch mixes up the sometimes staid niche of science fiction romance by adding nonstop humor, blockbuster action, and moments worthy of a soap opera."
—Dirty Sexy Books

DAW Books Presents GINI KOCH's
Alien Novels:

TOUCHED BY AN ALIEN
ALIEN TANGO
ALIEN IN THE FAMILY
ALIEN PROLIFERATION
ALIEN DIPLOMACY
ALIEN VS. ALIEN
ALIEN IN THE HOUSE
ALIEN RESEARCH
ALIEN COLLECTIVE
UNIVERSAL ALIEN
ALIEN SEPARATION
(coming in May 2015)

UNIVERSAL ALIEN

GINI KOCH

DAW BOOKS, INC.
DONALD A. WOLLHEIM, FOUNDER
375 Hudson Street, New York, NY 10014

ELIZABETH R. WOLLHEIM
SHEILA E. GILBERT
PUBLISHERS
www.dawbooks.com

Copyright © 2014 by Jeanne Cook.

All Rights Reserved.

Cover art by Daniel Dos Santos.

Cover design by G-Force Design.

DAW Book Collectors No. 1675.

DAW Books are distributed by Penguin Group (USA).

All characters and events in this book are fictitious.
Any resemblance to persons living or dead is strictly coincidental.

If you purchased this book without a cover you should be aware that this book may
have been stolen property and reported as "unsold and destroyed" to the publisher. In
such case neither the author nor the publisher has received any payment for this
"stripped book."

The scanning, uploading and distribution of this book via the Internet or via any other
means without the permission of the publisher is illegal, and punishable by law. Please
purchase only authorized electronic editions, and do not participate in or encourage the
electronic piracy of copyrighted materials. Your support of the author's rights is appreciated.

Nearly all the designs and trade names in this book are registered trademarks. All that
are still in commercial use are protected by United States and international trademark
law.

First Printing, December 2014
1 2 3 4 5 6 7 8 9

DAW TRADEMARK REGISTERED
U.S. PAT. AND TM. OFF. AND FOREIGN COUNTRIES
—MARCA REGISTRADA
HECHO EN U.S.A.

PRINTED IN THE U.S.A.

To the memories of all those we've loved who are gone from us too soon in this world—somewhere in the multiverse we're still together laughing.

ACKNOWLEDGMENTS

I know I sound like a broken record, but first and foremost I have to thank my wonderful editor and agent, Sheila Gilbert and Cherry Weiner, for always taking care of me and being incredibly fun, supportive, and patient while doing so. Couldn't do it without my fantastic crit partner, Lisa Dovichi and my main beta readers, Mary Fiore and Veronica Cook. Sure, they're my mum and daughter, but they don't *have* to read the final drafts in a day—they just do because they know I need them to.

As always, love and thanks always to all the good folks at DAW Books and Penguin, to all my fans around the globe, my Hook Me Up! Gang, members of Team Gini, all Alien Collective Members in Very Good Standing, Twitter followers, Facebook fans and friends, Pinterest followers, and all the wonderful fans who come to my various book signings and conference panels—you're all the best and I wouldn't want to do this without each and every one of you along for the ride.

Special shout-outs to: Joseph Gaxiola and Colette Chmiel for continuing to be the best assistants anyone could have, near and far both; Missy Katano for help with many things military and Lynn Crain for help with many things diplomatic and Alphabet Agency related; Tamara Baker, Moskintia, Dee Haddrill, and my other Aussie fans for helping me with all things Australian any time of day or night; Dan King, for hooking me up with Moskintia; Chrysta Stuckless, Missy Katano, Mariann Asanuma, Jan Robinson, Terry Smith, and Koren Cota for all the delicious and lovely things you've bestowed on me to keep me going; Oliver & Blanca Bernal for always having a welcoming home; Adrian & Lisa Payne,

Hal & Dee Astell, Andrea & Duncan Rittschoff, and Stacy Stolz & Gordon Drinovsky for always supporting me wherever I go; Jennifer Stuckless for some awesome fan art; Raul Padron for late night Cuban language assistance; my Paranormal Romance Dream Team pals—authors Caris Roane, Erin Kellison, and Erin Quinn—for laughs, advice, and solidarity; my Wyked Women Who Write friends—authors Jordan Summers, T.M. Williams, Sharon Skinner, T.L. Smith, and Marsheila Rockwell—for fun times at cons and while eating cupcakes, and for being there when I needed help, teasing, or someone to veg out with; all the members of The Stampeding Herd—Lisa Dovichi, Barb Tyler, Lynn Crain, Hal Astell, and Marsheila Rockwell—for ensuring that I always have someone to run with, metaphorically speaking; Mysterious Galaxy San Diego and The Poisoned Pen Scottsdale for support at cons, events, and book signings; Craig & Stephanie Dyer, Brad "My Man" Jensen, Joseph "Pick A Nickname" Gaxiola & Edward "GF #1" Pulley, Duncan & Andrea Rittschoff, Adrian & Lisa Payne, and Linda Johnson for fantastic and much needed help during Phoenix Comicon; Chris "Delicious" Swanson for extreme late night brainstorming; Robert Palsma for ensuring I know someone likes me every day; awesome author L.E. Modesitt, Jr. for excellent advice and friendship; Missy Katano (gettin' the hat trick) for her detailed work on cataloging and more for the earlier books in the series; and especially Emily Albee, aka Amadhia, for letting me bring her into Kitty's worlds.

Last but never least, thanks and love as always to my husband, Steve, and daughter, Veronica. I wouldn't trade the two of you for anything, not even superpowers and a host of hotties in Armani. Honest.

THE FORMER PRESIDENT OF INDIA, Abdul Kalam, shared a lovely sentiment—Look at the sky. We are not alone. The whole universe is friendly to us and conspires only to give the best to those who dream and work.

He's totally right that we're not alone, of course. But with all due respect, former president Kalam is dead wrong about the entire universe being friendly to us. There are a lot of "others" out there, and while some are all for helping good ol' Earth, there are plenty who think we should be avoided, enslaved, or destroyed.

George Carlin said that if it's true that our species is alone in the universe, then I'd have to say the universe aimed rather low and settled for very little.

I know he's right. I just know there's more out there than we've seen. I look for it, sometimes, when I feel alone. I look for all the "others" out there. So far, unless they're in a comic or a book or a movie, I haven't found them.

I'm not sure what's actually more surreal—that the universe is teeming with life of all kinds, or that I've somehow gone from being a single marketing manager to the wife of the Vice President of the United States in just under five years.

Oh sure, it was a long road between "there" and "here"—much of it filled with fights against many very bad things, both extraterrestrial and very terrestrial. Humans are really the worst though. We're devious and nasty on a scale that, thankfully so far, none of the aliens showing up to visit or move in seem able to manage. I'll take a fugly space monster over most of the human megalomaniacs I've dealt with over the years.

Being married to an alien, at least one from Alpha Four of the Alpha Centauri system, has definitely been the highlight. Well, our hybrid and scary-talented daughter is a highlight, too. Jeff and Jamie make all the change and general surreality that has become my daily life worthwhile.

Sometimes, I wonder what it's all about. I mean, I have a pretty great life, and I love my family. I'm a good wife, mother, and daughter, and I do things that matter. But there are days when I just can't do anything right, and I wonder what's wrong with me.

Oh, of course, I have bad days. Sadly, since becoming the Second Lady, or whatever I'm really supposed to be called now, there's a lot of pressure. Shockingly, with more public scrutiny comes more ways for me to screw up. And there are days when I wonder what's wrong with me.

Sometimes, I just want to see what it would be like, if things were just a little different. Maybe not a whole lot different, just enough to where I could do something more, be something more . . . be something else.

Sometimes, I just want to know what it would be like if I was me, but maybe a little less unwillingly famous and a whole lot more competent on the regular people things I sometimes seem incapable of managing with anything resembling smoothness or competence.

* * *

Some days, I just want to be somewhere else. A place where I do everything right.

Some days, I'd really like to be somewhere else. Where everything I do is right.

Hey . . . is there an echo in here?

CHAPTER 1

MY BRAINS OOZED out of my ears.

Not from being shot or something. From boredom. Massive, stultifying boredom. Boredom on a scale so epic I didn't think anyone could really fathom it. I could barely fathom it and I was living it.

Cheers went up from those around me. Well, not most of those immediately around me. I was surrounded by Americans. Sure, more than half of them were actually aliens only one, two, or zero generations out from Alpha Four in the Alpha Centauri system, but still, beings that lived in America and had been raised as Americans. And this was *not* an American pastime.

"You're sure this is cricket? I mean, the game. The game that millions of people around the world supposedly love?"

This earned me a dirty look from everyone near me, American or no. I'd tried to keep my voice low, but apparently cricket shared something in common with golf, that most boring of Scottish games that had infected the U.S., in that the fans were hushed unless something "exciting" was happening on the field.

I wasn't actually sitting next to my husband. As the newly minted Vice President of these non-cricket-mad United States, Jeff was sitting a couple of rows below me with now-

President Armstrong and the Australian Prime Minister. Technically, as his wife, I should have been sitting with them.

Wiser heads had prevailed, however. Despite a great deal of effort and patience on the part of the Head of the C.I.A.'s Extra-Terrestrial Division and the American Centaurion Public Relations Minister—otherwise known as Charles Reynolds and Rajnish Singh—and a week's worth of immersion therapy, I still hadn't been able to grasp or enjoy cricket.

Since we'd been in our mid-twenties Chuckie had lived half the year in Australia, and Raj had been born and raised in New Delhi. Ergo, they both actually enjoyed cricket. In fact, Raj was quite a rabid fan, and Chuckie had an Aussie team he supported. Meaning if anyone was going to get this game through to me, it should have been them.

Only, it took the complexity of baseball, the slowness of golf, and the bizarreness of croquet, and managed to turn them into something that, sports lover though I was, I just couldn't manage to follow, let alone like.

The hope had been that I'd pick up enough to have the light bulb go off while watching a live match and suddenly become an expert. Hope might have sprung eternal, but it was definitely being dashed against the wicket today, because I still wasn't sure where the wicket was, let alone what it was or why it existed other than to be the current bane of my existence.

It didn't help matters much that the entire point of this extravaganza was the Australian government's visiting to show support for both the new administration in particular but also aliens in general.

Because of Operation Destruction, the entire world knew aliens lived here. The entire world also knew that there were a lot of different alien races out there, and that some of them really hated humanity. Of course, some of them liked us just fine, in part because we'd given the exiled A-Cs a home.

However, there were still a lot of people around the world who felt that aliens were the worst things to hit Earth, and they wanted us gone. Off the planet, in work camps, or merely wiped off the face of the Earth, they weren't picky. What with Jeff and then-Senator and now-President Armstrong's surprise landslide win, knowing an alien was a heartbeat away from the presidency had all these anti-alien groups in a tizzy of epic proportions.

Australia had its share of alien haters. Club 51, our biggest, most coordinated anti-alien enemy, had made a lot of inroads into Australia, meaning one of America's biggest allies had a huge anti-alien population.

So it was vital for us to make the Australian Prime Minister and his retinue feel happy and comfortable. The PM was a huge cricket fan, hence this game. That I was supposed to feign excitement about.

Wished I'd studied acting instead of business in college, because, despite my desire to be a good wife and representative of my constituents, I was failing to convince anyone that I liked this sport.

The fact that we'd spent money to fix up the stadium where the Redskins played football to look like a cricket field didn't help. They weren't my team—we might live in D.C. now, but I remained true to my Arizona Cardinals and their tradition of usually losing—but I'd have committed many major felonies to have seen the Redskins trot onto the field and toss the pigskin around. I couldn't pick a Redskins player out of a lineup, but still, football was a sport I understood and enjoyed.

I loved baseball, too, but neither the Washington Nationals nor my beloved Diamondbacks were going to be showing up to save my day. There were lots of guys on the field who, according to the program, were quite cute. Not that you could really see them. So I didn't have that distraction going for me. And when I could see them, they were standing around in a giant circle or running back and forth along a small strip of dirt in the middle of the field far, far away. For whatever reason, this didn't make my Sports Gene go wild.

My phone beeped and I dug it out of my purse. At a normal sporting event I'd never have heard it. At this one, not a problem. Of course, I wasn't supposed to spend time on my phone when we were at public events, but our daughter wasn't with us and the text could be about her.

Sadly, it was from the head of Alpha Team. James Reader was none-too-gently suggesting I plaster a look of enjoyment onto my face. He wasn't technically at this event—Alpha Team's job was to protect, not to be the face of American Centaurion. Had no idea where in the stadium Reader and the others actually were, other than nowhere I could see them. However, they could see me, and I looked, if I took his text to be accurate, "like you're about to die while passing gas."

I replied with one word: "charming." Wanted to say other words. But my Secret Service detail had clued me in—I had no such thing as privacy anymore.

Dropped my phone back into my purse as people nearby gasped. Something was happening on the field. It appeared to be exciting, based on the crowd's increased murmuring. Couldn't tell what the heck it was. Looked around. Right now would be a great time for a parasitic superbeing to form, or for an intergalactic invasion to happen, or anything else that would alleviate the boredom. Waited hopefully. Nothing. Apparently the Powers That Be liked cricket. Or had been bored into inactivity.

"When is the halftime or intermission or whatever?" I asked Raj. Again, tried to keep my voice down, but apparently the acoustics in this stadium were great, because I got another host of dirty looks.

"There isn't really a break like that, as I've explained." He managed not to add "over and over again," but I could see the thought written on his face. "We're watching a T-Twenty game, so there will be a short intermission in about an hour."

We'd already been watching this for an hour and had been sitting here even longer. I wasn't sure I could stay conscious for another hour without moving around. And there were at least two more hours to get through after the short intermission. And this was a "short" game. "Real" cricket could go on for days. This game had to have been created to torture political prisoners. Wondered if I could invoke the Geneva Conventions as a way out of the boredom. Probably not. My luck never went that way.

Plus I was uncomfortable. Under normal circumstances— you know, before my husband had somehow become the Vice President—I'd have been in jeans, my Converse, an Aerosmith thermal of some kind, and my nice, warm snow jacket. Or I'd have been in what the A-Cs, who were love slaves to black, white, and Armani, always wore—a black slim skirt, a white oxford, and black pumps, with a long black trench coat.

Because we were now some of the most public of figures, I was required to pay a lot more attention to what I was wearing. I'd also been assigned my own color—iced blue. I was in iced blue as much as I'd been in black and white before. In fact, I missed black and white, I was in this blue so much nowadays. This meant that for this event I was in an iced blue pantsuit, an off-white Angora sweater, and neutral high-heeled boots. And pearls. Supposedly I looked great. I felt remarkably stupid dressed like this at a sporting event.

Chuckie got a text and grunted. "You need to pretend to be having fun," he said. Either his voice hadn't carried or everyone else agreed with him, because no one shot the Evil Eye toward us.

"I'm trying."

"It's not working."

Made up my mind. "Then, I'm out of here."

CHAPTER 2

"WHAT THE HELL?" Chuckie sounded ready to lose it, though he managed to keep his voice down.

"You can't leave," Raj said, as he tried to watch the so-called action on the field and look at me at the same time, with limited success.

"No freaking duh. I'm going to the concession stand. Now."

Raj, sensing that the emergency was about a negative three on a scale of one to ten, turned his full attention back to the match.

"Couldn't we just send someone?" Chuckie asked, sounding relieved. "You're going to have to go with a contingent, and that's going to be noticed."

"I need to piddle." I didn't, but I needed to splash cold water on my face and drink about a gallon of coffee to make it through this ordeal. Of course, I was in makeup, so cold water on my face was probably out. It was also February and we were outdoors in the freezing cold. I was at risk of dying from hypothermia as well as boredom. Hypothermia sounded better.

Chuckie heaved a sigh. "The Secret Service has to escort you."

"Fine. They probably want some coffee and to use the bathroom, too."

This earned me a dirty look I chose to ignore. I got up. The entire row behind me got up as well. There was some grumbling from the crowd behind us. I had no idea how, but we'd somehow packed this stadium with every cricket fan in, by my guess, the entire United States. Maybe we'd imported them from Europe or something. Regardless of the statistics Raj had thrown at me, I couldn't believe that more than about fifty thousand Americans liked this sport.

The row behind me was made up of my wide variety of bodyguards, of which my Secret Service detail was only a part. This detail included two women and four men—the wives of Vice Presidents rarely got as much security as I rated, but apparently, my reputation had preceded me.

All of the Secret Service agents assigned to us had picked up cricket in less than a day and understood the sport. They didn't love the sport, but they understood it. They, like everyone else, had given it the Old College Try in terms of teaching me. Unlike everyone else, they'd given up quicker. I respected their intelligence and ability to identify a lost cause quickly.

Two of the other men behind me were Len Parker and Kyle Constantine. I'd met them right before Jeff and I got married, when they were still playing football for USC. They graduated into the C.I.A. and had been the bodyguards Chuckie had assigned to me early on in our stint in D.C. Len and Kyle both understood cricket, but as former football players, felt it wasn't a real sport. This made me love them even more than I already did.

The others were from Centaurion Division. Four A-C agents, one human. The human guy was Burton Falk, who I felt actually reported up to the person who was most likely coordinating the majority of my actual protection—Malcolm Buchanan.

Buchanan had been assigned to me by the Head of the

Presidential Terrorism Control Unit, also known as my mother. Mom had put her best operative onto me and my daughter, Jamie, at about the same time Chuckie had assigned Len and Kyle to me. There was never a day I didn't appreciate Mom's protective instincts, because Buchanan had saved our lives quite a number of times.

He wasn't here, that I could see. He had Dr. Strange powers, and if he didn't want you to see him, you didn't see him. He insisted it was just training. I didn't believe him.

However, while I didn't see him in the stadium, I knew he was nearby, watching for threats to my safety. Sadly, Buchanan was no help in terms of the threat to my sanity currently being perpetrated on the field.

Of course, my getting up meant that everyone on one side of me had to get up, too. Because Chuckie was the smartest guy in any cricket audience, he'd put himself in the aisle seat and had me right next to him, meaning he was the only one who had to stand to let me out.

He heaved another sigh and offered his hand. "I'll go, too. Why not? It's not like this is the first match I've seen in ages or anything."

"Wow, bitter much? You can stay. I'm sure my thirteen other protectors can handle my trip to the bathroom."

"Advise Cosmos that Cyclone and Playboy are on the move," Evalyne said quietly into her lapel. She was the head of my Secret Service detail. The Secret Service gave out nicknames to those they were protecting. Based on Chuckie's wealth, position within the C.I.A., proximity to us, and personal relationship with me and the rest of American Centaurion, he was considered one of those under protection.

A Secret Service agent next to Jeff nudged him. Jeff turned around. Chuckie cocked his head, Jeff shared an obvious "go with her" sign. Chuckie nodded, and I gave up. Gave him my hand, he helped me out of the aisle, then took my elbow and helped me up the stairs to the concourse. Cameras flashed.

"Great," he muttered.

"Yes, this is us, off to have our torrid affair with my husband's blessing and a baker's dozen of witnesses. We're so smooth, you and me."

He laughed. "It's amazing how you make it sound ridiculous and the tabloids make it sound like we're actually committing adultery every five seconds."

"It's one of my many gifts. You know what's weird?" I asked as we reached the concourse level. "When it bothered Jeff, it didn't bother you. Now that he just finds it amusingly annoying, you find it distressing."

"One of us has to cover the worrying about our reputations part of this goat rodeo we find ourselves in."

"Thanks for taking one for the team. Crap. I left my purse under my seat." I almost never left my purse anywhere. Experience had shown that I needed to have it, and its contents, with me at all times. Sure, I might not need hairspray, a Glock and several ammo clips, the giant hypodermic needle and adrenaline I still had to slam into Jeff's hearts more often than I'd like, or most everything else inside it. But I sure needed my wallet to buy coffee.

Chuckie sighed. "I'll buy whatever, Kitty. I don't want to go back and forth any more than we have to."

"I have money for her," Len said. "Jeff gave it to me, just in case."

"I feel like an infant."

As I said this, Evalyne shot some hand signals at the agents with us and everyone fanned out. The three A-Cs disappeared. Well, they used hyperspeed to check out the concourse, but to human eyes, they were here one second and gone the next.

Of course, my eyes weren't fully human any more, just like the rest of me. Due to our enemies pumping Jeff full of Surcenthumain, what I thought of as the Superpowers Drug, he'd mutated. His sperm had mutated, too, so that Jamie was born extra with a heaping side of special. And she'd passed a lot of that along to me.

The A-Cs were back. They were all troubadours, meaning that they reported to Raj. "Cleared," Manfred said.

Falk wasn't looking at any of us but was, instead, staring at the TV screens that were installed about every fifty feet, so that spectators who were buying concessions wouldn't miss the action on the field. He shook his head. "Sorry, but we have a problem."

CHAPTER 3

"GOD, WHAT NOW?" Chuckie asked as he looked at the screen Falk was staring at.

I did the same. The game wasn't on. Instead it was the anchor team for whatever sports news station that was covering the game. Couldn't hear them, but the stadium had closed-captioning on all the screens, and I could certainly read.

The general insinuation was that it was obvious I hated cricket. The discussion centered on whether I hated the sport, hated the Aussies, hated politics, hated the Armstrongs, hated my husband, or hated Chuckie. Or some combination thereof.

"Wow, does it get any better than this?"

"Probably," Evalyne said as she took my other arm. "Heading to the Excuse Station with Cyclone," she said into her lapel.

Chuckie laughed as Evalyne led me away and to the bathroom, the rest of my Secret Service detail trailing us. "I really need to go," I lied.

She snorted. "Right." We got inside and she and Phoebe, my other female Secret Service agent, checked every single stall. The couple of women who were in there finished up and scurried out.

I knew without checking that the four male Secret Service

agents were blocking both doors to this bathroom, two to each entrance, meaning that no one else, other than Elaine Armstrong or another woman within our little Circle of Protection, could come in here until I left. Under normal circumstances, this meant I was the fastest woman in the world in here. Today, I didn't feel the need to rush.

"You don't have to pretend to go for our sakes," Phoebe said. "You're probably doing less political damage in here anyway."

Per Chuckie, and I saw no reason to doubt him, most Secret Service agents didn't act informally with their assigned subjects. However, I'd managed to stand the official Secret Service formality for about a day.

Then I'd had a very private and meaningful talk with those assigned to me, wherein, assisted by Len and Kyle, I explained that they would call me Kitty, I would call them by their first names, and we would act like normal people whenever we were in private, or I would make life a living hell for one and all.

They'd all seen the wisdom of being casual. Len and Kyle had also shared how I rolled with them. Falk had chimed in with his impressions of me, too. Basically, no one on my protection detail could claim that they didn't understand how I operated. Which, happily, appeared to be working out. We were, by now, one big informal family whenever we were in private. This meant, among other things, that I got honesty from the people who understood far more about what was going on than I did.

"Thanks, Pheebs. I appreciate the support. It's not my fault this is the most boring game ever created."

Evalyne shook her head. "It's not that. At all."

"Really? It is to me."

"No," Phoebe said. "Evalyne's right."

"Explain what you mean, Ev. It has to be more interesting than whatever's going on out on the field."

Evalyne sighed. "Look, if, before your husband moved into the Vice Presidency, you'd been bored, and the three of us had been wandering around, trying to find something to do, and we'd stumbled upon this game? You'd have suggested we give it a try, because it's something new. We'd have gone in, you'd have asked someone near us what was going on, you'd have listened and paid attention. Then you'd have looked at the program. You'd have chosen which team to root for based on which team had the cutest guys, or which team had the most impressive record, or, preferably, the team with both."

"Or you'd have supported the team of whomever we were sitting by," Phoebe said. "Then, you'd have gotten into the game. By the end, you'd be a fan. Maybe not a huge fan, but you'd have your team, have a favorite player, and have made friends with those sitting around us."

"How can you assume that?"

They both sighed. "We've read up on you, it's required," Phoebe replied. "Think about it. If the scenario we just described had happened, wouldn't you be having fun?"

Considered this. "I guess so. Probably."

"You're not enjoying yourself because you're being forced to be here," Evalyne said. "Everyone tried to cram this knowledge down your throat, so instead of it being a fun outing, it's a job. And it's a job you didn't sign up for."

Washed my hands slowly. Not that I needed to, but that way I'd be able to honestly say I'd used something in the bathroom. "I suppose you're right. So, how do I fix it? And, based on what Burton pointed to on the TVs, I need to fix it."

"Just pretend no one spent the last week trying to make you like and understand this sport," Evalyne suggested. "Look at it as a sociological experiment. You need to determine what it is that everyone likes about this game. Two of the men close to you love the game—why? Focus on figuring it out, not fighting against it."

"I can do that. I think."

Phoebe shook her head. "They've made you so tentative. I understand why you're rebelling."

"Jeff didn't become VP because he wanted to. He did it

because it was the right thing to do for our people and country."

"I didn't mean the Vice President. Or any of your allies." Phoebe shrugged. "But your enemies' attacks are taking their toll. And I don't mean their physical attacks. I mean the ones you're trying to handle here—the innuendo, the insinuations, the pressure to be some sort of perfect political wife."

"Yeah. All that sucks."

"And it's affecting you negatively," Evalyne said. "So, let's go out and get you some coffee. Then, try to figure out why much of the world thinks this sport is the best thing going. It'll at least make you look like you're paying attention."

"Sounds like a plan."

We left the bathroom to find Chuckie and the rest of my detail standing there. The A-Cs each had two cardboard trays with four cups each. We were carting a lot of coffee. Maybe I'd make it through after all.

Chuckie had a giant cup in his hand, which he gave to me. "They make lattes here. It's a triple vanilla latte with lots of extra vanilla in it."

"I love you. And I say that with full knowledge that someone's lurking in the shadows and that it will be on the news within the hour."

"Let's get back, I want to see what I can of the match."

"Oh sure, it's all about *you*."

We chuckled all the way to the edge of the concourse, me happily sipping my latte. To find that the crowd was very animated.

People were jumping up and down and acting like normal sports fans for the first time. There were a set of older men who were flashing the V for Victory sign at each other, only their palms were turned in, not out. Figured this was how the Aussies or cricket fans in general did it. Nothing else was normal about this game, so their "we're winning" sign being a little backward was par for the course. The crowd was, hands down, the most excited they'd been since getting inside the stadium.

Because the crowd was standing and we were no longer around the TVs, I couldn't actually see what was going on down on the field. However, clearly it was a big deal thing, and per my chat with my Secret Service gals, I needed to get with the program. And what better way to do so than to share in the joy of whatever had happened while we were getting coffee?

We hustled back to our seats, to see everyone in our section standing as well, meaning I still couldn't see what all the fuss was about. However, I was going to show willing or I was going to die trying.

Due to the fact that everyone had something in their hands, other than the Secret Service detail, who were doing their usual Threat Watch activities, Chuckie was ahead of me going down the stairs. To let me into my seat, he and Manfred walked down and handed Jeff one of the trays of coffees, clearly for him and the rest of the bigwigs.

I was taking a step down as the Prime Minister turned around and smiled at me. I flashed him the Aussie V for Victory sign.

And all hell broke loose.

Certain moments of your life move in slow motion. This was one of them.

As I held my hand up, I saw Chuckie go from relaxed to horrified. He lost his grip on the coffee tray as he lunged up toward me, shouting, "Noooooo!"

Peripheral vision showed that Raj who, like the rest of the crowd, was standing, had spun toward me at hyperspeed and was also lunging for me.

The Prime Minister's expression went from pleasant to seriously pissed off. Then it went to freaked, as Jeff, who barely had a grip on the coffee tray, spun around to see what was going on. This, of course, meant that the coffees flew out of his control and, seeing as this was my life, slammed into the Prime Minister and his wife, while managing to splatter the Armstrongs as well.

All of this happened in a split second, and in that split

second, I also managed to lose my balance. As I went down, my coffee flew into the air and, because of how I'd been standing and holding the cup, it sailed right at the Prime Minister. A direct hit, too.

I spun to try not to slam my face into a chair or concrete steps. Managed it, but wasn't able to tuck my head too well, which was a pity, because I hit, hard.

The last thing I saw before I blacked out was Jeff, Chuckie, and Raj, all looking freaked out and pissed off. Not the nicest vision, really.

CHAPTER 4

YESTERDAY HAD PRETTY MUCH SUCKED. I was glad it was past, and had no idea how today was going to go, but one bad day in the past was always better than a bad day in the present or future.

No matter what the day or even night had been like, though, we managed to keep one thing sacred—the morning. It's hard to train kids to get up a little later, and harder to train non-morning-people to wake up early, but we'd done both.

I loved this time, as my husband ran his hands over me, then pulled me close up against him. "Mmmm, morning, baby."

I turned over and snuggled my face into the hair on his chest. He was more morning compatible than me, so he took my kissing his pecs as a decent greeting.

Snuggling turned into more, quickly, helped by his hands stroking my breasts and his tongue stroking my neck. He knew all the right spots to spend time on. As I started to moan, he chuckled against my skin. "Sing for me, Kitty."

Our house was well soundproofed, and, really, he was on "the" spot, so I acquiesced. I was a good, totally turned-on wife that way.

I remained turned on while he slid my nightie and his pajama pants off. Of course, he was still stroking my neck with his tongue and nipping it with his teeth and touching me all over, which might have had something to do with my sounding like a cat in heat.

As he slid into me my wailing increased. All this time together and he was still the Gold Standard, and he proceeded to do all the things he knew I liked. Of course, I liked a lot, so he had plenty of options to go for in order to practice and perfect his technique.

We did have a bit of a sexual routine though, centering mostly around how fast he could bring me to orgasm the first time. This morning, as he rolled onto his back and put me on top of him, the first one arrived quickly. As he thrust into me and I rubbed against him it hit and I gasped. "Oh . . . God . . . so good."

"That's what I like to hear." He pulled me to him and kissed me deeply as my body shuddered.

Once I quieted, a bit, he moved us into a sitting position, my legs wrapped around his back. We'd used this position a lot when I was pregnant and still liked it. He was deeper inside me, but not in an uncomfortable way, and it was very romantic, too.

Our arms were wrapped around each other, and he kissed me deeply again as we rocked together, each little thrust sending him a bit deeper inside me, making me start to shudder from pleasure again.

His arms were tight around me, as one hand slid up the back of my neck and into my hair and the other went down to the small of my back. I clutched at the back of his shoulders as we went faster and faster. How long we were like this I wasn't sure because I was focused on all the feelings he created inside me and out. But ultimately the friction increased to the point where I couldn't have kept myself from climaxing if I'd tried. Not that I'd ever tried that in my life, and saw no reason to start this morning.

I flipped over the edge and he joined me. The feeling of him erupting into me made my legs tighten around him as I moaned into his mouth and he growled with pleasure in return.

We stayed like this, kissing each other and stroking each other's backs, until our bodies quieted. Then we untwined and lay back down, his arm around my shoulders, holding me close, my head on his chest, playing with the hair there.

He kissed my head. "I love you, Kitty."

I heaved a happy, fulfilled sigh. "I love you, too, Chuckie."

CHAPTER 5

"THINK WE'RE UP TO THE ZOO TODAY?" Charles asked as we enjoyed our snuggle time.

"No idea. Jet lag seems to get worse each trip, instead of better."

"And it doesn't help that we had to come back to the States earlier than normal, either, I know. And I'm sorry."

I hugged him. "It's not your fault. Well, I mean, it is because you're the smartest guy in every room, and government think tanks tend to get reliant on people like you. But otherwise, I know you'd rather be in Oz right now. In the nice weather."

He chuckled. "True enough. But, we'll make the most of our extra time here, I promise. Maybe we should see if there's decent snow still on the slopes up north and go skiing."

"While that sounds great, I don't want to get into the jet again for at least a week. A long car trip would be an even worse idea. And considering how cranky everyone's been these past two days, you and me included, I'm kind of hoping everyone sleeps in today in a big way."

No sooner wished for than denied. There was a soft knock at our door. Charles pulled the covers over us. "Come in."

Peter stuck his head in. "So sorry to interrupt, darlings,

but the little ones are up and bounding and I don't know how long I can keep them entertained and quiet. Emphasis on quiet. Even with your father's help, Kitty, I might add. Jetlag has officially worn off the entire family."

"Is James up?"

"Yes, he is. However, he's doing the market run for me this morning so we can all actually have, well, brunch by the time all the adults are truly up and ready for it. Your father and I have already entertained the children to the extent of our copious abilities while only allowing them a scrap of bread and sip of water so they'll still eat with the rest of us. Hence why they're past impatient to get to the two of you."

"We'll be ready in about five minutes," Charles said. Peter nodded and closed the door. Charles pulled his pajama pants on and helped me with the nightie, then settled the pillows on the bed so we could sit up against them comfortably. "Ready for the onslaught?"

"Always." I snuggled next to him. "Especially when you prep me like you just did."

He grinned. "It's one of my favorite things." The door opened and three blond heads bobbed into view. "And here are the rest of my favorite things."

"Daddy! Mommy! Get up! Get up!" Max shouted as he jumped onto the bed with us. He might have been our second child, but he tended to lead. "We took a vote and everyone wants to go to the zoo today!"

Charlie clambered up. "Not quite everyone. Uncle Peter says we need to wear lots of sunscreen even though it's cold outside. Grandpa Sol says we just need to wear hats." He reached down and helped his little sister up. "What do you think, Daddy?"

"I think you'll want to do what your mother says," Charles replied as he put Jamie onto his lap. "What do you think, Jamie-Kat?" Everyone felt Jamie looked exactly like me. Couldn't argue, but I knew I'd smiled a lot more at her age. Maybe we just didn't smile enough at her.

Jamie didn't answer, just leaned her head into his chest.

Max burrowed in between us, back against the pillows. Max was a real blend of the two of us—my eyes, chin and body structure, Charles' everything else. Per his father, and mine, he had all my personality, though.

Charlie sat between us, facing us, legs crossed. He looked just like Charles to me—same eyes, wiry build, facial structure, and personality—which was a nice stroke of luck, since he was named for his father. I recognized his Serious Face expression—I'd seen it on his father's face since we were both thirteen. "Jamie doesn't want to go."

"Did she say that?" I tried not to sound hopeful.

He shook his head. "But I can tell."

"Me too," Max said. "She wants to stay home."

I chucked Jamie under her chin. "I know you want to watch your mirrors, Jamie-Kat. But the animals will miss you if you don't go see them."

She shook her head. "Bad things are going to happen."

Jamie rarely spoke. But the few times she did, she spoke perfectly, as if she was a much older child. However, she never spoke to share fun, happy, or loving things. It was always to tell us something bad was going to happen. So far as we could tell, she'd only been right a couple of times. But those times had been devastating.

Charles hugged her. "Bad things happen all the time. But they're not going to happen to us today."

Before he could say anything else, Jamie sat up straight, then clambered off the bed and trotted out of the room. I tried not to notice that Jamie hadn't waited for or asked for a kiss from either one of us. That she'd let Charles hold her this morning was good enough.

The rest of us looked at each other. "I love her, but she's weird, Mommy," Max said finally.

Charlie shot a disapproving look at his younger brother. "She's our sister, no matter what. Besides, it's probably just that Uncle James is back." It probably was. Somehow, Jamie always knew when James was near.

Max shrugged. "I know." He hugged me. "It's okay, Mommy."

Charlie crawled over and hugged me, too. "Yeah, it'll be okay, Mommy. I promise."

"Wow, I guess I'm not doing a good job of not showing the two of you that I'm worried about your sister."

Charles hugged all of us. "We're all worried. But we'll fix her, or keep her safe, or do whatever we have to to keep our family safe and make it all right, right?"

"Right," the rest of us said in unison. Then the boys both laughed and shouted, "Jinx!" And, as kids will, kept on shouting jinx at each other as they got off the bed and left our room.

"Ready for a shower?" Charles asked me. I nodded and he laughed. "I won't pinch you if you break the jinx."

"Awww, you spoilsport." Sighed. "I didn't mean to let the boys know how worried I am. I just wish Jamie was . . ."

Charles put his arm around my shoulders and hugged me. "It's okay, baby. She loves us. She's just . . . slower with some things."

"Right. We'll see what the doctors here think. D.C. has really good doctors."

"Yes." He kissed my head. "Let's get cleaned up and ready to face the day."

"I wish I knew why she wanted that mirror so much more than she wants us." I hadn't meant to say this aloud. But sometimes the words slipped out.

We didn't talk about what was wrong with Jamie much, because it made Charles defensive for reasons I didn't understand and that meant we would fight, even though I hadn't meant to start a fight. We only really fought about Jamie, and never because we weren't in agreement for what to do—because we both had no idea—but because we were both so worried about her.

But this didn't seem to upset him. "Well, maybe she just wants to look at the prettiest girl in the world all the time." He stroked my cheek. "I know I do. All the time."

"Flattery will get you everywhere."

"Yeah? Will it get me lucky in the shower?"

"Scrub my back and you can have me any way you want me."

He grinned. "Never let it be said that I don't take advantage of the best deals offered."

CHAPTER 6

SHOWERED AND DRESSED, we headed downstairs. While I adored living in Australia and missed all our friends there the moment we got onto the jet to leave, I loved our home in D.C., too.

Charles and I had grown up in Phoenix, and I'd always figured that's where we'd live and raise our family. But life had led elsewhere. We spent half the year in Australia and half in the U.S., and we'd had to settle on the East Coast for Charles' job at the think tank. So all of us—Dad, Peter, and James included—had dual citizenship. Charles said that it was worth paying extra taxes if that meant cutting down on the hassles of inter-country travel and living.

Fortunately, we had plenty of money. Charles was a self-made multi-millionaire several times over, both in business and in the stock market. So we lived well, albeit not lavishly.

We probably could have lived in a ritzier neighborhood, but I'd fallen in love with Colonial Village the first time I'd seen it. Back then, just as now, it was beautiful—streets lined with incredibly well-maintained, gorgeous homes and beautiful, mature landscapes, butted up against Rock Creek Park. The neighborhood was safe, the people who lived in it pleasant and friendly, and I could honestly say that when we arrived, every time, it was truly like coming home.

My dad, James, and the kids were all in the dining room by the time we got downstairs. Dad came over and gave me a peck on the cheek. "Feeling a little better today, kitten?" he asked me quietly.

"Yeah, I think we all are. How are you doing?"

He hugged me. "As well as always."

"Sol's complaining that I'm hogging the kids," James said. He was still the handsomest man I'd ever seen, even handsomer than Charles. Which explained why he was the top male fashion model in the world. Jamie was snuggled in his lap and the boys were hanging off of him. James flashed us his cover boy grin. "Oh, and, morning, you two. We were all wondering if you were going to sleep forever."

"We were, but then we realized that you're a diva and would demand we witness you stealing our children's affections," Charles said with a grin.

"Again," I added.

"And to think I gave you control of my career." James shook his head. "It's a miracle I can afford to eat."

"And we force you to live with us, too, don't forget that," I added. "Because we want to make sure you're going to pay for the kids' educations. They love you best after all."

"It's all I have," James said dramatically, while the boys giggled. "If not for the love of the children, I'd be cast aside until you needed me."

Peter snorted as he wheeled in the large serving cart. "Yes, Jimmy, you're suffering so. My darlings, take your seats. Breakfast is served."

Charlie and Max went to their seats, Dad picked Jamie up and put her into her chair between him and James, while Charles helped me into my chair and then sat beside me. I sniffed. "Peter, that smells amazing."

"Just a little eggs Benedict made in our family's unique style for the adults, and scrambled eggs with lox and chives for our precious little ones." Our family's special eggs Benedict addition was lox. We all loved lox. And Peter's hollandaise sauce was to die for. I started to drool a little.

"And fresh-squeezed orange juice!" Charlie added.

"And cocoa, tea, coffee, milk, and whatever else we want to drink," Peter said as he put a perfectly arranged plate in front of me. In addition to the delicious-smelling egg dish, there were beautiful breakfast potatoes, sliced fruit, and a small serving of yogurt.

Peter was, as always, amazing. We'd only been in D.C. for a day or so and he had the household running like we'd never left. Peter could have had a full staff—we could certainly afford it—but he insisted that he preferred to ensure that he remained invaluable. Once we were all served and Peter was seated, Dad said a short blessing, then we all got to the business of eating breakfast.

Conversation centered around how good the food was and the weather, which was cold but clear. Charles brought up the skiing idea, which was met with enthusiasm from the boys. All the adults, however, were of my opinion— we'd rather avoid being in the jet or on a long car ride for a while.

"So, Dad, we're thinking we'll tackle the zoo today. You coming with?"

"No, kitten, I can't."

"Why not?"

Dad sighed. "Your Aunt Carla has a half-day layover and wants to see us. I told her that you all had unbreakable plans, but that I was free."

"Oh. God. Thanks for taking one for the team, Dad. You're the best."

"Is she coming here?" Charles asked, with absolutely no enthusiasm. I shared his reaction.

Dad shook his head. "I'm meeting her at the airport. She gave me the usual complaints about Colonial Village."

"How does Aunt Carla the Bigoted Snob come from the same family as Mom?" Colonial Village was mostly African-American. No one here had ever made us feel anything other than welcome, and we had a lot in common with our neighbors, seeing as they were all affluent and mostly in high-powered government jobs. Only my Aunt Carla or someone like her would complain about our having a home here.

"There's one in every family, kitten."

"Be glad Charles has money," James said with a laugh. "Or you'd never hear the end of how you shouldn't have married him."

"Yes, because the money's what motivates Kitty," Charles said dryly. He took and squeezed my hand.

"Right. Not brains, personality, looks, or, you know, anything else."

Charles grinned at me. I'd learned, fast, not to mention that I was motivated by our great sex life—Charlie had been far too aware, far too early, of what words meant. We weren't sure if he was smarter than me and Charles, but we were betting that he was. Max, too. Jamie . . . well, the jury was still out.

"Do you need us to drop you at the airport?" James asked.

Dad shook his head. "I'll drive myself. That way, if Carla's flight is delayed the rest of you won't have to worry."

"We could take her to the zoo with us. I'm sure the lions are hungry."

"Kitten, she's still your aunt. She loves all of us, even if she's not our favorite person. So, is everyone else going?" Dad asked, the other men, more than me.

"I can't," Peter said. "Much as I'd love to."

"Awww," Max said. "Why not, Uncle Peter? It's always more fun if you're there."

"You always say the nicest things, my dearest. But your Uncle Peter has discovered several issues with the house that must be taken care of immediately if not sooner. It's a good thing we came back earlier than planned," he said to me and Charles, "and thankfully we have wonderful neighbors here, because firing the maintenance company and hiring a new one is first on my agenda for today. Charles, should I try to stick with the same budget?"

"Whatever you want, Peter, you know that's what we want. Choose the service you feel is best, and then worry about what it costs."

"And get presents for whoever covered whatever for us," I added.

Peter waved his hand nonchalantly. "Already handled, Kitty darling. Pictures will be taken so everyone knows what we gave to whom. The neighborhood is throwing us an early return party in a few days. I'll be coordinating that, of course. So, today I'm homebound."

"That's two of us out," Dad said. "What about you, Charles?"

As Charles opened his mouth, Social Distortion's "Ball and Chain" started playing. This wasn't my ringtone—our ringtones for each other were the same, Queen's "You're My Best Friend." No, this was the ringtone for the think tank. He sighed as he stood up. "Let me get back to you on that."

CHAPTER 7

"HELLO?" Charles walked out of the dining room.

As he did so, James' phone rang as well—or rather, "Psycho Therapy" by the Ramones started. That was his ringtone for the main modeling agency he worked through. Charles had become James' manager years ago, for a variety of reasons, most of them centered around the fact that James was our best friend and we wanted to be together and take care of each other as much as possible. But the modeling agency preferred to call James directly—Charles said no a lot more than James did.

James followed Charles' lead—both with sighing and stepping away from the table.

Charlie looked at his grandfather. "No, Grandpa Sol. Daddy's not going. And neither is Uncle James."

I recognized the sounds of their conversations and knew my eldest was right again. "Looks like you guys are stuck with me and me alone."

"That's okay, Mommy," Max said cheerfully. "Even though you'll make us do field trip reports, you still buy the best treats."

We traveled so much, and Charles had suffered so much in school, that we'd made the decision to homeschool our kids as soon as Charlie was old enough to learn to read—in his case, at two years of age. Max had waited until he turned three. With Jamie, I hadn't taught her to read—she had just started taking books and appearing to read them when she was eighteen months old. From the little we got out of her, she was really reading, and comprehending.

So the kids liked going to different sites, but the boys knew they'd have to give some kind of report later. My mother had said that this probably lessened their enjoyment while improving their abilities to observe. She'd approved.

"It's always nice to be appreciated."

"Yeah, it is," Charles said as he came back into the dining room. "I'd just like to be a little less appreciated when we have family time planned."

My turn to sigh. "We came back because they needed you. It's not a total shocker that they want you now, as opposed to later in the week."

James returned. "Yeah, Chuck isn't the only one being called in." He handed his phone to Charles, who looked at whatever message was there and grunted. "Sorry to desert you, girlfriend, kidlets. Duty in the name of fashion calls."

Even though Charlie had predicted this, the boys groaned and Jamie looked unhappy. Before I could add in my disappointment, the sounds of Good Charlotte's "Girls and Boys" hit our airwaves.

I pulled my phone out. "Hey, Caro Syrup, what's shaking?"

"Kit-Kat! You're in town and you haven't called me. I take it we're no longer friends and I should slash my wrists or try to steal your husband, right?"

"Oh, of course, right." My turn to leave the room and drop my voice. "We had a tough flight in, Caro. Really tough. I'm amazed any of us are up to doing anything today, but all does seem well."

"Oh, I'm sorry. Jamie had a meltdown?"

"Of epic proportions. She did *not* want to leave Australia. The flight was horrible—turbulence the entire time, and if James wasn't a fantastic pilot and Charles the best navigator around we'd probably be in the news as a tragic crash. I think they're the only ones who didn't throw up, too. The kids were sick the entire trip. And it's a long trip. So that day was hell on earth. And then everyone was exhausted and jet lagged, and yesterday was worse. Not just one kid melting down, but all three, and the five adults lost it, too."

"Even your dad?" Caroline was my sorority sister and my best friend from college. She'd known me a long time, and knew how even-keeled my dad normally was.

"Yeah, even Dad. I think he couldn't take the rest of us, honestly. It was like an episode of *Jerry Springer*. I'm just thankful Charles' parents stay in Phoenix or Temecula during the U.S. winter, or they'd have gotten to enjoy the 'fun' and lose their minds, and their cool, too. Believe me, alcohol was imbibed. More for survival than for enjoyment."

"Sounds horrible. But you just made me feel great about still being single and childless."

"Glad I could help."

"Hey, I called because Senator McMillan's in a locked-door meeting and I was given the afternoon off. I was hoping to drag you off shopping or something." The senior senator from Arizona was married to a sorority sister, albeit one from many years before ours. But that sorority connection had helped—Caroline was his right-hand gal and I was über proud of her. She almost never got time off, so getting a whole afternoon free, right when I was in town, was a rarity not to be tossed aside.

"We were going to hit the zoo. Not that any of the menfolk can actually go, other than my little men. You want to come with?"

"If that's the only way I can see you, sure. But if the kids want to hit the Smithsonian instead, I think their Auntie Caro could arrange some special tours."

"On this short notice?"

"Kit-Kat, you wound me. I'm a mover and shaker. I've got connections. Besides, the guy who manages the Congressional tours has the hots for me."

"Despite my desire to see who you're stringing along at the museums and/or the Capitol, after the past couple of days, I think we want to vote for a location where, should a repeat of yesterday happen, we won't be nearly as noticeable."

"Good point. That's why you're Super Mom. Okay, I'll meet you at the zoo in how long from now?"

Checked my watch. "We just finished brunch and everyone's dressed. In an hour?"

"Sounds good. Don't drive too fast—you haven't been back long enough to be used to driving on the correct side of the road, you know."

"Everyone's a comedian." We hung up and I went back to the dining room. "Auntie Caro's going to meet us at the zoo." The boys cheered and even Jamie looked a little happier. "At noon, so we need to get moving."

Charles nodded. "We all have to get rolling. I'll drop James at his shoot. Sol, you sure you don't want a ride to the airport?"

"Nope, I'm looking forward to driving my birthday present." We'd gotten Dad a new Lexus hybrid for his birthday last year and he adored it.

With five adults in our household and three kids to drive around, we had a lot of cars. Probably meant we were conspicuously consuming, but whatever. We were really popular with our Lexus dealer in Silver Spring. Considering Peter wasn't happy with the maintenance company, I'd probably have to take the cars in soon—car care while we were out of the country was part of their service.

"You going to give the 'super spy' a call?" James asked.

"Wow, you're reading my mind. Well done. Yeah, I was just thinking that I probably better take the cars in to get serviced and visit with Jack."

Charles groaned. "That just means Ryan's going to show you another new model you want, while his wife drags you off on a shopping spree. Really, you can let me take the cars in."

"No way. Jack's just a grateful dealership owner and Pia's fun to shop with. She never tries to make me spend too much money."

"Nope, you can do that all on your own."

"I resent that. I don't deny it, but I resent it. Besides, I like the Ryans, and you do, too. Stop whining."

He grinned. "It's called teasing, but I'll stop. You're not taking the cars in today, so we'll worry about it later. And we can crack all the Tom Clancy jokes about his name when we're together—he lives for someone coming up with a new reference."

Everyone helped me get the kids ready to go then, fortified with a ton of sunscreen and snacks courtesy of Peter and a set of hats courtesy of Dad, hugs and kisses courtesy of everyone, and some great kissing from Charles for me alone, we got the kids into our LX570. It was built like a really attractive tank, but we drove our most precious cargo in it, so I was great with owning the road, so to speak.

It wasn't my favorite car—that was still my old IS300. That car was older than Charlie but still drove like it was on rails and turned on a dime. Charles could tease me about the Ryans all he wanted—Jack ran a great dealership and the service department was unparalleled.

Because it was just two of them, Charles and James could have taken the convertible, but instead they opted for the IS. Couldn't blame them—thankfully there was no snow on the ground, but it was crisp and cool. Definitely not "top down" weather.

My men drove off first, with admonitions to have a lot of fun. I dumped my purse onto the passenger seat, ensured my phone was actively connected to the LX's Bluetooth, then realized I'd forgotten my iPod. "I forgot our music. I'll be right back. You three promise to behave?"

"We promise!" the boys said. Jamie nodded.

"Super, back in a jiffy." I raced back inside. Heard Peter snarling politely at someone and decided not to bother him. My iPod wasn't where I normally put it, so I had to search for a couple of minutes to find where one of the kids had left it.

Back downstairs, Peter was still snarling about the lack of anything being cared for while we were out of the country, so I headed straight back to the car. Made sure my iPod was connected to our audio system, triple-checked that everyone was safely buckled in, then turned on our music. "What do we want to hear today?"

"Jack Johnson!" the boys shouted in unison.

"Mister Surfer Dude of Coolness it shall be, then." I turned on my Mellow Man playlist and the sounds of "Up-side Down" wafted over our airwaves.

"The song is right," Jamie said. "We're going to go upside down. We should stay home."

"We'll be fine, Jamie-Kat."

The boys chose to ignore their sister and sing along with the music. This was probably the better choice. As near as we could tell, Jamie didn't like music. A doctor we'd seen in Paris had said that she was listening to a different soundtrack inside her own head, and until we could match that, we wouldn't make any progress with her. Charles said he was a quack, and Dad and James had agreed. But sometimes I wondered if Dr. Marling was right.

Heeding Caroline's warning, I decided not to take Beach Drive and to go through all of Rock Creek Park to get to the zoo. Instead I headed for 17th Street to hit 16th Street and go that way.

While the boys sang along to the music I relaxed and enjoyed being back in this area. I was looking at the road, but I was also looking around, paying attention to everything. Which was why I spotted the black sedan behind us.

All of our cars were black—my favorite color for cars—but this wasn't one of ours. It looked like a Lincoln Town Car, so it was probably a limo of some kind. Only limos normally didn't have metal push bars on the front. And I was pretty darned sure this one was following us.

Reminding myself that I was probably just overreacting

based on the past couple of days, I did a test. The light coming up was yellow. Normally I'd have stopped, but the road was clear in front of me and in the intersection, so I floored it, and made our right turn onto 16th Street as the light turned red.

The black Lincoln turned right into oncoming traffic. My mother had always told me to trust my gut. And my gut said that whoever was behind us couldn't mean us any good. We were the family of an extremely wealthy man—that meant we were targets for kidnapping. We didn't spend our lives thinking about this, but the thought was always there in the back of my mind, the fact that someone could decide to use us to get money from Charles.

As I sped up, I hit the Bluetooth and made the call. "Miss me already?" Charles said as he answered.

Took a sharp left onto Alaska Avenue. What a pity that Walter Reed had moved to Bethesda—we'd have been conveniently close to a hospital otherwise. On the other hand, I wanted to avoid any of us needing medical attention. The Lincoln followed us, proving that something bad was surely trying to happen. Found myself wondering if I should head for Bethesda, just in case.

"I think—" I was going to share that I thought we were being followed and were probably in danger. Only the Lincoln slammed into our rear and my head slammed into the steering wheel before I could say anything else.

As I started to lose control of the car and consciousness, I felt something—no, really, some*one*—go through me. And then, blackness.

CHAPTER 8

I COULD SORT OF HEAR the sounds of panic around me. Same as when I'd given birth to Jamie, I could also see myself, because I was outside of my body.

Not far outside. So I couldn't see, say, the entire arena. Meaning that, whatever else was going on, I was going to miss the rest of the cricket match. I was okay with this.

What I wasn't okay with was everything else. Things were chaotic but I could see Jeff's expression, and he looked terrified. Could hear people telling him to wait for an ambulance. Could hear Chuckie calling for medical help and prepping Walter Reed to expect my arrival. Could hear Raj calling for Tito and telling him to meet us at the hospital. Heard my Secret Service unit telling Jeff to get me lying down flat.

Jeff scooped me up into his arms. "None of those will be fast enough. The hospital's in Bethesda. And it's an hour from here by car. Five minutes is too long. Deal with the fallout," he said to Raj and Chuckie. Then he ran, carrying me, at his fastest hyperspeed.

The beauty of A-Cs and their hyperspeed was that the idea of going as the crow flies was something they were quite familiar with and wholeheartedly approved of. Jeff was right— to get to Walter Reed from the football stadium was an easy

45 minutes without traffic. However, it was probably about three minutes or less when Jeff was running. His cousin, Christopher White, would have been faster, but Christopher had stayed home. Wish I'd followed his lead, but figured I'd better focus on staying home with my body.

"Hang on, baby," Jeff said as we ran. "It's okay. Don't leave me, Kitty. You stay with me."

I tried to, I really did. But as we neared what looked like the outskirts of Rock Creek Park I heard something else. The sounds of, of all things, Jack Johnson singing "Upside Down." This wasn't the song I wanted to die to. I didn't want to die at all, but especially not while Mr. Put You To Sleep was crooning.

Then I felt us go through something, though if what I was seeing was correct, nothing was there, and Jeff hadn't run us into anything. I mean, sure, we were on the street, but Jeff was going so fast the cars and people were as motionless as the buildings.

Whatever we went through didn't feel solid, but it felt real. Real weird and real tingly, but real nonetheless.

There was a flash of light. I saw the Universe Wheel, the same one I'd seen when Jamie was born and I'd basically died in the delivery room. The one that looked like the most gigantic slide projector wheel ever, showing all the different universes in the multiverse.

I'd forgotten all about the Universe Wheel until now. Didn't have time to marvel about this, or the Wheel, because there were other pressing matters demanding my attention. Just as before, there was a golden thread attached to me now, but it wasn't the only thread I saw. Another thread crossed with mine as I and the person attached to said other thread flew past each other.

Managed one quick look. She looked like me. Dressed a little differently, hair styled a little differently, but otherwise, me. Figured our expressions were probably the same—openmouthed shock.

We passed like those proverbial ships in the night, then the feeling disappeared.

And so did the Universe Wheel, the golden string, and presumably my doppelganger.

Something else disappeared, too.

Jeff.

CHAPTER 9

I SLAMMED INTO A CAR SEAT, hands on the wheel. I was able to think fast in many circumstances, and—head injury from landing on concrete steps or not—this was one of those circumstances.

There were what sounded like little kids screaming and Jack Johnson singing. God alone knew why, but that's what was on the sound system. There was also something hitting us from the rear. And into oncoming traffic.

Didn't ask what the hell was going on. Just did what I'd gotten used to for the past many years—I reacted. Spun the wheel and got us back into our proper lane. We missed a head-on collision by about a half a second. We missed side-swiping three cars by about a second. Yeah, I hadn't had to drive like a maniac away from crazed killers for a while, but I still had the skills.

We weren't out of the situation, however, so took no time to preen. A quick look into the rearview mirror showed a black Lincoln with all the windows blacked out trying to slam into us again. That it was the car that had slammed into us already was a given, based on the impressive push bar it sported on the front.

We were near the old Walter Reed hospital, which was on the same straight line from the football stadium as the new

Walter Reed, which explained why Jeff had been running this way. Had no time to wonder where Jeff was. I was too busy trying to keep the car from going out of control.

Fortunately, adrenaline rush being what it was, I felt okay now, which was good because this hospital was no longer active. A-Cs had faster healing and regeneration, and I'd reverse-inherited that from Jamie, too. So, while my head still hurt, I was pretty sure I wasn't bleeding anymore. And while it might be a good idea to race off to the new Walter Reed to get help and possibly find Jeff, if these were the usual alien-haters on our tail, driving into a hospital full of the sick and injured would just give our enemies helpless targets to attack. Besides, the hospital was a lot farther away than the Lincoln.

Someone was shouting, a man's voice. Chuckie's to be exact. Had no idea how he'd gotten here. I spun us into a 180 and watched the Lincoln speed past. Then I hit the gas. Once I had it floored, I realized I was driving a gigantic Lexus SUV. This was not the A-C brand of choice. Sadly, this car didn't seem equipped with the usual A-C bells and whistles, either, meaning I couldn't spot either a laser shield or cloaking button.

Risked a quick look in the rearview mirror—not to see who was behind us but to see who was in the car with me. Two cute little blond boys who looked about seven and five were strapped into their age-appropriate car seats. Each one was holding one of Jamie's hands. All three kids looked terrified.

Well. However the hell this had happened, I'd woken up from a concussion in a car with my daughter and a couple other kids, and whoever was trying to kill me was going to kill them if I didn't prevent it.

Chuckie was shouting my name. Realized I'd also woken up in a car with a good Bluetooth system, because he wasn't here, but on the car's speakers. "Got it under control," I shouted back. "Just have some agents meet us somewhere along the way."

"What are you talking about? Where are you?" Chuckie asked. He didn't sound calm at all. "What's going on?"

"No freaking idea. Kind of busy." Heard a noise that wasn't Jack Johnson. It was a familiar sound though. Checked a side view mirror—sure enough, they were shooting at us. Enough was enough. Hoped the entire audio system was voice activated. "Switch music to Aerosmith!"

Thankfully, the music stopped mid-snore and switched. "Dream On" hit the car's airwaves. Not the song I'd have chosen in this precise circumstance, but even the slowest Aerosmith song was better than the entire Jack Johnson oeuvre.

I had the opportunity so I turned us into Rock Creek Park. Maybe I could lose them in here, and worst case we wouldn't cause a gigantic pileup when they drove us off the road.

"I have no idea where you are, Kitty," Chuckie said. "Or why you're worrying about music at a time like this. I just heard you and the kids screaming . . ."

"Use the GPS tracking or whatever. Call my mom. She needs to know what's going on, I'd guess. If she doesn't already know, I mean."

There was a thudding silence on the other phone. "Kitty, baby, are you okay?" he asked finally, his voice extremely careful and precise.

"Um, no, and why are you calling me baby? Jeff will hurt you for that, you know."

"Who the hell is Jeff?" Now he didn't sound careful or even freaked out. He sounded like Jeff normally did if I mentioned another man's name—jealous.

Before I could share that this was a really lousy time for him to crack weak jokes, the Lincoln took some more shots at us. This was a two-lane road, meaning I was weaving in and out of the thankfully light traffic, both on our side and oncoming, which added a certain thrill that had been so lacking to this experience. But I had no guess for how long it would be before they shot some tires out, whether ours or someone else's.

I didn't know this area all that well. We'd done a couple of picnics here, but, nice though this area was, it wasn't our part of town. Though it was a lot better to be chased here than around Embassy Row. Of course, if I'd been there, I could have just gotten to the American Centaurion Embassy and this would all be over. Still was a workable plan.

"I'm going to try to get to the Embassy," I told Chuckie.

"What embassy? Why? Kitty, we're in America, remember?"

"Yeah, I do. I—" But what I was going to say was cut short by screaming, mine and the kids'. Their screams were of terror—mine was of rage. The bad guys had managed to shoot out one of our tires.

Naturally this happened at a point on the road where we could, and, of course, did, go over an embankment. There were a lot of highway railings along this road, but not right here, and we headed toward the water.

Rock Creek really was a creek. Even so, this could have been a big deal, but the car handled fantastically and, modestly speaking, so did I. Sure, we bounced a lot and I was happy my seat belt was on. Had no idea *how* it was on, but chose to not complain when the cosmos decided to do me a solid. It happened so infrequently.

Managed to keep the car from hitting any trees, rolling, or going into the water, but it was a near thing. We did spin out rather impressively, especially since we were on some rocks, and ended up with the back of the car at the water's edge and the front facing the road. So I had a great view of the people who were getting out of the Lincoln with machine guns. No one I recognized.

Survival instinct took over. I grabbed my purse that was somehow on the seat next to me, ripped out the iPod and phone that were connected to this car's systems and threw them in, got my seat belt off, and leaped out of the car, flinging my purse over my neck. At the fastest hyperspeed I had which, after a lot of practice with Christopher and in danger situations such as this, was really fast.

Ripped the passenger door behind me off its hinges. I'd
worry about apologizing for that to whoever actually owned
this vehicle later—I had three kids to get. The younger boy
was nearest to me, and I was able to unbuckle his toddler car
seat quickly. The older boy was in a simple booster seat and
he'd gotten himself unbuckled.

Jamie's car seat was more problematic, in part because it
wasn't her car seat and, amazingly enough, it was more complex than the one we had for her. Decided I'd already hurt the
car and ripped the car seat out, Jamie and all. Held her and
the seat in my left arm.

Flung the younger boy onto my back. "Hold on, legs
around my waist, arms around my neck but not too hard."
Reached through and pulled the older boy to me and held
onto him with my right hand. "Hang on, all of you!"

Then I ran us across the river at my fastest hyperspeed. And
kept going. I didn't look behind us. Firstly because I couldn't
with all I was carrying, and secondly because I was a sprinter
and I'd learned in high school that sprinters who looked behind
them lost their races. The only times in my adult life I'd ignored that adage had only proven why it was a wise one.

Heard the sounds of gunfire starting and congratulated
myself on getting the kids out of the car and out of range in
about five seconds. Potentially a personal best. Perhaps I'd
brag about it somewhere in the far future.

Heard what was absolutely an explosion and found the
ability to speed up. If my fuzzy memory served, there was a
golf course somewhere around here and I decided heading
for it was probably my best choice.

It was like a forest in here, which made sense for the kind
of park Rock Creek was, but it was hard going in a pantsuit
and boots, not to mention lugging all the kids and stuff along.
Absolutely none of the foliage was helping us in any way,
though I managed not to ram any of the kids into branches
and such. Could not say the same for myself. However, I'd
gotten some increased strength along with the hyperspeed, so
I managed to get us through and keep on going.

Sure enough, after I stumbled and bumbled us around for a while, I managed to find the edge of the golf course. Ran onto the nice grass that had no trees trying to stab me and the kids and made it about a hundred yards in. Then I stopped and put everyone down.

As I got Jamie out of her car seat, the boys threw up. Okay, they were human. As I put Jamie onto the ground, though, she threw up, too. So, maybe it was just fear. "It's okay," I said as I held her and stroked the younger boy's back. "It'll pass."

The oldest boy recovered first. "Mommy, what's going on? Why did those people try to hurt us?"

Looked around. There was no adult here but me. "Um, who are you talking to, honey?" I asked him.

He'd already looked scared, but his expression changed, to a different kind of fear. "I'm talking to *you*, Mommy."

CHAPTER 10

THE YOUNGER BOY STOPPED BARFING and got to his feet. He looked at me closely. Then he took Jamie's hand and pulled her away from me. "That's not Mommy," he said in a low voice.

I ignored him, since he was right, and took her back. "Jamie-Kat, are you okay? Tell Mommy if you got hurt."

She cocked her head at me. Then she smiled. "You did great, Mommy." There was something extremely off in how she'd said this, and as she leaned against me, I tried to figure out what it was. Realized that she'd said my name as if she'd made a decision to call me Mommy, not that she actually thought I was her mother.

Watched the boys out of the corner of my eye. The older one looked shocked and freaked out. The younger one looked suspicious and worried.

"Mommy, why don't you know us?" the older one asked, almost pleadingly. "It's me, Charlie. And Max," he pointed to the younger boy. Charlie looked familiar, but not because I'd seen him before. But I knew I'd seen someone who looked like him before. Possibly because my head still hurt, I just couldn't place who.

Before I could reply a couple of older men rolled up in a golf cart. "You and your kids okay, ma'am?" the driver asked.

"Not really. We were attacked and shot at and our car exploded and I need to call my husband. And the Secret Service."

The two men looked at each other and chuckled. "I'm sure the regular police will be fine, honey," the passenger said.

"I doubt it. We were attacked by men who drove us off the road and shot out our tires. And then they shot up our car so that it blew up. I think." I hadn't looked behind me to be sure, after all.

"Uh *huh*," the driver said. "I'm Hershel, this is Hymie." He looked at me expectantly.

"I'm Kitty. This is Jamie. And Charlie and Max."

"Okay," Hershel said. "Well, Kitty, Jamie, Charlie and Max, we have no guns, but I don't see anyone pursuing you, so I think you're in the clear. Let's get you and your kids back to the clubhouse, honey. I think we can fit you all in if your little girl can sit on your lap."

They both got out and Hymie put Jamie's car seat in the back of the cart with their clubs. As they helped me and the kids into the back seat, my brain nudged—something was off with this. Not with the kids—something was clearly off with them—but with the reactions from the two men.

I was the wife of the Vice President. I was now one of the most recognized people in the D.C. area. Sure, if we were in Des Moines, maybe no one would know who I was. But since the campaign, or what I thought of as Operation Defection Election, I couldn't walk outside without paparazzi following me, and they weren't the friendly, helpful kind like Mister Joel Oliver. Sure, maybe Hershel and Hymie didn't pay attention to the news, but considering they both looked older than my dad, it seemed unlikely.

The boys sat quietly on either side of me and Jamie perched on my lap. She didn't say anything, which was also odd. Jamie was a chatterbox.

"Can you call my daddy?" Charlie asked the men as we "sped" along the golf course.

"Sure, son," Hymie said. "Doesn't your mother have a phone?" He looked at me over his shoulder.

"Oh. Yeah. I do." Dug through the purse and pulled out a phone. It wasn't my phone, though, but it definitely was the one I'd pulled out of the car—the charging cord was still attached. Pulled the cord out and tried to unlock it. My code didn't work. Charlie took the phone out of my hand and put in the right code.

"It's okay, Mommy," he said quietly. "You hit your head and it was really scary. Daddy says that sometimes trauma can create an incredible adrenaline rush, but then after you're safe, you sort of collapse. It's just like that." He handed the phone to Hymie.

"Hello," Hymie said cheerfully. "No, I'm not Kitty, but I think we have her and your kids." I could hear a man shouting. "Whoa, whoa! Calm down, mister. We're not trying to hurt them. We found your family on the golf course. Your wife's pretty shaken up, said her car exploded." Heard more shouting.

"And that someone shot at her," Hershel added.

"Yeah, and she was shot at. Not by us, so stop yelling." Hymie eyed us. "Nope, they seem okay. Shook up, but okay." He dropped his voice. "You wife hit her head for sure. You need to get to Rock Creek Golf Course right away. Yeah, sure, we'll stay with them. Lost our spot on the course already anyway."

He hung up and handed the phone back to Charlie. "Hang onto that, son. Your dad said he'd be right to you but he may have to call again."

Decided now was as good a time as any to ask a pertinent question. "Excuse me, but is the Vice President an alien?"

We reached the golf cart parking area as I voiced my question. Hershel sighed. "Now's not the time to discuss politics, is it?" He helped Max out, then took Jamie from me, while Hymie went and got our car seat.

"No, and neither is the President," Hymie said. "Regardless of your political party, you really shouldn't believe everything you hear on Fox News, honey. Try thinking for yourself."

"Huh?"

Neither Hershel nor Hymie seemed interested in explaining what they meant. Hershel handed Jamie back to me and took both boys' hands, Hymie kept the car seat and put his hand on my back to keep me moving, and we headed into the clubhouse.

There weren't a lot of people here, but we made quite a stir with the few who were as we went to the front. I checked outside, but there were no suspicious looking cars in the parking lot and no one packing heat I could spot.

Risked a look in a mirror as I rejoined the kids, Hershel, and Hymie—I looked like the poster girl for dishevelment. My clothes were pretty much wrecked. Sure, we had the Operations Team, what I called the A-C Elves, and sure, they were actually one really superpowered being with a serious hard-on for free will. But even so, I doubted the bloodstains were going to come out, A-C Elves or no A-C Elves.

There was a lounge area with couches and a television and Hershel ushered us over there. I dumped my purse into Jamie's car seat and sat down with the kids. The adrenaline rush was starting to wear off. Hymie had someone change the channel to local news. There were no news reports of a high-speed chase through Rock Creek Park that ended with a car exploding. There was one mention that traffic was being rerouted from Beach Drive due to an accident, but that was it.

Hymie shrugged. "Guess the reporters aren't interested or aware of your mishap."

This, more than anything else that had happened, told me that something was very, very wrong. There was no way that the news media wouldn't be having a field day with this. Sadly, it had been a really long time since no one in the media had cared about what I did or didn't do.

A couple of years ago, I'd have just assumed that Imageering out of Centaurion Division had altered the footage. But events, and what appeared to be an outer-space virus, had conspired to cause pretty much every imageer to lose their natural talents. Meaning there was no one around to manipulate the images and hide my mistakes. I'd really missed this, especially since Jeff had become the Vice President.

But today it didn't seem to matter.

Before I could ask Hershel and Hymie some more questions they were probably going to ignore or give me inscrutable responses to, all three kids' heads swiveled toward the door.

I turned to see Chuckie running in. He looked stressed out of his mind. As he looked at us his face drained of color—I'd only seen him look like this a few times in our lives. Figured I looked a lot worse than I thought I did.

Speaking of looks, Chuckie looked slightly different than he had earlier today. His hair, for example, was shorter. Not a lot, but as if he'd had a haircut between my hitting my head at the stadium and now, which seemed unlikely.

He was also dressed differently. The A-Cs were love slaves to black and white, formality, and Armani, and Chuckie, as the Head of the C.I.A.'s Extra-Terrestrial Division, had adapted and wore the same "uniform" as all the other men who were aliens or worked for Centaurion Division.

However, I knew my designers, and Chuckie was not only not in a suit, but he wasn't in Armani, either. He was in a Tommy Hilfiger ensemble that made me think we'd dragged him off of someone's yacht. He was dressed more colorfully than I'd seen him, or anyone else I spent a lot of time with these days, in years.

However, I'd spotted who Charlie looked like. He was the spitting image of Chuckie. I just hadn't known Chuckie until we were thirteen, so I'd never seen him as a little kid, other than in some pictures. It was clear that how Charlie looked was exactly how Chuckie had looked. How Chuckie had a son who was this old that I didn't know about, however, was a mystery I had no answer for.

Before I could ponder all these mysteries anymore, Chuckie reached us and pulled me into his arms. "Kitty, baby, are you okay?" His voice shook and he hugged me tightly and kissed my head, very lovingly and possessively. I managed not to react one way or the other, mostly because my head really hurt and I had no idea what was going on.

He let go with one arm and pulled the kids in. Not that he had to work to do this—all three of them, even Jamie, had clearly been waiting for this and flung themselves at him. Jamie seemed reasonably calm, but both of the boys were trying not to cry.

"Chuckie, you need to stop calling me baby," I said quietly. "Jeff is going to pop a vessel as it is."

He reared back and stared at me, eyes narrowed. "I ask again, who the hell is Jeff? And why, if you're trying to tell me that you're leaving me for whoever the hell he is, are you calling me Chuckie?" His voice was cold and he sounded hurt and angry.

I blinked. "Um, I've called you Chuckie since ninth grade."

"Only in bed for the past seven years," Chuckie replied. He still looked and sounded upset.

"Mommy hit her head," Charlie said urgently. "She doesn't know me and Max, Daddy. No matter how she's acting, I think she's really hurt."

Chuckie's expression softened. "Ah. Hang on, ba—, ah, Kitty." He let go of me and hugged the kids tightly, doing the parental body check for broken bones and other injuries. "How badly are you three hurt?"

"Not at all," Charlie said. "Mommy got us all out." He looked at me nervously. "She did it really fast, Daddy. And she pulled the car door off. And carried all of us, running so fast we couldn't see."

"You know what we talked about," Chuckie said.

"I know, the adrenaline rush, like the Hulk," Charlie said. "I think it was like that, but Mommy isn't feeling . . . right."

"She's not Mommy," Max said emphatically. "I keep on saying it, and no one listens."

Realized that Max was speaking like I did. My head was starting to throb from all of this, and I rubbed my forehead.

"It's Mommy," Jamie said calmly. "Charlie is right—she's hurt her head."

Chuckie's jaw dropped. "You're sure, Jamie-Kat?" She nodded. "Okay. Kids, you three sit here and let me check on Mommy." He turned fully back to me. "Let's see your head," he said gently, as he stroked my forehead.

"It's not my forehead; it's the back of my head." I turned, and Chuckie hissed.

"Why didn't anyone call a doctor or an ambulance?" he asked, of Hershel and Hymie more than me.

The two other men shrugged. "She didn't appear to need one," Hershel replied. "She's not bleeding anymore and I don't know what they would do for her concussion."

"I don't have a concussion." Hopefully.

Hymie snorted. "She asked us if the Vice President was an alien. A concussion your wife has. However, we thought getting her and your kids off the golf course and to safety was more important than calling nine-one-one."

"I'm not his wife."

At this everyone stared at me. Other than Jamie, who was rummaging through my purse. Or what was passing for my purse. My purse was big, black, and made of cheap yet extremely durable leather. The purse Jamie was digging into was a large pink and purple Coach bag. I didn't own a Coach bag. I didn't own a Coach anything.

"Yes, you are," Chuckie said, voice strained. "We've been married for eight years. We have three children . . . the three children here. You know, the ones that look like us? The ones calling you Mommy?"

I was about to protest when Jamie handed me a wallet. Wasn't a wallet I recognized, but it kept to the purse's theme—it was multi-colored pastels and by Coach. "Here, Mommy. See?"

Took the wallet and opened it up. There was my driver's license. Two of them, actually. One was for the District of Columbia, and one had a yellow stripe on the top and some red flower in the middle, and shared that it was for the state of New South Wales, Australia. Both of them listed addresses I didn't recognize.

Both of them said the same thing. That I was Katherine Sarah Katt-Reynolds. And both of them had my picture on them.

CHAPTER 11

STARED AT THE DRIVERS' LICENSES for a bit. Then I stared some more. Finally felt able to speak. "I'm so confused."

As I said this, Reader came running in. "Chuck, I came as fast as I could."

"Uncle James!" The boys threw themselves on him, and he hugged them. Head hurting or not, I'd gotten really good at catching when people around me were passing signs to each other. And Reader absolutely was passing signs back and forth with Chuckie. Reader gave an almost imperceptible nod, and Chuckie's arm tightened around me.

"How's my girlfriend?" Reader asked. "Kitty, you okay?"

"I think there's been some sort of weird misunderstanding. I'm not his wife. I'm not these kids' mother. Well, I tell a lie. I'm Jamie's mother, but I've never seen your boys before about an hour ago or whenever we were attacked, shot at, and driven off the road."

"Kitty has at least a concussion," Chuckie said, voice tight. "And she's been talking about some guy named Jeff."

Reader shook his head, just slightly.

"Look, it's cool that James checked out the crash site while you came here to check on us, and it's nice that he's also confirming that he has no idea who my mysterious 'Jeff' is, but can we stop with the cloak-and-dagger stuff? Or, to put it another way, who have we pissed off that's trying to kill me and these kids? And why are you all pretending we're married? I need to know what's going on so I know whose butt I have to go kick."

Both Reader and Chuckie stared at me. Their expressions were very similar—shock mixed with just a tiny bit of fear and suspicion. It wasn't a look I was used to either one of them directing at me.

A throat cleared. "Ah, are we safe to leave you all to the weirdest family reunion I've seen in all my born days, and that's saying a lot, and get back to golf?" Hershel asked.

"Ah, sure, yes," Chuckie said. He let go of me and shook both men's hands. "Thank you so much for your help." He pulled out a couple of business cards. "If we can ever return the favor, please don't hesitate to call."

"Boys, instead of haranguing her, why don't you get her home, or to your doctor, or wherever?" Hymie suggested, as he shoved Chuckie's card into his pocket without looking at it. "I don't think this is the best place for . . . well, whatever your family has going on."

Hershel was staring at the card Chuckie had given him. "Trade Winds Financial." He looked up and he no longer looked amused. "I think you need to get your family out of here, son. Just in case they were followed."

Hymie nodded. "We'll let you know if we see anything." He smiled at me. "Good luck, honey." Then the two of them wandered off.

"Well, that was refreshingly vague and threatening all at once. Does anyone want to tell me what's going on?"

"Yes, but, as suggested, not here," Chuckie said, as a couple of women came over. Both were in their late twenties and holding magazines in their hands. Clutching, really.

They were hesitant, and they weren't coming over to me, the kids, or Chuckie. They were heading for Reader. "Excuse me," one asked, voice trembling. "But are you . . . ?"

Reader flashed the cover boy grin. "I am." He looked at

the magazines. "Would you two like an autograph? And a picture?"

Much squealing ensued. Reader did that almost imperceptible nod thing to Chuckie again, then focused on the women. As they squealed, more people came over.

Chuckie picked up Jamie's car seat, took the wallet from me, dropped it back into the purse, and took Jamie's hand. "Boys, hold Mommy's hands, will you?"

Charlie took my hand eagerly, but Max didn't. Chuckie shot him a very parental "do as I say" look and, with a sigh, Max complied. "I know you're not our mommy," he said quietly as the excited crowd around Reader grew and we headed out.

"You and I are the only ones," I replied in kind.

"Stop it," Charlie hissed at his brother. "She's hurt and confused and you're making it worse." He squeezed my hand. "It's okay, Mommy."

Was about to say that it really wasn't, when we reached the vehicle Chuckie was heading for. "What is my car doing here?"

He shot a worried look over his shoulder. "I took this car this morning, remember? You were in the LX. The big SUV?"

"The one we crashed in," Charlie added helpfully.

"Oh. Right. But I meant what are *you* doing with *my* car?"

"Like all the others, Kitty, it's *our* car." He put the car seat into the back while I contemplated what the heck was going on.

Looked down. "Charlie . . . was I wearing these clothes when you left the house this morning?"

"*No,*" Max answered. "It's how I know you're not our mommy."

Chuckie was done with the car seat and he looked at me. "You're right," he said slowly. "You weren't dressed quite like this to go to the zoo." His eyes narrowed. "Whatever you did with *Jeff* it was fast."

"Mommy didn't go anywhere without us," Charlie said,

sounding stressed. "She doesn't know anyone named Jeff, Daddy, I promise."

"I do, actually. He's my husband. He's the Vice President of the United States. And he's an alien, from Alpha Four in the Alpha Centauri system, to be exact. And you were *in* our wedding, Chuckie."

Chuckie's expression shifted. Relief was fighting with worry, but he no longer looked hurt or angry. "Ah," he said gently. "Got it. Kids, it's fine. Or, well, not really, but it'll be okay. Let's get home and take care of Mommy." The kids climbed into the back of the car, Chuckie made sure they were all buckled in. "We're going to drive slowly because you boys don't have your car seats. No fighting or horsing around."

The boys nodded. Charlie still looked worried. Max looked truculent. Jamie, however, looked pleased.

Chuckie shut the car doors and then came over to me. He pulled me gently into his arms. I kept my body stiff. "We'll figure out what happened with your clothes. Maybe you decided to change before you all left because you were supposed to meet up with Caroline. But I get it, baby, and it's okay." He kissed my head.

"Caro's here?"

"Yes. You and the kids were heading to meet up with her at the zoo. I'll call her when we get home and let her know what's going on."

"What *is* going on?"

"You have what I'm figuring is a major concussion and that means memory loss, confusion, and many other things are possible. You've mixed up our *Traveler* game with real life."

"Huh?"

"We roleplay a game called *Traveler*, Kitty. It's like *D and D* but it's set in outer space. In that game, I'm an alien, named Geffer, and you're a human warrior. Our characters got married in the game. We have a monthly game when we're in Australia. In fact, we played just a couple nights before we came back to the States. That's what's going on—you've confused the two in your mind."

"No. Look, there are aliens on Earth. You're the freaking head of the C.I.A.'s E-T Division."

He hugged me tightly as he chuckled. "Kitty, you know I don't believe there are aliens on the planet. I haven't for years."

"Stryker knows the truth. Call him."

"Eddy? He's on a book tour, Kitty. And he's as aware that what he writes is fiction as I am."

"Where is Hoffa buried?"

"What? I need to get you home. Or to a doctor. Both, really."

"There are both at the Embassy."

"Maybe, but we're on American soil, so there is no embassy for us here, baby."

"I mean the American Centaurion Embassy."

"I have no idea what you're talking about, Kitty. But I'm guessing it's related to the game. Just like everything else."

"Conspiracies, which ones are active right now?"

He hugged me again. "Many, I'm sure. I don't pay too much attention to all of that, now, Kitty. I have a wife and three kids who need my focus."

He was lying. I could tell only because I'd known him for over half my life. However, the only thing he was lying about was that he didn't pay attention to conspiracies. Which begged any number of questions. All of which I wanted to voice and have answered, only my head started throbbing in earnest.

"I hurt." Hadn't meant to say that aloud, but oh well.

"I'm sure, baby." Chuckie stroked my back and I leaned into him. "I know you think you're being unfaithful to your husband right now, but, trust me, you're not. I'm your husband, you're my wife, and I love you and our kids more than anything in the world. Now, I'm going to get you some medical attention."

"Is Tito around?"

"No idea who you're talking about. Is that another 'boy-friend' I should be worried about?" He walked me to the passenger's side, opened the door, helped me sit, buckled me in, then shut the door and went around to the driver's side and got in.

"No, he's a doctor. And our friend. How do you fit in this car? You're so tall."

Chuckie stroked my cheek. "This was your dream car. It'll be hard to deal with when the kids are older, at least if we want all five of us in it, but for now, having the seat all the way back works just fine."

He pulled his phone out and made a call. "Peter, hi. Oh? Yeah, I'm glad he called you already, saves me time. Oh, you did? Thanks, I'm sure she'll be worried. Have her come to the house, but tell her to be careful. Can you please call Doctor Zainal and have him meet us at Walter Reed? We should be there in fifteen minutes or less. Great, thank you. Yes, stay home, we need you there more than at the hospital. I'm hop-ing we won't be there long. Yeah, thanks." He hung up and put the car in gear.

"Who were you talking to? And why are you having the Bahraini Embassy's doctor meet with us?"

"I was talking to Peter. He's our, well, I'm not sure what we call him. Butler, I guess. Though he does a lot more than that. He's part of our family."

"He's our Mister Perfect, Mommy," Charlie said. "That's what you always call him."

"Or Mister Mary Poppins," Max added.

"Oh. Good." Had no idea who this man was, but figured I'd find out. Or wake up from whatever freak dream I was having. Only I didn't feel like I was asleep.

"And I want Doctor Zainal because he's the best physician in the D.C. area, and we only get the best, Kitty. He's not associated with any embassy, though he did emigrate to the U.S. from Bahrain."

We left the golf course parking lot and Chuckie drove carefully back up the way I'd sort of come. He was watching the road, and all the streets around us, and he was also checking the side and rearview mirrors a lot. Couldn't blame him—clearly someone was after us in some way.

We got onto the Beltway. "Where are we going?"

"Walter Reed, just like I told Peter. I was going to go home first, but I think I want you to see a doctor immediately and the kids should get checked out too."

"Okay, I guess. I don't know why my head is still hurting. My regeneration should have fixed me up by now."

"You're not Wolverine, Kitty," he said with a chuckle that didn't hide his concern.

"Sure I am. I'm Wolverine with Boobs, remember?"

"That was Halloween a few years ago, baby." His voice was very gentle. "Kitty, you've had a traumatic experience and you were injured. Your mind is jumbled right now. But we'll fix it, I promise." He reached over, took my hand, and gave it a squeeze.

Considered this. "My wedding ring." Checked my hand. I was definitely wearing the wedding set Jeff had given me.

Chuckie kissed the back of my hand. "This is the set I got you on our fifth anniversary, Kitty. When we went back to Vegas to celebrate."

"This is all wrong," I said quietly.

"Because you're not our mommy," Max said conversationally.

"Stop it," Chuckie said sternly. "You're not helping things, Maxwell."

"Mommy never left us to change clothes," Max said with more patience than I'd have had in his place. "She's in different clothes. Explain that."

"Well . . ." Charlie said slowly, "Mommy forgot our music and went back into the house before we left, remember? She was gone a few minutes. Maybe she changed clothes then and we didn't notice."

"Why doesn't she remember? Why didn't Uncle Peter notice?" Max asked.

"I didn't ask Uncle Peter about Mommy's clothes,"

Chuckie said. "And Mommy's head is hurt—she's not remembering us, so her not remembering changing clothes isn't hard to believe. So, Charlie's explanation makes sense. We're going to take that as being gospel for right now, until proven otherwise, okay?"

"Okay," Charlie and Jamie said. Max didn't say anything.

"Maxwell Solomon . . ." Chuckie said in a warning tone.

"Okay," Max said with a sigh.

"Don't be too hard on him. I can't blame him for thinking I'm not his mother. I don't think I'm his mother, after all."

Chuckie took my hand again. "You are, but it's okay. We'll get you treated and your memory fixed up, Kitty. I promise."

I wanted to say something else, but the motion of the car was relaxing and I started to slip off into sleep.

"Don't fall asleep, baby," Chuckie said. "Stay with me, Kitty. Stay with me."

CHAPTER 12

"STAY WITH ME, KITTY. Stay with me, baby."

I woke up in a man's arms. "I need my wife admitted, immediately." The voice was nice—deep, masculine, and commanding—but it wasn't familiar.

"We need to put her in a wheelchair—" whoever he was talking to said. Sounded like a woman, but I wasn't sure.

"No," the man holding me said flatly. "I'm not letting her out of my arms, or my sight, until we're in a hospital room. Now, take us to one immediately." His voice radiated angry authority.

"This way, sir," someone who was definitely a woman said. "We'll get you into a room right away. Your staff can do the paperwork once they arrive."

"Thank you." The man holding me sounded relieved and far less angry. The authority was still there, though.

I opened my eyes as we hurried along. My head hurt, but I could say he was absolutely the handsomest man I'd ever seen in my life. He had broad features, light brown eyes, and dark wavy hair. Based on the arms holding me and what little I could take in, he was big and brawny, too. He also wasn't my husband.

"Who are you? Where is my husband? Where are my children?"

The man looked at me with concern. "Hang in there, baby. You hit your head. It'll be okay." Now, talking to me, he sounded just this side of freaked out.

Medical personnel were racing about alongside us and they ushered us into a very nice, large hospital room. It looked familiar—I was fairly sure we were in Walter Reed.

"We'll get her taken care of immediately, Mister Martini," a nurse said, very respectfully. "Doctor Hernandez is on his way."

"Seriously, my children were in the same car as me. Where are they? Two boys and a girl." Tried not to panic, but I didn't hear any of the kids' voices.

"Jamie's at home," the man holding me, who I assumed was named Martini, said. "What car? And what boys are you talking about?"

"Charlie and Max!" I struggled to get out of his arms. Martini seemed to understand what I wanted and put me down on the bed in the room. He was as big and brawny as I'd thought. Maybe bigger and brawnier. So perhaps he'd pulled us out of the car when it had crashed. "And how did Jamie get home? Did her father take her? And if so, where is he? Where are my boys?"

"What are you talking about, baby? I'm Jamie's father."

"I've never seen you before in my life and stop calling me baby. You might be a little more muscular than my husband, but I'm sure he can take you in a fight." Charles had studied martial arts for years and was a black or high belt in multiple styles and systems. The kids and I did martial arts, too, though we weren't nearly as competent as Charles was. Even though he was less overly muscled than Martini, I was sure Charles could hold his own against Martini in a fight.

Martini gaped at me. I chose to ignore him and find my children.

I tried to get out of bed, but Martini wouldn't let me. He was very strong, and while I considered trying to force my way past him, the nurses in the room were clearly on his side. As I looked around for someone I could appeal to, his phone rang and he took the call. "Got it. Great." He hung up and looked at the nurses. "We'll take it from here. Secure the room, please." The nurses looked unwilling, but they all left.

The moment the door closed behind them, people appeared out of nowhere. Literally. One moment, no one was in a space, the next a bunch of men in black Armani suits and ties with white shirts showed up. All of them were incredibly handsome. Most of them fanned out, some staying in the room and some going out into the corridor, all looking like Male Models of the Secret Service, but only one of them came over to us.

He was giving Martini a run for the Most Handsome Man in the World award. Though Charles was still the best looking man in the world to me because of who and what he was, James was the only person I could think of who could compete with these two men in a national survey.

This new man was about James' size, so shorter and smaller than Martini, though he, like Charles, was lean and wiry and didn't look like he was a weakling in any way. He had light, straight brown hair, and green eyes flecked with blue. Said eyes narrowed to glare at me. Charming.

"She looks okay to me, Jeff," he said. "Raj is going to stay and handle the mess at the stadium. The others are going to take a floater and should be here in a couple of minutes." He shook his head at me. "Another fine mess, Kitty. I know, I know—it wasn't your fault, right?"

"What in God's name are you talking about? Some lunatic rams my car off the road and you want to say that it *is* my fault?"

He stared at me. "What?"

"She hit her head," Martini said. "Hard. There was blood, Christopher."

Christopher cocked his head at me. "Where?"

Martini moved me gently. "Ah . . . there *was* blood. A lot of it. On the back of her head."

"She's got a bruise on her forehead, but that's all I see," Christopher said.

"Fantastic. Look, I want to know what happened to my

children, and I want to know now. Or I'm going to start screaming."

"I want to know how she changed clothes," Christopher said. "Because that's not the outfit Kitty left the Embassy in this morning."

"I have no idea what you're blathering about, but if someone doesn't tell me what's happened to my children, heads are going to roll."

Martini winced. "Calm down, baby. You're so upset it's smashing through my blocks."

"What the hell are you talking about? And really, stop calling me 'baby' or my husband is going to kill you, financially, figuratively, and probably literally, too."

Christopher stared at me. "Jeff . . . seriously, something's wrong."

Before Martini could reply or I could start screaming my head off, I saw a shimmering in the air, and then a group of men appeared again out of thin air. They all looked stressed and rather grim. Only this time, I knew two of them.

I shoved Martini away from me, leaped off the bed, ran to them, and flung my arms around my husband. "Oh Charles, thank God you're here! Someone tried to kill us and no one will tell me where the kids are and that man has been pawing me." I pointed to Martini. "I think he might have gotten us out of the car, but I don't remember anything since I hit my head and blacked out."

Charles stared at me. "Excuse me?" He looked at Martini. "Is this some kind of joke?"

Martini and Christopher were gaping. "I have no idea what's going on anymore," Martini said.

Looked to James, who had arrived with Charles. "James, make everyone stop fooling around. The kids are missing. Are they . . . hurt or . . . worse?"

"What kids?" James asked. "Jamie's at home where she's supposed to be."

"How? She was with me in the car. And even if she's somehow home safe, where are Charlie and Max?"

"Who are Charlie and Max?" Charles asked me. Sounding as if he truly didn't know.

I backed away from him. "Our sons. Jamie's older brothers. Our children." Looked at his hand. "Where the hell is your wedding ring?"

"Ah . . . I took it off." Charles looked freaked out. "You and Jeff and everyone else insisted I had to, to move on."

"Move on from *what?*"

"My wife's death."

"I'm alive, in case you haven't noticed."

The men all looked shocked, Charles most of all.

"Jeff," Christopher hissed. "Read her. Read her now."

"It won't prove she's not an android," Charles said. "But I agree with White."

Martini seemed to focus on me. I had no idea what he was doing, but I didn't feel anything. "It's Kitty," he said slowly. "But . . . she . . . doesn't know me." He sounded like this was breaking his heart.

Christopher put his hand onto Martini's shoulder. "She hit her head, Jeff," he said gently, and for the first time he seemed like he might actually be a nice person. "She may have a concussion, and you know that means potential memory loss."

"The loss of the last five years?" Martini asked, sounding almost frightened.

"We have enemies," Charles said, voice strained. "I have no idea how anyone could have gotten to her in the short time all of this has gone down, but for all we know, someone slipped something into the coffees I got us at the stadium. Or somewhere else. By now I put nothing past Titan, Gaultier, or YatesCorp."

Before I could ask, again, what in the world they were talking about, a normally cute Hispanic man who was about my height appeared, medical bag in hand. "Tito," Martini said, sounding relieved. "You need to run the OVS over Kitty immediately if not sooner."

Tito didn't argue or question, just pulled out something

that looked a lot like the wands TSA used to do non-intrusive body searches, only it had a lot more blinking lights. "This won't hurt," he said to me with a nice smile. "Just relax, Kitty. I'm sure everything's fine."

"I'm not," I snapped as he waved the wand around me. "I have no idea who any of you other than Charles and James are, and, much more importantly, I have no idea where my children are. My sons are seven and five and my daughter is three. We were in a car crash, at least I'm pretty sure we were. And no one will tell me where my children are, if they're hurt, or . . . worse."

"You have one child," Charles said. "Her name is Jamie."

"No, Charles. *We* have three children, and our daughter's name is indeed Jamie. Are you seriously going to stand there and pretend you don't know me, or our children?" I was too angry and scared to cry, but I wanted to.

"She thinks you're her husband," Martini said to Charles. "Seriously, Chuck, she believes it."

"I don't understand." Charles looked completely confused.

"Neither do I," Martini said. "But her feelings aren't masked, so she's certainly not wearing a blocker. And as long as she's not an android, I don't think she's wearing an emotional overlay, either—mostly because her emotions are going off the charts but I don't think they'd be the emotions our enemies would use to fool me."

Tito finished. "She's ninety percent organic, meaning this is Kitty. Only . . ."

"Only what?" Christopher asked.

"Only Kitty's ninety-five percent organic. Meaning either she got a couple fillings or a pin in her leg in the last week that I don't know about or . . ."

"Or," James said, "this isn't our Kitty."

CHAPTER 13

"WELL, FRANKLY, I'm not most of 'your' Kitty. I know exactly two of you in the room, and why those two are acting insane is beyond me. Is anyone going to tell me one damn thing about what's going on? And, keep in mind, the most important thing I want to know is where my children are."

More people appeared. The room was quite large—we were clearly in some sort of VIP room—but it was now packed to capacity. This time there were three women along, surrounded by another group of men, five of whom looked like they were in the military. There was a big, black, bald man built like Martini, an older man who truly exemplified the term Silver Fox, and a regularly cute guy who winked at me.

Cute and gorgeous or not, the men paled against the women. These were the most gorgeous women I'd ever seen in my life. One was about my height, blonde and buxom. Another was a willowy brunette. And the last was kind of a cross between the two, a slender blonde who looked a little like Christopher.

I steeled myself for the Cheerleader Experience, but the women ran over and hugged me. "Kitty, are you okay?" the buxom one asked. She was holding a big, black purse made out of cheap leather. I'd had a purse just like it in high school and college.

"The stadium's in an uproar," the willowy one shared.

"Raj will handle it," the third Beauty Queen said comfortingly.

"Awesome. Who is Raj? What stadium? And who the hell are you guys? And, I swear to God, someone had better tell me where my children are or I'm going to tear this place apart while I sue you all for everything you're worth."

The three Beauty Queens gaped at me. "Ah," the buxom one said finally, "huh?"

"She hit her head and has no idea who anyone other than Reynolds and James are," Christopher said. "Jeff says she's not wearing an emotional blocker or overlay. And Tito says she's organic but not the same organic as our Kitty."

The three Beauty Queens all blinked. The buxom one handed me the purse. "I figured you'd want this."

"Why?" This question earned me a room full of WTF looks.

She cleared her throat. "It's your purse. And, ah, I'm Lorraine."

"I'm Claudia," the willowy one said.

"I'm Serene," the third Beauty Queen said. "We were all in your wedding. To Jeff. Your wedding to Jeff. All three of us. And others. But all three of us. We're, ah, among your best friends."

"Really." Didn't know what else to say.

"Everyone in the room is your friend," Lorraine said, sounding almost as stricken as Martini had.

Tito, out of everyone, seemed the least confused. He took the purse from me, put it onto the bed, and rummaged through it. He found what he wanted quickly, pulled out a wallet, and handed it to me. "Let's take a look at this, okay, Kitty?"

I took the wallet—there really were too many of them for me to bash my way out, and with Charles acting basically insane, I had no good idea of what to do. Plus my head hurt, and so did my back and neck. Meaning I had whiplash, but I wasn't about to ask for a chiropractor recommendation from these people.

I opened the wallet because that certainly seemed to be expected. The driver's license picture was of me. However, it said I lived at the American Centaurion Embassy in Washington, D.C. I'd never heard of American Centaurion.

Of course, it also said I was Katherine Sarah Katt-Martini. Meaning that, at least if this was to be believed, Martini wasn't lying and I was his wife.

I continued to stare at the license. I had no idea what I was supposed to say or think. "Is this a really elaborate practical joke?" was the best I could come up with.

Tito cleared his throat. "No. You're the wife of the current Vice President of the United States, Kitty. Do you remember any of that?"

I shook my head. "The Vice President isn't named Martini," was all I could manage.

"Jeff," Charles said, "did anything odd happen while you were running Kitty over here? Anything you can think of that was off, anything at all, even it was a small thing, could give us a clue to what's going on."

"No," Martini said. "Well . . . there was one thing, near the old Walter Reed hospital, where it felt like Kitty was weightless, just for a moment."

Considered what he'd said while I stared at this proof that I wasn't who I thought I was. "I remember feeling like something or . . . someone went . . . through me. Just before I blacked out."

One of the men came over. "Look at me a moment, would you, Megalomaniac Girl?" he asked in a gentle tone. Decided I should play along and maybe someone would tell me what was going on.

I looked up. It was the guy who'd winked at me. "That's a hell of a superhero name. Or are you saying I'm a supervillain?"

He shook his head. "My name is Tim Crawford. You call

me Megalomaniac Lad. Because we figure out what the bad guys are doing."

"If you say so."

He looked at my left hand. "Wedding set looks like the one you normally wear, in other words, the set Jeff gave you." He took my hand and looked at it closely. "But it's not actually exactly the same." He looked at Charles. "But I know this isn't the ring he would have given you when he proposed."

Had no idea how he knew, but he was right. "Charles bought this set for me for our fifth anniversary." My throat felt tight. We'd gone back to Vegas to celebrate and Charles had proposed all over again and given me a second wedding set. He'd promised to do the same thing every five years.

"Right. You like baseball?"

"Sure, I love sports. I used to run track in high school and college, so I'm a jock. It kind of keeps hold of you."

"Favorite band is Aerosmith?"

"Well, yes. But I like a ton of different kinds of music."

He nodded. "You read comics?"

"Oh, yeah, of course." I looked at Charles. "It was the first thing we ever bonded over." Charles smiled at me weakly.

"Yeah," Crawford said. "So, aliens . . . do you think they're on Earth?"

Couldn't help it, I snorted. Loudly. Probably meant I wasn't going to be invited to lunch with the Beauty Queens, but oh well. "Of course not. Charles figured out that was all a hoax years ago."

Everyone looked shocked to stricken. Other than Crawford, who merely nodded. "Kitty, I think I know what's going on. And I can explain it at least for you, James, and Reynolds, and maybe for Jeff, too."

"Okay, I'm all ears."

Crawford cleared his throat. "You're in Bizarro World."

This was met with confused looks from everyone in the room other than those Crawford had named. Charles, James, and Martini all looked as if light bulbs had gone off over all their heads.

"Excuse me?"

"Bizarro World," Crawford said. "You're in it. In this world, aliens from the Alpha Centauri system are living on the planet. You're not married to Reynolds, though you two are still best friends. You're married to Jeff and, as Tito said, he's the Vice President. Just elected last November. You've also been an, ah, alien monster killer, the Head of Airborne for Centaurion Division, which is the military, science, and research side of American Centaurion, and an ambassador."

"Pull the other one, it has bells on."

He grinned. "I'm serious."

James came closer, and he had a funny expression, like he was trying to remember something important. "It's a multiverse out there," he said slowly. "Meaning that there can be many versions of ourselves, over and over again, with just little things different." He looked at me and Charles. "Some people you're connected to over and over again." He looked at the others in the room. "And some you're not."

Let this all rev in my mind for a little bit. Head hurting or not, I was able to think fast when I needed to, and I clearly needed to.

I took a long look around the room. "Ah, Tim?"

"Yes?"

"All the really gorgeous ones are, um, aliens?"

"Yes."

"Prove it."

Martini stepped closer and took my hand and put it against his chest.

"Oh, my God, you have two hearts!"

He nodded. "I do." He looked at me intently. "I think Tim's right. And so do you. I can feel it."

"How?"

"I'm an empath, the strongest in the world, probably the galaxy. And I can feel everything you're feeling." He stroked my face. "I can read your mind, too." He looked at Charles. "She's not 'my' Kitty—she's yours."

Charles shook his head violently. "No. If what Tim's saying is right—and until we have a more rational hypothesis, I'm willing to go with the multiverse idea—then she isn't mine, she's married to another version of me in another universe."

"So, in this world, Jamie is my daughter, but . . . Charlie and Max don't exist?" Shoved aside the horrible way this made me feel. Right now, I needed to determine if this was really what was going on or if I'd woken up in an insane asylum filled with America's Top Models.

"Yes, but Jeff is Jamie's father. You're not married to Reynolds, so the children you had with him aren't here," James said. "You married Jeff almost four years ago."

"How is Jamie here, then?"

"What day was she born?" Crawford asked.

"Christmas day, three years ago."

"Same as your Jamie here," James said. "And she's basically your little clone."

"Externally," Charles said. "Internally, she's Jeff's daughter."

"The ties to the mother are always strongest," Tito said.

The door opened. Someone was actually entering this room via conventional means. I turned to see who it was, and as I did so, the wallet fell from my hands. She looked normal, hale and hearty, and I felt like the room was spinning.

"What in the Sam Hill is going on?" she asked, all brisk authority. "Kitty, are you alright?"

"Mom?" I went to her slowly. "Mom, is it really you?"

She looked at me like I was crazy. "Of course it is, kitten. Who else would it be?"

I didn't question it any more. I just grabbed her and held on as tightly as possible. "Oh, Mom. I've missed you so much." As I started to cry, I had to accept that Crawford was right—I was indeed in Bizarro World. But at this moment, it suddenly seemed worth visiting.

CHAPTER 14

THE FIRST NURSES WE SAW at Walter Reed didn't like my head injury, but they felt it looked worse than it was. Once they cleaned me up it was decided that I didn't need stitches, and by the time the RN who was doing my pre-check for the doctor came in to see us, Chuckie was pointedly asked why I was even here.

When Dr. Zainal arrived he recognized me, but I was greeted as an old friend, not as someone he sort of knew. Dr. Zainal didn't mentioned aliens, Jeff, the Bahraini diplomatic mission, or anything else I'd have thought he would. He did ask how we'd enjoyed Australia and said he was glad we were back early, despite the circumstances. Just added this onto the Weirdness of the Day column and didn't even remark on it.

My head still hurt, but not like it had. Chuckie was clearly freaked out by my rapid improvement, but he just told Dr. Zainal about the car accident and the doctor seemed forgiving of my taking up his time, in part because the kids needed to be checked out, too.

The kids were checked first, and all declared fine and just shaken up. Then it was my turn. "The chart says that Katherine's head was cut open when she arrived," Dr. Zainal said. "How did you receive your injury, Katherine?" he asked. "I would have thought the airbags in your car would have caused a different injury, depending on where your hands were on the steering wheel."

"The airbags never deployed."

Chuckie stiffened. "What? Are you sure?"

"I'm freaking positive."

"Mommy's forehead hit the steering wheel," Charlie offered helpfully. "Then her head went back, but she didn't really hit the seat."

"And no bags opened anywhere," Max added.

"But it's the back of her head where the injury was," Chuckie said.

"Interesting," Dr. Zainal said. "As I examine her, I see nothing. However, the amount of blood on the back of her head and on her clothing is consistent with a more severe head injury than she appears to have."

"I'm a fast healer."

Dr. Zainal gave me the "really?" look. "Not in my experience," he said. "Not like this. However, even though there is no actual external injury we can see, the risk of a severe concussion is still there. If the hematoma doesn't go out—and you have no bump forming—then it tends to go in, and press upon the brain."

"Would that explain why Kitty has memory loss and confusion?" Chuckie asked, sounding almost desperate.

Dr. Zainal nodded. "Yes, very likely. We still know so little about what affects the brain, but a trauma such as what you described could cause many issues. But let's see what we have otherwise." A variety of tests were performed, and as far as I could tell, I passed them all.

The doctor shook his head. "Her reflexes are excellent, her eyes display no signs of concussion, and she displays no other signs of trauma or even injury."

"I told you, I'm a fast healer."

"Apparently so." But he didn't ask any more questions. At least of me. He pulled Chuckie aside and they spoke quietly. If I was still fully human, I wouldn't have been able to hear them. But A-Cs have enhanced hearing, so these days I did as well, and I could hear them easily.

"She needs an MRI," Dr. Zainal. "For starters. Potentially many other tests, especially if the MRI isn't definitive. I've never seen anything like this."

"She looked much worse when I got to them," Chuckie said. "I was amazed she was upright, but I just figured it was adrenaline rush."

"Maybe, but the rapid healing . . . I have no idea what could have caused that. It's a good thing, a miracle, at least it seems so, but until we study her more, I have no guess for what's truly going on."

Aside from the fact that they were discussing my health-care without consulting or including me, it occurred to me that I didn't want any regular hospital having a sample of my blood or tissue or anything. The less known about my improved physical makeup the better.

"I just want to go home," I said, before Chuckie could agree to anything. "Now. Please. The kids and I need to get home and regroup."

Dr. Zainal shook his head. "Katherine, you may have a severe concussion and we should probably do an MRI."

"No. I want to go home. Immediately if not sooner. I will not allow you to perpetrate any more medical procedures on me. Or the kids." They didn't need to discover that Jamie was also extra with a nice side of special, either. "Let's go, Chuckie. Now."

Chuckie stared at me. "Ah, okay," he said.

Dr. Zainal clearly didn't approve, but he stopped arguing. "Call me, day or night, if anyone feels worse. And a visit to your chiropractor would be a wise choice for the children. Katherine probably needs a visit as well, but I'm concerned about manipulation affecting her concussion negatively."

"Gotcha, we'll be cautious."

Both men stared at me, but we were allowed to leave. Of course, it took longer than anyone wanted to get released, but we managed it. Chuckie also managed to fit in a phone call to someone that he thought I didn't know he'd made. I could hear most of his side of the conversation and it consisted of a fast, high-level recap of everything that had happened and everything I'd said or done. My strong suspicion was that the person on the other end of the call was Reader.

"Please stop calling me Chuckie outside of the bedroom, Kitty," he said quietly as we were finally heading toward the car. "It makes me really uncomfortable when you call me that in front of the kids."

Decided to not complain about this. Everything was weird, odd, or suspicious, why not this, too? "What would you prefer then? Chuck?"

"No. What you've called me for the past many years, baby—Charles."

"Check. Charles it is."

He sighed but said nothing else, got the kids into the car and tucked me in as well, then we headed off.

The car ride wasn't filled with an overabundance of chat. Chuckie seemed worried and a little preoccupied. The kids were quiet, though I could hear Max grumbling that no one ever listened to him about anything. And I didn't feel like talking, since the answers I gave and got didn't make me or anyone else feel any better about anything.

Apparently we hadn't been that far from wherever we lived when we'd been run off the road, as we got off at the same highway exit we'd gotten on at earlier. We turned off the main street quickly and pulled into a lovely neighborhood with mature landscaping and nice, large homes. Was fairly sure this was the Colonial Village area, but wasn't positive. I was used to living in A-C facilities and they were gigantic, but these homes were still probably double the size of the house I'd grown up in.

Which reminded me. "Have you called my mom yet?"

Chuckie's hands tightened on the steering wheel. "Let's get home first, okay?"

We pulled up to a large house with a five-car garage. "This is a pretty house."

"Glad you still like it, since you picked it out." One of the garage doors opened and we drove in. "You wait in the car while I get the kids out."

As he got out of the car, a man came into the garage from, I assumed, inside the house. It was a man I knew. He rushed to my door and opened it. "Kitty, darling, what did Doctor Zainal say? Are you and our precious little ones alright?"

"Pierre! It's so good to see you! Can you explain—"

"Pierre? Why are we speaking French?" He sounded genuinely confused as he started to help me out of the car.

"I'll do that, Peter, please. And like I told you, she hit her head," Chuckie said, as the boys crowded near Pierre and Chuckie got Jamie out of the car. "Hard. Doctor Zainal says the amount of blood he saw on the back of her head and clothes indicates that Kitty's lucky she didn't crack her head wide open. However, nothing seems wrong externally now. But she needs rest and to be watched for signs of major concussion."

Pierre cocked his head at me. "How did you hurt the back of your head if you were in a car accident? And if there was so much blood—and I can see that there was by the horrid state of these clothes—why don't you have stitches?"

"These are question no one's going to like my answer for—I was at the football stadium, watching a cricket game, and I fell onto the steps. After I caused Jeff to spill coffee on everyone. And I have faster regeneration than regular people."

Pierre stared at me. "Who's Jeff?" As I looked at him I noticed he looked a little different than he had when I'd left this morning. Like Chuckie, his hair was slightly different, and he wasn't in the Armani Fatigues. He was dressed fashionably, but not formally.

"That's the question of the day," Chuckie said as he handed Jamie to Pierre and carefully helped me out of the car. "I'm fairly sure she's gotten our *Traveler* game mixed up in her mind with reality."

"Ah, interesting."

"Is it?" I asked. "Can we call my mother now?"

Pierre and the kids stared at me. All of them looked upset.

Chuckie sighed as he helped me into the house. "Kitty . . . I'm sorry, but . . ."

"But what? What's wrong? Did Mom get hurt? Is Dad okay?" Maybe whoever was after me and the kids had been trying to get to or hurt my mother.

Chuckie put his arm around me and led me into what appeared to be the living room. "Kitty . . . baby, I'm so sorry that I have to tell you this, again, but . . ." He hugged me and kissed my forehead gently. "Your mother has been dead since Jamie was six months old."

CHAPTER 15

MOM WAS DEAD? This did not compute. At all. "There's no way! I just saw her last night! Is this some weird covert op?"

"No," Chuckie said gently. "I wish it was."

"Look, my mother is the head of the P.T.C.U. If she was dead, wouldn't the President have a problem with that?"

"P.T.C.U.?" Chuckie asked. He was clearly asking for everyone else in the room.

"Presidential Terrorism Control Unit. She's the head of it."

"Ah. There's no such unit, Kitty."

"Look, I realize that it's extremely covert. I mean, I didn't find out about it until I was freaking twenty-seven and discovered aliens were on the planet. But is now the time to pretend? Surely the kids are aware of what you do and I did for a living."

"Daddy works for a think tank, but only 'cause Papa Sol thinks he needs to make his mind available," Charlie said. Clearly he'd heard this a lot.

"How do we afford this house?"

"Charles made his money in convenience stores and then in the stock market," Pierre said. "As you proudly tell anyone who asks. You're multi-millionaires many times over, as the bank cheerfully tells me every time I pay our bills."

"Okay. What do you all think I do for a living?"

"You don't work, Mommy," Charlie replied. "You take care of us."

"She homeschools us," Max added. "Our real mommy, I mean."

"I told you to stop that, Maxwell," Chuckie said sternly.

"Uncle Peter, did Mommy go change clothes before we left this morning?" Max asked.

"Ahh . . ." Pierre looked as if he wished he'd been briefed on whatever story he was supposed to tell.

"She forgot our music and went back into the house after Daddy and Uncle James left," Charlie added.

"That makes sense." Now Pierre looked relieved. "I was on the phone dealing with the worst customer service in the world, so elephants could have gone in and out and I wouldn't have noticed. Speaking of which . . ." He took my jacket and made the tsking sound that indicated he felt this item was probably beyond repair.

"That's it, then," Chuckie said to Max. "Mommy decided to change to look nicer for Auntie Caro and that's why she's in different clothes than she was in at breakfast. Speaking of whom . . . Peter, did you reach Caroline?" He helped me sit down on a very lovely sofa. Had to admit, I liked the décor. Didn't mention it because I had a feeling everyone would tell me I liked it because I'd picked it out.

"Yes, she went to get Sol from the airport. She took a cab there and she'll drive them both back here."

"Why would Caro have to get my dad from anywhere, let alone the airport?"

Both men gave me the look I was becoming familiar with—the "oh dear, it's worse than I thought" look. Pierre cleared this throat. "Ah, your father went to meet up with your Aunt Carla during her layover today."

"Why?"

"Ah, so none of the rest of us would have to see her."

"Well, that makes sense. So, Aunt Carla's alive, well, and exactly the same as I remember, but you insist that my mother, her younger sister, is dead?"

Peter nodded sadly. Chuckie, meanwhile, was on his phone. "Caroline, hi. Are you with Sol? Great. Is Carla gone? Oh. Wonderful." He didn't sound like it was truly wonderful, which boded in the Aunt Carla department. "Well, the car's totaled but they're all amazingly okay. Kitty's hit her head, though, and is having some, ah, memory issues. You're going to need to prep Sol, and probably Carla, too, I'm sorry." Aunt Carla department confirmed. "Yes. Ah, she remembers who you and I are, but, ah . . . yeah. She thinks she's married to an alien." He swallowed. "And until a couple of minutes ago, she thought Angela was still alive."

"I don't believe she's dead yet. I only believe that you've all *told* me she's dead."

"Yeah, you heard that right. Please. Thanks, see you soon. Drive safely, and I really mean that." He hung up and sat down next to me. "Caroline's got your dad and they're on their way here, baby. It'll all be okay, I promise."

"Aunt Carla's along for the ride, too, isn't she?"

"Yes." He said this with absolutely no enthusiasm.

"Truly, I cannot wait." Leaned against Chuckie. "I don't understand what's going on."

He put his arm around me and held me close. "I know. We'll get it taken care of."

"I want to know who's trying to kill us. Because in addition to the airbags not going off—meaning that car was tampered with—the people who ran us off the road had machine guns that they used on the car in a clear attempt to finish the job they started. And I didn't recognize any of them."

"Why would you recognize crazed killers?" Chuckie asked, sounding as if this was potentially the craziest thing I'd said so far.

"Um, by now I have a long history with hit men and women. Some who don't like us, most of whom are very dead now, and some who do. Speaking of whom, we should probably contact my 'uncles,' Peter the Dingo Dog and Surly Vic."

"Why are you calling Uncle Peter a dog?" Charlie asked.

"I'm not. Different Peter."

Chuckie put his finger to my lips. "Kitty, you need to stop, baby. You're babbling and you're frightening the children."

"Not just the children," Pierre said quietly. He was texting. "Kitty, darling, we don't associate with paid killers."

"They prefer to be called assassins. And yeah, actually, we do."

Pierre's phone beeped. "James is on his way. He should arrive when Caroline and Sol do, if not before."

"Fine. Look, the car was clearly tampered with. Assassins went out of their way to kill us. First by trying to drive us into a head-on collision, then by actually driving us off the road, and then by shooting us and blowing our car up. I'd sincerely like someone to take this seriously and stop acting like I'm crazed or concussed."

"Let me worry about that," Chuckie said.

"Not just no but hell no. People tried to kill me and these children today. As far as I'm concerned, that makes it totally my worry. I'm used to people trying to kill me on a regular basis, but it never stops being annoying."

The "oh dear" looks were on everyone's faces. "Mommy," Charlie said, "no one ever tries to kill us."

Jamie nodded her agreement. "*We've* never gone through this, Mommy." Again, everyone looked shocked. And again, there was something in the way she said this—something off. I needed to figure out what was going on with her and I needed to do it soon.

"She's not our mommy," Max said, stomping his foot. Just like I did when it got to be too much and no one was paying attention to the obvious. "Listen to her! She talks wrong, just a little, but it's wrong. She looks wrong, just a little, but it's still wrong. Daddy said that's her wedding ring, but it's *not*. It's just a little different, but it's still wrong. She knows she's not our mommy."

"She *is*," Jamie said strongly.

"She *isn't*," Max retorted. "Ask her who she thinks she is."

Chuckie opened his mouth, probably to tell Max to behave, but I put my hand up. "Until I believe it, stop telling Max he's being inappropriate. Because right now I feel like he's the only one listening to me."

Chuckie took my hand and looked at the wedding set more closely. "Max is right," he said slowly. "This isn't the set I bought for you. It's close, but not quite the same. Where did you get this?" He sounded jealous and suspicious again.

"From my husband. My actual husband."

"Tell them," Max pleaded. "Tell them who *you* think you are."

"I *know* I'm Katherine Sarah Katt, only I'm married to a man named Jeff Martini. He's an alien from Alpha Four of the Alpha Centaurion solar system. The positives are that they're here to protect and serve, and have given us a tremendous amount of technology. Oh, and they're all, every one of them, drop-dead gorgeous. And they think brains and brain capacity is the be-all, end-all, and, lucky us, they therefore feel that humans are da bomb, which is kind of a super bonus."

"Kitty," Chuckie said patiently, "there are no aliens on the planet. It's a hoax. I'm sure they're out there, somewhere, but they're not here."

"Yes, actually they are. Aliens have been on the planet, en masse, since the nineteen-sixties. You, Chu—, ah, Charles, are part of the C.I.A. As I told you earlier, you head their Extra-Terrestrial Division. This has made you a target because we have a lot of enemies and you protect us. You were recruited by my mother."

"Your mother wasn't in the C.I.A." He was lying. Again, I could tell, but the unsettling thing was that this was, so far, the only thing he was lying about.

"She is or was, and my father is a cryptologist for NASA, specializing in alien languages."

"Sol is a history professor."

"Yes, but that's his cover. We aren't married because I thought you were joking when you proposed in Las Vegas and I found out you weren't after I'd already met and fallen in love with Jeff. You've been married, to a half-alien named Naomi. She died due to one of the many megalomaniacs that are constantly trying to destroy the A-Cs and take control of our world."

"I don't know anyone named Naomi," Chuckie said gently. "I've told you many times—I've never cheated on you, Kitty. Is that what this is all about? That old fight about why I'm occasionally gone for long periods where you can't reach me?"

"No, because I know nothing *of* that old fight. Let's move on, but I'll be happy to revisit that later. James is the Head of Field for Centaurion Division, the military branch of American Centaurion, which is the principality or whatever all the aliens fall under. He, like me, killed a parasitic superbeing—basically an alien monster—which was our introduction to our new supersecret lives. Following me so far?"

"Not at all," Peter said. "I mean, I can't speak for anyone else, Kitty darling, but this sounds like you're trying to pitch a new TV series for the CW."

Heard a step and turned to see Reader enter the room. "I'm following it," Reader said. "At least, I think I am."

"How long have you been here?" Chuckie asked. He didn't sound angry. He sounded like he was verifying that Reader had been backing him up.

Reader shrugged and passed one of those little signs to Chuckie. "Long enough." Chuckie looked relieved, but only for a fleeting moment. I only saw this exchange because I was pointedly looking for it. "Based on what you and Peter have told me, something's very off, more than a concussion or the confusion of the *Traveler* game and real life. Based on what I just heard Kitty say, she has an entire life that she feels she's lived that is completely different than the one we know of."

"And whoever you think I am, she has no knowledge that the two of you are in the C.I.A., or similar, does she?"

CHAPTER 16

THE KIDS LOOKED CONFUSED, Pierre looked suspicious, and Chuckie had heard this from me already so he had his poker face on. But my C.I.A. accusation caused Reader to jerk. He pulled it together quickly and slapped an innocent and confused expression onto his face, but his reaction was the final proof I was looking for.

"No idea what you're talking about," Chuckie said.

"Bunk. How did my mother die?"

"She was in an accident—" Chuckie started.

"Bunk again. If she didn't die of a disease, and I didn't witness this death—and based on you saying that you hated having to tell me that she was dead *again*, I didn't know about her death until you broke the news—then she died on a covert op. One I'd imagine she had both of you working."

Both men were ready to lie to me, I could tell. But Dad, Aunt Carla, and Caroline entered the room, forestalling the fibbing.

The kids ran to our new arrivals and got hugs and confirmation of their well-being. Chuckie helped me up from the couch—I didn't need it, but he seemed to think I did, and I didn't want to have an argument or the discussion we needed to have in front of Aunt Carla.

I examined the three newcomers. Each looked slightly

different than the last time I'd seen them—mostly hairstyles and clothing choices. All off, just a little, but off from what I knew to be reality.

True, I didn't see Aunt Carla a lot, but she was wearing a wedding ring—the ring I remembered was from her third marriage, indicating she was still married, which wasn't the case as I knew it.

Caroline looked happier than I'd seen her since Michael Gower had died. Not that she'd spent the past year and a half moping but still, some of the light had gone out of her eyes when she'd lost the only man she'd found that she'd wanted to marry, and that light was still in those eyes here.

And Dad . . . Dad looked like he'd been heartbroken and trying to hide it for a long time. Had no idea what was really going on, but whatever it was, it hadn't been good for my father. Meaning that Chuckie's insistence that Mom was dead had a lot more weight.

Dad came over and hugged me tightly. He was shaking. "To think we almost lost all of you . . ."

Decided that, regardless of what I was thinking, my father needed comforting and reassurance, not me to sound crazy. I could save that for later. "It's okay, Dad. We're all alright."

"You're a wreck, Katherine," Aunt Carla said as she extracted me from Dad and hugged me as well. "Why haven't you all had her get cleaned up?" she asked the men chidingly.

"We were waiting for you and Caro to get here," I replied quickly. "So you two could help me."

Caroline looked confused by this, but Aunt Carla beamed. "I'm happy to cover what Angela would have, dear."

Saw Chuckie wince out of the side of my eye, and felt Dad stiffen next to me. Chose to use the diplomacy I'd been forced to learn these past several years. I hugged Aunt Carla again. "Thanks. That means a lot to me."

Every jaw in the room dropped, other than Aunt Carla's—and I knew that because I didn't feel her jaw hit my shoulder—and Jamie's. Even the boys looked shocked. Jamie, however, looked pleased.

"Okay," Caroline said, sounding as confused as she looked. "Normally you want Charles to help you."

"Not today. He has to figure out who ran us off the road and why." Figured now was a terrible time to say that I didn't think he was my actual husband and wanted to avoid intimacy, because that was only going to lead to bad things.

Chuckie sighed. "She's hit her head, as I keep on saying. Right now, Kitty doesn't remember us correctly. She doesn't think I'm her husband. In fact, she believes she's married to a space alien and has a completely different life." Apparently Chuckie felt the Full Disclosure Option was the way to go. Nice of him to cover that for me. "Until proven otherwise, I still think her concussion—which I'm certain she has—caused her to mix up our *Traveler* game in her mind." He was set on this one.

"Wedding rings," I reminded him.

"You lost your set and got one to replace it without telling me," Chuckie said. "You've done similar with other things we like that got lost or broken. That's just one reason, but it makes sense."

"Does it?" My head throbbed, which it shouldn't have, since I was basically all healed up. Of course, there was always the nagging possibility that he was right and I just had a major concussion and wasn't as healed up as I thought I was. "My head hurts again."

Aunt Carla raised her eyebrow. "Really?" She gave me a long look. "She looks peaky, I'll give you that. Caroline and I will help you and hopefully we can reassure you that Charles is your wonderful husband and the father of your beautiful children."

"Yeah." We stood there for a couple of seconds. Everyone looked at me. "What?"

"We're waiting for you three to leave to get you cleaned up," Reader said.

"I have no idea where to go. I've never been in this house before."

Aunt Carla, Caroline, and Dad exchanged the "oh dear"

looks. "Not to worry," Aunt Carla said gently, as she put her arm around me. "Caroline and I will show you."

Max opened his mouth—to tell everyone I wasn't his mother, I was sure—but I caught his eye and shook my head just a little, and he closed his mouth. Chuckie and Reader weren't the only ones who could pass little signs around.

We went upstairs and Jamie came with us. She trotted into a room, but it wasn't the one Aunt Carla was heading me toward. "Can I see where Jamie's headed?"

"Certainly, Katherine. It's her room." Aunt Carla was being much nicer and far more solicitous than I was used to. Chose to accept this as the way things were wherever here was and go with it.

Jamie's room was a shock. First of all, it wasn't pink. Jamie loved pink. To the point where we weren't sure that, if she had the means, she wouldn't remove all other colors from the spectrum. This room was pretty—clearly done up in Little Girl Pastels, but it wasn't the Shrine to Pink that I was used to.

The other oddity was the mirror. There was a very large three-way mirror dominating this room. Jamie was sitting in front of this mirror, just staring at it. She looked happy and intent. She also didn't turn around or even look at any of our reflections in the mirrors.

"What's she looking at?" I asked softly.

"Herself," Caroline said. "At least, we think so."

Aunt Carla backed us out of the room and headed us down the hall. We passed three more bedrooms, all larger than Jamie's. Aunt Carla had me look into each room.

One was clearly for Charlie and Max—the bunk beds and Junior Science Wizard and Future Sports Star motifs were in full force, as was the proof that Legos were the model airplanes of this generation. Unlike Jamie's room, this room was pretty normal. Filled with all the top-of-the-line stuff little boys liked, but still, normal.

The bedroom across the hall from the boys' was Reader's. I'd never seen how he decorated outside of Centaurion Division properties, which tended to conform to the Elves' preferred Functionally Austere style. The evidence showed that Modern Hipster Chic was apparently Reader's personal look. There were framed prints of a selection of his fashion covers all over, too. Some I recognized—the Calvin Klein ad that I'd had up in my dorm room, for example—but most I didn't. He looked fantastic in every one, of course.

The next bedroom was Pierre's, or rather, Mini Paris Done Tastefully. Had to admit I liked it, but then, Pierre never made a misstep in anything as far as I'd ever seen. Monet was the artistic theme here.

"What's wrong with Jamie?" I asked as we entered what was clearly the master bedroom. This was decorated exactly like I'd expect a room where Chuckie and I spent a lot of time to be decorated. Framed rock posters on the walls—all of them signed—were mixed up with eclectic artwork, much of which looked original. Smaller art pieces and little knick-knacks adorned the tops of the gigantic bookcases, all packed with books, along the longest wall, a king-sized bed that looked extremely comfy, a lounger that reminded me of the one I used when Jamie was a baby, and a gigantic walk-in closet, attached to a bathroom reminiscent of the one I'd shared with Jeff in Vegas, right before we got married.

"We're not sure," Aunt Carla said carefully. "You and Charles don't like to talk about it a lot."

"Ah. Okay. Um, I have to say, this is a great house. And I've only seen some of it."

"Yeah, you guys love it," Caroline said. "Your place in Australia's great, too. Do you remember it at all?"

"No. I know no one believes me, but I don't belong here."

Caroline hugged me. "It's okay, Kit-Kat. We'll get you cleaned up and then you can relax and we'll show you pictures and remind you of things. It'll all come back to you."

Aunt Carla cleared her throat. "Ah, Katherine? Is there a reason you might not remember? Aside from a concussion, I mean."

"I honestly have no idea what you're suggesting."

She sighed. "Pressures due to all of Jamie's issues. Your nagging concern that Charles might sometimes . . . stray. The loss of your mother." She looked very sad. "You and Sol haven't handled it well. It's why I try to come by when you're in the States, at least as much as my travel schedule allows. This is the first time you've . . . let me help. I'm just wondering if there might be a trigger Caroline and I can discover that would have caused you to have this complete memory loss of so many things that you treasure."

"No, not that I can think of. In the world I'm from, Mom isn't dead, I don't worry about my husband cheating on me because A-Cs mate for life, and Jamie is a precocious, happy little chatterbox, who has no issues." Well, she was potentially one of the most powerful hybrids around, and was housing a superconsciousness in her mind, but those were very par for our particular course.

"Ah." Aunt Carla and Caroline exchanged a look. Or rather, a "look."

"What? I mean, seriously, you both seem to have reached the same conclusion."

"It sounds like you've made up a life that's just a little better and more exciting than the one you have in reality," Caroline said carefully. "It's a natural thing, especially because you told me earlier what a tough trip home you'd all had. I can understand wanting to escape for a little bit, even if it's just into your own imagination."

"I'm not making any of this up."

"Is anything in here familiar?" Aunt Carla asked.

"Well, sure. The bathroom is a lot like one at The Hotel when I was there right before I got married. To Jeff Martini. Not to Chuckie. Sorry, Charles."

"You've told me you only call him Chuckie in bed now," Caroline said. "Because it didn't sound adult enough and he was a successful businessman and deserved respect."

"Yeah, he said the same. I call him Chuckie all the time where I'm from."

"Or else you still want to call him Chuckie and don't because you feel pressured, and so in your fantasy, you call him the name you prefer," Aunt Carla suggested.

"Maybe. I think I just want to get cleaned up. Do I wear jeans, concert T-shirts, and Converse here?"

They both nodded. "When you're relaxing," Caroline said.

"Great. Then I'll change into that. I think I'm okay to shower alone, but I promise to call if I need you guys."

Aunt Carla shook her head. "We've both seen everything you own. Leave the bathroom door open. Just in case."

Chose not to argue about this compromise. Got out of these clothes and into the shower. It was a great bathroom and I felt physically better after showering using the highest-class hair and personal care products I'd ever seen. Contemplated using hyperspeed for it, but decided that it would be better to wait, in part because I needed to relax a little.

Shower done, I dried off with the fluffiest towels in existence. If this was really the life I was "trying to escape," I had to ask myself why anyone would think I'd want to.

Contemplated things Chuckie had said to me before I got married. He'd mentioned that he'd have found a smooth, casual way to get me used to living a wealthy lifestyle. Clearly, he'd managed well. Though nothing was overdone—unostentatious was still Chuckie's watchword and apparently it was this family's as well.

Combed my hair back into a ponytail and trotted out. They'd laid clothes out for me and I stared. The underwear, jeans, and Converse were not an issue, nor was the Aerosmith hoodie. It was the T-shirt they'd picked that had me confused.

"Why the hell would I wear, let alone own, a Jack Johnson T-shirt?"

Both women stared at me as I started to get dressed. "Ah, because he's a personal friend?" Caroline asked. "You guys went to a concert a few years ago, went backstage, bonded. You never miss him when he's on tour. The kids know him. He's their favorite."

This did not compute. "Jack Johnson? He of the slow and boring?"

"You all think he's cool." Caroline sounded ready to cry. "He's the nicest guy—he's your friend, Kitty. I count him as my friend because of you. How can you be insulting his music all of a sudden?"

Wow. Not only was everything else messed up, I suddenly liked a musical artist I found to be stultifyingly dull. It was like I was in Bizarro World.

I froze, my jeans halfway on. "Oh. Wow. That's it."

"What's it?" Aunt Carla asked.

Didn't answer and finished getting dressed instead, though I took the Jack Johnson shirt back into the ginormous walk-in closet and hung it back up in the rock T-shirts section. Chose a Mötley Crüe shirt—had a feeling I was going to need double rocking support today.

Put on the hoodie and looked around for my purse. Remembered that it wasn't my purse and it was downstairs somewhere. Maybe still in the car. Couldn't recall. Decided not to care, since the likelihood that it contained a Glock was slim. Still, one never knew.

"Where do I keep my Glock?"

"In your purse," Caroline answered. "Though I don't know that you've ever fired it except at the shooting range."

Interesting. Apparently the wealthy had some serious security issues. Then again, I'd been run off the road with clear intent to kill, so those concerns seemed less like paranoia and more like brilliant planning. And, hey, I had a Glock. Chose to look at this as really good news.

Also chose to look out the bedroom window. In time to see a dark sedan with an impressive pushbar in front and blacked out windows driving slowly up the street.

"Um, Caro? Aunt Carla? Tell me . . . do we happen to have a safe room in this house?"

CHAPTER 17

"YES," Aunt Carla answered promptly. "Angela insisted that you have a safe room here and in Australia."

More proof Mom had been in covert and clandestine ops before she was killed. Murdered, more likely. Felt rage growing. Good. I was going to need it.

"Super. Where, exactly, is the safe room? And how many can it hold?"

"Downstairs, at the back of the house," Caroline replied. "And it can hold at least twenty people. It's stocked to support those people for at least a week. And it also has full medical supplies."

"And weapons," Aunt Carla added. "Because, if you're in a safe room . . ."

"Yeah, you're not there for the thrill of playing hide and seek. But this is great news. By the way, the nausea will pass."

"Huh?" Caroline said, as I grabbed her and Aunt Carla. Contemplated grabbing Jamie, but I only had two hands and no idea if either woman would follow orders from me, ever, let alone right now. I'd come back for Jamie—those downstairs would be the first targets. Besides, I had to find the room anyway.

Took off at hyperspeed. Zoomed downstairs and ran

around for a second or two, then realized I had no idea where
the room was and safe rooms were supposed to be disguised,
so I had no chance of guessing where it was with the limited
time I had. Stopped in front of Chuckie and Reader. They
both jumped as if we'd appeared out of nowhere, which, considering how hyperspeed worked, we had.

"The safe room! We need everyone in it—right now!
Don't question, just go!" I shoved Aunt Carla and Caroline
at them, then ran back upstairs. Grabbed Jamie, realized I
hadn't seen the boys downstairs, and went to their room.
Sure enough, they were in there.

Grabbed Max and threw him on my back, while I took
Charlie's hand in my free one. "It's just like in Rock Creek,
kids. Hang on, no strangling me, Max. Charlie, lead me to
the safe room. You steer, I'll handle the speed."

Had to hand it to these kids—they didn't question. Max
held on, Charlie nodded, Jamie squeezed my hand, and we
took off. Charlie led me to the room the adults were thankfully heading for. We got there first, but the others were right
behind us. Naturally there was a combination. Stopped and
put the kids down. The running had been short, so while the
kids and women were gagging, no one was tossing their
cookies.

Ran back to find Chuckie starting to head upstairs, to grab
the kids no doubt. Grabbed him and ran him back to the
room. "Get it open," I told him, "get everyone in, then get
your guns. We're about to be attacked."

He opened his mouth, and I put my hand up. "I did all this
at something called hyperspeed. I'll explain it later. Just get
in the damn room. If I'm crazy, super, it's a fun family excursion right before Mommy goes to the Special Hospital for a
Little Vacation. If, however, I'm not—and I guarantee that
James can tell you that I wasn't making it up about those
freaking machine guns—then the assassins are on our street.
Move it!"

Spun around and ran back to the living room. Sure
enough, the purse was on the sofa. I dumped it out and, joy

and rapture, a Glock .23 dropped out. Grabbed it and ran back to the safe room. Chuckie had just gotten it opened. Hyperspeed was a great thing.

Contemplated the options. Sure, they weren't the Reader and Chuckie I knew, but they were still clearly Reader and Chuckie. Meaning some things would be the same, including who was likely to be the most adaptable and shift into teaming with me the fastest. Plus, I had the children to consider.

Grabbed Reader and shoved Chuckie inside. "Take care of everyone and if I sound totally scared, sweet, or clueless, or James doesn't give you the right password or whatever you two use, then assume we're hostages and come out with guns blazing. Otherwise, we'll let you know when it's over."

With that, I slammed the door. Sure enough, it locked.

Took Reader's hand and ran upstairs, to the same window where I'd spotted the car in the first place. It was just parking across the street. Hyperspeed remained the best superpower ever.

"See that car?" I asked as he gagged. "That's the car that drove us off the road. And it was filled with assassins with machine guns. I have one Glock and, as far as I saw, a single clip. I have no idea what firepower you and Chuckie possess. But I have something else that I'm now convinced this world does not have."

"Kitty, I realize something's off, and I can agree that this looks highly suspicious, but—"

"Bizarro World."

"Wait, what?"

"Bizarro World. I've switched places with the Kitty in this universe. Should we survive this attack, I'll tell you all about it, at least, what I can remember. However, survival is not a given. But, what these assassins don't know, or know how to counter, is the fact that I have hyperspeed, increased strength, and superfast healing."

"Excuse me?"

"I'm Wolverine with Boobs, James. In the world I come

from. Because, I think I may have mentioned, I'm married to an alien and there was mother-and-child feedback and all that jazz I'm living to tell you later. You need to back me up. I'm going to take these bastards out before they kill anyone, especially anyone in this house. By the way, should I kill them or incapacitate them? If given the option, I mean?"

He stared at me. "Incapacitate," he said, sounding shaken. "But if you have to kill them, we can take care of it. You're really not our Kitty, are you?"

"No. Welcome to the New Reality. I'm really hoping that your Kitty and I don't have to die in our respective Bizarro Worlds in order to get home, but the way my luck runs, I don't count on it. Where do you want to be—up here or downstairs?" I had my guess, but it never paid to assume.

"Here. Our weapons are stored in my room."

"I knew it!" I went to take off the safety off on my gun—sometimes I was prepared. Only . . . "What the hell? Is this gun defective?"

"No, why?"

"Where the hell is the safety?"

He stared at me. "Glocks don't have safeties. Well, not external safeties. It's one of their best features."

"The hell they don't. Dude, I've used Glocks for the past, like, five years, and every one of them has had a safety."

"Well, girlfriend, in *this* universe, Glocks don't have safeties."

"Wow. No safeties on the Glocks and no aliens. Can't wait to find out what else you're lacking."

Reader managed to shoot me the cover boy smile. "Let's survive this attack and then we can compare universal notes."

"Works for me." With that, I took off.

Hyperspeed was such that it couldn't be caught on video or film, so the human eye didn't stand a chance. I normally needed to be enraged in order to get my skills working well, but not only had Christopher and I been working on this for ages, but I'd been on edge all day and thinking about my mother being dead had started my anger revving already. It was nothing to flip over to rage—I'd been holding that emotion back for hours.

Didn't have time to find out how many entry doors this place had—I needed to ensure that the assassins weren't able to set up or surround us. Zipped out the front door so fast I was pretty darned sure no one could have spotted it. No one started shooting, so I took that to mean I was going so fast I couldn't be seen by anyone other than an A-C, and apparently they were in extremely short supply here.

Of course, if there were no A-Cs, and therefore no A-C technology, and my Glock was different, that meant that other things were potentially different as well. However, as with most of the events of the past few years, I was going to have to find out what was going on and adapt on the go.

So, you know, routine.

CHAPTER 18

"A IR... KITTY... NEED AIR," Mom said.
I released my hold a little but didn't stop hugging
her. "Sorry, Mom. I just . . ." Couldn't stop crying. Decided
to blame hitting my head and changing universes or whatever. Saw Martini out of the corner of my eye—he looked
freaked out and upset.

Mom hugged me back. "What's going on, kitten?" she
asked me softly. "Whatever you did with the Prime Minister
can be fixed, I promise."

Crawford cleared his throat. "Ah, Angela? It's all a long
story, but the fastest explanation is this—this isn't 'your' Kitty.
She's from an alternate universe and has, as far as we can guess,
changed places with the Kitty we know and love. Not that we
won't learn to love this one, I'm sure," he added quickly.

Mom grabbed my upper arms and moved me back so she
could examine me. Just the way she'd acted any time I didn't
want to tell her about something bad that had happened when
I was younger.

She nodded. "Looks like Kitty, but with a much better dye
job than you usually manage for yourself."

"It's highlights, Mom. And I didn't start doing this until . . ." My throat closed up and wouldn't let me say the next
words.

Her expression softened. "Ah. I'm dead in your world, aren't I?"

Felt the entire room stiffen. Looked at Martini again—he'd already known, I could tell. His whole empath thing must have clued him in the moment I saw Mom. Felt bad for him—if what he'd said was true, then my emotions were undoubtedly affecting him and, from how he looked, they were affecting him negatively.

I nodded. "For the past two and a half years." Forced myself to pull it together. "So, I have no idea what's going on here, but from the number of people in suits in this room, it's a lot."

"Yes, it is." Mom removed herself from my grasp, spun around, and went to the door. "Secret Service are to remain on duty outside. That's an order." Then she shut the door and came back to me.

"Uh, why are you giving the Secret Service orders, Mom? In fact, why are they even here?"

"I'm the head of the Presidential Terrorism Control Unit, or the P.T.C.U. It's clandestine, and all forms of covert and clandestine ops report into us, some directly, some dotted line. And I take it by your expression that you had no idea I did this kind of work until right now."

"Right. Uh, do you think you did it in my world?"

"Am I married to your father, Solomon Katt?"

"Well, yeah."

"Then I did. I was in Mossad when we met."

"But you're neither Jewish nor Israeli."

"No. I'm just special, kitten. Like you are."

"You're also married to the Vice President, remember?" Crawford asked. "Hence the Secret Service outside."

"Oh. Right. You know, someone was trying to run me and my children off the road in, uh, my universe." The panic about the kids that I'd managed to ignore for a few minutes resurfaced.

Martini winced. "Baby, please, stop . . ."

Was about to tell him to stop calling me baby when the

full ramifications of what was going on hit me. "Oh. Crap. I have to pretend to be your wife, don't I?"

"Please and thank you," Crawford said. "Angela, I know why you kept the Secret Service details outside, but we may have to take them into our confidence."

"Absolutely not." Mom looked around the room. "Good, we only have Centaurion Division personnel here. I want no one other than those in this room to know that anything has happened beyond Kitty hitting her head, hard, and getting a concussion. Memory loss and confusion are a natural outcome of that. We can brief her on everything else."

"Raj needs to know," Serene said. "And Pierre will guess. Mister Joel Oliver might, too."

Mom shrugged. "Raj, I agree. If Pierre or Oliver guess, then we can choose if we tell them or not. But otherwise, no one else. Too many know what's going on right now."

"I don't know what's going on. And, more to the point, I have no idea what's going on with my children."

"Your kids are safe," James said with conviction.

"How would you know?"

"If Tim is right, and it's the only explanation that actually makes sense, then you and our Kitty switched right when you were being attacked, right?"

I nodded.

"Then she was put into your place in order to do exactly what I and everyone else here knows she did—she handled it and she and your kids are all safe."

"You have no way of guaranteeing that. Why would she be more likely to be able to keep from being run off the road than I would?"

Christopher walked over to me and picked me up. With one hand. Easily. "We're aliens. From another planet. Compared to humans, we're stronger, faster, and have accelerated healing. Due to a drug that some of us were . . . given . . . a few of us have mutated." He put me down. "Jeff is one of those people—he's the strongest empath in the universe, most likely. He's also stronger and faster than the average

A-C. I am, too. Jamie's birth affected our Kitty and gave her most of our powers."

"So she's faster and stronger than you are," James said. "And she's been trained to handle these kinds of situations for the past five years."

"And I've worked with her on her powers for the past three years," Christopher added. "She can handle whatever is being thrown at her in your world."

"Especially if there are actually no aliens in your world," Charles added. "Because if there aren't, then she's probably the most powerful person on Earth right now."

"I shudder to contemplate that," Christopher muttered.

The Silver Fox came over and gave me a warm smile. "I'm Richard White, Christopher's father. I'm also Jeffrey's uncle, and Paul Gower's." He indicated the big, black, bald guy. Who happened to be standing close to James. Got the distinct impression they were a couple. "Paul is our current Supreme Pontifex, meaning our religious leader. I used to be, however, I retired when Jamie was born. Katherine and I also partner up when it comes to butt-kicking, as you like to put it. She is more than capable of protecting your children as she would her own."

Took a deep breath and let it out. "Okay. So, why did we switch places? As in, why not have her just show up, save the day, and come home?"

"We have no idea," Richard said. "This is, to our knowledge, the first 'switch' that's happened."

"Lucky me."

"Truly. Could you tell us what your life is like where you come from?"

"Uh, sure, I'll aim for high-level. Charles and I have been married for eight years, we're wealthy—he made his money in convenience stores and then more of it in the stock market."

Martini nodded at Charles. "That's the same, then."

"We live half the year in Australia and half the year in D.C. We're normally not in the States right now, but Charles' third career is being part of a think tank, and they needed him back." Everyone I could see looked like they didn't believe this. Decided to forge on. "I homeschool our children. James is the top male model in the world, and Charles manages his career. My father is a history professor, though he's been on sabbatical since . . . Mom died."

"What are the odds?" Martini asked Charles.

Who looked at Mom. "High. Angela, would you have recruited me into the C.I.A. if Kitty and I had gotten married when we went to Vegas together that time?"

"Yes, and for the same reasons—you were too intelligent and looking into too many things the government needed to keep hidden. I'd have recruited you faster, because you were absolutely on a watch list until you came inside."

"How did you and Reynolds meet me?" James asked.

"We went on a worldwide honeymoon. We met you in Paris. You were horrified that we hadn't had a real church wedding, so you arranged one for us. You were our best man. You're our best friend. Why are you calling him Reynolds? You call him Chuck, you're one of the only ones who's allowed to."

"We didn't meet in that way in this world," James said gently. "So I'd have known you almost as long as you've been married. Angela?"

She nodded. "I'd have recruited you, too, I'm sure. Your being a fashion model would be a great cover and allow you to go everywhere. Charles being your manager screams 'cover story' to me, too."

"Are all of our friends in Australia in the C.I.A., too? Or are they all just in ASIS?"

"Not sure," Mom said. "They could be in Australia's Secret Intelligence Service. What do they do?"

"Well, the freaking Prime Minister and his wife run the damn country, but the rest of our friends there are doctors and lawyers and government workers and such." The entire room drew in their breath. Ignored them. "We've known most of our circle since we hit Australia. We discovered I was preg-

nant with Charlie when we were in Australia and everyone
was so great to us, and they loved that Charles was brilliant,
so we just sort of . . . stayed."

"So," Richard said carefully, "you're intimate friends with
Australia's Prime Minister?"

"Yes, as I said. We met through their eldest daughter and
they sort of took us under their wings. Are you going to tell
me that he's a space alien or a spy?"

"No, not at all. However, I believe that you may be here
to save our day as well." Richard looked around. "We're all
thinking the same thing, yes?" All heads nodded.

"Kitty," Charles said, "our Kitty, just insulted the Prime Minister in a really huge way. International incident kind of way."

"What in the world could she have done? Tony's like the
coolest guy in the world." Well, that depended on which
party you belonged to and which socioeconomic level you
lived in. Dad, Charles, and I all felt that Tony was a true
politician, with all the negatives that came along with that
career choice, but the Costellos had been wonderful friends
to us, and ultimately, that mattered more.

"She did this." Charles made the V for Victory sign, only
he had his palm turned in.

"Oh my God. She did *not!*"

"Half of us have no idea why you and Raj freaked out
about that, by the way," James said.

"James, seriously, are you high? She flipped him off in
Australian!" I turned to Richard. "What did Tony do?"

"Before or after Jeffrey accidentally spilled coffee all over
him and his wife? Or before or after you threw your entire
cup of coffee at and on him?"

"Both happened because Kitty was falling," Martini said
quickly. "But, yeah."

"So, let me get this straight. The wife of the Vice President, in other words, me, flipped off the Australian Prime
Minister and tossed her coffee at him, then her husband, the
Vice President, threw coffee onto the Prime Couple?" Everyone nodded. "God, I hope their kids weren't around, too."

"No, they were spared." Richard seemed to find this funny.

"So not amused. So I insulted my friends? Fantastic."

"No," Charles said. "Our Kitty, who has never met these people prior to these past couple of days, insulted them. You, however, can hopefully help us figure out how to fix this situation, which has basically made one of our closest political allies incredibly angry."

"Well, most of the Australian people probably think this is fab, since they, like the people here, live to pick on their leaders."

"This happened at a cricket match," Charles added.

"Who won? Was it our team playing?"

Everyone looked at each other. "More than anything else she's said," Martini said, "this convinces me that Tim's theory is correct."

"He's not a popular politician," Mom said, sort of hopefully.

"Name one who is," Charles countered.

Martini shrugged. "To Chuck's point, I'm not popular, and neither is Vince. And we had an amazing come-from-behind victory, which would make you *think* we were popular, only you'd be wrong. Vincent Armstrong, our current President," he said to me.

"Whatever you say. So, really, back to the cricket match. Who was playing? Who won?"

"That needs to stop," Crawford said. "Look we need to brief her on what she does and doesn't like. And we need to do it fast."

"And then we need to get things fixed with Australia," a new voice said. Spun around to see an incredibly handsome guy who was probably from India via the aliens in some way. "Because the Prime Minister is mad enough that he's making noises about sending all their A-Cs back to the U.S., and that's not good for anyone."

CHAPTER 19

"RAJNISH SINGH," Richard said. "He prefers to be called Raj."

"Why are you introducing me to Kitty?" Singh asked.

"Bizarro World," Crawford said.

Singh's eyes narrowed, he cocked his head a bit to the right, stared at me, then nodded. "Okay, how did it happen?"

"Wow, does everyone here read the comics?"

"Many of us did before we knew you, or rather, your counterpart," James said with a grin, "but everyone else has been forced to in order to keep up. It does make some things easier. Raj, this falls under the highest need-to-know orders and that means no one outside of this room needs to know."

Singh nodded. "That makes sense. Embassy personnel will figure it out, though."

"Not if we do our jobs right," Crawford said.

"Look, the biggest issue that we're all sort of stepping around is that this Kitty thinks she's married to me, not Jeff." Charles rubbed the back of his neck. "We're already dealing with rumors of our 'affair.' Kitty acting like she doesn't want Jeff touching her is only going to fuel that."

"What, you want me to commit adultery just to make it easier with the press?"

"No," Mom said quickly. "But you do have to pretend to be in love with Jeff."

"You two are big on the public displays of affection," Lorraine said. "So, you'd better get used to hanging onto him and kissing him, at the least."

"I haven't kissed another man since Charles and I got married." A horrible thought occurred. "What if she doesn't realize she's in Bizarro World? What if she's sleeping with my husband?" All the old fears—that Charles was cheating on me whenever he went away on trips and I couldn't reach him—surfaced. What if he'd figured it out and wanted to sleep with a different and, apparently, far cooler version of me?

"Technically, it would be you doing it," James said.

"The hell it is."

"Look," Christopher snapped, "this isn't a game. We're in the midst of a huge political situation. Worry about your sex life later."

One of the military guys nodded. "Jerry Tucker. I'm your favorite flyboy, just so you know. And, Christopher's right—who's zooming who isn't important. Making sure America and Australia remain friends and ensuring that the A-Cs in other countries aren't rounded up and shipped to America is vital."

"The precedent for that kind of thing isn't good," Claudia said.

"The Holocaust. And all other forms of ethnic cleansing. Yeah, I know history. At least mine."

"It's the same here," Singh said. "And that means that, yes, you're going to have to do uncomfortable things for the good of your country and your people. In your case, for the good of both your countries, and people you don't realize are yours."

"But, you know, no pressure."

Crawford grinned. "You sound like our Kitty, so that's a huge start."

"We need to get her back to the Embassy," Serene said.

"We need to stop having clandestine meetings in the middle of Walter Reed. I'd prefer to take her to the Science Center, by the way, but I'm not sure if that won't cause more problems."

Charles shook his head. "Actually, that will solve most of them. We tell the press that she's really hurt her head and being taking back to Centaurion Division for medical care. No one will question it, other than the staff here, since a bruised forehead isn't all that big a deal."

"Nice to know you care. I have whiplash, too, I'm pretty sure. And if we weren't anti-drug I'd down a couple of Valium if I could get my hands on them."

Charles gave me a funny look. "I do care, Kitty. But I can't care like you want."

"Why not?"

Charles looked lost. "Because . . ."

"He married my sister," Paul said, as he put his arm around Charles' shoulders. "She was . . . murdered by our enemies. They'd only been married six months."

Charles had said something about this earlier, but it hadn't really registered until now because I'd been panicking and thought he was being flippant toward me for some reason.

"You married someone else?" Tried not to sound hurt or heartbroken. Failed, based on most of the expressions in the room, Charles' in particular. He looked like he'd been punched in the gut, repeatedly.

"He did," Martini said gently, as he came over and took my hand. "So did you. Here. It took him a long time, but he'd finally moved on. I'll explain it all later, when we debrief you. You're going to have to accept that things are different here, but I promise I won't do anything that makes you uncomfortable."

"Okay. I guess." It wasn't, but there was nothing I could do about the situation right now. Besides, Charles looked ready to break down, and I had a feeling both Paul and Martini had realized this. Before I had. Time to pull up the Big Girl Panties and deal. "So, now what?"

"Now," Martini said, "we take a gate to the Science Center, Raj and Angela cover the press and join us later, and we figure out how to fix everything—our problems and yours, too."

"Promises, promises."

Martini chuckled, then James made a call. There was a weird shimmering in the air again, and everyone in suits began stepping through it and then disappearing.

"This is how you guys appeared out of nowhere, isn't it?"

"Yes," Martini confirmed. "You normally get nauseated by the transfer and I, ah, carry you through. You say it makes you feel better. The other Kitty you, I mean."

"Yeah, I figured that out. Um . . ." Looked at Charles.

Who looked uncomfortable. "Jeff, I'll go through before you. Kitty, really, if I'm essentially the same man in your world, I'll understand."

"The hell you will, Mister Jealous."

Everyone else started laughing. Martini looked embarrassed and Charles looked like someone had just discovered some deep, dark secret.

"So, you really do like just one type," Lorraine said as she stopped laughing. She was about the only one. "Amy was right."

"Amy who?"

"Amy Gaultier, now Gaultier-White," Claudia replied, still giggling. "One of your besties from high school, now married to Christopher."

"Speaking of whom," Christopher snapped. He didn't appear to have a sense of humor he was aware of. "We'll have to brief her. She'll know this isn't our Kitty right away." As he said this, a different part of the air shimmered and a tall, willowy redhead appeared out of nowhere.

"What are you talking about, Christopher? Kitty, are you okay?" she asked, looking and sounding worried.

My fists clenched. "Just what the hell are you doing here, you bitch?"

The laughter in the room ceased immediately. "What?" Christopher asked. "Kitty, what the hell?"

I was too angry to speak. What the hell was Amy doing in this life, intertwined with it, apparently? Martini held me back from attacking her, which I'd kick him in the shins for later.

Amy gaped at me. "Kitty? What do you mean? And why are you calling me a bitch?"

"You know why," I managed to growl out.

"This isn't actually our Kitty, this is the Kitty from Bizarro World," Crawford said to Amy. He gave her a fast update while I contemplated if I could pound her face in before they all pulled me off of her or not. Sadly, had to bet on not.

"Got it," Amy said when Crawford was done. "Glad we've all learned to be instantly adaptable to whatever weird gets tossed at us."

"Some adaptation isn't going to happen," I snarled under my breath.

"Kitty, why are you mad at me?" Amy asked. As if she didn't know.

I could see the wheels in Charles' head turning. "Oh. You and I got married in Vegas, right?" I nodded. "And I'll bet you called Amy to ask her to come out to be in our wedding." Nodded again. "And she was likely . . . less than complimentary about your choice of a husband."

"That's a polite way of putting it."

Amy had the grace to look guilty and embarrassed. "Yeah, I probably wouldn't have been . . . supportive at that time, if what Tim just told me is true."

"It's true," James confirmed.

"You said Charles was a loser and that you hoped I was marrying him because he now had money," I confirmed through gritted teeth. "I verified that you weren't joking and you verified a lot more nasty things about Charles, and me, for loving him. We haven't spoken since, and I intend to keep it that way. Keep this heinous bitch away from me because I will beat the ever-living crap out of her if she comes near me."

CHAPTER 20

"NOT AN OPTION," Mom said. "And you're going to get over it, all of it, right now." Mom had her No Nonsense Voice going strong. "I don't care what relationship you and Amy do or don't have in your world. In this one, you're best friends and you will act like such for the foreseeable future. Do I make myself clear?"

"Yes." My fists were still clenched. So were my teeth.

"Kitty, I'm sorry. For the me in the other world, your world, I mean. I'm sure that she did say terrible things. I've said them about Chuck for years, even after I discovered aliens were on the planet. But . . . Chuck and I are friends now. I've realized what you saw all those years ago—he's really the smartest guy in any room and he's not Conspiracy Chuck so much as totally in the know. This change in my attitude was made a lot easier since he's literally never wrong and I've seen that proved over and over again."

"I was wrong about where Hoffa's buried," Charles said calmly, as he gave Amy a smile I could honestly say was fond.

"Really? Where is Hoffa buried, then? You have a theory in my world—"

"*If* we could get back to what matters," Mom snapped. "Amy's apologized. Kitty?"

"Oh my God, really? I'm not a teenager anymore."

Mom gave me the Hairy Eyeball Look, crossed her arms over her chest, and tapped her fingers. Based on this posture, I was one word away from being grounded.

I caved. "Apology accepted. If this world's Charles has forgiven you, and only if."

He nodded. "I have. We're all dealing with things so much more important than how I was treated in high school, that it's relatively easy to get past."

Martini snorted. "Yeah, right. They've come to an accord in the recent term, baby, but before then, believe me, I have no issues believing that the Amy in your world hated the Chuck in that world and had no problem telling you so. And the dislike was definitely mutual. They get along now mostly because of you."

"You mean my Cosmic Alternate, but fine. Politics makes strange bedfellows and all that."

"And we're in a political situation," James said. "So let's get going. Amy, you'll get fully briefed along with Kitty. There was no way she wasn't going to have to know anyway, so all of you who are glaring at me and Tim for 'telling the secret' can just cool your jets."

"We already have too many in the know," Mom said, but she sounded resigned, not really mad. "Stop gleefully adding in more."

James shrugged and shot Mom the cover boy smile. "We'll handle it, Angela. We always do. And we'll get your Kitty back, too. I promise."

Mom nodded and I felt a lump in my throat. She wanted me to leave. Guess I couldn't blame her—I wasn't really her daughter. Martini squeezed my hand.

"That's good, but remember—they're both my Kitty," Mom said. "Don't think I'm willing to lose one over the other. Just call me an overprotective mother bear. In any and all universes."

Martini let go of me and I went to Mom and hugged her. "Thank you."

She hugged me back, her breath-taking bear hug. "It'll all work out, kitten. You focus on getting up to speed on the kind of things you do in this universe, and I'll keep the wolves at bay as long as I can." She let me go and jerked her head at the others. "Get moving. Raj, you're with me. Everyone else, get to Dulce and get everyone's stories straight. Pronto."

Those still in the room nodded and started through the shimmering air. They faded slowly into nothingness, which was kind of fascinating and icky at the same time.

"Are they being diced up or something?"

"No," Martini said. "The gates don't work that way."

Christopher sighed. "Stop coddling her. We didn't coddle our Kitty and she more than managed. They work via the same method the Operations Team—which we'll explain to you later—uses to get us whatever we need pretty much before we need it. A subatomic, spatio-temporal warp process, filtered through black hole technology causing a space-time shift with both a controlled event horizon and ergosphere that allows safe transference of any and all materials. All gates also use a form of harmonic frequency. Floater gates, such as the one we're about to go through, require more intense harmonic frequencies in order to exist and hold. This is why all gates have to be calibrated before anyone or anything goes through them. There's more to it, but that's the gist."

"Interesting." Everyone stared at me. "What?"

"We're not used to you grasping the scientific stuff so . . . quickly," Claudia said.

"In other words, you all think I'm an idiot. Got it."

"No," Charles said. "You haven't had to hide how smart you are in the world you come from, because you're married to me. But in this world, you carried on your use of, ah, protective coloration, and it's second nature to you now." He grinned. "It works well for you and allows you to make logical leaps that others miss, so it's a good thing."

"Oh. I have to be a ditz again? Fantastic."

"Not a ditz. Just be yourself, Kitty. From what I can tell, you're still the you I know here, just with some different life experiences." Charles looked sad for a moment, then he nodded to Martini and walked through the shimmering.

"No one here thinks you're stupid," Martini said as the others followed Charles. "Like Tim said, you've been the Head of Airborne for Centaurion Division, the Co- and then Head Ambassador for our principality, and now you're the wife of the Vice President. And in all that time, you've saved the day, and all of us, over and over again."

The room was empty other than Singh, Mom, me, and Martini. Mom nodded to us. "We're going to go stress out the Secret Service and hospital staff. Don't dally." She and Singh left, closing the door firmly behind them.

"Why would we dally?"

"Ah . . ." Martini looked embarrassed. "We tend to, ah . . . make out. Sometimes. Before we go through a gate."

Examined his expression. "You mean we make out every time."

He shrugged and grinned. "I can't say I've ever thought it was a bad thing."

I laughed. "I'll bet." Considered what everyone had been telling me and I leaned up and kissed his cheek. He seemed shocked, but in a good way. "That'll have to do for now. But it's probably bad luck if I don't kiss you in some way."

He hugged me. "I'm willing to be superstitious." With that, Martini swung me up into his arms and walked us through the shimmering. And I was instantly reminded that I'd hit my head.

The nausea hit, hard and fast, and—married to other people or whatever we were or not—I buried my face in his neck. It helped a bit, and him tightening his hold on me helped more.

Thankfully, it was over fast. Martini put me down gently and rubbed the back of my neck. "It'll pass, baby, I promise. And yes, I'm calling you 'baby' because I always do and you're going to have to get used to that."

"Charles calls me 'baby,' too."

"Glad both versions of you like that."

"Yeah." Looked around. "Where in the world are we?" We were in what seemed like a huge cavern loaded with more computers, desks and screens than I'd ever seen, even in the movies. There were tons of people bustling about and most of them were women who were all, regardless of age, as hot as Lorraine, Claudia, and Serene. Meaning I'd landed in the Land of the Beauty Queens. Hoped the rest of them were as nice as the three I'd met so far appeared to be, but I didn't count on it.

"This is the Dulce Science Center for Extra-Terrestrial Studies. Our main science, research, and medical facility. We're in New Mexico now, by the way."

"This looks like the biggest version of the Bat Cave ever. Though I imagine it's a highlight of the UFO Tour or something."

Martini laughed. "Oh, in some ways, this isn't going to be as hard as everyone fears."

CHAPTER 21

I DID A QUICK PASS AROUND the car while the assassins were getting out. I wanted them out of the car before I attacked, in part so they couldn't drive off and in part because if I could conserve my strength and not have to rip off the doors of their car, so much the better.

Three men and a woman got out. They were dressed all in black, wearing dark sunglasses, and packing serious heat. Unless they were filming a gangster movie on this street and no one had advised the neighborhood, these people meant serious killing business.

Up reasonably close they remained unfamiliar. Didn't know if this was good, bad, or indifferent. Also didn't know if I'd recognize any of them once I could get a closer, calmer look. Made the executive decision to take them out and check their IDs later.

How, was the question, particularly since Reader had asked me to incapacitate them if possible. I wasn't feeling kindly toward anyone in this car, of course, seeing as they'd just run me and the kids off the road and then gunned us down. Realized it was a really damned good thing I'd somehow switched places with my counterpart in this universe, at least for her and all the people I'd left in the house.

ACE? I asked in my head. ACE, are you there? Did you

help me get here so I could save the day? Nothing. Algar? Why not give it a shot to reach the King of the Elves? Algar, if you can hear me, my free will could use an assist. Nada. Chose not to freak out about this—maybe they could both hear me and were just playing possum for some reason, probably related to the fact that my luck remained consistent.

Had no more time to spend trying to reach benevolent superconciousnesses or rakishly handsome other-dimensional beings. I had some nasty assassins to take care of.

The woman was the closest to me. I grabbed the machine gun she was holding, wrenched it out of her hands, and slammed the butt into her stomach. As she buckled, I used the gun to give her an uppercut. She went down and out.

My hit caused her sunglasses to fly off, along with the blonde wig she appeared to be wearing. And now I did recognize her. It was Bernie, she of the pretend friendship in order to steal my baby and kill me during Operation Assassination. I kicked her in the head, just because I hated her guts.

Bernie being here meant that there was a really good chance that Raul the Pissed-Off Assassin was one of the men. He might not be that pissed off, either, since Bernie was alive. He might also be able to tell me who the Mastermind was—because if someone was controlling things in my universe, that same someone could be doing similar in this one, especially if the Mastermind was a human.

Used the gun I'd taken from Bernie to smash the nearest man in the back of his head. He went down, I gave his head another side blade kick to ensure he was out, grabbed his gun, and went on to the next. I'd search all of them for more weapons—which I was more than positive they had—once they were all down.

The remaining men were just realizing something was wrong when I body slammed one of them into the other. As they went down, I hit them both on their heads and grabbed their guns. They were both out and I was in possession of four machine guns before they hit the ground. Hyperspeed was the best. Enhanced strength wasn't so bad, either.

Machine guns were heavy and I had no idea what weapons Chuckie and Reader actually possessed. Ran the guns into the house, dumped them on the living room floor, then came back to do a body search of the hit squad.

A search of all the places I could think of on each person was going to take longer than I felt safe doing alone and out in the open, hyperspeed or no hyperspeed. Plus this was a residential neighborhood and someone was going to spot four strangers unconscious on the street sooner as opposed to later.

Dragged each of them back to the car and tossed them into the back seat. I wasn't particularly nice about it. Decided I'd feel bad later.

Four assassins in, doors closed, I got into the driver's seat, intending to move this car into our driveway. Only, as I turned the car on, the passenger's door opened and a man joined me. He had a gun out and it was pointed at me. "Hands where I can see them."

I stared. "Excuse me?" Him being here shouldn't have shocked me, but it did.

"Hands. Where I can see them. Now. I don't know how you just did what you did, without being seen and so quickly, but I'm highly skilled with rapid-fire, and I guarantee I can hit you."

"Wow. Even in this Bizarro World you have Doctor Strange powers."

He blinked. "What?"

"I just can't believe that you're working with the bad guys, Malcolm. Did you switch before my Mom was killed, or after?"

He blinked again. "What the hell . . . ?"

I jerked my head toward the back seat. "Are these your friends? If they're your friends I'm sorry. For you. If they're your targets, then I have some questions for them before you do whatever it is you're planning to do, and a couple other dudes probably will as well."

"How the hell do you know—?"

"How the hell do I know who you are? I've known you for

three years. You're Malcolm Buchanan, aka Mister Skills, aka Doctor Strange. No one sees you unless you want to be seen. You can kill people in like fifty different ways." On that I was just guessing, but my experience with Buchanan was that if it was possible, he could do it. "You're a superspy. At least, I hope. If you're a super assassin our beautiful friendship is going to be in jeopardy."

"What friendship?" His eyes narrowed. "How do you know my name?"

Heaved a sigh. "Okay, I'll try to fill you in before the assassins who tried to kill me and three little kids earlier today and were clearly coming back to finish the job wake up. But first, are you with them or with the C.I.A. or whatever? I'll still tell you what's going on, regardless of your answer, by the way."

"You will? Why is that?"

"Because, seriously, we're friends."

"Sure we are."

Decided this was getting us nowhere. Time to test a technique Christopher and I, along with my Secret Service detail, had been working on—taking someone's gun from them without getting shot or beaten up. I was pretty good at it by now.

Reached out and grabbed the hand and wrist holding the gun, pointed it up, hit a pressure point that caused his hand to release, twisted his wrist, snagged the gun, and turned it back on him. All in about one second. As per usual, when the skills were working at optimum, there wasn't anyone around, Christopher in particular, to impress.

Buchanan gaped at me. "How the hell—?"

"How the hell did I do that? And without you seeing or having time to react? It's part of the story I'm going to tell you. But first, you're going to tell me who you work for."

The passenger's door opened again. Only this time Reader was standing there, with a gun pointed at Buchanan's head. "Hands where I can see them."

"Wow, that's a running theme with you guys, isn't it? James, do you recognize Malcolm Buchanan here?"

"Who?" Reader grabbed Buchanan and pulled him where he could see his face. "What the hell are you doing here?"

"Trying to keep the Corporation from killing all of you."

"Which one? Titan Security, Gaultier Enterprises, or YatesCorp?"

Both men looked at me blankly. Reader recovered fastest. "He means the Cuban Mob." Buchanan nodded.

"Ah. Gotcha. So, James, is Malcolm C.I.A. or is he with another Alphabet Agency or has my friend here gone to the dark side?"

"He's C.I.A. Well, he was. He went rogue."

"What the hell are you doing, telling her that?" Buchanan sounded furious.

Reader rolled his eyes. "Kitty, what's the garbage in the back?"

"Four assassins. I do actually know one of them and that means I sort of know one of the others. I knocked them out but we really need to get them tied up and all their extra weapons removed. Soon." I could hear the sounds of people starting to come to.

Reader nodded and let go of Buchanan. He opened the rear door and karate chopped everyone back there. The sounds of awakening ceased.

"I like your style, James, I've always said so. I was planning to drive this car onto the driveway before Malcolm interrupted me."

"Put it in the garage. There's room, since the SUV was destroyed." Reader shot Buchanan a derisive look. "Where were you earlier today when these four attacked?"

"Where were *you?*" Buchanan sounded pissed. "You were called back because of this threat, and instead of doing anything to protect the innocents, you and Mister Brilliant headed off to a meeting."

"Wow, I can't wait to get all the juicy details—and I mean that sincerely, because this sounds like a Very Special Episode of As The C.I.A. Turns—but we need to get the hell off this street before some nice person comes over to see what's going on."

Reader nodded. "I'll get the garage opened up." He trotted across the street and into the house while Buchanan got back into the car.

"Can I have my gun back?"

"Nope. I like it. And I can drive one-handed. I'm skilled." The car was already started, so putting it into gear with just my left hand wasn't hard. Drove the short way into the garage with the gun trained on Buchanan.

"I thought you said we were friends."

"We are, where I come from. Here? I'm not so sure. And it sounds like you're not exactly BFFs with James and Chu—ah, Charles."

Buchanan stared at me. "You're not her. You're not Kitty, not the real one."

"Wow, you *are* good. And, points to your team or whatever, because it took a hell of a lot more convincing for James and I'm not sure that Charles is on board yet. What gave me away, besides everything?" The garage door closed and I turned the car off.

"Kitty doesn't call him Chuck or Chuckie, not in public. It's Charles, all the time. How did they find someone who matches her so completely?"

"Oh, that's all part of my fun story I'll tell you when we have a moment's breathing space. Does the Kitty that you've been shadowing know you exist?"

"No." He looked away. "No, she doesn't."

"Why not?"

"She doesn't need to know that I'm there."

Considered what Reader had said about Buchanan going rogue. "You left the C.I.A. after my mother, Angela, was killed, didn't you?"

"We were set up. And I know it was an inside job. Hell yeah, I left."

Thought about how who Mom had on her team in my world. "So . . . is Kevin Lewis on the team?"

"He was."

Was. "Um, what happened to him?"

Buchanan turned back to me, and pain and anger flashed out of his eyes. "As with the rest of our team—other than Reader, Reynolds, and myself—he and his entire family were murdered. By the same people trying to kill all of you."

CHAPTER 22

"**OKEY DOKEY**," I said as Reader opened the rear door. "I just want some questions answered, and then I have no problem killing all of them. Ugly." I'd met most of the folks in the P.T.C.U. by now, and Kevin, Denise, and their kids, Raymond and Rachel, were my friends, and I loved them. The idea that someone had murdered them in this world made me want to hurt whoever had done it in a very real, very painful, and very personal way.

Reader sighed. "We have no actual proof that we were set up. That's the story he's telling you, right?"

"Yeah. I have no problem believing it. Where I come from, this kind of crap happens all the time."

"Where *do* you come from?" Buchanan asked, as I indicated he could get out of the car and help Reader haul assassins out.

"Check them, James. I only grabbed the machine guns. I'm sure they're all armed to the teeth. And cyanide capsules aren't out of the question, either."

"Jeez, did you and Buchanan drink the same conspiracy theory Kool-Aid?"

"You're not going to stand there and say that Charles isn't still the Conspiracy King, are you?"

"No, he is," Reader admitted. "But not like Buchanan here is."

"It's not a theory if you can prove it's real."

"Good point, Malcolm. Hold onto that mindset, because when I answer your question, you're going to need to have that open mind going strong."

The men searched our captives and found an impressive arsenal strapped and hidden about their various persons.

New household armory established in the living room, Buchanan drew all the blinds and curtains and locked all the doors while Reader gave me zip ties and duct tape. I had our assassins trussed up like Cajun Turkeys by the time Reader was back with Chuckie and the others.

"Kids, no one touches any of the weapons, or else being spanked and grounded will be the least of your worries."

"We try not to spank the children," Chuckie said.

"I'm all for that, as long as none of them touch the guns, knives, or explosives. However," I shot Mom's Hairy Eyeball Look at all three children, "all bets are off if this particular 'don't touch' order is disobeyed."

The three kids nodded and clustered around Dad. Good choice.

"Malcolm, it's good to see you," Dad said. "How have you been?"

"He's been out in the cold, apparently, and I mean that totally in the spy talk way, Dad. I think everyone in the room is about to hear a lot of interesting things that are going to make most of you go 'no way!' and similar. Trust me when I say that what I'm going to tell you is true, and I'm sort of betting on Malcolm being right, too." At least, in my world, he was always right. Why not here?

"Should I take the children elsewhere?" Dad asked.

"No. They deserve to hear what I'm going to say, Max in particular."

"Could we move the guns and such, Katherine?" Aunt Carla asked. "At least so we can all sit down?"

"Sure," Chuckie said. He jerked his head at Buchanan and

Reader, and the three of them moved our arsenal off the couch and onto the dining room table. The table had a really pretty tablecloth on it. Chose not to whine about how the weapons were probably going to wreck that, even though Pierre's expression said that this, more than anything else that had happened in these past few minutes, was the most horrible thing ever. Then again, the couch and floor looked okay, so maybe the tablecloth would survive, too.

While they were doing this I contemplated what to do with the assassins. I didn't want them hearing anything Buchanan or I were going to say, but at the same time, I didn't want to keep on knocking them out, lest we cause brain damage. I didn't care about their brains, but, as I'd been repeatedly told today, people with concussions had memory issues, and I wanted what was in their memories.

The idea of putting them into another room was appealing, only every TV show and movie was a crash course in why this was a bad idea. Keeping your enemies where you could see—and stop and/or kill—them was the way to go.

"Do we have any wax or anything?"

"Uh, why?" Chuckie asked.

"Dude, to put into the assassins' ears. I don't want them hearing anything we're going to be saying. Seems obvious to me." Bernie was coming around. Realized I didn't want any of the assassins looking at the civilians. I didn't want them looking at the house, either. "Do you have an unfinished basement or weight room or something?"

Chuckie nodded. "But I don't want to leave them down there unattended."

"I like where your head's at. And, I agree, but I don't want them knowing where they are, either." I grabbed Bernie's legs and dragged her off at hyperspeed. This conveniently knocked her out again. Oh well, we'd just have to risk the brain damage.

It was easy to find the door to the basement, which was a pleasant surprise. You entered via the kitchen. Wondered if I could ask for a snack—I was getting hungry.

Broke down and dragged Bernie downstairs holding her
under her armpits, versus letting her head hit each stair,
though being nice like this took effort. Deposited her in a
really nicely furnished and actually finished basement that
appeared to be doubling as both a workout room—which
came complete with a gigantic bathroom that had five toilets,
sinks, and showers—and an impressive wine cellar. Wondered if one of the walls spun around to reveal a superspy
lair, but figured I'd find out later.

Passed Reader and Buchanan carrying one of the male
assassins all nicely. Well, they didn't have the history with
Bernie that I did.

Got upstairs and grabbed the next assassin. "If we got
lucky and they had ID on them, can you figure out if one of
them is named Raul, or if one of them is married to Bernie,
or if any of them are named Dier or Diaz?" I asked Chuckie,
who was keeping everyone else in place. "It's important."

He nodded and I dragged off Assassin #3. Passed Reader
and Buchanan on their way back up. Dumped my dude next
to the other dude, and contemplated options.

The weight room had a mirror on the wall that opened up
to the Super Bathroom, so I didn't want them facing that.
Happily, there was a wall that went three-quarters of the way
across between the wine cellar and the workout room. Moved
the assassins so that they were facing this wall, which meant
their backs were to the mirror. So far, so good.

Reader and Buchanan brought the last one down. Buchanan moved a weight bench so that we could sit the four of
them up and lean them against the bench to keep them in a
sitting position.

I'd done prisoner interrogations before, but I'd had Jeff,
Christopher, Gower, and Reader helping me. Of course, I'd
also had Chuckie helping me. The thing was, I knew I
couldn't count on either Chuckie or Reader to react how I
needed them to, and Buchanan was currently the textbook
definition of Loose Cannon.

Reader trotted upstairs and came back with Chuckie. "Kitty, do you want to tell us what's going on now?" he asked.

"Nope. I want to know who, if anyone, is named Raul in this group."

Chuckie pointed to the guy we had on the opposite end from Bernie. Good. I didn't want them near each other in the first place. "Raul Diaz. Bernice Diaz is the woman. The other men have no ID on them. Why these two do is suspicious."

"Super. They have ID because they're married and they like to get up close and personal with their targets, and that means you need to have a driver's license on you just in case the cops pull you over for speeding. Do we have chloroform or something? Trust me when I say we do not want these guys hearing what we're going to discuss."

Chuckie and Reader exchanged one of their signs and Reader went to the wine cellar. I followed him. He shifted five different bottles in five separate areas of the wine rack on the far wall. On the sixth bottle, the wall opened to reveal a room that was set up as a computer center with many extras.

"Nice setup," Buchanan said from behind me. "Company approved?"

"No," Chuckie replied. "Angela thought it would be wise to have. Off book."

"I just knew you guys had a secret room here somewhere. You have one in your house in Australia, too, don't you?"

"Yes, we do." Chuckie rubbed the back of his neck. "You're not my Kitty, are you?"

Wondered just how dense my counterpart was, then thought about it a little more. I'd been clueless about what my parents and Chuckie were actually doing until I was twenty-seven—later even for Chuckie—and if I hadn't been around a forming superbeing, I'd probably still be clueless. She trusted the people she loved the most, just like I had. Wondered how she was handling the discoveries she was undoubtedly making. She was me, in that sense, so I figured she'd roll with whatever punches came along.

"No, I am Katherine Katt, but I'm not *your* Katherine Katt, thanks for joining Team Reality Check. Let's drug these creeps and then I'll share the wonder that is me."

"Truly," Chuckie said, "I can't wait."

CHAPTER 23

CHLOROFORM WAS PROCURED and put over the assassins' mouths and noses. They all went back to fully out. "We have a little while now," Reader said. "What's the story?"

"Bring the rest of the family down here. They need to hear what I'm going to say and I need the kids to verify something."

"I don't want—" Chuckie started.

Put my hand up. "I don't care what you want right now. I'm telling you that your secrets need to come out, completely. Your children almost died today. If what I'm going to tell everyone about hadn't happened, your family *would* have died today. You can work with me and we can fix this, or you can work against me and leave the people you love the most in mortal danger. Your pick, but I have no idea how long I'm here for, and if it's a short-term loan, speed is going to be of the essence."

Chuckie looked like he was ready to argue, but Buchanan spoke up. "Everyone upstairs knows what's going on, at least to a certain degree, based on what's just happened. Trying to hide this, or lie to them about it, is the definition of stupid."

Chuckie sighed and nodded. "Fine. You're both right." He trotted upstairs and came back with everyone. "Okay, we're all here."

"Kit-Kat, are you okay?" Caroline asked me. "You haven't done anything remotely normal since . . . you ran us to the safe room. And, right now . . . you're looking at all of us like you've never seen us before."

"I've seen you all before, just not the yous that you are."

"Katherine, whatever are you talking about?" Aunt Carla asked.

"Before I answer that, kids, I need you to look at the woman here. Have you ever seen her, or this man," I pointed to the guy Chuckie had identified as Raul, "before? Anywhere, here or in Australia or even just in passing?"

The kids all gave it their attention. "I have," Jamie said. "She tried to kill us."

"When?" Charlie asked, sounding shocked.

"A long time ago," Jamie replied.

"No way," Max said. "But I've seen her. I don't remember where."

"We know her, Mommy," Charlie said. "We met her in the park last week. She gave us candy, remember? She wanted to have us meet her kids and do a play date, but you told her we were heading back to America and it would have to be a rain check."

"It so figures. And, no, honey, I don't remember. Because Max is right. I'm not your actual mother." Charlie looked stricken, Max relieved, and Jamie . . . Jamie looked a little disappointed.

"I *told* you she wasn't our mommy," Max said to Jamie.

"She's the mommy we needed," Jamie replied stubbornly.

Everyone stared at her, me included. "What, sweetheart?" Chuckie asked carefully.

But Jamie just shook her head and wouldn't speak.

"My Jamie is a chatterbox," I said to Chuckie. "What's going on with this Jamie?"

Everyone looked uncomfortable. Max heaved a sigh. "Jamie doesn't talk a lot. And . . . other things."

"She's spoken more today than she has in recent weeks," Pierre said, sounding sad and worried.

Shoved worry about this Jamie to the side and took a deep breath. "Fine. We'll move on. You may not understand it, and don't ask me how, but the best I can give you is this—I'm in Bizarro World. Oh, and this is Malcolm Buchanan. Like Charles and James, he's C.I.A. Just like my mother was. I'm not from this world—on my Earth, aliens exist and I'm married to one of them. I'm sure aliens exist here, too, though I don't think they've come to Earth to live. Have they, Dad?"

"How long have you known?" Dad asked.

"Me? I've known since I was twenty-seven and I discovered aliens were on the planet."

"Kitty, for the last time, aliens are not on this planet," Chuckie said.

"No, but they're out there, and they're communicating with us . . . aren't they, Dad?"

He nodded. "We're far from being able to visit, and communications take a long time, but intelligent life is out there, and, for us, quite nearby."

"In the Alpha Centauri system, which has a lot of populated planets, doesn't it?"

Dad nodded again. Pierre, Aunt Carla, and Caroline looked shocked, but not nearly as shocked as Chuckie and Reader. "I'm sorry, boys. It's need-to-know and you didn't. Really, you still don't. Kitten, Charles is right—there are no aliens on this Earth."

"Dad, I can't tell you how much I appreciate that you were a good father and read some comics just to keep up with me. You said 'this' Earth. Meaning that you're feeling fairly confident that there's more than one universe out there."

He gave me a small smile. "The current thinking is that we're part of a multiverse. And I'm looking at the proof. You're here." He shook his head. "You're not my daughter. I mean, you are, clearly, but you look just a little . . . off. You're acting off, too, and not because of a concussion. How you moved . . ."

To her great credit, Aunt Carla wasn't arguing with Dad. Had a feeling it was because she also thought I wasn't the "right" Kitty. Which showed a rare ability to be insightful that the Aunt Carla I knew didn't have or never bothered to use.

"Yeah, it's called hyperspeed. I have it because my particular alien is both very powerful and was given a drug that mutated him. Our daughter, Jamie, who is the exact same age as this Jamie, did a mother-and-child feedback thing. So, I'm sort of part alien now." Looked at Chuckie. "I really *am* Wolverine with Boobs."

"Then where's *our* mommy?" Charlie asked in a little voice.

"I . . ." I was going to say that I wasn't sure, but my head throbbed. Had a feeling it wasn't hurting because of slamming into concrete. "Well, like your Grandpa Sol said, there are a lot of universes out there. And many of us are in all of them. Sometimes we're the same, and I guess sometimes we're not, but . . ." I winced as my head throbbed again.

Then I saw it. I saw the Universe Wheel. And I remembered it, and every time I'd seen it. And I also remembered that I never actually remembered it once I left the place where I was floating and watching the Wheel turn.

So, someone was trying to help me. Had two guesses for who, though others might be assisting as well. Sent a mental "thank you" out, and then got back to the business at hand of freaking out everyone in this basement.

"Katherine Katt is in a lot of universes out there. I've seen them. I'm one of the Katherine Katts that exists. In my universe, aliens from the Alpha Centauri system live on Earth." My head throbbed again. "In fact, they're only on Earth—or I only know about them being on Earth—in my universe. So, in this one, they haven't come here." Meaning Ronald Yates had never come to town. The implications of which might or might not matter right now.

"And . . ." I remembered more. "I saw her, your mother, your Kitty. She and I passed each other, just at the instant when she was knocked out, I think. So, that means she's in my world while I'm in hers."

"But, if this is true and we're not all choosing to believe

some bizarre fantasy, how did you get here?" Chuckie asked finally. "I mean that in the Bizarro World way, by the way. As in, was there a portal, were you both in the same place at the same time, or what?"

"Chuck, it's true," Reader said. "You know in your gut it's true. And I saw her in action, you didn't. And by 'saw' I mean watched things happen in the blink of an eye when I couldn't see Kitty, because she was moving so fast. There's nothing on Earth that could do that. At least, not on our Earth."

"I felt . . . something, when we switched. That's all I've got right now, I'm sorry."

"Why were you switched?" Buchanan asked thoughtfully.

"I think we were switched because the Kitty in this world and all her kids were about to die. I've been trained for five years to handle impromptu emergency situations. I handled it. She'd have died."

"You don't know that," Charlie said defensively.

Looked at Jamie. Who looked smug. "Yes, I do. Don't I, Jamie?"

She didn't reply. Chuckie cleared his throat. "Okay, I can believe that. My wife is a great driver and has excellent reflexes, but she's not trained to handle assassins. Speaking of whom, why did you know the kids would know the woman?"

"Because she exists in my world. She tried to kill me and Jamie when Jamie was just an infant. Well, she tried to kidnap Jamie and kill me. Because my Jamie is amazingly talented, in a very alien talents way." Looked up at Buchanan. "You saved us from her, by the way. That's how I found out what you really did. So, how long have you been shadowing the me in this world?"

"Since your senior year of high school."

Everyone, even Chuckie—hell, even Dad—looked shocked. "Dude, you're not that much older than me."

"No, I'm not, but I'm older than you by enough. You were my first solo assignment, after your mother recruited and trained me. Protecting you, or rather, the Kitty from this world, has been my job for a decade." He looked over at Chuckie. "And it's been necessary. You were added on as a protection target once you two got married. And the children, of course."

"But you worked with us on missions," Reader said. "You going to tell us you're Multiple Man and can be in more than one place at a time?"

"He's Doctor Strange, actually."

"Whatever," Buchanan said with a short laugh. "No, Angela had others doing family guard duty when we were on missions. She only pulled me in for the really tough ones."

"So you're saying you've been protecting us from threats for a decade?" Chuckie asked. "I call BS. You worked too many missions with us for that to fly."

Buchanan shrugged. "By the time Max was born, Angela had a team covering you. I was the head of it." His eyes flashed. "And all my people are dead, too, just like all of hers. Out of her entire team, the three of us in this room are all that remains. Someone just tried to take you and your entire family out. That would include Reader, here, wouldn't it?"

"But we were called back because of the threat," Reader argued. "If what the kids and Kitty say is true, and we have no reason to believe it isn't, then these assassins were going to hit us in Australia. Coming home saved us from them."

"Did it?" Buchanan asked, speaking for both of us. "We're all only standing here, alive and in one piece, because an alternate version of Kitty—one with superpowers, I might add—just traded places with her. Otherwise, your family's dead and the murder-suicide that would have happened in this house later wouldn't even be questioned."

"Malcolm is right, Charles," Aunt Carla said quietly. "And as insane as it is to say this—I believe this Kitty. She moved me and Caroline at a speed that's impossible. She lifted things far heavier than she should be able to. And what she says makes sense. It's never sat properly with me, the story that Angela died in an accident. Based on what I know of my sister, this all seems more likely than not."

"Aunt Carla, please let me welcome you to Team Mega-lomaniac. I'll explain the name later, but suffice to say, I'd like you thinking of every weirdo thing that's happened around our family for the past, oh, forty years or so, please and thank you."

"There's a lot," Dad said quietly.

"I'm sure there is. Start thinking of it, and writing it down. We may need to cross reference for connections and such. Caro, same for you, only focus more on politics. Charles – and you have no idea how hard it is for me to call you that— and Malcolm, let's get the Most Promising Conspiracy Theories lined up and ready for review."

"I believe we can start with the company we hired to take care of our home and vehicles," Pierre said. "The lack of anything being cared for combined with your airbags not opening screams suspicious to me."

"I totally agree. Oh, and I hate these people, whoever they are, who have put these plans into motion. I say this a lot, by the way. There's a conspiracy afoot, gang, and it's been afoot for a while. Chu-, argh, Charles, once our prisoners wake up I'm going to question them. But, while we're waiting, how's your Wi-Fi situation down here, and do you have a spare laptop I can use?"

"It's excellent, Kitty the Alternate," Pierre said. "And we have a plethora of computer equipment you can use. But why do you need it?"

"Because we're outnumbered and outgunned. And that means it's time for me to try to see if any of our reinforcements are out there."

CHAPTER 24

WE'D WANDERED THE BIGGEST RAT MAZE in the world, entered a gigantic library that would make the Library of Congress feel inadequate, and were now in a conference room that looked like a giant fishbowl. Somehow, the people I was with felt this was more secure than the hospital room at Walter Reed had been. Perhaps aliens couldn't read lips.

I'd met more people than I had a prayer of remembering, especially because ninety percent of them were gorgeous, and it was getting hard to differentiate one stunning beauty or amazing hunk from the other. Was grateful the A-Cs ran the gamut in skin tones and attractive body types just like humans did, because otherwise I'd have had less of a chance of remembering them than I already did.

Everyone was brought up to speed, at least insofar as how I was here and where we assumed "their" Kitty actually was. I'd gotten a very high-level overview of what the past five years had been like for my Cosmic Alternate. Apparently, even more complex than homeschooling two preternaturally bright boys and a little girl who was likely autistic. It was kind of nice to know that I rolled with the punches wherever I happened to exist, though.

Amy was still persisting in the idea that we were pals, which was more than a little annoying, especially because I knew Mom wanted me to fake it. I hadn't seen my mother for far too long—disobeying her direct orders right now seemed . . . ungrateful. And I was hugely grateful for whatever had flung me here, because, despite everything else, getting to be with Mom and to know that she loved me, even though I wasn't the same me as her daughter in this universe, meant everything to me.

Amy was picking up that I wasn't on board with our becoming BFFs again. She was wisely across the conference table from me, meaning I couldn't lunge at her, so she was still smart.

"Kitty," she said during a brief lull in the barrage of information, "I swear to you that I'm not your enemy."

"So your mother tried to tell me when Charlie and Max both were born. But I didn't care then and I don't care now. Your parents? I still like them. You yourself? I'll fake it just like my mother wants and everyone here says I have to, but in reality, you've been dead to me for eight years."

Everyone gaped at me and Amy's face drained of color. Christopher put his arm around her and hugged her to him. "What did you say?" Charles asked slowly. "About her parents?"

"They still keep in touch with us, in the hopes that Amy and I will somehow reconcile. We won't, but why hurt Herbert or Solange's feelings?"

"Holy God," Crawford said. "Kitty, is Herbert Gaultier doing any, ah, untoward experiments in your world?"

"No. He's a freaking humanitarian. He's got one of his research facilities focused on curing cancer. They've made some real breakthroughs. He got into it when Solange got sick. He found a cure for her, which works, but only if you have a specific genome type or something. The FDA can't approve it, therefore, so he's treated people in France, sort of illicitly and sort of not. Successfully each time, though. He's how we met Doctor Marling."

"Doctor Marling?" Martini sounded shocked. "Antony Marling?"

"Yes. He's the leading pediatrician worldwide for children with . . . autism."

"Why would you need to know a doctor like that?" Tito asked.

No time like the present. This Charles would hopefully not react defensively and get us into a huge fight in front of all these people. And if he did, maybe Martini or someone could reason with him and explain that saying the word didn't make either one of us bad parents. "Because, while we aren't sure, it seems that Jamie is autistic. Haven't you noticed anything wrong with her?"

"Ah, our Jamie is not autistic," Martini said. "Precocious and, ah, talented and more. But not autistic."

"Do both you and the . . . other me think that?" Charles asked.

"I think so. Charles is extremely . . . touchy on the subject. We can't talk about what's really wrong with Jamie without fighting. He thought what Doctor Marling suggested was crazy, but I think he might have been right."

"What did Marling say?" Martini asked.

"Sorry, but I need us to get back to the Gaultier and Marling thing," James said, voice tight but loaded with authority. It was clear he was saying this as Top Dude in the Room. And all the others nodded and turned to him, so apparently he was the Top Dude in the Room. Interesting. I'd have pegged that role for Martini, Richard, Charles, or Paul. "Kitty, in our world, those men were two of the most evil around, and they caused a tremendous amount of damage, pain, and suffering, much of which we're still dealing with."

"Well, in my world, they're both dedicated to saving lives and are humanitarians of the highest order."

"In our world, my mother is dead," Amy said in a small voice. "She died when we were sophomores in college. Chuck verified that my father murdered her."

"Oh. Wow. God, I'm so sorry." I was. I knew what it was like to have lost your mother far earlier than you ever thought you would. "If it helps at all, your parents are still madly in love in my world."

Tears rolled down Amy's cheeks. "It does. A little. They're both dead here."

"I killed her father," Christopher said. "Because he was going to kill all of us, starting with Amy."

"I can understand that. I mean, I guess. If he was like you say he was here, killing your only daughter would be par for the course. Herbert would die for Amy in my world."

"How could he be the man I remember him being when we were young in another universe, but one of the most evil men around in this one?" Amy asked plaintively.

"Is LaRue Demorte around?" Crawford asked. "She might be working for either Gaultier or Marling."

"Never heard of her."

"You're sure?" Martini asked.

"Chick named Street of the Dead? I'd remember a name like that. And no, as I said, I've never heard of her."

"That explains a lot," James said. "She may have been the person that flipped Gaultier toward the dark side here."

"She was Gaultier's assistant, then his mistress, and then his wife," Charles explained. "She's brilliant, and extremely evil."

"Glad we've never met."

"And if Ronald Yates never came to that Earth," Richard said, "then perhaps that means the people he'd have influenced stayed on a different path."

"Who's Ronald Yates?"

"My father," Richard said sadly.

"And our grandfather," Martini indicated himself and Christopher. "Most evil man in two solar systems. Makes Amy's father and Antony Marling look like small change, and that's saying a lot. Seriously, we'll continue to brief you on what it's like here while we marvel at how nice and calm your world is at the same time."

"Our world is hardly calm."

"Great, then we'll play World Badness One-Upmanship as we go along."

I couldn't help it, I laughed. "You talk like I do."

He nodded. "You've rubbed off on me. Don't worry, I like it."

"Let's go over our list of megalomaniacs," Crawford said. "I'd love a rundown on who's a saint and who's still a sinner."

Lorraine hit something and a screen descended. There was a long list of names on it. "Wow, you guys have a lot of enemies."

"We do," Claudia said. "You—well, the other you—have helped us defeat most of them and hold the others at bay."

"Go my Cosmic Alternate." Looked at the list. "Leventhal Reid. He's an American politician, or he was. He died in a drunk driving accident right around the time my mother died." Checked all the expressions in the room. "Ah. You think my mother was protecting him or after him?"

"Based on our experiences," Charles said, "she was after him."

"As a warning," Martini said quietly, "my Kitty is terrified of him. It doesn't stop her, but she considers him the most evil man alive or dead. And in our world, he's back from the dead. She preferred our grandfather to Reid."

"Wonderful. What are the odds I'm going to meet this charmer?"

"I'm hoping zero, baby."

"Works for me."

"It's the same situation for LaRue," Charles said, also speaking softly. "And I'm hoping you don't run into her, either."

"Apparently visiting Bizarro World isn't nearly as fun as I was led to believe. Okay," I said in a louder voice, "never heard of Madeline Cartwright, but Cybele Siler Marling is Antony's wife. Her sister is Madeline Siler, and based on that née Siler I see behind her name on your list, I assume it's the same woman. She works with Cybele and Antony doing cancer research. She's a huge activist in Europe and lobbies in the U.S. all the time."

"So, she's a good guy?" Crawford sounded shocked.

"Yes, as far as I know." Continued to peruse the list for people I hadn't already talked about. "Ronaldo Al Dejahl I've never heard of, the Al Dejahl Terrorist Network doesn't exist—and believe me, we're world travelers so we pay attention to the various terrorist organizations. John Cooper is a really common name, so I have no idea, but I don't know one personally. Esteban Cantu . . . vaguely familiar, but that's not that uncommon a name, either. No one I can place. Vincent Armstrong—hey, didn't you say he was President?"

"Yes, he is," Serene confirmed. "He was an enemy. He's not anymore."

"Nice to know people can change. Don't know him, he's for sure not our President, however he could be a Congressman or a Governor—I certainly don't know all of them by name. Lillian Culver, no idea, Abner Schnekedy, are you kidding and who could forget that name? No idea who he is. Guy Gadoire, name's vaguely familiar but I have no idea why. Vance Beaumont, Edward Brewer, Nathalie Gagnon-Brewer, Leslie Manning, Bryce Taylor, Eugene Montgomery, Lydia Montgomery, Marion Villanova, Langston Whitmore, Marcia Kramer, and Zachary Kramer are all people I don't know. All of them could exist in my world, by the way, I just don't know them. I'm not sure that this means anything. Or that my doing this is useful at all."

"Just keep on," James said. "Better safe than sorry. They're not all our enemies, most of them are politically connected, and two of those people are high up in the U.S. government. Here, I mean."

"If you say so. I haven't heard of any of them, so they can't be that high up where I come from. Casey Jones, Howard Taft, Harvey Gutermuth . . . my God, who names these people? No idea, unless you've got issues with a long-dead president. Club Fifty-One, never heard of it. Farley Pecker . . . him I'm pretty sure I know. He's the head of the worst bunch of so-called religious lunatics this country has come up with in a long time."

"Yeah, he's exactly the same here," Christopher said.

"How awesome for both of our universes." Ran through a zillion more names—there were a lot of people on the A-C's Potentially Sketchy Humans List. I knew none of them. Then I hit a couple that I did recognize. "Wait—Jack and Pia Ryan? What the hell?"

"You know them?" Charles asked.

"Yes, they're friends of ours. Jack owns the Lexus dealership in Silver Spring where we buy all our cars. Pia's in sales. He lives for jokes about his name and how he's the same Jack Ryan as in the books. They're cool. Why are they on your Enemies List?"

"Ah . . . they weren't actually . . . on our side," Crawford said.

"Well, he might have been," Serene said. "We don't know for sure."

Looked around the room. Everyone looked kind of uncomfortable, and the A-Cs weren't looking at me. "Oh, for God's sake, what is it?" No one answered. Most of them were looking at the conference table or the ceiling. Decided to do the math for myself. "They're both dead here, aren't they?"

"Yes," Charles said. "I'm sorry. They weren't our friends. Pia worked for the C.I.A. We think she killed Jack because he found out what she was up to. She was murdered by the Mastermind."

"The who?"

"That's a long explanation—" Christopher started.

Charles put up his hand, shutting Christopher up. "We have a Sith Lord active, and Pia was eliminated during Apprentice tryouts."

Allowed this to compute. "I should probably be embarrassed that this explanation was the most understandable of all that you've given me since I woke up, but it was. Got it. Wow, things really suck here. At least in some ways."

"They do," Richard said. "But so far, we've been able to combat them. What I find interesting is that while some people, such as Charles and James, seem the same in your world, many do not."

"I think it's the Yates Factor," Charles said.

Martini nodded. "Granddad isn't here to spread his evil, people who maybe could have gone either way flipped toward good."

"And maybe some flipped toward bad without him." Everyone stared at me. "What?"

"How would not having an evil influence mean that some would flip toward bad?" Claudia asked.

"Sometimes people fight against a stronger force, just because it's there. So, if there was a stronger evil, maybe someone would be good because of it. And without that stronger evil, the temptation to *be* the evil might have won."

"Maybe." A man who I really hadn't registered as being in the room was the speaker. He was about Martini's size, brown hair and blue eyes, and he was handsome. Human handsome, like Charles. Realized he looked familiar and that he'd been at the hospital, though I hadn't really registered that until now. But it was more than that—had a feeling I knew him, somehow. "Maybe the evil person just doesn't have to hide in the same way, because there are no A-Cs to stop him."

"Um, okay. Have we met?"

"Not really. I'm Malcolm Buchanan. Your mother recruited me when I was in college. And that means that it's likely she did the same in your world."

"What does that mean? Other than that you're C.I.A. or P.T.Whatever or something?"

"I think the Mastermind is a human. Just because you don't know most of the humans we've listed doesn't mean they aren't on your world—it's obvious your husband has kept all of this away from you. So that means there's a good chance that the Mastermind is on your world, too. And he might be doing the same things there as he is here, only without anyone to stop him."

CHAPTER 25

ALL THE MOUTHS IN THE ROOM started to open, but Martini beat them all to it. "It doesn't matter."

All the mouths stayed open, in shock as far as I could tell. Christopher recovered first. "What?"

"Look, it does not matter. We've allowed the fact that things are different in this Kitty's world to distract us from what's going on. But what we have to fix, right now, is the situation with Australia. Once that's taken care of, then, yeah, I'm all for us going back to the hunt for the Mastermind. But until our major diplomatic issue is resolved, we're at risk of making one of our country's closest allies into our enemy. That cannot be our legacy."

Martini's voice was filled with the same authority I'd heard at the hospital. And everyone, including James, all closed their mouths, nodded, and obviously shifted mental gears.

Lorraine pushed some buttons and new data appeared on the screen. I didn't pay much attention to it. Now that I'd spotted him, I watched Malcolm. He was the only one who hadn't really agreed with Martini. Not that I thought he disagreed. But I got the impression that he was hoping to learn something from me that would solve their biggest problem. I just had no idea of what that could be. Because he was also right—my family had been lying to me for years, and I'd bought it, so what the hell could I know that would help a different world?

A flowchart appeared onscreen that brought my attention back. It showed the various levels of command in Centaurion Division. There were several versions of this, starting with the year prior to the one when my Cosmic Alternate had joined up. It was the most helpful of the data they'd been shoving at me, because I could see both her progression through the ranks and that of the others in the room. Based on what Richard was saying for these charts, my CA had been a major force in this group. Felt kind of proud. Sure, it wasn't me doing it per se, but clearly I'd represented in this world.

"Show her your Centaurion Files," Crawford said to Charles when the hierarchy discussion was done. "She got the Sith reference, she'll get those, too."

"I will, but I don't have them loaded into Centaurion's systems." Charles patted my hand. "I know you'll understand it, Kitty. I just think we need to do what Jeff said—focus on how to fix our political situation. You know the Prime Minister and his wife. What do you think we should do?"

"Saying, 'gosh, I'm so very sorry' and giving someone a little present doesn't work in this world?"

"Kitty," Amy said, voice sugar sweet, "I'm so very sorry for the other me. I'd love to take you to lunch and buy you a little present to make up for it. We back to being friends?"

"Wow, you got that out without your voice dripping in sarcasm. I'm impressed. But, yeah, okay, it's at that level? From one bad morning?"

"Kitty flipped off the Prime Minister after insulting the game of cricket—the special game we'd arranged to show how much we love Australia, I might add—for hours, tossed hot coffee on him, and *then* Jeff dumped hot coffee on him and his wife," James reiterated. "Seriously, this was a major screwup."

"So, I can't like cricket while I'm here, right? Because

that would be too much of a switch and everyone would think I'm faking it."

"Right," Crawford said.

"Katherine, I'd like you to think of a more personal fix," Richard said. "You're frankly the only person who knows what's going on who also has the means to solve this problem in an honest fashion."

"In other words," Charles said, "help us, Obi-Wan Kenobi. You're our only hope."

"Okay, let me think." Took a deep breath and tried to let my mind wander. But everyone was staring at me. "What?"

"Ah, we're used to you talking while you think," Paul said. Nicely. But still.

"What? Seriously?"

"Yes," Claudia confirmed. "All the time. Nonstop, really."

"I'll be insulted for my Cosmic Alternate later. Look, I became a mother really fast and in my early twenties, and Charlie has the combined brainpower of me and Charles. He was comprehending everything at a very young age. Max is the same, and I have to figure that Jamie is as well, since her first words were late but in perfect, fully formed sentences that made sense. I've learned to keep whatever I'm thinking to myself."

"Think that will be a problem?" Crawford asked James.

Who shrugged. "If it all goes well and we can figure out how to get her home safely and quickly, no."

"Guys, I'm in the room."

They both grinned at me. "Go ahead and think, Kitty," James said. "We can handle the silence. I think."

"Ugh. Now I can't think because you're all staring at me. Look, I feel over-briefed and I can guarantee I'm not going to remember everything you've all info dumped onto me. My head still hurts, as does my back and neck. I realize your Kitty heals fast. I don't. I'd love a couple of Advil and a chiropractor, and then to go somewhere sort of normal, relax for like five minutes, and then try to figure out how to save the world and all that crap."

Everyone looked contrite. They all also shot Martini looks that said he should have known this already and done something about it. "I have my blocks up. High," he mumbled.

"Oh my God, you're all blaming Jeff for not knowing I was in pain? I told you *all* at the hospital that I'd been in a car accident. That no one chose to do the math is not my problem. Where's that doctor guy, Tito? Why isn't he in the room?"

No sooner were these words out of my mouth than the conference door opened and Tito stuck his head in. "I was off getting a chiropractor we can trust to both be discreet and help, not hurt," he said with a grin. "Jeff, Chuck, I want to get her to medical. Doctor Li is here, and I want to get Kitty taken care of and Doctor Li back to Pueblo Caliente as soon as possible."

"Where is Pueblo Caliente?" I asked as Martini and Charles stood. They both looked shocked.

Martini helped me up. "Um, it's where you're from, baby. In Arizona."

"I'm from Phoenix. So is Charles."

Jaws dropped. "Ah, is Phoenix in the middle of the state and the state capital?" Charles asked.

"Yes. Prescott used to be the capital, though, way back when."

He nodded. "Phoenix is named Pueblo Caliente in this universe."

"Oh. Great. I think this means I have Bizarro World Bingo."

We walked through the rat maze again and headed off to the elevators. Everyone was giving Martini funny looks both while we were waiting for and then in the elevator car and he looked kind of depressed. I didn't get it but decided not to question. Charles seemed incredibly uncomfortable in here, too.

More wandering led us to what appeared to be a huge medical wing. I could understand why the world would believe they'd take the wife of the Vice President here—this looked far more impressive than Walter Reed.

Dr. Li turned out to be a pretty Chinese woman about my age who was waiting for me in another room that resembled a fishbowl. Privacy wasn't an alien thing, apparently. Per Tito's introduction, she was a leading practitioner in all the holistic and natural types of medicines, including chiropractic, acupuncture, and acupressure, along with being an herbalist and holding a PhD in Chinese Medicines from two universities. Wanted to ask her when, if ever, she slept, but I was married to a brilliant man and it wasn't a leap to figure that she was in the same brainy stratosphere.

She was also a great chiropractor and, after X-rays were taken, she adjusted me so that I only sort of ached. Martini was given a bunch of natural meds for me to take to reduce inflammation and get the lovely bruise on my forehead to diminish quickly. Had to hand it to this world—their medicine seemed somewhat advanced compared to what I was used to.

Medical perpetration over, the discussion ensued for where to go next. I wanted to take a nap, and Martini supported that desire. "And, besides, isn't Jamie going to be worried about why you and I have been gone so long?"

Martini shrugged. "No. She's used to it. She's at daycare."

"Excuse me? Are you saying that you have all of one child and you're dumping her off at some daycare every day?"

This ensured that everyone stared at me again. I was really batting a thousand on this particular skill. "Ah, yes," Martini said. "We have active jobs and we're in danger situations all the time. It's safer for Jamie. The daycare is in our Embassy, and she's there with all the other Embassy and Alpha Team kids. She loves it."

I wasn't convinced but decided not to have this argument here, or in front of all of these people. Technically this wasn't my fight anyway.

We went up to a floor that had a lot of cars and a lot of things that looked like the metal detectors in airports—big metal doorways to nowhere. "These are what stationary gates look like," Martini said, as he led me to the metal detectors.

We weren't alone—apparently many of the people with us lived at the Embassy or in the D.C. area and were going back with us, Amy and Christopher included. While all these people were filtering through, Paul pulled me aside.

"Kitty, I know it's been explained that I'm our religious leader. I just wanted you to know that if you need to talk to someone and you don't feel right talking to Chuck or Jeff, I'm here for you. And Richard is, too."

"Thanks. That's really very nice of you."

He smiled and shook his head. "No, it's my job. When our people need support and guidance, the Supreme Pontifex needs to be there for them. Every one of them. Even those who aren't sure they are one of our people yet."

"That seems like a huge responsibility."

"It is. But it's worth it. Most of the time." He looked very sad for a moment.

"When is it not worth it?"

"When we lose people we love." He hugged me gently. "I know you have to feel lost and stranded and more than a little like the weight of a world was just dropped onto your shoulders. I just want you to know that precedent has already been set—you'll do everything we need you to."

"I'm worried that I'll mess things up worse, not make them better."

He chuckled. "Oh, you might. But the thing is, I know you'll still manage to save the day."

"How can you be so sure?"

He kissed my forehead, though not where I was bruised. "Because that's who you are and what you do."

"Then I guess I'd better do my best."

He smiled. "Or, as we call it, routine."

CHAPTER 26

ANOTHER HORRIBLE GATE TRANSFER made better by Martini carrying me through it. Being around Charles while acting as Martini's wife was starting to get to me emotionally, and finding him waiting for us as we exited the gate into what appeared to be a dark basement made it worse. He was alone, so I assumed the others had gotten upstairs into the light.

"Jeff, it occurred to me that Stryker and the others are going to know this isn't the real Kitty almost immediately," he said as Martini put me down gently.

"Eddy's here? I thought he was on book tour."

Both men stared at me. "Ah," Charles said finally, "what does Stryker do in your world?"

"He's a hugely successful author. He helped my Charles debunk all the aliens on Earth theories a long time ago. He's a close friend, the kids love it when he visits."

"What conspiracy theories is he into?" Martini asked.

I shrugged. "Not a lot, really. I mean, he pretends for some of his fans, but, really, while he's certain intelligent life is out there, he's equally certain it hasn't shown up on Earth."

"Betting that's wrong," Martini said under his breath.

Charles coughed. "Um, is he in shape?"

"Well, Eddy couldn't run a marathon, I'm sure, but yeah,

he does a lot of public appearances and he takes care of himself."

"She won't be able to fake her reaction," Charles said to Martini. "Guaranteed."

"Guys, I'm in the room. Speaking of which, why are we in a basement?"

"Most gates are in bathrooms—in every bathroom in every airport in the world—or in basements," Charles replied. "Most basement gates are in residences."

"Why?"

"Just our thing," Martini said. "We don't have to have her go over to the Zoo."

"I love the zoo. I was on my way there when I was run off the road. I was kind of hoping I could take Jamie there."

"Maybe," Martini said. "But that's not the zoo I meant. I can't believe we didn't brief her on the layouts of the Science Center or the Embassy. But we didn't."

"My God, there's more information you want to give me? Pass." I headed for the only staircase I could see and went up. Exited into a short hallway that led to a bigger hallway and a gigantic kitchen. Someone I knew was in there. "Peter!" I ran to him and hugged him.

"Kitty, darling, why are you calling me Peter?"

Looked up at him. He wasn't joking. "Uh . . ."

"She hit her head, Pierre," Martini said quickly as he and Charles raced into the kitchen. "She's a little addled from it."

Peter's expression went from confusion to concern instantly. "Have we seen a doctor?"

"Yes, Doctor Li."

"Excellent. Hand over the medicines. I'll make sure you take them on time."

Martini so handed. "Has the trouble gotten back here?"

Peter shook his head. "I wasn't watching the news. Tried to keep tabs on all of you, but that cricket match was so deathly dull, I couldn't manage it, and neither could anyone else who was Embassy-bound. I thought the Princesses were going to lose their minds."

Charles and Martini looked at each other. "We didn't cover personnel too well, either," Martini said.

"Why would you need to?" Peter asked politely.

"I'm having memory issues Pe—ah, Pierre. Like with your name. I'm sure it'll pass, but for right now, I'm not remembering things right. Jeff and Charles were helping me."

"Charles?" Peter raised his eyebrow. "Are you two fighting?"

"Uh, no?"

"She was trying to call me Charles while we were with all the dignitaries. Feels a lot stuffier than Chuckie, but it seemed to impress a couple people."

"Need to check on Jamie," Martini said, as he took my arm and led me quickly out of the kitchen. Charles followed us. "You call him Chuckie," Martini said in a low voice as we headed for the stairs. "You're the only one allowed to and you've said many times why you won't call him Chuck or Charles."

"Seriously? I only call him Chuckie in bed." Both men winced. "Sorry, but it's true. But, fine, Chuckie it is." Hoped I could call him Chuckie without feeling amorous or awkward. Checked Martini's expression—it was clear he was hoping that, too.

"She hit her head hard, on concrete, and that was witnessed by everyone around us and by now thousands of people on TV, minimum," Charles said, sounding as if he were trying to reassure himself as much as Martini. "Any slipups can be explained by the whole 'major concussion' excuse."

"I say again, Bizarro World sounded a lot more fun in the abstract."

"True enough," Martini said. He took my hand, grabbed Charles' arm, and suddenly we were moving at the fastest speed I'd ever encountered.

It was over quickly, but like the gates, it wasn't fun for my stomach. We stopped outside of what appeared to be the day-care center. Fortunately, I saw a bathroom nearby, wrenched out of Martini's hand, and ran for it. Made it into a stall just in time.

"I'm so sorry," Martini said from behind me, as I barfed my breakfast into the toilet. "Kitty's enhanced and all the other humans take a pill Tito created . . ."

"What . . . ever . . . ," I gasped out between heaves.

He knelt down next to me and pulled my hair back for me, while he put his other hand onto my forehead. It helped and I finally stopped throwing up. Martini got up and walked away. I heard water running, then he was back with wet paper towels. He moved me into a sitting position instead of a kneeling position and wiped my face off. He looked so sorry and also so sad I couldn't help it—I started crying.

He pulled me into his lap and rocked me. "It's okay, baby."

"No it's not," I sobbed out. "I'm the wrong person and somewhere along the line I'm going to blow it so badly that I'm going to make things worse for all of you. And you seem like a great guy but I don't know you, let alone love you, and I don't know how I'm going to pretend when I have to."

Martini continued to rock me. "I know how hard this is, and you're doing great, much better than you think you are. You're just genetically predisposed to rolling with whatever happens and handling it, and you've been doing a great job. This was my fault. I'm letting myself pretend you're 'my' Kitty, but in doing so, I'm forgetting that you're really not. I have to remember what it was like when we first met—I'd never have just grabbed you and run off at hyperspeed, not without warning, not when we weren't in danger. Hyperspeed is hard on humans—everyone throws up from it, not just you. That's why Tito created a drug to combat the effect."

"Hope I can get some."

He kissed my forehead. "As soon as you're feeling composed, yeah, I'll get you some." He leaned my head against his shoulder. "Just relax now."

Had to admit, him holding me was comforting and comfortable. But at the same time, it wasn't right. "I feel like I'm cheating on my husband."

"I know. I can feel everything you're feeling, trust me, blocks or no blocks. And I feel the same way, really. But we'll manage. Without breaking the vows that matter to us. I promise."

Heaved a shuddering sigh. "Okay. It's hard on Charles, damn, I mean Chuckie, too, isn't it?"

"Yes. And it's probably going to get harder. I don't know how long you're going to be with us. Alpha Team is going to focus on trying to determine if there's a rip in the space-time continuum or if there's another reason for how you traded places with my Kitty. But that could take some time."

"Or I could get sucked right back as soon as she's saved the day in my world, right?" Martini didn't reply and I thought about this. And the fact that these people didn't seem able to lie, and they weren't comfortable trying, either. "She's solved it already or she's dead, right? That's what you're thinking."

"Yes. I honestly believe that she can handle anything tossed at her, and what you described would be something she'd be more than capable of surviving. And she'd protect the children at all costs, because she'd see your Jamie as hers, and she'd never leave two little boys, either."

"So, we assume she and the children are alive and that leaves us with the obvious hypothesis that either there's more going on over there that she has to handle or that whatever switched us is going to switch us back whenever it feels like. Or never."

"Yes."

There was something in his tone—I was fairly sure that he was avoiding telling me something. The idea of being stuck here wasn't horrible. But to be here and not be married to Charles, to not have my sons, to leave my father and friends without me, was the horrible thing. Then again, she'd hit her head worse than I had, to the point where Martini had clearly thought she was badly hurt. So she might have that terrible concussion and not know who she really was. Which created a lot of jealousy and panic that I could do nothing about.

Shoved that worry to the side. I could take it out and enjoy it any time things got dull or I got comfortable, after all.

Of course, there was another option. "What you're not saying is that she hit the back of her head on concrete and was unconscious when you were taking her to the hospital. So she could have ended up blacked out in my car. And if that's the case, then she and my children are all dead."

Martini held me more tightly. "No. She has fast regeneration, just like we do. She wasn't dead or dying. She was hurt, and bleeding, but she was okay."

"You're lying, I can hear it in your voice. She was knocked out, and you're just saying this because you want to believe it. And you want me to believe it, too. In part because it's what we both want, and in part so I don't freak out."

"Yes." This time I could tell he was telling the truth. "Keep in mind that I can run faster than you can see. Kitty was unconscious, yes, but really not for very long, at least if we assume you switched at the moment she felt weightless to me. I think she would have been out for about a minute. Which means she was probably coming around. After all you, were also unconscious when I . . . got you."

"Or whatever switched you two wanted you both in an unconscious state and therefore kept her in said state longer," Charles said as he joined us in the bathroom. "There are other things here that we haven't told you about, and they would be powerful enough to do something like that, especially if they felt it would be safer for Kitty. And yes, I was eavesdropping, I'm in the C.I.A., it's just a natural habit. Besides, I was worried about Kitty. This Kitty. As well as the other one."

"Some things never change," Martini said, but he didn't sound angry. "You mean ACE, don't you?"

Charles nodded. "She's about to meet Jamie, our Jamie. She needs to know."

"Know what? I thought you said there was nothing wrong with your Jamie?"

"There isn't," Martini said soothingly.

"Other than that she's more talented than her father or uncle. Jamie may be the most powerful A-C we have. She's done some amazing things. And she's also housing a super-consciousness in her mind."

"Excuse me?"

"We mentioned ACE, during the briefing," Martini said.

"No. You mentioned powerful aliens of all kinds, including some that were godlike or so far advanced that they were hard for our minds to comprehend. You never said one of them was living in my daughter's head."

The bathroom door opened and a little girl trotted in. My little girl. Dressed differently, hair cut and styled a little differently, but still, my little girl. She came straight to me and sat in my lap and gave me a big hug. "Hi, Mommy."

"Jamie . . ." I hugged her back. "Mommy's missed you."

"I know. But you're with me now. Can we go to the zoo?"

"Uh, sure. Not necessarily today, though."

"Jamie-Kat, does Missus Lewis know you're out here?" Martini asked.

"Yes, Daddy, she does. Mommy, how do you like it here? Is it nice for you?"

Saw Charles stiffen and felt Martini do the same. "Ah . . . yes. It's nice here. How do you like it here?"

"If you like it, then why were you crying?" Jamie reached up and patted my cheek. "Don't cry anymore. You'll do it all right, Mommy. Don't worry. You're the right Mommy for the job." Then she leaned up, gave me a kiss, stood up, gave Martini a kiss, hugged Charles' legs, and trotted out of the room.

We were all quiet for a few long moments. "Okay," I said finally, "is Jamie able to tell what people are feeling, like you can, Jeff?"

"Yes," he said. "And other things. But definitely she's got empathic talent."

"Okay. The amazing things she's done, describe some of them."

"As my Kitty would put it, she time warped from New

Mexico to D.C. and kept a gigantic flying saucer from leveling all of the Mall area. And also from leveling her parents."

"During the second alien invasion we told you about," Charles added. "The one Kitty calls Operation Destruction."

"Gotcha. So, uh, I have a crazy question."

"Go ahead," Martini said. Charles nodded.

"Am I the only one who thinks that Jamie just basically told us that she's somehow involved with the Great Mommy Switch?"

But before either one of them could answer me, a different male voice echoed through the bathroom. "Excuse me, Mister Vice President, but the President is here to see how Missus Vice President is feeling. And he's not alone."

"Who's with him, Walter?" Martini asked as he and Charles helped me up off the floor.

"The Secretary of State, the Secretary of Defense, the Director of Alien Affairs for the F.B.I., and the Head of Special Immigration Services for Homeland Security. And there are more reporters on the street than Pierre and I can count."

CHAPTER 27

APPARENTLY IT TOOK LONGER to wake up from be-ing chloroformed than from being kicked in the head. More new knowledge.

The delay was good, because the thing I was really noting was how slow everything and everyone was. Sure, no one in the room had hyperspeed in my universe. But we had the Elves and a wide variety of Field agents who were living to serve, and I'd gotten used to asking for a thing and having it right there by the time I was done with the words. Here, it was working at good old human slow.

But, Pierre got me set up with a chair, card table, and wireless laptop. Then he scurried off to join Dad, Aunt Carla, and Caroline, who had taken the kids upstairs. In addition to their assigned "come up with the weird" tasks, I had them keeping an eye on the street, just in case our assassins had backup coming. The kids seemed excited by this assignment, the adults less so.

Thankfully, my counterpart had that iPod I'd saved from the car, and it contained most of the same music I had. She even had the newest Neon Trees album, which seemed like the right choice for right now. Plugged the iPod into the com-puter and hit play. As "Love in the 21st Century" started, I relaxed. A little, at least. And, all things considered, a little was better than nothing.

"So, who are you looking for?" Reader asked. "We may know some of them."

"People who are part of our team in my universe." I was searching, but the realization that the names Timothy Crawford, Jerry Tucker, Matthew Hughes, Joseph Billings, and Randall Muir were really common was being shoved at me. Realized that I had no idea what Chip Walker's real first name was. What a great boss and friend I was.

And amazingly enough, not everyone had a picture on social media or similar, making identification close to impossible. Decided to try some educated guessing.

Leonard Parker was also a common name, but Kyle Constantine wasn't, at least, not as much. As the Neon Trees' "Living in Another World" came on, I found Kyle, and therefore found Len. "Wow. So they went pro."

"Who?" Chuckie asked, looking over my shoulder. "What, you know some professional jocks in your world?"

Len was the incoming quarterback for the Jets, and Kyle was their new defensive end; they'd been acquired from Oakland in a trade that was considered the smartest move the Jets had made in recent years. They were both considered great players, and the Jets were touted as being Super Bowl bound for the upcoming season.

"Yeah, I do. They work for you, though, not the NFL. In my world." Had a feeling I wasn't going to get anywhere trying to contact them—they were both popular players and their social media feeds were gigantic. I'd have to catch them in person, and that was probably going to be hard. Though, not as hard as it might be, since I could use hyperspeed. But creeping on public figures could backfire, in more ways than I could count.

"Right. As if I'd hire brainless jocks?"

"They're not brainless. They're both really smart, Len especially. They're good guys." Got a lump in my throat as "I

Love You, But I Hate Your Friends" came on. I missed my
team. "Do we have any way of hacking into the Navy's
records? Five of the guys I'm searching for are Navy pilots."

"Sure," Reader said, producing a laptop from somewhere,
the Secret Armory presumably. "Give me their names and
ranks."

"Captain Jerry Tucker, Captain Matthew Hughes, Captain
Randy Muir, Lieutenant Joseph Billings, Lieutenant Chip
Walker."

"Wait, I thought you said they were all pilots."

"They are. Why?"

Reader shook his head. "In the Navy, the title of Captain
is only given if you're commanding a ship."

"It's not like that where I come from. They're all from Top
Gun and they're all pilots. If they've been on a ship, it was a
long time ago."

Reader shook his head. "Bizarre."

"Dude, I did mention that I'm in Bizarro World, right?"

Received a nice shot of the cover boy smile. "Right. Okay,
that might be why you couldn't find them. They could have
different ranks and even be in different branches of the service here." He was intent for a few minutes while the Neon
Trees shared that some things were "Unavoidable."

While Reader searched for my flyboys, I looked for
Hacker International. Proving that they were either dead or
still the top hackers around, the only one I could find was
Stryker, and only because of his *Taken Away* series. "Charles,
is this Eddy?" I showed him a picture of a guy who—if I
squinted and allowed that I was in an alternate universe—
looked like a slimmer, well groomed, incredibly confident,
and rather suave version of Stryker.

"Yes," Chuckie confirmed. "He's a successful author."

"Does he think aliens are around?"

"Like I told you earlier, no, Kitty, he doesn't."

"Right. It's just . . . you're *sure* this is Stryker Dane?"

"As sure as I am that it's also Eddy Simms, yeah. Why?"

"No reason. He still has great hair."

"So you've always said. My Kitty took him wardrobe shopping and for a makeover when he hit the *New York Times* Bestseller list. He's basically never looked back."

"Nice to know he's still smart in this world." My counterpart had managed this level of change in Stryker? She was amazing. I was proud of my other myself.

"He's actually in Australia right now. He'd planned his tour so we could spend time with him, then I got called back, so we'll miss him."

As "Voices in the Hall" started, I heard Reader breathe in sharply and looked over at him. He seemed upset, but as he saw me look at him, he plastered on a bland expression. "Nope, sorry. Can't find them." He closed his laptop and stood up.

"What is it? You found them, didn't you?"

Reader shook his head and I was prevented by following this up by the assassins starting to come to. Tabled for later, then. Turned off the music—no reason to make it remotely pleasant for them.

It was interesting to watch Chuckie and Reader do an interrogation. Reader played Good Cop and Chuckie took Bad Cop. Buchanan took the role of Looming Muscle Who Likes to Hurt Prisoners.

They scored names—after the usual "my name is Putin" or "Abraham Lincoln" crap. So, in addition to the two we knew, we felt confident we had Luis Sanchez and Julio Lopez. Maybe. Those were pretty common Cuban and Hispanic names, so there was no way to prove that they were telling the truth.

Decided this was going far too slowly. Walked over to Bernie and picked her up. By her throat. And I held her off the ground. "This is me calm. Imagine me seriously pissed. Then understand that I'm going to know when you're lying."

Her eyes were wide. "What?" she gasped out.

"Leave her alone," the man we'd identified at Raul snarled.

"Or you'll do what, exactly? Kill me and all the kids? Kill

everyone in this house? Yeah, you've tried that already. You've failed." Looked over at Raul while Bernie tried really hard to get free to no effect. She tried to hit and kick me. I hit her thigh, hard. She stopped trying. Superpowers rocked.

"What do you want from us?" he snarled.

"We want the obvious. Who hired you and why?"

"We don't ask why," Sanchez said.

"Right." Gave Bernie a little shake. "I happen to know this is your wife, Raul. I also happen to know you love her. A lot. What would you do if I killed her?"

"I'd find a way to kill you, ugly."

I nodded and tossed Bernie down. Went over to Raul and punched him, hard, in the gut. He doubled over. "Guess what, asshole? I'm not going to give you that chance. You can tell us what we want to know and maybe we'll turn you over to the proper authorities, which would give you a fighting chance to get free, wouldn't it? Of course, not turning you over to the authorities and just taking our frustrations out on you is also appealing."

Chuckie put his hand on my shoulder. "There's an easier way. Much easier."

"Oh, tell me you have truth serum here!"

"We do." Reader was tapping a hypodermic. "Who do you want to hit first."

"Shoot up Bernie over there. I hate her a lot."

"All I did was offer your children some candy," she said peevishly. "Which you didn't let them take."

Go Other Me, for not trusting strangers with candy. She was, apparently, smarter than me in a whole variety of ways. "Yeah? You did that so you could get up close and kill us very personally on a 'play date.' I'm really against that kind of crap, Bernie."

Bernie looked surprised, presumably that I knew her game plan. But she also looked a trifle smug. The thought occurred that she may have been trying to do to these kids exactly what she'd wanted to do with my Jamie—to kidnap them, not kill them.

Moved to where I could see all their expressions. "So," I asked casually, "why did you decide to change from kidnapping the kids to killing them?"

Bernie's eyes opened a bit wider and Lopez jerked just a little, but that was confirmation as far as I was concerned. But none of them spoke.

"Time for the Sodium Pentothal," Buchanan said.

Raul sneered. "That won't work on us." Sanchez nodded and added his sneer to Raul's. But Bernie didn't look nearly as convinced, and neither did Lopez.

"You have a lot of that?" I asked Reader. He nodded. Took the syringe from him and put it at Raul's neck.

"Don't!" Bernie shouted. "You could kill him or paralyze him if you don't know what you're doing!"

"Ah, now there's the thing, isn't it? Do I know what I'm doing? I'm getting seriously pissed at the delay . . . I promise you, I can indeed ram this into your husband hard enough to kill him. And I don't want to bother untying him to find an arm vein. So . . . what's it going to be?"

"We work for the Corporation," Bernie said.

I pressed the needle against Raul's skin. "He twitches, this probably goes in. No freaking duh, Bernie. We know you're assassins for the Cuban Mob. What we don't know is who, exactly and precisely, told you to go kill us. Or why. We want to know both. There are four of you. If I screw up shooting the truth serum into Raul's neck, I can just try again with you. And then your other boys here."

"So," Buchanan said, falling nicely into the role of Badder Cop, "I guess the question is, who wants to die first? Or last?"

"You'll just kill us?" Lopez asked.

"Sure. You're assassins. If you're not going to tell us what's going on, then you're not going to tell the F.B.I. or the C.I.A. or anyone else what's going on. Meaning you have absolutely no value to us as people to hand over to our superiors."

"And the Corporation isn't going to want you back badly

enough to make a deal with us," Reader added, sounding a little regretful. Was pretty sure it was faked—he was trying to be Good Cop, after all. "And what we want they won't give us anyway."

"So what?" Raul asked through gritted teeth. "You're just going to kill us anyway. Why should we make it easy for you?"

Of course, this was the issue. I knew without asking that Buchanan would kill all four of them if he was allowed to. For all I knew, Chuckie and Reader would, too. Frankly, so would I—I, more than the three men, really knew what these assassins were capable of.

Chuckie took the needle from me and grabbed Raul's arm. "Good point. You're the one in charge." And with that he slammed the needle into Raul's neck.

CHAPTER 28

RAUL JERKED, went rigid, and Chuckie dropped him to the floor, so that Raul was facing away from the others. Bernie screamed and Lopez jerked, big time. Sanchez kept his cool, but I could see him sweating.

Because I was enhanced, I could see things that were faster than the normal human eye could catch. Which was how I'd seen Chuckie switch the syringe with one that seemed like a prop—as far as I could tell, the needle didn't penetrate. However, Chuckie had squeezed a pressure point on Raul's arm at the same time he slammed the needle onto another pressure point in Raul's neck. Raul was still alive, but he was knocked out and temporarily paralyzed.

This wouldn't last long, but it didn't have to. Buchanan and Reader lifted Raul's deadweight and moved him into the wine cellar. I heard what sounded like something ripping and assumed they'd found some duct tape and were ensuring that Raul wouldn't be able to share when he woke up.

"Who's next?" Chuckie asked.

"The Corporation isn't run out of Cuba anymore," Lopez said, sounding freaked out. Clearly he was the rookie in the group. Good. "We're run by an American politician."

"Shut up," Sanchez snarled.

Reader came back in. "I say we burn the bodies. Less mess and no one's going to be looking for them anyway."

Lopez went pale. "Look, I don't wanna die. You let me cut a deal, I'll tell you everything."

"You'll tell us everything now," Chuckie said, "and then we'll decide if your information is worth us calling up our superiors."

"Some of your superiors are dead, just as ours are," Sanchez said.

I had him by the throat and up in the air in less than a second. Unlike Bernie, who was about my size, he was built more like Christopher. Did not matter. I had him up and off the floor. "*Now* I'm seriously pissed. Are you saying that you're the ones who killed my mother?" My voice was a growl, not even on purpose.

"No," Bernie said, sounding freaked out. "No, we didn't. We wouldn't—"

Shut her up with an excellent side blade kick to her head. While still holding Sanchez off the floor. Well, at least this awesome move had witnesses. Not the ones that mattered, because Christopher would never believe it and Jeff probably wouldn't, either, but still, I had someone around to impress.

Not that I cared about that so much. What I cared about was getting some answers before I got so angry I ripped someone's throat out.

"One more chance," I growled at Sanchez. "And then you join your buddy Raul in the deader pile and I see how good old Julio here likes talking."

"I'll talk," Sanchez choked out. "Just put me down. Please."

"Wow, they teach the magic word in assassins school? I'm impressed." Put him down, not nicely at all. "Spill it."

He nodded. "When Señor Battle went to prison, control of the Corporation moved."

"José Miguel Battle, Sr.," Chuckie said quietly to me. "He worked with the C.I.A. originally during the Bay of Pigs fiasco, and then he became the godfather of the Cuban Mob."

"Fantastic. So, who did ownership pass to?"

Sanchez shook his head. "Doesn't matter. He was killed and then the next ones after him. Turf wars, you know how it is."

"Yeah. I'd still like names."

"I don't know the name of Señor Battle's first head man. But the one who took over was what Julio told you—an American politician from Florida."

Had a funny feeling. "And his name?"

"Leventhal Reid."

Managed not to totally freak out, though it took effort. "So, did you kill my mother on his order?"

"No. We didn't kill your mother. His right-hand man did that, in retribution for her shooting Reid. He's the one who hired us. He wanted everyone who ever worked with Angela Katt wiped off the face of the Earth. But he wanted her family to die last."

"Why?" Reader asked.

Sanchez shrugged. "So he could enjoy it, I guess."

"The government thinks the Corporation is basically shut down," Chuckie said, voice tight. "Angela didn't believe it. We were investigating them, and had proof that Reid was involved, but we didn't know he was the man in charge."

"So who is this 'he,' Reid's right-hand man?"

Sanchez didn't look willing to share.

"Look, you give us a name, one that we can believe, or else this is all BS and you've just tossed out the name of a dead politician to try to fool us." Put my hand on Sanchez's throat again. "And if that's the case . . ."

"We're not allowed to know his name," Sanchez said. "Or see his face. He wears a mask when he gives orders."

"Oh my God, pull the other one." My hand tightened on his throat.

"It's true!" Lopez said. "He's loco, scary loco, but we don't get to see him."

"I don't buy it. You don't run an entire criminal organization wearing a mask as if it's Halloween every day. I mean, sure, they do that in the comics, but in real life?"

"He wears a mask," Sanchez insisted. "No one sees him."

"Someone does," Chuckie said. "Who?"

"His woman," Lopez said with a nervous giggle. "She sees him."

"And what's *her* name?" I asked, hoping it wouldn't be the name I was expecting and dreading at the same time.

Sanchez smirked. "Bernice."

I tightened my hold on his throat. "You get to go bye-bye now, Mister Liar." He struggled but I was stronger. Besides, Chuckie wasn't the only one who knew how to knock someone out. Sanchez passed out and I tossed him toward Reader and therefore away from Lopez, who was looking freaked out.

"That's two down," I said as Reader dragged Sanchez off to be with Raul. "Let me be clear. I know that Raul was not the head man of the Corporation. I also know that you were trying to follow good old Luis' lead and try to lie to us." Put my hand on his throat. "Do you really want to see if I'm strong enough to strangle you while I have you up in the air? I am, by the way. But if you're, heh, dying to find out . . ."

"No," he choked out. "I don't want to die. I just don't want any of them to be able to say that I was the *hutia*."

"The what?"

"Big Cuban rat," Chuckie supplied. "Okay, fine, your only other witness is unconscious. Who's the man supposedly in the mask?"

"Not supposedly. Luis wasn't lying. He wears a mask, so no one can identify him. I think they're loco, both of them, but they're in charge. They have plans." He shuddered. "Killing people for a reason, that I understand. Killing babies for revenge? That's wrong."

"Oh, so good to know you have a moral standard. I note it didn't stop you from trying today, however. Tell us about his woman."

"I don't know her real name. She's tall and blonde. Everyone calls her *Señora de Muerte*. But, really, they both wear masks. Just the kind that cover half the face, not like Halloween. But enough so they're hard to identify."

Got a very bad feeling. I was far better with French than Spanish, but Lady of Death was a pretty close matchup to LaRue Demorte, languages-wise. "What's he look like? He's American, right?"

Lopez nodded. "Tall, built like him," he jerked his head toward Chuckie. "Dresses well, they both do. But nothing that stands out."

"And the dude's name? The new Head of the Corporation? What does he call himself?"

"*Papa Patrón.*" Lopez shrugged. "I know, it's a stupid name."

The bad feeling cemented itself. Because this was easy to translate. "Father Boss."

CHAPTER 29

CHUCKIE PULLED ME ASIDE. "You just went pale," he said quietly. "What did that ridiculous name mean to you?"

"It's a really long story, but the easiest explanation is that, in my world, we have a Sith Lord active. We call him the Mastermind. He's the third generation of Sith, by the way. For us, the first Sith was an alien, named Ronald Yates. But his apprentice and the second Sith Lord was Leventhal Reid."

"So that creep was in your world, too?"

"Creep would be the nicest thing I could say about him. He remains the most terrifying person I've ever dealt with. Jeff was only able to save me from him by about a second, and even then, even after Jeff killed him, Reid found a way to come back."

"What? Is your head hurting or something?"

"No. In our world, Herbert Gaultier and Antony Marling, among others, were able to create legitimate clones and androids. We're still finding out what else they created and who else is continuing on their sick and twisted work."

Chuckie jerked. "Who did you say?"

"Antony Marling and Herbert Gaultier."

"There's no way, Kitty. Herbert Gaultier is a successful businessman, yes, but he's focused on saving people and the planet. Very focused. Herbert and Solange keep in touch with us, even though you cut Amy out when we got married. He's a humanitarian, focused on curing cancer among other things. True, I think Marling's a quack, but he's considered the top doctor in the world for autistic children."

"Really? They're good guys?"

"Yes. Very much so."

"And . . . go back. I've cut Amy out in this world?"

He nodded. "She . . . insulted me when you called to tell her we were getting married. You two haven't spoken since. Herbert and especially Solange keep on trying to get you two to make up. But I can't say that I'm eager for it. It's been nice to not have your friends insulting me constantly."

Couldn't stop myself, I hugged him. "I'm sorry. And I'm sorry to say that it happens in my world, too." Hugged him harder. "But I'm still your most ardent defender."

He hugged me back and kissed the top of my head. "Thanks. That's kind of nice to know."

Realized we were hugging just a little too long and gently pulled away. "So, um, Solange is still alive? The woman who Julio over there just ID'd as the Lady of Death sounds a lot like LaRue Demorte, who in my world got to tack Gaultier onto the end of her name."

"She's not Amy's mother there, is she?" He sounded horrified. If he only knew LaRue he'd be grossed out, too.

"Oh, hell no, she's too young to be a mother of someone our age; she's only a few years older than us. Well, supposedly. She was Herbert's secretary, then mistress, then second wife, after he murdered Solange. Per you, by the way. In my world, if you say it, we know it's so."

"Wow. It's nice to know that I'm considered infallible somewhere."

"Oh, I'm betting you're infallible here, too."

"So, back to that name. Why did it make you go pale?"

"Because we discovered the clones of Reid and LaRue when . . ." Had no idea how he was going to take this, and wondered if I could talk around it. Realized I was going to have to tell him sooner or later. Might as well be sooner.

Chuckie cocked his head at me. "Ah. What did they do to me? Am I still alive in your world?"

"You are, yes. Your wife, however . . ." Swallowed hard and went on. "She loved you so much. And Jamie, too. We have human and alien godparents for Jamie. James and Amy—who I'm still besties with in my world—are my Jamie's human godparents. Jamie's named for James. And me."

"Same here. Jamie Katherine."

"I figured on the first name, but it's nice to know on the second. Jeff's cousin and Amy's husband Christopher is her alien godfather. And your wife, Naomi, was her alien godmother. And, like the best fairy godmother in the world, she sacrificed herself to save you and Jamie from the Mastermind."

"Ah. How long were we married?"

Swallowed hard again. "Six months."

Chuckie got a funny look on his face. "How long ago did she die?"

"About a year and a half ago."

"Took me a long time to get married. Why?"

"Ah . . ." There was truly no good, or modest, way to answer this question.

"Oh. I was still in love with you, wasn't I?"

"Yeah. In my world, our timing sucked."

"Figures. Am I . . . still mourning?"

"Yeah, you are, actually." He looked kind of ill. "What is it?"

"She's going to want to take care of him, isn't she? She'll see him as me, as her husband, and even if she's clear on everything else that's going on, it's me, like you're her, in that sense. She'll want to stay where it's exciting and things are so much better than here."

"Whoa there, big fella. I haven't been in this world very long, but I have to say that, other than the fact that you've been lying like a wet rug to her about what you actually do in your third career, and the fact that Mom is dead in this world, it's pretty great here."

"Really? She and our children would be dead if not for this switch. You've made that abundantly clear. She already has Jamie there. She can have more children . . . a new Charlie and Max. With him." He sounded stricken, as if he really believed this was going to happen.

"Wow, dude. Seriously, until just a couple years ago, I honestly had no idea that you were the jealous type."

"I hide it well."

"Not so much right now. And I'm betting not at all to Other Me. Look, I deal with this all the time because Jeff is a jealous man, too. He was majorly jealous of you, for years. He's finally gotten past it, at least most of the time. You need to trust the two, well, three of them as much as they have to trust you and me, you know."

He shook himself. "You're right. I'm sorry."

"It's okay. That's what friends are for, remember? And in every universe that we exist in, no matter what, you're always my best friend."

He gave me a slow smile. "Then that makes the multiverse sound a whole lot better." He cleared his throat. "So, the weird name? You still haven't told me why it freaked you out, just that it has something to do with my . . . other wife's death."

"Yeah. While we were doing the usual Mexican standoffs that I seem unable to avoid, both Reid and LaRue called the man in charge 'Father.' He's not their real father—it was clearly what Yates, our Alien Patient Zero for Evil, had told Reid to call him, and, when I killed Yates and Reid took over, it was what he told his then-Apprentice to call him."

"Wait, what? You killed someone?"

"Hells to the yeah. More than one someone, to be honest."

"How many someones have you killed in this alternate reality my wife is in?"

"Dude, I'm losing count. Definitely in double digits. They were all bad guys, if that helps any. And by bad, I mean horrifically, terribly evilly bad. Just like the guys we're going after now."

"Okay. I guess."

"You guess. If I'd realized there was a Glock in Other Me's purse this morning, I'd have killed all four of them already for what they tried to do to me and three innocent little children. *Your* innocent little children."

"I'm not trying to sound disapproving, Kitty, I'm sorry. I can just see where this is going. You want to take down whoever's in charge of the Corporation. And by 'take down' I mean 'kill.' "

"Probably. Because of the explanation you interrupted."

"Oh, pardon me. Do go on."

"I do sarcasm so much better than you. At any rate, with Reid being dead—and I note you didn't freak out when I said that my *husband* had killed him—said Second Apprentice is now the Master, and he's doing an endless clone loop with himself, Reid, and LaRue. Not Yates, though—they don't appear to want the competition, or the control, for whatever reason. All of this was basically confirmed by the Reid and LaRue clones. So, if we take Father Boss to its obvious conclusion . . ."

"Frankly, I didn't want to sound like I was running your husband down and besides, you indicated Reid was attacking you so that was acceptable. And no, I don't need a feminist tongue lashing, so you can close your mouth. You're right, I was being sexist, and I'm sorry and I'll do my best not to do it again. But, yes, I see where you're going with that name. And, based on all of this, you need to realize that whoever is running the Corporation in this world has an extremely high probability of being the Sith Lord in yours."

"Got it in one, but then I never had a doubt. By the way, the chances are incredibly high that it's someone I know, and know well, in my world. From all we've learned, the Mastermind knows pretty much everything we're doing and planning to do."

"Well based on your reactions to Gaultier and Marling, be prepared for this person to be someone you think is a good guy in your world."

"Yeah, that had occurred to me, too. You know, this is sort of like *Days of Future Past* or *Age of Apocalypse*. Some people are still doing the jobs they were doing in my universe, some are still evil and some are still good, and some, wow, just wow. I'll do my best to not assume at this point. But anyway and speaking of Marling, why would you guys interact with an autism specialist?"

Chuckie looked down. "Jamie," he said quietly. "We're not sure what's wrong, and we don't discuss it a lot, but I think it's autism and I'm pretty sure my Kitty does, too. And . . . if Jamie's autistic, it's all my fault."

CHAPTER 30

"WE'LL DEAL WITH THE REPORTERS** somehow, Walter," Martini said. "We'll be down momentarily."

"So much for that nap idea." The three of us looked in the mirrors. "Well, you two look great. I, on the other hand . . ."

"Look like someone who's had an accident and is therefore shaken up," Charles said.

"My clothes are a mess. And the less said about the state of my hair, the better."

"They're also wrong," Martini said with a jerk. "We need you to change clothes before we go downstairs. And your hair is cut differently."

"I'll put it up in a banana clip, if you have those here. That should hide any differences."

"We do," Charles said. "You two take care of that, I'll stall." He raced off before I could say that if I was going to be undressing in front of a man, he was the man I was going to be far more comfortable with.

"It'll be fine," Martini said, as he took my hand. "I won't look. Though I've seen everything you have, since you're, you know, the same. In that sense. I think, anyway."

"Let's just stick with you not looking, Mister Smooth." We went to an elevator this time. And once again, Martini seemed uncomfortable and sad. "Why are you unhappy in elevators?"

Now he looked embarrassed. "Ah, we, uh . . ."

"Oh, wow, you guys do it in the elevator?" It had been a long time since Charles and I were able to be that adventuresome. "It's got to be better than an airplane bathroom." Though those were damned fun times, and I had extremely fond memories of a few airplane bathrooms. I was fairly sure Charlie had been conceived in one.

Martini still looked embarrassed, but he grinned, too. "We like to find as many places as possible to, ah, ensure the relationship is still solid."

The doors opened and we got out. "Works for me. And, wow, is this place really an embassy, or is it just a gigantic luxury hotel?"

"I guess it's a little of both. Does it bother you?"

"Not really. It's not like our houses are miniscule, and Charles ensures we always have the very best. We're not ostentatious, but we have three kids and family and friends living with us—we need a lot of space."

"Interesting. My Kitty can barely handle it, and she's been living here for three years."

Considered this as we entered a penthouse apartment that, frankly, was probably as large as my home in D.C. "Charles made his first millions right before we got married. He made the next ones right after in the stock market. We're careful with our money, but we have a lot, so maybe it's just that I'm used to this by now, and she hasn't had the same time to adapt."

"Sounds about right. Here's our closet. As a race, we like formality and the colors black and white. You, well, my you comments about that all the time. The standard outfits for women—"

"Are what I saw all the Beauty Queens wearing, right? White oxford shirt, black slimskirt, black pumps. The clothes are all Armani. In fact, that's the only designer I've seen on anyone since I woke up here. Did Armani win the Fashion Wars and those lines are all that's left?"

"No, all the other designers are around, at least we have a lot. We just prefer the way Armani looks. Again as a race. In many things we're extremely conformist."

"Okay. What if they don't fit me?"

"They will. Including your underwear. Our Operations Team will make sure of it."

Looked around. "I don't see anyone."

"You won't. They're very discreet. But, trust me, if you need something that's not in here, just ask for it and it'll show up. Fast. And put your clothes into the hamper—they'll be cleaned and back waiting for you shortly."

"Okey dokey. Um . . ."

He grinned. "I'll leave you alone here. I'm going to leave the bedroom door ajar, because the soundproofing is excellent, and if you need me, I don't want you calling and my not hearing you. And yes, I'll probably feel it if you're in trouble, but I'd prefer to err on the side of over-caution."

"Works for me. And thanks." Leaned up and kissed his cheek again. "I really appreciate how you're acting with me."

He hugged me gently, but didn't say anything. The hug wasn't a long one, and then Martini left the closet and the bedroom.

I got undressed and dumped my clothes into the hamper. Grabbed a robe and went to the bedroom door. "Do you think I have time to shower?"

"Honestly, no. But you're fine."

"You guys really can't lie at all, can you?" Trotted into the bathroom and did as fast a sponge bath as I could manage. Combed out my hair and put it into a ponytail, then into a banana clip. That way, if I had to lose the clip for some reason, my hair would be back and hopefully no one would notice that it was different from my CA's.

Considered putting on makeup to hide the bruise, but it was our excuse for everything, so figured I shouldn't bother.

As I left the bathroom I noticed several gigantic cat trees, sort of arranged like their own condominium block against one wall. There were no animals on them, but they could have held a couple dozen cats. There were four dog beds against the opposite wall. No dogs in evidence, but four big ones lived here, if I went by what I was seeing.

Back to the closet. Sure enough, there was underwear waiting for me. I knew this because it was sitting neatly on top of the dresser and hadn't been there before. "Uh, thank you, whoever you are. Thank you very much."

Underwear on, I found the set of clothes that were for me, because they were hanging alone, with shoes under them, and I knew they hadn't been like this a few minutes ago.

The outfit was nice and quite flattering, and the pumps were comfortable, so one thing was going right. There was a purse sitting there—looked like the same purse they'd tried to hand me at the hospital. Had no idea where that had gotten to, but when I looked inside, it sure looked like the same purse. There were no other purses in the closet. So either my CA just asked the Operations Team for a new bag every time she wanted a change, or she was a one-purse girl. I'd been a one-purse girl, before I'd married Charles. Decided this was, therefore, my purse for this universe, slung it over my shoulder, and went out to Martini.

"Will I pass muster?"

His eyes went wide and he nodded slowly. "Yeah. You look . . . perfect."

Felt my cheeks get hot. "Thanks." This was not good. I shouldn't be feeling all fluttery around Martini. Then again, maybe it was a good thing and would let us fake out everyone we had to.

He stood up and took my hand. "Let me take the lead on everything downstairs. You just stand there and look sexy and I'm sure we'll get through it." He squeezed my hand. "Not that I'm telling you not to add in when you think you should. Then again, I've never needed to tell you that."

Now was definitely not the time to mess up him thinking of me as his Kitty. "You got it."

He kissed my cheek, and we headed for the elevator. This time, he put his arm around me while we waited. Figured he was nervous about my fooling the people we were about to meet with. Put my arm around his waist.

"The President is Vincent Armstrong, you call him Vince. The Secretary of State is Monica Strauss, and you call her Monica. The Secretary of Defense is Fritz Hochberg. We call him Fritz when things are serious, but when we're relaxed it's Fritzy."

"Really?"

"Yeah. They're not our enemies but this screwup should mean they're not happy with us. The Homeland Security guy is Cliff Goodman, he's one of Chuck's best friends. The guy from the F.B.I. is Evander Horn. He's black, and has burns over most of his body, but you can't see them when he's in a suit. Regardless of the situation, you call him Vander."

"Even if I'm being formal?"

Martini chuckled as the elevator doors opened and we got in. We kept our arms around each other and he seemed more relaxed in here now. "Depends on the situation. When you're making a 'we're going to kick your butts' statement, you tend to go with titles and extreme formality. Hoping we won't have to deal with that today."

"Me too."

"Cliff and Vander are our friends, so expect them to be supportive, but they still have jobs to do and we've made those jobs harder today. You have a full Secret Service detail, two women, four men, and you're close to them. Worry about remembering the women's names—you can use the concussion excuse for the men, and we'll use it for anything where you don't know who someone is or what to say to them. The blonde is Evalyne, you call her Ev, and she's in charge of the detail. The brunette is Phoebe, you call her Pheebs. They give us all codenames. I'm Cosmos, you're Cyclone, Jamie is Cutie-Pie, and Chuck is Playboy."

"Really."

Martini chuckled and hugged me. "Really. But that's just his cover."

"Like Batman."

"Yeah, that's what you always call him."

"What do I call you?"

He grinned. "Superman."

"Well, that seems to fit." We left the elevator still holding onto each other. Steeled myself, because we were going to see Charles in a couple of seconds, and I couldn't look guilty or jerk away from Martini.

There were men and women stationed about, all in suits, but none of them were Armani. They all looked really official. "Secret Service," Martini murmured as he nuzzled my ear. Realized that us being the poster couple for Public Displays of Affection was great, because he could slip me clues and just look normally lovey-dovey. "Not yours. Assume yours are waiting for us with the President."

Peter met us in the hallway and led us to the room where everyone was. "They look rather grim," he said quietly.

"Thanks for the warning," Martini said. "It's not a surprise."

We entered a decent sized parlor, but it was packed with people. Some were clearly Secret Service—they were lined against the walls. Two of the women made eye contact with me and gave me tiny nods. Assumed these were Evalyne and Phoebe and gave them fast smiles back.

The people who were here to meet with us were with Charles and Singh, who was back from whatever he'd been doing with my mother. One of the visitors was tall and distinguished—and he looked like a career politician. Based on how the room was focused around him, figured this was President Armstrong.

There was an older man who was clearly military, or former military, by his bearing. Took a wild one and assumed this was Hochberg. The woman with them was wearing the typical power suit female politicians favored. She looked to be in her late forties and was attractive in a steely way. Had to guess this was Strauss.

There was a handsome, medium-skinned black man who

looked about Richard's age and was built like Richard, Martini, and Paul. He had close-cropped hair and sparkling brown eyes. He shot us a look that seemed supportive, so I assumed this was Vander.

He was next to a guy about Charles' age who gave me an encouraging smile. Assumed this was Goodman. Now that I saw him in person, the name registered. I knew this man in my own universe.

Before I could marvel at the differences between my reality and this one, the President nodded to us. "Bad business today, kids."

"Accidents happen," Martini said. No one looked like this was close to being a good enough answer.

"I'm so sorry—" I started, but the President cut me off.

"You have to go to Australia, Jeff," Armstrong said. "Right away. And if Kitty's up to it, she needs to go, too."

CHAPTER 31

"WHAT? WHY?" Martini sounded stressed. Couldn't blame him.

"Why? Are you kidding?" Armstrong shook his head. "Don't act naïve. I realize Kitty got hurt. Right now, that's the only thing that's keeping the Aussies from rounding up their A-Cs and shipping them off to us. And if they do that, you know what happens."

Tried hard to keep my mouth shut, but I couldn't stop myself. "I'm Jewish, so yes, we do. And I'm *so* glad that my cracking my head open was in everyone's best interests. Oh, and I have a concussion and feel like I've been in a car crash, but, seriously, don't bother to ask how I'm feeling. Anyone at all."

"You flipped off the Prime Minister *and* you tossed your cup of coffee at him," Strauss said. Decided I didn't like her.

"Not on purpose. Any more than Jeff spilled more coffee on him and Margie on purpose." Martini squeezed me. Remembered that this Kitty didn't know the PM's wife.

"We know that," Armstrong said. "And, I'm sorry, Kitty. You weren't representing well at the event to begin with. And then with everything else that happened . . ."

"You mean when I fell onto concrete and hit my head?"

"Yes, and we're sorry you got hurt," Hochberg said, showing at least some ability to fake caring. "But you were insulting the Australians the entire time."

"Cricket's a boring sport for those who aren't into it," Vander said, earning my instant loyalty, even though I, personally, liked the sport. But even I could admit it wasn't as exciting as any form of football. "Golf's boring to watch too, unless you're into it. I realize that Kitty was bored. From what I've heard, half of the Australian people find cricket to be boring. Choosing to create an international incident over this screams 'easy opportunity' much more than real insult."

"It was the combination of events," Strauss said. "My office has been deluged."

"So sorry to put you out and force you to do your job and all, but, my God, how juvenile are all of you people? This is something that I'm sure can be resolved, easily, by simply apologizing in whatever stately way we're required to."

"Exactly!" Armstrong beamed and I got the feeling I'd just locked us into doing whatever he wanted. "Which is why you and Jeff need to get on a plane to Australia immediately. Bring Jamie, too. I think the whole family representing will be better. I hear Margie likes kids."

"She has three, I'd think she's fond of them, yeah."

"Vince, I'm not against our going," Martini said. "But why right away?"

"Because, just like Vander said, we think this is being used as an excuse," Goodman answered. "American Centaurion has a lot of enemies and they're all jumping at the chance to show how horrible all aliens are."

"I'll be going with you," Strauss said, ensuring that I was going to hate this trip. "To ensure that the two of you actually manage to stay on script."

That did it. I'd dealt with people treating Charles like dirt when he was so much smarter and more successful than they were. I wasn't going to allow anyone to do the same to Martini, not if I was his wife in this universe. I pulled away from him and got right up into this woman's face. "You will rephrase that or you will get out of my house. Forever."

Strauss looked shocked. "I beg your pardon?"

"Yes, you'd better, only in a believable fashion. I don't care how important you think you are, but the man in this room who actually *is* a heartbeat away from the Presidency is my husband. Therefore, you will speak to him, and to me, and to our friends and family, with respect or you will get your happy ass out of my home or I will set the dogs on you. Is that clear?" There were four dog beds. That meant there were real dogs around somewhere, I hoped.

The room had gone incredibly still. It was clear everyone was waiting for Strauss' reply. I was holding eye contact with her—and though she was a worthy opponent, there was no way she was going to win. We played the Staredown Game at home for fun. Sure, Charles usually won, but not always. No one other than him or my mother had ever been able to beat me and this woman wasn't going to make it into that hallowed echelon.

Sure enough, she broke first. "I'm very sorry . . . Kitty. And Jeff. I didn't mean to come off as insulting or to indicate that I felt my position was higher than that of the Vice President. I honestly wasn't prepared to have to deal with fallout from this event—normally, you two are always on top of your game."

Based on everyone's reactions at the hospital when they'd thought I was "their" Kitty, I found this last one hard to believe. However, I knew when to take the apology and move on. "Thank you, Monica. It's been a very difficult day for everyone."

I went back to Martini. The two female Secret Service agents shot little "atta girl" signs to me. Decided they were joining Vander in my Instant Loyalty section.

"I really think we need to wait at least a day," Martini said. "Just to be sure that Kitty's feeling alright."

Realized he was hoping my CA and I would switch places before a trip to Oz. But I couldn't believe I'd been sent here just to hang around. No, if I was here, I was supposed to do something—and saving the A-C's diplomatic day seemed like it was probably my cosmic job.

"I'd like the time so that we can determine the right things to do and say in order to apologize. Us stampeding to Canberra in order to beg forgiveness without a good plan—a plan that clearly needs to involve me in a big way, I must add—seems remarkably stupid. Along the lines of making someone who is not a trained actress pretend to love a sport they hate and then being shocked, *shocked* I say, when she doesn't succeed. I ask again, just how juvenile are all you people?"

Everyone in the room, including all the Secret Service agents, stared at me. "Ah, what Kitty means—" Singh started.

The President put up his hand. "What Kitty's saying is that we're acting like a bunch of immature assholes. And she's right. And, by the way, I realize I haven't really said this properly. Elaine and I are both sorry you were hurt, and I'm relieved to know you've bounced back as you always seem to. Elaine will be relieved, too."

Didn't take genius to figure that Elaine was the First Lady. "Thank you. Yes, we'll go to Australia. No, we are not running off like crazed wolverines just for the thrill of it all. We will, in all haste, determine what we feel is the best way to apologize, run it by everyone in the room, and then, once we're confident we have a Plan A, B, C, *and* D in place, then we will head off to Australia to make things right."

"Cliff and I will work with you on the planning," Vander said quickly. Armstrong and Hochberg nodded, Strauss looked relieved. Really hated her. Wondered if my CA could stand her or not. Decided it didn't matter right now, but I was betting on no.

"Sounds good," Charles said. "Now, if we can, I'd like to suggest we adjourn, because Kitty needs some rest."

Tried not to shoot a loving look toward him, but it took effort. I was fine thinking of Martini as my husband when I was angry, apparently. The moment I wasn't, however, it was difficult, especially with Charles right there.

Paws were shaken all around, then Martini walked Armstrong, Strauss, and Hochberg out, trailed by their many Secret Service agents.

Goodman clapped Charles on the shoulder. "Nice job.

We'll get it handled." What interested me was that Charles allowed and even seemed to like it.

Charles smiled. "Yeah, thanks for the support. I do think Kitty needs to rest. Why don't we get started and then she can weigh in once we have something?"

"Sounds good to me, buddy," Goodman said with a wide grin. Charles didn't object to the friendly term, which was hugely shocking.

Vander nodded, but looked a tad uncertain. "The apology will directly involve Kitty. I think she needs to be involved the entire way through. Kitty, what do you think?"

I thought that I liked Vander, wanted to kick Goodman in the balls, and was really wondering how different things were in this world. "I'm with Vander. I think the idea of a bunch of men figuring out how I should apologize to anyone, let alone the PM couple, sort of screams of chauvinism. Don't you think?"

Goodman laughed. "That's right, you're our feminist throwback."

"I wouldn't call it a throwback," Singh said. His tone was very soothing. "Feminism isn't exactly nonexistent right now."

"And it's still very necessary, since some men seem to think they're the boss of everyone, not just themselves." Decided that—regardless of what Martini had said and how Charles seemed to feel—I wasn't loving Goodman. At all. I'd spent too many years identifying who was trying to befriend us because they wanted to use our money, connections, or Charles' brain without giving us any form of reciprocation in terms of loyalty, support, or real friendship. Goodman struck me as one of these. Plus, I knew what he was in my world. Sure, some people here were different, but he wasn't striking me as one of them.

Goodman seemed to catch on that he'd pissed me off. "Sorry, Kitty, and you're right. Believe me, I know who I'm the boss of and who I'm not. And you're right—everyone has their part to play, and yours is the biggest right now. So, what do *you* want us to do?"

"Nice recovery. Frankly, I'd like to work with Vander, Evalyne, and Phoebe on this. And Raj and Pierre, of course. Only." Vander looked pleased, the two female Secret Service agents looked shocked and flattered, and Singh looked relieved. Goodman kept a very pleasant, bland expression on his face. Interesting.

"Why no one else?" Charles asked, looking slightly worried.

Shrugged. "Because a smaller team of people who get what's going on and can advise me will be better than a gigantic room full of talking heads."

"Can't argue with that," Martini said as he rejoined us. "As always, I just figure whatever Kitty wants to do is the right thing. So far, I've never been wrong about that." He gave me a smile that told me he was incredibly pleased with and proud of my performance. Felt myself flush like a schoolgirl. Hey, he was incredibly handsome and had bags of charisma. I was starting to see how my CA had fallen for him. "Baby, you want to start that now or take that nap you wanted?"

"Frankly, that Strauss woman pissed me the hell off and I'm no longer tired. So now will work. Depending on how fast we can come up with what to do, I'll sleep at night or on the plane." It seemed unlikely we were going to take a gate for this, but who knew? However, figured I should err on the side of assuming that the VP was going to have to look as normal as possible for this excursion.

"Figured," Martini said with grin. "Pierre is prepping as we speak. He said to tell you that he has a gigantic amount of my mother's brownies hot out of the oven, lots of milk, plenty of Cokes and other sodas, plus other snacks all ready for you."

And it was nice to see that some people were exactly the same in this world. "As always, Pierre's the best." Looked at my smaller team. "Let's go eat. And plan. But eating sounds like our first order of business."

Martini laughed. "Only my girl."

CHAPTER 32

HAPPILY, we were doing our meeting in the humongous kitchen. Peter had everything Martini had described and more on the table. Martini kissed me on the cheek, and then he and the others, including the male Secret Service agents, left us alone.

"Any chance of some tunes around here?" I asked as I devoured a brownie. They were, possibly, the best I'd ever had. I needed this recipe. For when I got home. So I could give it to my Peter. As if I was going to make these, or have any shot of them turning out as delicious if I did?

This question got me some looks. "Kitty's having some memory issues due to her concussion," Singh said smoothly. "Just shout 'com on' like you always do and ask Walter for whatever you want to listen to," he told me with a reassuring smile.

"You sure you're up to this right now, Kitty?" Vander asked, sounding concerned.

"Yeah, I think so. I'll let you know if I'm not, okay?" Everyone nodded. "Great. Com on!"

"Yes, Missus Vice President Chief?"

Decided not to question this kid's choice of titles. "Hi Walter. Can I have some music, please?"

"Sure, Chief. What do you want to hear? Band or play-list?"

Dawned on me that this was a big test moment. If I chose a band my CA didn't actually have or like, I was going to have to spend a lot of time on explanations. But she was me, so that had to mean we liked a lot of the same music. The 80s seemed like a safe choice—all the oldies stations were big on 80s music at home, and I had to figure it was here. "How about the Psychedelic Furs?"

"You got it, Chief. You want only them or the playlist that has them and some others?"

"Let's do the playlist." That way, I'd get an idea of some of the other bands my CA liked. The sounds of "All That Money Wants" hit the airwaves. Singh and I both relaxed. "Thanks Walter. Com off." Hoped that was the right thing to say. Singh remaining relaxed indicated it was. Go me. "So, in the opinion of the three people who witnessed my screwup firsthand, how bad was I, really?"

The blonde Secret Service agent who I took to be Evalyne shrugged. "You were about the level of the first President Bush barfing on the Japanese."

"That bad, huh?"

The one I was hoping was Phoebe shook her head. "That wasn't the worst thing ever. It was more embarrassing for the President personally than anyone else."

"So, what Vander said is right—them getting all offended is an excuse."

"Maybe," Singh said. "But you did flip them off. I know you don't know that the way you did the V for Victory sign was insulting, but it was."

"Frankly, you and Jeff showering them with hot coffee had to have been worse," Vander said. "It just came off car-toonish, Kitty. But yes, I think it's an excuse."

"I believe that some of their reaction may be because the general consensus of the Australian people is that you're both heroes," Peter said as he slid another brownie my way.

"How so?" I asked with my mouth only sort of full.

"Since discovering what happened, I've had everyone in the Zoo monitoring. From what they tell me, the majority of the Aussies think you and Jeff are fantastic. Your popularity scores are going through the roof."

"Wait, so why is everyone freaking out?"

"*Your* popularity is high," Evalyne said, as "Sins of My Youth" by the Neon Trees came on. "But Prime Minister Costello's is not, and this is feeding the very vocal constituency that doesn't like him."

"Meaning, you made him look bad and his people loved it, so he's even more pissed," Phoebe translated.

"Ah. So, politically, we're great if Jeff and I wanted to run for office in Australia, but we've made our ally look bad and because his people loved it, he wants to make a point."

"Pretty much," Vander said. "It's fixable, Kitty. It always is."

"So you guys always say." Figured this was a safe bet. Everyone's grins indicated I'd guessed right. Go me. I was batting a thousand. Did *not* expect this winning streak to last.

"So, what are our thoughts?" Singh asked. "Obviously we need to craft a very good apology, but we also need to give them some kind of gift."

The others started brainstorming presents, some grandiose, some small, all expensive. But as the Psych Fur's "House" came on, I ignored them and thought back. We were talking about people I knew well, and it was wounded pride that was giving special interests a wedge in they were capitalizing on.

If we wanted Tony back on our side, we needed Margie to come around first. And Margie wasn't going to come around based on some lavish gift. She'd want something personal and meaningful, not something that was showing off.

So what could we get a couple who had pretty much everything? Thought about what was in their home. No, that wasn't right. Matching wasn't the key.

As "The Ballad of Mona Lisa" from Panic! At The Disco came on, I thought farther back. When we'd first hit Australia we'd run into Lulu, their eldest daughter. She was younger than us, but we'd hit it off and hung out, met her friends, and their friends, and had found ourselves within a group where we fit.

When we'd found out I was pregnant, both my mother and Chuckie's were far away. Lulu had introduced us to her parents then, and Margie, the mother of three, had taken me under her wing. She'd become our "Australian mother" even though she was a little too young to *be* our mother. But she filled that role happily and willingly, and we loved her for it.

And, to thank her for that, I'd given her a gift on Mother's Day. It was a gift she treasured, and I knew this because it hung with the things her own daughters had given her over the years. And every year, when we exchanged gifts, she still told me that this first Mother's Day gift from me was her favorite.

Touched Singh's hand and leaned toward him. He leaned in to me, so I could speak softly. "Do we have a way to see if there's something specific in the PM couple's home? Without their knowing, I mean."

"Yes. Why?"

"Because I think I know what will work, but first, I have to make sure they don't have one already."

"If you can describe what they're looking for, I can have their house searched in the next fifteen minutes." He grinned at my expression. "Yes, we're really that fast. And yes, they'll never know *because* we're that fast."

He got me a pad of paper and a pencil and I scribbled a description and even did a serviceable drawing. "It's made of crystal, and if it's there, it should be hanging up."

"I'll have them search everything in case it's packed somewhere." Singh took the paper and walked off, presumably to make the call.

As he left, "Sugar, We're Goin Down" by Fall Out Boy hit the airwaves, and Malcolm came in. "Hi, where have you been?"

"Around." He looked at the others. "Can I steal Missus Chief away for a minute?"

"Sure, everyone else is handling the brainstorming." I got up and we also left the kitchen. Singh was nowhere around. "Where did Raj go?"

"His office," Malcolm pointed to a nearby door. He walked us down the hall toward the basement.

"Uh, why are we going here?"

"I need to talk to you, and I don't want anyone else hearing us."

"Okay. Why?"

"Because I saw how you looked at one of the people in the room today."

"How could you? You weren't there."

"No, I wasn't. However, I was watching."

"Why?"

"It's my job. Watching over you and your daughter is my mission. Period. I generously include your husband, both of them," he added with a grin. "But only because they matter to you."

"Well, that's nice. You know, do I know you? In my world, I mean. You seem . . . familiar. Beyond having met and interacted today, I mean." We headed downstairs to the dark and creepy basement.

"You probably do. Like I told you, your mother recruited me out of college. She assigned me to watch Missus Chief and Baby Chief when you all came to Washington. But if you were married to our resident genius as young as you say and were living half the time in D.C., I'd bet Angela assigned me to watch over you then. So you may have noticed me, off and on, but we'd never have actually interacted unless I had to physically get you out of danger."

Malcolm flipped a switch and there was light. Which didn't make the basement any better but at least it was a lot less creepy now. Also noted that I couldn't hear the music down here, which was disappointing.

"Ah. Okay. And no, not that I can recall. So, why are we here?"

Malcolm sighed. "Because I don't just think the Mastermind is a human—I know he is. In fact, I'm pretty sure I know *who* he is. And while both of your husbands think this situation with Australia is top priority, I don't. Stopping the person responsible for every action against Centaurion Division and, by extension, the P.T.C.U. and other organizations is the most important priority we have."

"How do you know that if the others don't? And if you know, why haven't you told them?"

"I know because I look at people, things, and situations very differently from the rest of the people involved. And I'm willing to believe the word of a parrot."

CHAPTER 33

"WHAT DO YOU MEAN, it's your fault if Jamie has autism?"

Chuckie shook his head and didn't answer. Thought about all the various conspiracies he'd told me about over the years, especially those about the C.I.A.

"You think the C.I.A. gave you some drug, don't you?"

"I do." The words sounded dragged out of him, and his voice was very low. Got the distinct impression he hadn't shared these thoughts with Reader. It was clear he'd never shared them with Other Me. I could tell by how he was acting.

"Did my mother approve that? Is it something you remember happening?"

"No to both, but there's no other explanation that makes sense." He sounded desperate, and desperately scared. I wasn't used to Chuckie being this emotional—he was normally laid-back and cool. Intense in bed, yes, and in a good way, but otherwise, he'd learned to keep his cool before I'd ever met him.

Considered my reply carefully therefore. "Autism could be caused by someone slipping you some LSD or something you don't remember, sure. But there are so many other factors." Extremely high intelligence, for example. Figured that wasn't going to be a comforting alternate, so kept it to myself. "Besides, I realize that your Jamie is a lot quieter than mine, but she doesn't seem off."

"Really? Have you seen her room?"

"Yeah. The mirror is a little . . . odd, I'll give you that. But she's clearly functioning at a high level."

"She's not a normal kid, and not in the way Charlie and Max aren't normal. Her interactions with us are limited—she'd rather stare at that mirror all day and night than leave the house, let alone interact with any of us. It's like she's addicted to TV or video games, but at least with those there would be something we could deal with in a straightforward way. When we try to limit her mirror time she gets . . . difficult."

"You mean she throws a temper tantrum."

He nodded. "Of epic proportions. And it's not just that. She's listless and uninterested most of the time unless she's in front of her mirrors. The few times she really communicates she comes out with these proclamations of doom. Never of anything good, and certainly not all the time. Usually she's wrong. But there are times she's been right. Charlie told me that Jamie said you were all going upside down today, in the car, before they left the garage. She wanted everyone to stay home. And, she was right. It was a dangerous situation."

"Yeah. One I realize Other Me wouldn't have survived. Okay, we'll deal with that as we can, but I want you to look at me, right in my eyeballs." He did. "You are not responsible for this, any more than Other Me is. If your Jamie really *is* autistic, this is not a 'fault' situation. This is a 'pull together and figure it out' situation, but you aren't to blame. And I can guarantee Other Me would feel the same way. If, you know, you actually told her."

"I can't," he muttered, as he dropped his eyes again. "She'd never forgive me."

I snorted. "Dude, seriously. She's going to have the same 'what the hell?' reaction I did when the truth comes out, but that's all. I'll tell you what she's going to be mad about—you lying to her about what you and James do and Mom did. That's going to be something you need to apologize for. I'm sure she'll understand—I did, when I found out. But at the same time, that's the betrayal. Not this."

"She thinks I'm cheating on her, when we're on missions I can't tell her about." He sounded ready to break down. This was not good.

"Dude, stop doing this to yourself. And to her. Tell her the damn truth. Sure, she'll worry, but she worries now. Let her worry about the reality, not the lie. I mean, unless you *are* cheating on her."

He looked up and his eyes flashed. "Kitty, you've been the only woman I've ever loved in my life. No, I'm not cheating on you. Her. You know what I mean."

"Yeah, I do." Heaved a sigh. "It took the you in my world a long time to get over me, so I can easily believe this. What I can't believe is that you haven't worked together to fix your Jamie. And you haven't by the way you're acting, and by the way everyone else is acting. Use the word. Own the word. Find out if the word is right. But stop hiding from the word. Not saying the word doesn't change the reality. Only doing something positive, or negative, can change the reality."

He nodded and gave me a weak smile. "I suppose you're right."

"You said you thought Marling was a quack. Why?"

"Jamie doesn't seem to like music, even though Kitty and the boys do. He said that she's listening to a different soundtrack in her head, and once we can find that frequency, then we can really get through to her."

"Yeah, I can actually understand that—both why you think it's crazy and why I think it could make sense. Though, honestly, there hasn't been one thing I've said to her or done with her today that she's hasn't fully comprehended and been involved with."

Chuckie eyed me for a long couple of seconds. "Yeah. She's responding to you much more than she does her real mother."

"Yeah, and I think that—unlike Charlie, who thought I

was Other Me, or Max, who was sure I wasn't—Jamie knew from the get-go that I was someone else, but she *wanted* me here."

Chuckie rubbed the back of his neck. "It's getting more complicated, the more we talk about it, not less."

"True, but when you switch universes, some complication needs to be expected. We need to stop powwowing, by the way. James has been blocking us from Julio and Bernie, and Malcolm seems to be indicating that the other two are conscious, so we need to decide what we do with them."

"We'll have the Agency pick them up."

"That sounds good, but I have another question for Julio before we go that route." Chuckie's concerns had brought up something I needed to check.

Trotted back to Lopez and Bernie. She was glaring at me, he looked worried. Showing he was smarter than he looked. "Julio, have a question for you. Bernie, I've tortured stuff out of him while you were unconscious. I don't want to have to do that again. So, your choice—I knock you out, which I am *all* for, or you don't blame Julio for wanting to not have to drop trou again."

"Fine," she snarled. "It doesn't matter what he tells you— I'll get you for murdering my husband."

"Oh, blah, blah, blah. I hear that a lot. Don't care. And, trust me, it's taking everything I have to not just break your neck right now. I'd shut the hell up if I were you." Bernie subsided and I turned back to Lopez. "So, Julio, the people we were discussing, the ones running the Corporation, where in the government do they work, do you know?"

"No idea. Really."

Saw Bernie smirk out of the corner of my eye. So she knew. "Bernie, I have a proposition for you. You give me something I want, I give you something you want."

"What's that?" she sneered. "To let me live?"

"Actually, no. To let Raul live."

"You killed him already," she snapped.

Showing he was paying attention, Buchanan dragged a

body with a black bag over its head in front of Bernie. He pulled the bag up, showing Raul, alive if not overwhelmingly well. Bernie and Lopez both gasped. Nice to know they really thought we'd killed him. Told me that these were probably enemies it wasn't going to be wise to show mercy toward. Worked for me.

Buchanan put the bag back over Raul's head, pulled a gun, and put it against the bag. "Tell her what she wants to know, or I get rid of this piece of trash for real."

"There aren't real bullets in your gun," Bernie sneered.

Buchanan turned the gun on her and shot her in the thigh in less than a second. Apparently Buchanan was on the "show no mercy" mindset already.

I managed not to let my jaw drop while Bernie screamed. Didn't look to see if Chuckie and Reader approved of this—because if I showed weakness now, Buchanan was going to actually have to kill these people. And while I was willing to do it, I didn't want us to have to.

"It's a clean shot," he said. "You can get patched up and be fine. If you tell us what we want to know. Otherwise, I shoot him in the head with the rest of the very real bullets in my very real gun."

"They work for the C.I.A.," Bernie said through gritted teeth. "Somewhere in there, we don't know where. But when Reid was in charge, he always indicated that his right hand was hidden in the C.I.A., and from all that he's done since taking over, it sounds right."

"What are their names?" I asked. "Papa Patrón and Señora de Muerte. What are their *real* names?"

She shook her head. "I don't know." But her eyes flicked to Raul.

"Raul knows," I told Buchanan. He pulled off the bag and ripped off the duct tape covering Raul's mouth. "I know you've heard everything. Tell us the names, or my friend here gets to shoot your wife wherever he wants."

"You claim to be better than us, but you're not," Raul growled.

"No, see, we *are* better than you. We don't have your little kids here and we aren't trying to kill them. We also didn't attack you without warning—you attacked us. These are simple distinctions. You're just bitter that we were able to stop you and turn the tables, so to speak. Now, answer my question or watch what happens to your wife."

Buchanan pointed his gun at Bernie's other thigh. "Hard to walk if you're shot up in both legs," he said conversationally.

"The woman, no one knows her real name," Raul said quickly. "They call each other by their Corporation aliases at all times and she didn't show up until Señor Reid was killed. The man, though, I've heard different names for him. But they're all aliases, too, I can guarantee it."

"Give them to me."

"Señor Reid called him Michael Corleone, I heard him introduced as Farallón Tipobueno to a few businessmen, but mostly it was *Menor Patrón*, Junior Boss, until he took over."

"Why does he wear a mask?"

"Same as for the all the aliases—so we can't identify him and therefore can't betray him. He's not Cuban and he's not Mexican. He's a white American, like all of you. Señor Reid was white, too, but he understood Cuba. This one?" Raul shrugged. "He understands how to make the Corporation strong again, and we respect that."

"Why would your identifying the head of the Corporation be a problem?" Chuckie asked from behind me. "It's not like you all didn't know the Battles when they were running things."

"Papa Patrón isn't trusting. Now, I've told you the truth. Are you going to let my wife bleed out?"

"Oh, it's tempting, but I guess not," Reader said. He'd procured a med kit, presumably from the Secret Spy Room, and knelt down near Bernie. Chuckie moved Lopez away from her so he couldn't try anything.

While Reader performed battlefield medical treatment and Buchanan covered everyone with his gun, I went back to check on Sanchez. He was awake. Picked him up and brought him back out with the others. "Look, another party favor."

Raul glared at me. "You think you're funny."

"No, I think I'm hilarious. I also think your loyalty was to Reid, not to Battle or to Mister Aliases."

Raul shrugged. "Señor Reid helped me when I was young. I show my appreciation."

"What has Papa Patrón done for you lately?"

"Paid us well to kill off everyone on Angela Katt's team."

This wasn't news, but it still made me see red. "Which one of you killed her?"

"I told you, Papa Patrón did that himself. I would have, if he'd let me. She killed Señor Reid."

"Actually," Chuckie said, and his voice was tight, "she didn't. I did."

CHAPTER 34

RAUL STARED AT CHUCKIE for a long moment. "Then I'm doubly sorry we didn't kill you and all your family today."

That did it. I punched Raul as hard as I could, which was pretty hard. Uppercut. He went back, down, and out.

"I think you broke his jaw," Buchanan said conversationally. "Nice hit."

"It was that or kill him. Okay, we can't turn these four over to who you normally would—their benefactor is in the C.I.A., meaning that the hunt for all of my mother's team was essentially put in place by a mole. And said mole will ensure they 'escape' and come after us again. I'm not willing to risk that." Especially because Other Me and I might be back in our own worlds when that happened.

"Mole hunts are never pleasant," Chuckie said.

"And I'd figure this mole has it set up to make it look like whoever the last man standing out of the team is the one who killed everyone else. Malcolm, based on James' reactions when he saw you, I'd say that you drew the Tom Cruise role in the first *Mission Impossible* movie."

He nodded. "So, what do we do with them? I'm fine with killing them."

"Make up your mind," Reader said. "I'm putting a lot of effort into not letting Miz Charm here bleed out."

"I think we need to call in friends from overseas. I suggest Mossad, but MI Six is also a great option."

"We have Mossad contacts," Reader admitted.

"I'm sure you do. My mom was in Mossad when she was younger, wasn't she?"

"Yes," Chuckie said. His voice sounded funny. Looked at him. He looked funny, too.

"James, the moment Bernie's patched up, make the call to Mossad. Tell them we need these people picked up fast and we're only turning them over if we have their assurance that they will not be handed right back to the Corporation or to the C.I.A."

"You got it, girlfriend."

It was nice to hear Reader sounding like my Reader. But Chuckie was not acting like my Chuckie. Grabbed him and went back to our whispering corner. "What's wrong?"

"I can't tell her I'm C.I.A. If I do, then I have to tell her it's my fault her mother's dead. And she'll never forgive me for that, ever."

"Chuckie, seriously, you're losing it." He winced. "Sorry, look, I've only used that name for you since the first day of high school. Not embarrassing you is an adjustment we don't have time for. Unless you pulled the trigger or shoved her in front of a bullet, how the hell is these assholes murdering Mom your fault?"

"It was my operation. Things went wrong . . ." He looked old, very old, suddenly, and I realized he'd been carrying this guilt for well over two years.

Thought back. I remembered how Mom had been during the Party of Death that was the start of Operation Sherlock— she'd given me a giant bear hug for no real reason, and hadn't been able to tell me about what mission she'd been on at that time. The timing wasn't quite the same, but then again, Reid was dead by then in our world. Didn't matter—Mom had probably almost died on that mission, whatever that mission was. If there had been a mole in the C.I.A. or P.T.C.U., maybe my mother would be dead in my world, too.

Of course, the Mastermind was somewhere high up in the government. Meaning that Mom probably survived because there were aliens on the planet and Centaurion Division always ensured that the P.T.C.U. had Field agent back up.

I took one of Chuckie's hands. "Look, what you do and what Mom did is highly dangerous work. And it sounds like there's a mole in the C.I.A. In fact, if you guys were after the Corporation, then it's a guarantee that nothing you guys could have done—regardless of who'd planned the operation—would have gone right. It was set up for all of you to die. That you only lost Mom is probably miraculous."

"She'll never—"

"Stop selling us short!" I hissed this as vehemently as I could, hopefully without sharing it with everyone else. "You know what I see as the problem in your relationship? The fact that you've spent so many years lying to the person you love the most under the guise of protecting her that you can't believe that she can roll with whatever you throw at her. But she *can*, and I know that because she's freaking me. I handled aliens on the planet without batting an eyelash." Okay, I'd fainted, but that was because Jeff had implanted some memory in me and besides, that wasn't important now. "She can certainly handle this."

"What if she can't? What if this, combined with Jamie and everything else makes her . . . ?"

"Makes her what?"

"Makes her want to stay in your world?"

"My God when did you become a Drama Llama?"

Reader came over. "Sorry to interrupt the domestic dispute, but I've sent a message to our main contact at Mossad, complete with pictures of our four friends over there. Waiting to hear back."

"What do we do with them in the meantime?"

Reader shrugged. "No idea. I'm more interested in translating the aliases they gave us."

"They're worthless," Chuckie said morosely.

Channeled Mom. "Snap out of it, and that's a damn order."

Both men jerked and straightened up. "What?" Chuckie asked.

"I said to cut it out, and I mean it. Stop moping and wallowing in drama about all the many 'what ifs' you've decided are so all-encompassing and, instead, put the best mind in the multiverse to the task at hand. We need to figure out if those stupid aliases give us anything to work with to identify the mole in the C.I.A. who happens to be running the Cuban Mob. Unless you're just too busy feeling sorry for yourself, that is."

Chuckie blinked. "My Kitty never talks to me like that," he said finally.

"Maybe she should. Maybe she will. I can *guarantee* she will if you're still trying to blame yourself for every problem in the world when she gets back. Now, focus. We have four aliases to work with. Chop, chop, time's a wastin'."

Chuckie nodded slowly and gave himself a little shake. "Okay. Papa Patrón is obvious—Father Boss. Junior Boss is the right translation for Menor Patrón, and that seems both obvious and not like we get anything more."

"Other than confirmation that Reid was your first Sith Lord and that the current Papa Patrón was his Apprentice. Which the Michael Corleone name indicates, too. The son who will actually take over the mob."

Reader nodded. "Yeah. It also could indicate there were other 'sons' who didn't survive."

"Then they, like all of Reid's rivals in the Corporation, are dead. This isn't a group that sends their competition off to rest homes or vacations in Aruba."

"True enough," Reader said. "So, what about our last name, Farallón Tipobueno?"

"That name isn't one I've heard before," Chuckie said. "Either first or last."

"Frankly, like Raul said, it sounds made up." Thought about it. "LaRue Demorte must be a made up name, too. It never occurred to me before, because she was working for Gaultier and at the time I met her I didn't think of her as an evil genius. So, it's a safe bet she's Señora de Muerte. Gaultier was French, so she put her fake name into French. Now she's tied up with the Cuban Mob, so she's put her fake name into Spanish . . ."

"What?" Reader asked. "Oh. Wait. You think Papa Patrón has done the same thing, don't you?"

"Yeah, I do. I just don't speak Spanish well enough—well, at all, really—to be able to translate it."

Chuckie clenched his jaw. "It would figure," he snarled.

"What would?"

"Hang on, I need to be sure." He had his phone out. "Give me a minute, Google has a nice translation program."

Reader's phone rang while Chuckie's phone was connecting. Apparently A-Cs on the planet meant that telecommunications was a lot better. "Yes? Hey. Yes. Yes, we'll only release with your guarantee that they won't be extradited to either Cuba or the U.S. Frankly, we want them on ice forever. Oh? Really? Well then, we're pleased to have done a favor for our friends. Yeah, please, as soon as possible."

Reader hung up and chuckled. "Turns out the Israelis are looking for all four of them. Something about some high-ranking operatives being assassinated over the past couple of years."

"Think they were going after Mom's friends in Mossad?"

"I think it's very possible," Reader said. "Your Sith Lord seems to have a real hatred of Angela, to an almost insane degree."

"They were absolutely going after all of Angela's friends, but not because of her. Because of me." Chuckie sounded furious, though not guilty. So, one for the win column. "I should have seen it—this guy's been jealous of me since we met and spent the first part of our careers constantly trying to one-up me. He's a loose cannon. Brilliant, but unhinged. I always felt he got in due to political connections, and if Reid pulled strings, that would fit."

"James and I are breathless with anticipation to learn who this guy is so we can go kill him. So, you know, in your own time and all that."

Chuckie looked at me, and his eyes were flashing with rage. "Farallón Tipobueno translates in a Spanish-Cuban fusion to Cliff Goodman."

CHAPTER 35

MY TURN TO BLINK. "Wait, what? Cliff Goodman? He's a tall blond guy a little older than us, usually dresses like every other go-getter in D.C. and normally has his hair just this side of a Marine high and tight? That Cliff Goodman?"

"That's the one," Chuckie growled.

"Bizarro World is officially more bizarre than I was prepared for. Cliff works for Homeland Security, not the C.I.A., and he's your best friend in D.C. In my world, anyway."

"No idea of how," Reader said. "He and Chuck are like oil and water."

"Um, you two aren't close in my world. You didn't meet through me in that universe, and that may be why. You don't all-out hate each other, but you're not buddies—it's more like you two tolerate each other, in a friendly way, but still. And Gaultier and Marling are good guys here. So, the precedent exists for good in one and evil in the other."

"Why are you defending him?" Chuckie asked. Angrily.

"Because . . . he's your friend. You trust him . . ."

"What?" Reader asked softly.

"Um, I need to be able to talk out loud. And I don't want our prisoners hearing me. How soon are the Israelis getting here?"

No sooner asked than Pierre came running down. "We

have a very suspicious-looking van arriving. Should I get everyone into the safe room?"

"Yes, just in case," Chuckie said. "I think they're friendlies, by the way."

Pierre nodded then looked at Bernie. "Oh, there's blood. Wonderful. I hope I can get it out of the flooring." With that he raced off.

"You two stay with the prisoners," Chuckie said to me and Buchanan. "The agents coming know me and James, and they're a suspicious bunch with great aim and itchy trigger fingers."

"You know, just like Buchanan," Reader added as they headed upstairs.

"Hilarious," Buchanan said.

Went over to him. "Think Mossad will keep their word?"

Buchanan nodded. "They tend to be less . . . forgiving than we are."

Bernie looked freaked out. "Please, don't let them take us." She was pleading.

Knelt down in front of her. "If we'd begged to be spared, if we'd asked you not to try to murder three innocent little children, would you still have killed us?"

"No." But she wasn't looking at me.

"Look at me," I growled. She did. "Don't look away. Now, answer my question again."

"No." But her voice trembled and the lie was in her eyes, and besides, I knew her in my world. And in this one, she was still the same.

I leaned closer. "I know you, what you and Raul are. In your souls. And so I know that you're lying. Julio here, maybe he wouldn't have killed the children. Only, he would have tried because he's more scared of what you all think of him and will do to him than he is of losing his soul."

"So what are we?" she asked defiantly.

"You're murderers. Gleeful murderers. You get off on it, both of you." I stood up. "You're not redeemable. You're just evil."

"More evil than the one who hired us?"

"Oh, hardly. But I'll wager if we did a headcount, you've killed a lot more innocent people than we have. So, you go to the people who understand why sometimes mercy isn't a wise choice."

"They'll torture and kill us," Bernie said, a bit desperately.

"Yeah? Here's some wisdom you and Raul, in particular, can appreciate. An eye for an eye, a tooth for a tooth. Enjoy getting some Old Testament justice. And just remember this—whatever Mossad does to you will be a hundred times nicer than what I'd do to you if we were alone and there were no witnesses."

"Good attitude," a familiar voice said.

Looked up to see Reader, Chuckie, and three people I knew. Managed not to shout out their names, but only just.

"Kitty, this is Oren, Jakob, and Leah," Reader said. Indeed, my three pals from Mossad were here. Bizarro World wasn't completely turned around, at least. The three of them looked a little more grim and battle worn than I remembered, however.

It was Oren who'd spoken, and he gave me a friendly smile that had no recognition in it. "Charles says that you've discovered the truth. Welcome to the Family. Officially."

"Thanks. Did you know my mother?"

They all nodded. "Very well," Jakob said. "She was an amazing woman. James says you're just like her."

There was something in the way Jakob was standing near Reader—got a suspicion, but decided voicing it could wait. However, Reader had someone at Mossad on speed dial, and that someone had dropped whatever to come right over.

Leah walked over to our prisoners. "I recognize you," she said to Bernie. "You befriended my best friend. And then you killed her."

"Yeah, that's their MO. What are you guys going to do to them?"

"Nothing good," Leah said, and both Lopez and Sanchez shuddered at the tone of her voice. It was an impressive tone.

Hoped I'd heard enough of it so that I could practice and add it to my repertoire of Terrifying Vocal Inflections to Use on Evildoers. "And they will never be going anywhere else. We'll give you what we get out of them, of course, as long as it doesn't betray our own state secrets."

"You guys rock, thanks."

"What about their car?" Buchanan asked.

"Oh, I'd like to hang on to that. I think we can use it."

Bernie glared at me. "A car won't tell you anything."

"You may be right, Bernie. Then again, you don't know what I'm looking for."

Buchanan duct taped everyone's mouths and black bagged them. Then the men carried them upstairs. Leah stayed with me. "How has discovering what Charles and James do affected you?"

"I'm rolling with it."

She nodded and handed me a card. "In case you find that you're not rolling with it as well as you think, you can call me any time. If Angela was here, I know she'd handle any issues for you. But with her gone, while I'm in no way her equal, I'd do anything for her, and that means anything for you."

Couldn't help myself, I hugged her. Leah and I were friends in my world, and it was weird to pretend that we'd just met.

She hugged me back. "I won't let them escape or be traded," whispered to me. "I'll put bullets in their brains before I allow them to ever get the chance to kill any more people, all of you especially."

"Thanks. I appreciate that, truly. Because I know their first targets would be my children."

We unclenched and she nodded. "They would be. They've murdered several families in these past two years. They're on some kind of ethnic cleansing campaign."

Thought about Papa Patrón, and who Chuckie thought it really was. "The one giving the orders is trying to remove anyone who can stop him. You kill someone's parent, they grow up, search for the truth, find it, and then they'll hunt you down until the day they die." It was what he was essentially doing to my mother and her team, after all. "You wipe them out young, then there's no way for the genes to pass on and no one to enact vengeance."

Leah gave me a small smile. "They forget that we Jews understand that mindset, far too well. And we avenge our own, regardless of bloodline."

"Bad guys of the world beware. And all that."

She grinned. "Exactly." She gave me another hug then trotted upstairs, leaving me alone with my thoughts. However, I still enjoyed thinking aloud, and doing so alone just made a girl sound crazy. So, decided to wait until the others returned.

Which they did shortly, with Pierre and a ton of cleaning stuff in tow. "You carry on," he said. "I need to get these stains out before they set."

Chuckie jerked his head and we went into the wine cellar. "Okay, you thought of something, Kitty. What was it?"

"Well, first off, James, are you and Jakob an item?"

Reader grinned. "We were. We're still close. But our jobs made a long-term relationship too difficult. Well spotted. I didn't think we gave off any signals."

"You don't, really, but I'm getting better at looking at the little things. And that brings me to what I was thinking. Because I think I've ignored all the little signs about Cliff in my world, because in that world you, Charles, like and trust him, and if you think it, ninety-nine percent of the time, therefore so do I."

"How?" Chuckie asked, shooting me a grateful look, presumably for calling him Charles in the group. "I can't stand him. He started the rivalry with me early—even before I knew who he was."

"How so?"

"I was in a long-distance chess championship. We never saw our opponents or knew their names. All moves were mailed in. Yes, that's how long ago it was. I won. Turned out

I was the youngest participant and so the group that had put the contest on really made a big deal about it, and they released my name and picture, with my parents' permission, of course."

"I've never heard this story. Maybe it only happened in this world."

"I doubt it. It happened when I was in grade school, Kitty. I'd told my teacher and she told the class. I was never given a moment's peace from that point on. I learned then not to talk about how smart I was."

"Ah. Okay, that makes sense." Tried not to be bitter that, in this world as well as mine, Chuckie was an outcast because he was brilliant, instead of being touted as the greatest guy around. "And Cliff was one of the participants?"

"Yeah. He was a freshman in high school and he came in second. He'd expected to win, protested that I was too young to have been in the contest, accused my parents of cheating, and basically made a gigantic scene. He's been in competition with me ever since. When Angela first brought me into the C.I.A., he was already there. He mentioned the contest, which is how I realized who he was. No one else was going to remember that I'd beaten them, not fifteen years later."

"So . . . if that happened in my world, then the likelihood would be that the Cliff there probably had the same jealousy reaction. And that fits, because we've clearly determined that the Mastermind has a serious hard-on for hurting you. Everything is being done to hurt, discredit, destroy, and kill you."

"We loathe each other. We're absolutely enemies in this world."

All the pieces fell into place. "Oh, wow. It all fits. All of it." Bellie saying "good man"—it was indeed Cliff's name she was saying. Colonel Hamlin feeling that he knew who the Mastermind was—again, he knew and worked closely with Cliff, he'd have the best insights into how Cliff worked. "But Jamie lets him hold her . . ." But the first time I'd ever tried to hand her to Cliff, when she was still a baby, she hadn't wanted to go.

"So?" Reader asked. "She's a little girl."

"My Jamie is special with a heaping side of extra in those departments. But in my world, the bad guys have created emotional overlays and enhancements, to avoid the A-Cs with empathic talent, Jeff in particular. And maybe they want to ensure they can fool Jamie, too. Maybe Cliff has been wearing one for far longer than we've known they existed."

"Makes sense," Chuckie said. "Plus, he's good at faking people out. Just not me. He hasn't been able to fake me out."

"But in this world, there were no distractions to keep you guys apart. And no Ronald Yates to teach Reid, and therefore, Cliff, how the idea of pretending to love your enemy is a good way to get close to them. And, more to the point, there were no empathic aliens around who could read your emotions. I'll bet cash money that the Cliff in my world has spent years learning how to control his emotions, to focus love and friendship toward the people he hates the most. He's brilliant, and clearly he's focused."

"That fits," Buchanan said. "But we need to be sure, because if we're going after the wrong guy in either the C.I.A. or the Corporation, then we're screwed in more ways than I can count."

"Well, as our Mastermind seems to like to say, everyone has their part to play. We'll figure out how to do what we have to without hanging ourselves."

Both Reader and Chuckie jerked. "Goodman says that all the time, a part to play or a variation," Chuckie said. "All the time. I can't think of a conversation where he hasn't found a way to use it."

Looked at Buchanan. "Someone who knew who the Mastermind was and was working closely with him used that phrase, and I realized he'd picked it up from someone. Then his daughter said it as well. The Mastermind made sense as the source, based on everything that was going on, both times." Meaning Stephanie knew the Mastermind personally. Closed my eyes and really concentrated. "Cliff said it to me. During Operation Defection Election. We were in the middle of something big and it didn't register to me then. Why it's come back to me now, I can't say."

"Your subconscious mind is working on this problem along with your conscious mind," Chuckie said without missing a beat. "It makes sense. Go on, what else?"

"Richard—an alien—insists that whoever the Mastermind is, we met him after we got to D.C. But he meant me and Jeff—he wasn't thinking of Chuckie." Who winced. "Dude, I'm doing my best. Sorry about the sexytime slipup. But . . . Cliff's car blew up during Operation Sherlock. So maybe I'm wrong?"

"Was he in it?" Reader asked dryly.

"No. He'd just bought it. He was supposed to take me, Jeff, and Charles home and it was cold and wet and he was showing off the car's automatic start feature . . . Oh my God! He sacrificed an entire new car just to ensure none of us could possibly think he was the Mastermind, didn't he?"

"Sounds about right," Chuckie said. "And that would be worth it if he's running a huge crime cartel. He's got more money than anyone realizes."

"Yeah and this particular cartel would make the Corporation green with envy." And he'd had Clarence put Pia Ryan's body in his car. Talk about planning. "But . . . we were going to take Cliff back with us and brainstorm what to do, but he said he didn't want to know so he wouldn't have to tell us we couldn't do something. He's the Head of Special Immigration Services reporting directly to the Secretary of Homeland Security in my world, so he can indeed tell us no and make us obey him. So, why not take the opportunities to know exactly what we're doing?"

Chuckie snorted. "I can tell you why, easily. Where's the fun in that?"

CHAPTER 36

I **STARED AT MALCOLM** for a moment. "Huh? What do parrots have to do with anything?"

He gave a short laugh. "Long story, tell you later. I'm in very tenuous and complicated communication with the person who told us a Mastermind existed in the first place, and I've confirmed my suspicions with him, and he agrees with my conclusion. I haven't told anyone else because I have absolutely no proof. To bring the Mastermind down, we have to be able to prove that he *is* the Mastermind."

"So, why would my reactions matter? I just got here, remember?"

"Oh, I do. But, based on your reactions, I'm pretty sure he's the Mastermind on your world, too. And right now, your reactions are the only thing I have to go on. So, why don't you like Clifford Goodman?"

"He's a bastard in my world. He's in constant competition with Charles. Charles doesn't hate a lot of people, but Goodman's absolutely at the top of his Enemies List." Considered the implications. "We don't have the same kind of conspiracies going on in my world. I don't think we have an evil genius in charge of everything bad."

"Maybe not. You don't have aliens on your world. They're the reason the majority of our conspiracies and control the world plans are in action—to try to control the most powerful beings on this planet. And make no mistake, they're worth controlling, if you're of that mindset. Stronger, faster, smarter, and far more resilient than humans, and yet they're here to protect and serve."

"You think they're naïve."

"They are. I don't say it's a bad thing. But they are. You can't afford to be. I can guarantee that Goodman's going to do his best to go along with the rest of us to Australia."

"You said 'us.' Are you going for sure?"

"Wither Missus Chief goes, so goest I. Both of your husbands approve of this by now and it's just assumed that I'll be along, whether they see me or not."

"Okay, I'm great with that. But you think Goodman's going to try to sabotage the fix with Australia, don't you?"

"Yes. Missus Chief and I both firmly believe that the Mastermind wants to destroy Reynolds, and you've just confirmed that it's the same on your world."

"But why are he and Charles friends here?"

"Chuckie. You call him Chuckie. It's important that you not slip up in front of Goodman. But why are they friends? You want my honest opinion?"

"Of course."

"Reynolds has had one friend in his entire life—Missus Chief. He wanted to marry her, but she married Martini instead. I think Goodman took advantage of Reynolds feeling like he might lose his only friend by sneaking in and pretending to like him for himself. Reynolds fell for it, hard. Can't blame him, really. An assassin tried something similar with Missus Chief when she first got to D.C., when she was feeling lost and overwhelmed. Said assassin would have succeeded in killing her and kidnapping Jamie, but I was there and I saved her."

"You mean you killed the assassin, right?"

"Right. It's my job."

"Did I sound horrified? The term 'assassin' isn't normally assigned to people I want to hang with."

He laughed. "In this universe, Missus Chief's been 'adopted' by the two top assassins in the world, and a third one joined Team Kitty recently. But they have a strict code and treat killing as business. These others? It was pleasure for them."

"Wow, I hope there's not a quiz later. So, you think Goodman found Charles, sorry, Chuckie at a vulnerable time, and because of that Chuckie fully believes in this friendship?"

"Yes. And if Reynolds believes it, so does Missus Chief. He's pretty much never wrong."

"He was wrong about where Hoffa's buried."

"And he's wrong about Goodman. But he has an impeccable track record otherwise. Making the Hoffa thing seem like the only exception to the rule."

"So, no one suspects Goodman because Chuckie trusts him?"

"No. *Missus Chief* doesn't suspect Goodman because Reynolds trusts him. The others are taking their cues from her. Meaning you. Until your alien husband finally caught the clue that Reynolds was no longer a romantic threat he was as likely to kill Reynolds as the Mastermind, by the way. They're friends now, which is good. Reynolds is going to need to lean on Martini when the truth about Goodman comes out. He's lost his wife—to discover the person he thought was his true friend is the *reason* his wife is dead?" Buchanan shook his head. "People have gone on a rampage or killed themselves for less. And Reynolds has been dealing with depression for over a year and a half now."

"Is there anything you don't know?"

Buchanan sighed. "Sadly, yes. I don't know how to prove that Cliff Goodman is the Mastermind and have the people who need to believe it buy in. And I don't know how to do all that without getting some or all of us killed." He gave me a weak grin. "That's normally Missus Chief's job."

"But, you know, no pressure."

He laughed. "From my experience, there's no pressure you can't handle."

Heard voices and footsteps. "What are the odds they're looking for us?"

"High. Let's go. Do your best to hide what you think of Goodman—if he thinks Missus Chief has caught on to him, he'll accelerate his plans, and I'm not sure we're ready for that."

We headed upstairs. Once we were on the first floor I was aware of two things—I could hear music again, "Here Come Cowboys" by the Psych Furs, and, sure enough, Singh and Peter were looking about. "Ah, there you are," Peter said, sounding relieved and shooting Malcolm a suspicious look.

"We weren't downstairs making out. Malcolm just wanted to be sure I was really okay."

Singh nodded. "That makes sense." Figured he'd realized that Buchanan couldn't verify my alrightness in front of those not in the know, and applauded myself for a good one. "But we have some ideas, and I have the results of the house search. The answer is a firm no—there's nothing like what you described anywhere in the PM couple's homes, nor in their children's."

"Awesome. Then I know exactly what to get. If we can find it. Or find someone who can make it." After all, I'd found this item a good eight years ago now.

"I had a team search for it online," Singh said. "We've found nothing like it anywhere. And by anywhere I mean worldwide."

Thought about it. "The shop I found it in was small and the owner was older." Made up my mind. "Can those gate things go anywhere?"

Peter stared at me. "Why are you even asking that question?"

Saw both Malcolm and Singh passing me the "shut up, shut up" sign. "I don't know." I rubbed my head. "I'm feeling kind of . . . addled."

Peter went to solicitous in a heartbeat. "Of course you are, increased healing or not. And that bruise on your forehead is still visible, meaning you were hurt far worse than anyone wants to share with me." He put his arm around my waist. "However, enough's enough. You're getting that nap, and you're getting it now."

Malcolm and Singh looked relieved. "That makes sense, Pierre," Singh said. "I'll keep the others moving and tell them Kitty needs to rest."

Peter led me to the elevators as "Sleep" by My Chemical Romance hit the airwaves. Malcolm came with us. Peter shot him a warning look. "I'm sure you don't need to guard her in her bedroom."

Malcolm laughed. "Nice to see that Mister Vice President has you around to cover the jealousy crap when he's busy." He nodded to me. "I'll be nearby if you need me." He wandered off down the hall.

Peter fussed over me the entire way upstairs, but I was used to this. When we got to my rooms I hugged him. "Thank you for always being you."

He hugged me back. "Always, Kitty, darling. Now, you rest. The world will continue to turn if you take a nap."

"Let's hope, right?"

Went into the bedroom—still no animals around, despite the evidence that they were here. Took off the clothes and went to the closet to hang them up. However, there were several sets, shoes included, waiting there. Chose to take the hint and dropped my slightly used clothing into the hamper.

"Thanks, whoever you are. Really appreciate it."

The music was still playing, albeit not too loudly. So I heard both the song changing to "Lessons in Love" by the Neon Trees and the front door opening at the same time.

Looked around wildly for a robe. One was hanging there. Only, I could swear it hadn't been there a second prior. "Uh, thanks again." Chose not to add that I hoped whoever was doing this wasn't getting a lot of cheap looks. Then again, there was a lot to be said for perfectly cleaned and pressed clothes being there for you at any moment you needed them.

Flung the robe on as Martini came into the bedroom. "Hey, Pierre told me you were lying down after all. He wanted you to take your pills that the doctor gave you before you did."

"Thanks. Where are they?"

He grinned. "I put them in the kitchen. My Kitty hates taking pills. I figured you might be the same way."

"Yeah, I kind of am." I was also really aware that I was naked under this robe, and that I was, therefore, basically nude in a bedroom with a man I wasn't actually married to.

Martini shook his head with a chuckle. "While Kitty and I take every opportunity, you don't need to worry." He took my hand and led me out of the bedroom and to the kitchen. "As I keep on mentioning, I'm not going to force myself on you, and we're doing nothing untoward."

"Sorry. Not trying to insinuate you're a rapist or anything. It's just . . ."

"Just what?" he asked gently as he helped me onto a bar-stool at the counter, then sat down on a stool next to me.

"What if she doesn't remember?" Hadn't meant to blurt this out, but I was uncomfortable, and that was partly because I honestly found Martini very attractive. There was no way she wasn't going to find Charles attractive—she was me and I'd always thought he was handsome since senior year in high school. "What if she thinks she's me, his wife? What if they're sleeping together and they don't know?"

Martini sighed as he handed me a ton of pills, some big, some small, and a large glass of water. Clearly he'd prepped this before he got me. "Why are you so worried about this? In our relationship, I'm the jealous one. Kitty is occasionally, but she doesn't spend a lot of time worrying about me stray-ing."

"I don't know," I said in between downing pills. "I guess . . . I've spent so long wondering if Charles was cheat-ing on me when he was gone and I couldn't reach him. He always had such lame excuses."

"Because he was off on covert operations and he couldn't tell you the truth." Martini ran his hand through his hair. "Look, for what it's worth, it took him a long time to get over the fact that Kitty married me. He was able to let it go because they're still close friends. And because he fell in love with my cousin."

"And then she was killed." By the man Charles thought was his best friend.

Martini jerked as "Trust" by the Neon Trees came on. "What?"

"Uh, you know she was killed, right?"

"No, that's not what I'm asking you about. You broadcast your emotions—it's just something some people do. They tend to be the more honest out there, the ones who don't hide. Chuck's emotions are strong when he's around or thinking about Kitty. But otherwise, he's not that easy to read."

"Okay, nice to know. Not clear on what you're asking me."

"When you mentioned that Naomi was killed . . . you think you know who did it. And I want to know how you know, and who it is. And I want to know now."

CHAPTER 37

CRAP. I had no idea what to do. Wished I'd had the fore-sight to ask Malcolm about this. Because Martini had his In Charge voice on and he also sounded like he was angry and stressed, and I felt very vulnerable all of a sudden.

Martini's eyes narrowed. "Why do you want Buchanan here to protect you?"

"Ah . . ." I had no answer I could give. I wasn't used to someone acting like they were reading my mind.

"I can read Kitty's mind because I'm enhanced and be-cause I'm so close to her. You're her, I'm reading you. You're a little harder, but you're her—some different life experiences in the last decade, but still, her."

"Great. Uh, do you always threaten her?"

"What?" Martini jerked back as "Ready To Go" from Panic! At The Disco came on. "I'm not threatening you."

"Okay, maybe you don't realize that you're looming over me suddenly, and that your voice is lower, and that you're glaring. But you are. All of those things. And I'm not wear-ing any clothes other than this robe."

Martini blinked and shook his head. "I'm sorry. But if you know who killed Naomi, then you know who the Mastermind is. And that's vital information."

"Then why did you tell Malcolm it wasn't important?"

Martini shrugged and I saw him visibly force himself to relax. "Because the political situation was more vital. Raj told me you felt you had a fix, and you handled everyone else already, so we're not in panic mode anymore."

Malcolm definitely thought finding proof so we could officially identify the Mastermind was the most important thing. "Sorry. You're just throwing me. I don't know you. Really at all. I can't differentiate between intensity and anger with you."

Martini took a deep breath and let it out slowly. "Okay. Not angry. Just stressed and worried. This is as hard for me as it is for you. Harder in some ways."

"Yeah, I have two husbands here, you sort of have half a wife." Once again, I hadn't meant to say that, it just came out.

But he laughed. "Yes. Exactly. And, honestly, I wasn't pretending—I'm jealous. Of pretty much everyone, I guess. Definitely of Buchanan. It's an ego hit when your mother-in-law assigns someone to protect your wife and daughter, and then he does a better job at it than you do."

"From what you all told me earlier, you do most of the saving when my Cosmic Alternate needs it."

He smiled. "She saves me more than I save her, honestly."

"Then why worry about Malcolm?"

"Why are you worried about my Kitty?"

"Because she's me, and they both might not notice the difference. Or else he may like her more. She could do everything he does with him. I can't."

Martini cocked his head at me. "I can't swear to it, of course, but I truly doubt that your Chuck is cheating on you." He leaned nearer and chucked me under my chin. "Once you go Kitty, you never go back. And, trust me, you're his and he wants you, the real you, back. I promise."

"Okay. I have no choice but to take your word on it." Tried to figure out what to tell him as "A Pain That I'm Used To" from Depeche Mode came on. "Look, I don't think Malcolm wants me telling. We have no proof. Yet."

"Did he tell you not to tell me?"

"No, not specifically or anything. He doesn't want the Mastermind to know that I know who he is, because the Mastermind thinks I'm your Kitty and if he knows your Kitty knows, then he'll activate his doomsday plans or whatever. I think. And I realize that was a completely confusing explanation."

Martini chuckled. "It was, but I've heard worse. Look, unless you think the Mastermind is me for some reason, why couldn't you tell me? Is it someone close to me?"

"No, I don't think so." He was close to Charles, but Malcolm hadn't indicated that the Mastermind was tight with Martini. One small blessing. Hopefully. "He's a human, not an alien." Worried that I'd said too much.

Martini sighed. "Do you really want a nap or were you just getting out of a situation smoothly?"

"I know I should be tired, but the medicines are helping. Eating all of your mother's brownies helped a lot, too. I had a ton of them. And three glasses of milk."

"Not a Coke?" He sounded worried.

"Not with brownies that good. Trust me, I drink them. I assume my CA is as addicted to them as I am."

He grinned. "Yeah, she is. It appears to be the drink of choice for the sexiest girls in their universes. And that wasn't a come-on."

I snorted. "Right. But anyway, why were you asking?"

He pulled out his phone. "I'm going to solve this. Go get dressed. When she's going casual, my Kitty wears jeans, Converse, and a rock T-shirt."

"Sounds good. Oh, by the way, how do I get the recipe for your mother's brownies?"

He laughed. "She'll never give it out until she dies, I don't think. And my parents are named Lucinda and Alfred. Just in case."

"Good catch, thanks. Work on her for that brownie recipe, will you?"

As I headed for the bedroom I heard him chuckle. "Only my girl." Of course, that was the problem, in a nutshell. Well, as Mom always said, it was time to focus on solutions, not problems. As if to confirm this, "Foolish Behavior" from the Neon Trees came on.

Trotted into the closet and found a set of clothes laid out for me. Just as Martini had described, only with an Aerosmith hoodie as an addition. "Mötley Crüe? Okay, if you insist. And thanks again."

Looked through the T-shirts, all of which were hung with care. Saw a lot I owned, though most were slightly different. No Jack Johnson shirts, though, nor any Amadhia shirts. Oh well, we couldn't match 100 percent. Hopefully she had their music. Amadhia was my favorite female singer and all of a sudden I really wanted to hear her voice. However, now wasn't the time to ask for a musical switch.

The Crüe on my chest, my beloveds on my back, and My Chemical Romance singing "Mama," I trotted back out to Martini, who gave me a big smile. "That's better. Now you look like you."

Decided not to argue—we'd had our first fight, and I didn't really want to have a second any time soon.

He shook his head. "That was a misunderstanding, not a fight. At least, I didn't think it was a fight. Did it really feel like a fight to you?" He looked worried and sounded more so.

"For me and Charles, that was a fight."

"Oh. I'm even more sorry, then." He didn't look happy anymore. "I didn't mean to frighten you and then fight with you, ever, let alone in the space of a few minutes."

I patted his knee. "It's okay. I'll make a note that, for you, this was just you being jealous and insecure."

He laughed. "Pretty much. Buchanan's on his way up. We'll discuss it and then determine if we should tell Angela now or wait."

"Wait, you want to involve my mother?" Panic hit, and I couldn't stop it. Felt tears coming and held them back.

Martini noticed, of course. He was off the stool and holding me in a moment. "Shh, shh, it's okay. We won't let anything happen to her. I promise." He patted my back. "It's okay."

"What is?"

"To cry."

"I've done too much of that today. Has it only been a day?"

"Not even a full day. Despite how it feels, it's just early evening. But it's been years' worth of emotional hits. Crying is a release. So cry if you need to, baby. It doesn't make you weak, not to me or anyone else who matters."

Leaned my head against his chest, but him holding me reduced the panic enough that I could calm down. The double heartbeats were unusual but also soothing. "Yeah, it has. I can't . . . Jeff, I can't lose her again."

He kissed my head. "I swear to you, I won't let anyone hurt your mother. Not that she needs a lot of protection—and you're definitely her daughter, because you don't, either. Not that that stops me, or Chuck, or anyone else from protecting the two of you, and everyone else that we can. We're a family, all of us, and we're in this together. Forever." He hugged me tighter. "And no matter when you go back to your own universe, you'll always be part of our family. No matter who you're married to."

A knock at the door caused us to separate. But I felt okay. Looked at the time. "Where is Jamie?"

"Pierre is giving her dinner because he thinks you're napping and I'm taking care of you. We'll get her soon, but I don't want her hearing this discussion."

"No argument, just wanted to make sure she was okay. I'm sorry I didn't think of it sooner."

"It's okay. She's safe and in good hands everywhere in the Embassy." As the music changed to "Not Falling Apart" by Maroon 5, Martini opened the door and let Malcolm in.

Who looked at us. "First fight, huh?"

"Wow, were we really that obvious?"

Malcolm shrugged. "To me, yes."

"That's what I wanted to talk about," Martini said. "Because Kitty tells me you've been far more observant than the rest of us. And those observations need to be shared. Now."

Malcolm shrugged. "You're not going to like it. And I'm not sure you're going to be able to hide that you know. Very few A-Cs can lie believably and you're absolutely not one of them."

Martini sighed as we all moved to the living room. He sat on the couch and I sat with him. Malcolm took a comfy-looking chair. "Okay," Martini said. "I can buy that reason, honestly. But at the same time, Kitty insinuated the Mastermind is someone we know well."

"He is. But that means he knows you well, too," Malcolm said. "Look, if I thought you'd both believe me and be able to hide the information, I'd have told you about my suspicions three years ago."

"Three years?" Martini sounded shocked and a little angry. "You've known that long and haven't done anything?"

"I've done a lot, including being attacked and put into a coma that took some of my memory away. But knowing and proving aren't the same thing, and Angela would be the first one to tell you that. And I still have no proof."

"Does my Kitty know?"

Malcolm shook his head. "But you two need to practice. Hold hands."

"Why?"

"So you get used to it. You're going to be observed the moment you leave the Embassy in a normal, human way. Practice makes perfect."

Martini looked at me as he did as Malcolm asked and took my hand in his. "And yet you've told this Kitty. Meaning that she's proved something to you, or confirmed something. So the Mastermind *is* in your world, too, isn't he, Kitty?"

"Yes, as far as we know."

"Then tell me, so we can take care of him, once and for all."

"She can't," Malcolm said. "The problem is that you, Martini, will not be able to control your protective instincts. Once I tell you who we suspect, you'll never be comfortable with him again. Meaning he'll know that you know. And then he'll escalate whatever he's planning this time, and that's likely to end badly for all of us."

"Now I'm just going to suspect everyone," Martini muttered.

"Better that," Malcolm said. "Even better that you prove you can fake it." He looked at me. "He can't lie. Most of them can't. Missus Chief jokes about it all the time, but she uses it, too. So does the Mastermind. You can't tell him, no matter how much you want to." He looked at Martini. "And you can harangue me about it, but not her. Clear?"

Martini eyed him, and I felt a stag fight coming. They were both Alpha Males, that was clear. But instead of fighting, Martini squeezed my hand gently and nodded slowly. "Yeah. I get your point. And you're right—if you tell me who it is, I'll just get rid of him before he hurts anyone else, my wife and child in particular."

"Charles is in the most danger, he's who the Mastermind wants to hurt."

Martini shook his head. "Hurting you and Jamie? That would hurt Chuck as much as losing Naomi, trust me." He sighed. "So, I have to pretend I don't know that you know, and then, if I do that well, maybe you'll tell me who's trying to destroy all my people?"

"Pretty much," Malcolm said. "But you have political garbage to handle, so that should be a distraction."

"Speaking of which, I need to get to Paris really soon."

CHAPTER 38

BOTH MEN STARED AT ME. "Why?" Martini asked finally.

"Because the gift we need to give Margie Costello is there. Somewhere. I'm pretty sure I can find the shop, but I couldn't tell someone else how to find it."

"We can't do time travel," Martini said. "So it's around midnight there. Unless the store you're looking for is open twenty-four-seven, we're out of luck for a while."

"Would it work to go there on the way to Australia?" Malcolm asked.

"Yes, but I don't want to be followed by photographers. If getting this gift is turned into a media circus it won't do what we need it to."

"How are you with the early morning hours, before it's light out?" Martini asked me.

"I'm not in love with morning, but I have three children. I'm used to getting up at all hours. If I can go to bed early, I should be able to get up hella early, too. What are you thinking?"

"We gate over to the general area you think this store is in, find it, buy what you want, and get back before anyone in D.C. is actually awake."

"I like that plan. That's a good plan."

"You two can't go alone," Malcolm said. "And don't even try to argue about it. Who, besides me, do you want?"

"Richard," Martini said without missing a beat. "He works best with Kitty, and he's the best at smoothing problems over." He grinned at me. "At least so your Cosmic Alternate tells me."

I laughed. "Works for me." I could handle hanging with the Silver Fox some more. Hey, I was married, not dead.

Martini groaned. "It doesn't matter which Kitty it is, they all lust after my uncle."

Leaned over and kissed his cheek. "Don't worry, you're lust-worthy, too."

"What time do you want to launch this particular mission?" Malcolm asked.

"Three a.m. our time is nine in the morning there," Martini said. "Sounds like the right time."

Malcolm nodded. "You'll advise White, Senior?"

"Yeah. Is that enough, just the four of us?"

"The Minister of Sulky Looks would be a fine addition, but I won't want to hear him complaining at that time of the morning. Never, really, but at three in the morning, I'll punch him. At the least."

"Who's the Minister of Sulky Looks?" This was a new one.

Martini chuckled. "It's what Buchanan here calls Christopher when he's being . . . difficult. But I'd rather keep Christopher here, to protect Jamie. Who we are not bringing with us on this little side trip."

"Yeah, I noticed that the guy glares a lot." Maybe it was because he was married to Amy. "Now, of course, every time I look at him I'm going to think of that nickname. Thanks for that."

Malcolm grinned. "You're welcome. What about the Secret Service? They're not going to like you two sneaking out."

"Do they know about the gates and the hyperspeed?"

Martini nodded. "Yeah. We haven't been able to hide that from them." He sighed. "I already had to deal with Cliff bawling me out for us going to Dulce earlier without them. After taking you to the hospital without them. At least he was upset with me, not our Secret Service details, since it's not their fault when we take off without them."

"Why would he care about that?" Hoped I wasn't showing any reactions, mentally or emotionally. Focused on the music playing, which was "In the Next Room" by the Neon Trees.

"Secret Service reports into Homeland Security," Malcolm explained, betraying absolutely nothing. "It makes sense that Goodman's running point for the Secret Service. Especially when you two don't behave."

"The regular details will be off, and the nighttime details are far more focused on external activity than internal," Martini said. "We usually don't slip out in the middle of the night. Hyperspeed and gates will solve the problem."

"Aren't they supposed to be, well, hovering around us a lot more than they have been?"

"We have so much security in the Embassy that they can relax somewhat," Martini said. "And, Vice President or not, they're not allowed in our bedrooms. They're a little more lax with us because we have our own people in here guarding too—Field agents, Alpha Team, Buchanan and your C.I.A. detail, and so on. Not everyone's here all the time, but some of them are on hand around the clock. We're the most secure of all the public officials."

"Depends on your perspective," Malcolm said. "You're also the main focus for domestic terrorism right now."

"Comforting. Uh, where's Jamie? Exactly, I mean."

Martini sent a text. His fingers moved so fast I couldn't see them. "Pierre's bringing her up." He sent another text. "And Uncle Richard's on board and he'll make sure Christopher knows what we're doing and that he and Amy come into our rooms after we've left."

"Doesn't sound exactly clandestine."

"We know how to do this, baby. We do it all the time. Which is why Cliff and the Secret Service aren't happy with us."

"I thought they basically tapped your phones."

Malcolm laughed. "They try. But the A-Cs are scientifically adept, to put it mildly. They have their own phones. The moment Martini got the nomination as V.P. they've been running two sets of phones each—one for the Secret Service to listen to and one for their real network."

"Wow. They must hate our guts."

"No, they don't, actually," Malcolm said. "They like you, both of you. You treat them like people, and important, part of the team or family people. It's one of your gifts. Your details are actually very loyal to you both, and to Jamie. However, if one of you gets hurt while on their watch, not only will that upset them personally, it will ruin their careers. And you two are possibly the hardest politicians to keep tabs on in the history of America."

"Go us." The music switched to the Psych Furs purring "Pretty in Pink" just as Peter arrived with Jamie, who was indeed in pink. She ran to us.

"Mommy, Daddy! Can I sleep in bed with you tonight?"

Martini and I looked at each other. "Sure," I said. "Why not?" I was convinced Jamie knew I wasn't her real mother, and I was also pretty darned sure she'd suggested this so that Martini wouldn't have to sleep on the sofa.

Martini nodded. "Don't expect it every night, Jamie-Kat, but sure. It's been a tough day on Mommy. I think she'll like cuddling with her little girl."

Jamie beamed. "Good. The pets will like that."

"Speaking of which—" I was about to ask where all the animals were, when I heard them. And then I saw them.

Four large dogs were being controlled by a big guy who looked like he'd played football in college. He was followed by another guy who wasn't quite as big but still looked like an athlete, who was pulling a giant wagon that appeared to have a cat carrier in or on it.

"And here is where I leave you," Peter said. "Enjoy the parent and child, fur, and feathers reunion, my darlings. Call if you need anything." He left as the dogs dragged their handler to us.

Realized I'd met these two guys already, during the massive information session at Dulce. They hadn't registered and I realized they'd been hanging in the back, guarding, like Malcolm did. Did manage to remember their names, though. The bigger one was Kyle and the slightly smaller one was Len.

"You guys are my C.I.A. protection detail, right?"

"Right," Len said as Kyle gave up and let the dogs go.

The dogs were all over us, wagging, howling with joy, and slobbering. It had been a long time since I'd had dogs. But I still remembered how to control them. By channeling Mom. "Dogs . . . *sit!*" Four dog butts hit the floor. "Good dogs. Who's who?"

Everyone stared at me. "What do you mean?" Martini asked slowly. "They're your dogs. Well, they were your parents' but when we all moved here, they went into a no pets building and we got the dogs."

"And the cats," Len said as he opened what was apparently the Feline Winnebago and three cats sauntered out. But they weren't the only animals in there.

An enormous number of fluffy balls of fur were piling out of the Winnebago, too. More than it seemed that it could have carried. They resembled kittens. Kittens with no ears or tails that I could see, but with bright, black eyes that looked almost like buttons. Or they were balls of fur on paws. But regardless, they were adorable. And they were like nothing I'd ever seen before, at least, not real and alive.

"What are those? And why did Pierre say 'feathers'?"

"Ah," Martini said, as "Animal" by the Neon Trees started. "As to that . . . well, there are a couple of other reasons the Secret Service isn't as worried about our security as they could be."

CHAPTER 39

"OKAY, I CAN BUY THAT. It's all about competition with you, right? That's Cliff's motivation for . . . everything?"

"Right," Chuckie said. "But he's sporting about it. Why take an unfair advantage?"

"Especially since he already has a ton of advantages over us, over you. Yeah." My stomach clenched. "He's there, and Other Me is there and totally unprepared for this."

Chuckie snorted again. "She hates him, because I hate him. Nothing he can do or say will fake her out."

"And I'm there," Buchanan said.

"Yeah, but that doesn't mean that the you that is there doesn't trust Cliff."

Buchanan dug into his pocket, pulled out a folded piece of paper, and handed it to me. It was old and very dog-eared.

Opened it and read aloud. "If I'm found dead, the guilty party is or is associated with Clifford Goodman of the C.I.A." Looked up. "Wow, dude, you rock the conspiracy stuff. Possibly even more than Chu-, ah, Charles here."

"I'm a suspicious bastard, what can I say? Besides, my job is protecting you. Your husband's enemies are, as today has aptly proved, yours as well. So, I've been investigating, in a very low-key manner, for years. After Angela was murdered and the rest of the team started going down, I was able to solidify my thinking. I didn't know that Goodman was the head of the Corporation, but I was pretty sure he was a mole."

"Why didn't you say something to us?" Reader asked.

Buchanan shot him a very snide look. "What, and have you two ridicule me for being a crazy, trigger-happy lunatic?"

"Yeah, let's all stop the Bag on Malcolm Party, shall we? Clearly he's neither crazy nor trigger happy, considering I'd have willingly killed Bernie at any time today."

"Right." Reader shook his head. "You're awfully bloodthirsty."

"Dude, you have no idea, but today? It's an average day for me."

"Your world sounds infinitely more dangerous than ours," Chuckie said, sounding incredibly worried.

"Never fear. Other Me has far more protection around her at all times than any of us do. Speaking of which, no dog, no cat, no hamsters?" Hadn't seen or heard an animal since we got here.

Chuckie shook his head. "Quarantine isn't kind to animals, and we travel too much."

"What, you're loaded and you haven't figured out how to grease some palms to ensure your pets are given preferential treatment? I'm disappointed in all of you. But anyway, right now it's less things for our enemies to kill, so I'll let it go. Though a pet would probably do Jamie a world of good." Chuckie opened his mouth. "It's tabled for later. So, now what? I say we go find Cliff Goodman and LaRue of Death or whoever she really is and make them really most sincerely dead."

"I love how you think," Buchanan said, with complete sincerity as far as I could tell.

"I'm sure you do," Reader replied. "However, we have no idea where he is and, in this world, murdering someone in your own agency, or any other for that matter, carries some serious penalties."

Chuckie nodded. "We need proof that he's the mole."

"Depends on what we're hoping to achieve." They all looked at me quizzically. Sighed. "If we want to humiliate Cliff and get him out of the C.I.A., yes, by all means, we need proof. If, however, we want to stop him from becoming the Mastermind here that he is where I come from, then we need to put a Final Solution into action. Because, like those assassins he sent after all of you, the dude won't stop. I guarantee it."

"You're right," Buchanan said. "But we still need proof. I haven't hunted him down and killed him because I don't want to discover I'm wrong."

"You're not," Chuckie said. "But before we become judge, jury, and executioner, we need to know, for sure, that he's the one in charge."

"And knowing what else he has going on wouldn't be a bad thing, either," Reader pointed out.

"Anything that can help us in your Secret Lair?"

"Not really," Chuckie said. "We need to figure out what to do with our family. They're in danger, and if we're going after Goodman that means they're left unprotected. I'd suggest that Kitty guard them, but honestly, I don't think we have a chance without her along to help us. And leaving one of the rest of us behind isn't going to be a good choice, either."

"What about the Israeli Embassy?" The three men stared at me and, couldn't help it, I rolled my eyes. "Dudes, they just dropped everything to come help us out. Leah told me she was there for me if I was having issues with transition. In my world, when we're in trouble we run to our friends, and vice versa."

"Hard to beat Mossad for protection," Buchanan pointed out.

"Jamie won't be able to handle it," Chuckie said quietly.

Considered this. "Leave Jamie to me. If I can't get through to her, okay, we'll shoot for Plan B. But if I can, James, you need to see if Jakob, Oren, and Leah can do us another solid."

Semi-plan of action agreed upon, we rejoined Pierre, who was just finishing the cleanup. "I assume that horrible woman was one of those trying to kill our precious darlings?" he asked.

"She was," I confirmed.

He nodded. "Sorry you only shot her in the leg. I hope the Israelis are less kind."

"They will be," Buchanan said. "Trust me on that."

We headed upstairs to find the rest of the family still on watch—Caroline and Aunt Carla were stationed downstairs, Dad and the kids were upstairs.

"I'm making dinner," Pierre said. "We all need to eat. Unless we need to run or more assassins are on their way, in which case I'll just prepare snacks to go."

"Sadly, I vote for the snacks. Hopefully the people in charge aren't aware that their assassins have failed and been captured, but we need to use any extra time we have to get to safety, not to chow down."

"Katherine, what should Caroline and I do?" Aunt Carla asked. "I've missed my flight—which is fine, because I told those waiting for me that you'd been in an accident. But Caroline has a job to get back to, and if I don't show up eventually, without you and the children being hurt or dead, it's going to be questioned. Not," she added quickly, "that I'm anything other than relieved that you're all alright."

Hugged her. "It's okay, I know what you meant. I think, honestly, you two need to be protected. And I doubt anyone's going to believe us if we tell them what happened."

"I can call in sick," Caroline said. "There's always a bug going around, and I pretty much never take sick days unless I'm at death's door, so the Senator will believe it's real."

"I'll give whatever excuse you need," Aunt Carla said. "Solomon brought my luggage with us, so I'm taken care of and no one will be wondering why it isn't claimed. I just need a legitimate excuse for why I'm no longer going to Paris."

"You two rock, and Aunt Carla, I'm not sure there's a

good excuse to avoid Paris. But I truly appreciate you taking one for the team." Looked at Dad who'd come downstairs to join us. "Um, you know, why don't you just say that Dad and I aren't doing well and that you feel that we need you with us right now?"

"Because you tend to not want me to stay an hour, let alone longer." Aunt Carla had a sarcasm knob. She wasn't at eleven on a scale of ten, but she was surely at an eight and rising. Bizarro World was loaded with surprises.

"Makes it all the more believable that you're staying," Reader said quickly. "Tell them that the accident—which Kitty and the kids miraculously walked away from—is causing Sol and Kitty to finally deal with Angela's death and that's why they asked you to stay."

She nodded. "That sounds reasonable. It'll fly with the family and friends I'm visiting."

"What about your husband?"

She gave me a small smile. "He died last year. I . . . still wear my wedding ring because you two don't have a monopoly on mourning." She gave Chuckie a fond look. "We don't all find our soul mates on the first try, Katherine. For me, third time was the charm." She took a deep breath. "But, we do go on. And it makes this easier."

"Are we going with you guys, wherever it is you're going?" Caroline asked.

"No. We want you and the kids in a safe house of some kind. We're still setting that up, but you should get your excuses done now."

They both nodded and stepped away to make their calls. "I'll call the Israelis," Reader said, also stepping away.

"I'll start packing what we'll need to survive for, how long, a week?" Pierre asked.

"Let's hope it's that or less," Chuckie said. Pierre nodded and zipped off.

Dad sighed. "I'll go back upstairs and tell the children they can pack one small bag each with toys and games. Pierre will handle clothing, toiletries, and anything else pertinent.

We're barely unpacked anyway. But . . . Jamie isn't going to want to leave."

"I'll talk to her." No one looked like this gave them any hope that I'd get through. Dad kissed my cheek and headed upstairs.

"You need to clear anything?" Chuckie asked Buchanan.

"No. I've got safe houses and I've been floating between them since I, as you put it, went rogue."

"I think it was James who put it that way."

"I did," he said, rejoining us. "Jakob said that, with what we just gave them, Mossad would take us to Israel and back if we needed them to. Housing our civilians at their embassy with full Mossad protection is, and I quote from his superior, merely a small favor they're happy to oblige. So, once we get the kids, Sol, Pierre, Caroline, and Carla safely tucked away, where do the four of us go? Cuba? Jakob said Mossad will drop us wherever we need."

Thought about it. "No. Cliff's here in D.C. First of all, because he works here, but mostly because he wanted you guys brought back here so he could see you dead."

"Why, do you think?" Reader asked.

"Because in my world, this is my skill. I'm Megalomaniac Girl—there's not a psycho or evil genius mastermind I can't feel the love with. For whatever reason, I'm just this kind of skilled." Missed Tim something fierce. Which reminded me. "James, what did you find out about my flyboys?"

"Ah, we should determine if we want Mossad to help us. They've offered."

"Oh, nice try at the distraction. Tell me. It's something bad, isn't it? Are they working for Cliff or something?"

Reader didn't look like he wanted to share. "Tell her," Chuckie said, in a tone that brooked no argument. "She's a big girl. Frankly, she's Wonder Woman, based on what I've seen. Tell her—I'm sure she can handle it."

"I'm not," Reader muttered. "But fine, have it your way. I found them. All of them. And . . . they're all dead. Killed in action in Iraq or Afghanistan over the course of the past five years."

CHAPTER 40

MY THROAT WAS TIGHT and I had tears in my eyes. But I didn't let them fall. "You're sure? All of them? Jerry and Matt and Chip and—"

"Yes." Reader stopped me. "I'm positive. Kitty, I'm so sorry. First your mother and now this."

"There's no one I can hurt to avenge them, is there?"

"No," Chuckie said as he put his arm around me and hugged me to him. "There's not. They were in wars, and unfortunately, wars have casualties. I'm sorry, baby. I'm so sorry."

Swallowed hard. I knew about casualties, of course. Understanding that this was how the world worked was easy from a logical perspective. However, from an emotional one, any time someone was lost it was a tragedy.

Tragic or not, however, I knew what my guys would tell me to do if they were, somehow, here. And that would be to save the day and not let the bad guys win. "Okay. I'm going to go talk to Jamie. James . . . search for Tim Crawford. Maybe he's not dead."

"Common name. What does he do?"

Great question. I had absolutely no idea what Tim had done before he'd joined Centaurion Division. "Ah . . . I don't know." It was official—I sucked as a boss and a friend.

"We can get Mossad as backup," Chuckie said soothingly. "You don't have to find every person here you know in your world."

Considered this. "Maybe I do. I mean, some are good and some are bad. So the possibility exists that they may be hooked up with Cliff in some way."

"Cross that bridge when we get there," Buchanan said. "We need to clear out before Goodman figures out his team's failed and sends a better one."

"A better one, that's it!" All three men looked at me blankly. "James, see if you can find Peter and Victor Kasperoff. They're cousins, probably out of Russia. Sometimes they go as Keller, but always Peter and Victor."

"Who are they?" Reader asked. "In your world I mean."

"The best assassins out there. And my adopted uncles. Long story. But if they're here, I think I can get them on our side again. And we may need them."

Reader and Chuckie exchanged an "OMG" look. "I'll try." Reader didn't sound enthused.

"Look, I'll write out a list of every other human operative and ally I have in my world. I had no luck finding anyone but the two guys who turned pro and while I'd love to call in the Jets for backup, I doubt we can score help from that corner. But one thing I do know—the Mastermind is a master chess player, and we're going to need all the pieces we can get."

"We'll get backup," Chuckie said soothingly. "Why don't you try with Jamie? If she doesn't want to go, we're going to have to come up with another plan, because I doubt the Israelis want to move in a three-way mirror."

"I'm sure they could roll with it." But I wanted to talk to Jamie anyway, so I trotted upstairs, leaving the men to discuss their worry about my insane desire to call on scary people who wouldn't know me for help. They probably had a point.

Found her in her room, watching herself in her mirrors. "Hey, Jamie, can I talk to you for a minute?" She nodded but didn't turn away. Went to her and sat down next to her. "What are you looking at?"

"Me."

"Ah. Well, do you like what you see?"

"Sometimes."

"Okay. We need to go and we can't take your mirrors with us. But we can come back for them."

"I can't leave them."

"Why not?"

"They need me."

Pondered my next move. She was a little girl and I was quite capable of picking her up and just taking her to safety. I was also the adult and the mother, so, technically "because I said so" was also a very viable and legitimate response. However, we needed to avoid Jamie having a meltdown, and besides, there was something more going on here.

Other Me and Chuckie had come to the conclusion of autism, and I could see why. But I was from a world where, if someone started behaving oddly, you had to question if they were an alien, an android, an enhanced human, or something else entirely. Therefore, I'd learned that the obvious, easy answer wasn't always the right one.

So, had to figure out my next move, and make sure it wasn't the move that Chuckie or Other Me was likely to choose. Not that I thought they were doing a bad job as parents, but if they'd known the right things to do or say, they wouldn't think Jamie was autistic, or they'd have confirmed it and would be getting her professional help.

Looked into the mirror. It was set up so that the mirrors reflected not only the person in them, but each other. In fact, the way the mirrors were set created what appeared to be an infinite number of Jamies, curving out and around. I'd seen something like this before. Recently. And at least one time before.

It looked like the Universe Wheel, only closer up and on its side, truly like a round cassette that you'd use in an old-fashioned slide projector.

But Jamie wasn't looking at all the other images. She was staring straight ahead. So I stared straight ahead, too. And I saw what she was seeing.

In front of me, not so much. But in my peripheral vision? Worlds were spinning past, and I could see myself in them. Just for a moment, and then the next worlds moved into place. And if I looked directly at a world, what I was seeing turned back into the general reflection of the mirror.

"It's like *Through the Looking Glass*. Times a million. Or more."

Jamie didn't turn, but I saw her beam at me in the mirror. "I knew you'd understand, Mommy!"

"I think I do. What, um, do you see, Jamie?"

"What you're seeing, Mommy. All of us, all over. I'm always with you," she said happily. "Even where I have two mommies. You're always the mommy who is my mommy."

In most of the other worlds I was married to either Chuckie or Reader. Mine was the only one where aliens were on Earth, so it was the only one where Jeff was. But I'd seen a few worlds where I was married to guys I didn't know, and a few where I was married to girls I didn't know. I was too busy to try to spot those worlds right now, but I remembered them from when I'd given birth to my Jamie.

"Who's your daddy in those worlds?"

"Usually Daddy. Sometimes Uncle James."

Made sense. Chuckie and I were in every world I could see, and Reader was in most of them. If I was going to be artificially inseminated, or just have sex with a guy I liked in order to conceive, they'd be the obvious choices. And choosing the smartest guy in any room as your baby's sperm donor made sense, though, clearly, in some worlds, I'd gone for slightly less brains and perfect cheekbones instead. That was me, mixing it up and keeping the multiverse guessing.

Cleared my throat. "Why haven't you told Daddy or . . . your Other Mommy about this?"

"They don't understand." She looked sad. "They think I'm broken."

Wanted to stop looking into the mirrors and just pull her into my arms and tell her how much I knew Chuckie and Other Me loved her, that they were frightened because no parent wants their child to suffer and they thought she was suffering.

But I didn't. Instead, I picked her up, keeping her facing the mirrors, scooted myself under her, bent and crossed my legs, and put her down onto my lap this way. Then I put my arms around her and held her. "Parents want the best for their children. And I can understand why they're scared. They love you so much."

"I know. I love them, too. That's why I asked."

"Asked what?"

"For help." She said it as if it was obvious. I'd changed universes—perhaps it *was* obvious.

"Who did you ask to help you?"

"Who we all know to ask."

We all. Interesting. "I don't know who that is, Jamie-Kat." Was she in contact with ACE or Algar? I could but hope.

"Yes, you do, Mommy—Auntie Mimi."

CHAPTER 41

I WAS THE ONLY ONE in my world who knew that Naomi wasn't actually dead. Well, ACE and Algar knew, of course. But I was the only non-superconsciousness and non-Black Hole Person who knew. She'd taken so much Surcenthumain that it had done what we'd nicknamed it and then some—it was the superpowers drug and she'd become like Dark Phoenix, so powerful our world couldn't contain her.

Naomi had left us and saved ACE. But ACE had told me she could never return to our world again. However, he'd never said she couldn't travel the multiverse.

Chuckie and Naomi had wanted to have a little girl who would be Jamie's best friend. Maybe Naomi had compensated for that loss by watching over not only my Jamie, but every Jamie out there. She loved Chuckie and Jamie both, and any jealousy and insecurities had to have burned off when she became, if not a god, then a powerful superconsciousness.

"So, ah, how do you talk to Auntie Mimi?"

"I don't."

"Um, Jamie, you just said you asked Auntie Mimi for help."

"No," she said in the stubborn way little kids have, "I didn't. I said I asked for help and that we all know that it's Auntie Mimi who will help."

"Okay. So who did you, specifically, ask to help you?"

She shot me a look in the mirror that I recognized. It was my Jamie's "oh Mommy, you see but you do not observe" look. Thought about it. "Oh. Wow. You're talking to, ah, yourself? In all these worlds?"

She nodded. "I can see everyone. That's my job," she added rather proudly. "I'm the one who can see us all."

"Who has what other jobs?"

"We're all a little different. Because of who our Daddies are, and because of how it is where we live. So we each do different things."

"Are all of . . . you . . . powerful?"

"Sort of. I'm the only one who can see everyone, though."

"Have others tried?"

"Uh huh."

"Has my Jamie tried?"

"Yes. Your me is who connects us, but she can't see everyone. Only I can."

This made sense. Jamie was incredibly powerful, and now she housed ACE in her mind. "When did Jamie connect with you?"

"Oh, I saw everyone first. I saw your me, and you, before I had the mirrors though."

"How?"

"I heard your music and I concentrated. That's how I knew that mean lady. She tried to kill us when I was a little baby."

Maybe this Jamie *was* autistic. But if she was, this was autism taken to an amazing degree. Then again, maybe all autistic kids saw other worlds and no one had figured that out yet. "So, you hear the music I play? Not the music here?"

"Uh huh. I like the music here, but I like yours more. When Mommy took me shopping with her is when I first saw the mirrors. I made her take them home with us."

Tried not to imagine the temper tantrum that would have had to have been thrown in order to get Other Me to literally buy a somehow special three-way mirror set out of a department store. But if your child is having hysterics, sometimes you do whatever you can to make said hysterics stop.

"Is that when you saw all the other worlds?" She nodded. "And is that when you talked to my Jamie?"

She shook her head. "It wasn't until Auntie Mimi died that Jamie found me. She was looking for Auntie Mimi and found me. She can see me in her mirror sometimes. But not all the time. But I can always see everyone all the time."

So ACE had either given my Jamie the boost she'd needed or she'd taken that boost from him. Hoped it was a mutual thing, however it had happened. I didn't want ACE harmed or abused any more than I wanted Jamie harmed or abused. Any Jamie.

"So, why have you been staring at your mirrors, and yourself, all this time?"

She gave me the "duh" look. "Because it's fun. And it's important. I can see what's coming, too, sometimes." She looked sad. "Only bad things, and only if they're going to happen soon. When I was littler, I thought all of the things were going to happen to us. But then I figured out they were different mes."

Chuckie had said she occasionally proclaimed doom but tended to be wrong. "So, you told your Daddy and Other Mommy about bad things you saw coming up, and they didn't believe you, did they?"

"No, because they didn't happen to us most of the time." She looked sadder. "If I'd known how to talk to Auntie Mimi, I could have saved them."

"Saved who?"

"People we love."

Decided this might not be the best line of discussion. I hugged her tightly. "It's not your fault, if you couldn't save someone, Jamie-Kat. You're not responsible for everyone in the multiverse." Her expression said she didn't agree with me. Tried another way. "You saved your Other Mommy and your brothers today, though, as well as yourself."

She brightened up. "I did! And you did great, Mommy! I knew you would, too!"

"So, how do you talk to the Jamie in my world?"

"I don't know, I just can."

"Even if you're not looking in your mirrors?"

She nodded. "Sometimes. My mirrors make talking to her a lot easier. But I only know what needs fixing if I look in the mirrors."

"Well, right now, we're the ones that need fixing. And in order to do that, we have to take you, and Charlie and Max, and Papa Sol to another house. Just for a while. While Daddy and I go save the day and stop the bad people. But your mirrors need to stay here."

"But I *need* them."

"I know. But you know what? Charlie and Max need you, too. They need you to pay attention to them right now, just like Daddy and I do. You can't save everyone else if something bad happens to you, or to us, right?"

"Right," she said doubtfully. "But what if something happens to them?"

"Are these special mirrors?"

"No," she said impatiently. "I mean Jamie and my real mommy and Jamie's daddy. They need me to watch."

"Are they in danger?" We were always in danger, so the odds were good for a big yes.

"No. But they could be. They're trying to fix things and stop bad people like you always do. And my mommy's not like you, Mommy. She needs me to watch."

It took everything I had not to agree with her. But if this Jamie was ever going to have a chance at, if not a normal life, then a more engaged one, this was a moment of truth. "No, Jamie, she doesn't and they don't. I know it feels like if you don't watch everyone all the time then bad things are going to happen. But the truth of the multiverse is that bad things happen all the time. Many times to good people. And though we want to save everyone and make sure nothing bad happens anywhere, that's not actually possible."

"But it's not fair!"

Ah, the rallying cry of children. I hugged her again. "I

know, sweetheart. Life's not fair. But if we fight and do our best and take care of each other, we can sometimes even the odds. You brought me here, and I'm going to even the odds for your family, I promise. And your mommy is going to fix things in my world." She certainly couldn't make them worse, of that I was sure. "And my Jamie's daddy will protect her, and your daddy will, too. But I have to protect you and your daddy and family here. And to do that, you have to help me."

"How?"

"By being brave and trusting that everyone can survive without you watching them for a while." I kissed her head. "Besides, your mommy and daddy need you to show them that you do love them, and not just by watching the many thems in the mirrors, but by being with them and focusing on them here in this world more. Can you do that? Can you be brave enough to take a chance and deal with this world, only for a while?"

"But I like my job," she said in a little voice.

"And it's an important job! I'm not saying to never look into your mirrors again. But there can't be danger happening every day. Even in my world, we get days when nothing happens and we're sort of bored." I loved those days. They happened so infrequently.

"No," she admitted. "Most days nothing much bad is going on. But I like watching everyone. You especially."

"Aw, thanks. And, I know it's all interesting. It's like the Jamie Channel all the time, with slightly infinite variety."

She giggled. "I like the Jamie Channel."

"I know. But you need to watch the Real Life Right Here Channel, too. I know you can, because you're my daughter, and you're Nana Angela's granddaughter, and we can do anything we set our minds to do."

"I guess so." She sighed. "How long will we be gone?"

"I'm not sure. A few days maybe."

She nodded. "Okay. But it's going to make it hard—" She stopped talking and looked as if she'd just had a brilliant idea.

"Make what hard?"

Jamie shook her head and didn't answer. Instead she got up and trotted over to her bed. There was a big Hello Kitty backpack on the bed. She started to put some toys into the backpack. Decided I wasn't going to get an answer out of her on what other thing she felt was going to be harder if she left her mirrors.

Took one more look and watched the worlds swirl past. I could understand why Jamie didn't want to stop watching. I didn't really want to stop, either.

But we had a world to save, and I had my mother's murder to avenge. I got up and helped Jamie pack.

"Will you do a favor for me?" I asked her as we finished up.

"I guess."

I laughed. "I'm not trying to trick you. Can you talk more to your brothers and everyone else while we're gone and you're not watching?"

"I guess. Why?"

Took her hand and headed downstairs. "Because it will mean a lot to all of them. And that's part of taking care of the people you love—doing things that make them happy. And you talking more, really interacting with them, will make them happy."

"If you say so, Mommy. By the way—take the kitty with you."

"Your backpack?"

"No," she said as we rejoined the others in the living room. "Not Hello Kitty. *The* kitty."

"Um, okay. I guess."

Chuckie picked Jamie up. "I'm so proud of you for coming with Mommy like a good girl." He gave her a kiss. Jamie kissed him back and Chuckie looked so happy it made my heart hurt.

"Do we have everything?" Buchanan asked. Confirmation of everyone else being packed was given.

"I haven't packed. Anything."

"I handled most of it, Kitty darling," Pierre said. "But just in case, you may want to take a quick look."

"I can do that." Zipped upstairs at hyperspeed. Looked like Pierre had grabbed everything that made sense, at least as far as I could tell. Besides, I wouldn't need as much or the same things as those staying with the Israelis.

Did a quick search of the upstairs before I went back down. As I looked out the back hallway window I noticed that there was an orange tabby cat huddled on the windowsill. Based on what Chuckie had told me, this wasn't the family cat. But it looked cold and hungry and it had no collar. And besides, Jamie had been pretty clear.

Opened the window and the cat mewled pitifully at me. "Come on, Stripes, let's get you into the warm." The cat purred as I picked it up, and snuggled next to me. Zipped back downstairs. "Good thing I did a check. Meet Stripes."

Everyone other than Jamie stared at me in a confused manner. Jamie looked pleased. "Kitty, I told you, we don't have a cat," Chuckie said. "It must be a neighbor's."

"I think it's a stray."

"Then leave it here," Chuckie said.

I looked at Jamie. "No. We're taking Stripes with us."

"What?" Chuckie sounded exasperated. "Why? We can't have a pet, Kitty. We travel too much."

Stripes and I looked at each other. Then I looked back at Chuckie. "We'll work it out. For now, Stripes comes with. He's good without a carrier, but James, could you call ahead to the embassy? Stripes could really use some food."

"Oh, anything for you and your new sidekick, girlfriend."

"We have an issue with the cars," Buchanan said, possibly to get us off the feline argument. "With the SUV destroyed, there's no single car that can hold everyone."

"Then we divide up. Who's the best driver?" Everyone looked at me. "Okay, so, does that mean I take the civilians, or does that mean I'm the one who's going to run interference if needed?"

"Interference," Chuckie said. "You take the two-seater."

"I wanted the IS."

"I'm sure you did. However, it seats five, so I'm driving it. The kids will be with me. James will take the hybrid—it's the slowest but he's the best driver after you."

"Wow, in my world, James is the best. At pretty much everything."

"I'm touched," he said as he finished texting. "Jakob says that you're lucky Leah likes you. Cat stuff is being gathered for the sidekick. But I'm not indestructible and you seem to be, and the interference car has the most risk. Besides, I think someone who can run as fast as you can will lose her mind in a hybrid, no matter how good its acceleration may be for its class."

"Fine, fine, not really complaining. So, that's three cars. Malcolm, did you drive here?"

"Actually, no. I took public transportation because I was fairly sure my car was tampered with this morning."

"Great! Not that your car was messed up but that means you can drive the assassins' car. It'll give us more space for the weapons, which we are absolutely taking with us, and anything else you guys have hidden about that we may need."

The men sighed and nodded. "We'll pack the cars," Reader said. "But we could take Peter's car."

"We can, but I want to ensure we hang onto Raul's car, too."

"What do you expect to find in it?" Chuckie asked.

"An entrance."

CHAPTER 42

AS MARTINI SPOKE, a bunch of birds that looked like peacocks and peahens on steroids appeared out of nowhere. Couldn't help it, I screamed a little. The birds gave me hurt looks. "Swear to God, no one told me you were running a real zoo here."

Now all the animals looked hurt. Jamie crawled into my lap and hugged me. "It's okay, Mommy. I told the pets you hit your head and might not remember them. They'll forgive you."

Stared at Martini. "Bizarro World just reached new heights for me. Tell me what's going on. Right now."

"You don't have pets in your world?" Martini sounded shocked out of his mind. Decided he'd figured that Jamie knew what was going on, too. Or this news was so surprising he'd forgotten we were supposed to pretend we were married and that I was the mother she was used to.

"Uh . . ." Looked down at Jamie.

Who beamed at me. "It's okay, Mommy." She looked over at Martini. "Daddy, can I go play in my room?"

"Ah," Martini gaped. "Sure. Yes, Jamie-Kat, go ahead." Jamie kissed us both, then trotted off into our bedroom. One of the fluffy balls of fur was on her shoulder.

"Well," Malcolm said, "that was interesting."

"I'm so lost."

Kyle cleared his throat. "The dogs are Dudley the Great Dane, Duke the Labrador, Dotty the Dalmatian, and Duchess the Pit Bull. Your parents were into the whole same first letter for all the fur babies thing."

"The cats are Candy and Kane," Len held each one up, "and Sugarfoot. Oh, and you can talk to them."

"Excuse me?"

"All of them. These are Poofs." Len pointed to the furballs. Noted he had one on his shoulder, as did Kyle. "They're from Alpha Four, just like the Peregrines," he indicated the big birds. "Bred to protect the Alpha Four Royal Family."

"*Excuse me?*"

"Oh, right," Martini seemed dazed. "We forgot to mention that. Didn't seem relevant earlier."

"Jeff's a prince," Kyle said conversationally, as if this was no big deal. "So is Christopher. Jeff could have taken the throne on Alpha Four but he stayed to be with you."

"Wow, that's really romantic."

"You thought so, yeah," Len said. "We've heard about it enough, at any rate."

"I see that sarcasm remains a go-to move in the multiverse."

"Wherever you are, Kitty, so is the sarcasm." Len grinned. "Sorry, and I realize you're thrown, but the Poofs and Peregrines are great. Jamie insists on having all the Embassy pets that aren't on some kind of guard duty with her at all times. Hence why they've been at daycare all day, too."

"The animals do guard duty?"

"Yes, well, the dogs to a degree, but the alien ones absolutely," Malcolm said. "The Peregrines are able to go invisible. So are the Poofs. They all have hyperspeed. They're also willing and able to not only take a bullet for you, but in the case of the Poofs, to ingest it and spit it out later. Oh, and the Poofs have a giant size, too. Might be a good idea to show her now," he said. To a fluffy ball that somehow appeared in his hand.

His Poof mewled, then jumped down out of Malcolm's hand and went Martini-sized. At this size, it had a mouth full of razor-sharp teeth. It purred at me—loudly. Then it went back to small and back into Malcolm's hand. "Thanks, Killer," Malcolm said to the Poof. It purred at him.

"Uh, how many, ah, Poofs and Peregrines do we have?"

"Twelve mated pairs of Peregrines," Len replied promptly. "They were a gift from the King of Alpha Four. We're considered an Alpha Four principality, by the way, and the Peregrines are a subtle reminder of that whenever politicians get uppity. We have more Poofs than anyone can count. Poofs are willing and able to eat people. The Peregrines can probably take on an elephant and win, let alone something smaller."

"The male Peregrines normally shadow their, ah, assigned protection targets." The way Kyle said this, I got the impression the Peregrines didn't feel they were "owned." "Unlike the Peregrines, the Poofs are androgynous and supposedly only mate when a Royal Wedding is coming, but you can't prove it by Earth Poofs. They mate all the time, as near as we can tell."

Two Poofs jumped into my lap and started purring, but in a worried kind of way. One mewled at me. "I'm sorry. I don't know who you are."

"Harlie, the Head Poof, who is technically Jeff's," Len pointed to one that looked no more or less impressive or cute than the others. I could spot differences, though I wasn't sure how I was doing it. "And Poofikins, which is your Poof. Even though they're supposedly only for the Royal Family, the Poofs attach to whoever names them. And they sort of choose their names, based on what you say to them when you, ah, meet. Jamie's Poof is Mous-Mous."

"And you say I can, what, Doctor Doolittle it and talk to them?"

"Yes," Martini said. "You can. You're the only one they listen to, for the most part. I'm curious, though—your reaction to the Poofs and Peregrines I get, but why are you shocked by the dogs and cats?"

"We spend half the year in Australia and half here. It's not fair to an animal—both countries have quarantines and that would mean that any animal we had would spend half of its life in some horrible kennel. And once the pets we had when I was in high school died, Mom and Dad didn't get any more. I guess because of what Mom really did. Maybe because we were traveling. I don't honestly know, but I don't know these animals, in any world. I haven't had a pet since Charles and I got married."

The cat Len had called Sugarfoot came over and settled himself on my lap in between Harlie and Poofikins. Didn't want to, but couldn't stop myself from petting him and the Poofs. All three started purring.

"I have a different set of questions," Malcolm said. Only he wasn't looking at any of the humans. Instead he was looking at one of the male Peregrines. "Bruno is normally always by your side, Kitty, whether you realize he's there or not."

"Yeah," Martini said. "So?"

"So, does that mean when you grabbed Missus Chief and ran, was Bruno along for the ride? And if so, did he see what happened? And if he did, does that mean the animals are aware that this isn't the 'real' Kitty? And if they are so aware, what else do they know that they haven't told us?"

All the animals, cats and dogs included, looked at Malcolm with the most innocent looks I'd ever seen. It was like a Sea of Animal Innocence. I had three kids. There was no way this was real.

"They know something, I can tell you that."

This earned me some betrayed looks, some satisfied looks, and some "you go, girl" looks.

"Interesting," Martini said. "We thought that Kitty could talk to the animals because she was enhanced."

There was a knock, the door opened, and Richard came in. "Pardon me for interrupting, but Jamie asked me to come up."

"How?"

"She's good at asking for the com to be turned on, too,"

Richard said, with more than a little twinkle in his eye. "She's learned that from her mother. And I see that, based on the number of animals here, you're discovering more exciting things, aren't you, Katherine?"

"More and more every second."

"I did hear what Jeffrey said, and, while most of you assumed that our Katherine's talent was brought out by her enhancement, frankly, she was communicating with the Poofs well before she gave birth. No, I believe that this is just something Katherine is good at."

"What, my special skill is communing with the Animal Kingdom?"

"The animals won't harm you," Richard said. "You're their favorite."

"I'm not the 'me' they're used to."

"They know," Martini said. "I'm not as good with animals as I am with humans and A-Cs and all, but I can tell they know. They're trying to make you relax and like them. It's why the dogs haven't all leaped on you like they normally do. Every single time they see you. Or me. Or anyone, for that matter. And why the others are keeping their distance—they don't want to freak you out."

Duchess heaved a doggy sigh and jumped up onto the couch, between me and Martini. She settled in and put her head on my thigh. Two Peregrines came over and flew up onto the couch, on my other side, and settled next to me.

"Are we posing for a picture?" Wanted to resist petting them, but I couldn't. Used one hand for Duchess and one for the birds. They all seemed to like it. The two Poofs and Sugarfoot were all still purring.

"Oh." Martini looked a little upset.

"What?" Richard asked him, as "Miss Missing You" by Fall Out Boy came on.

"We're asking her to get attached to things she can't have in her real life," Martini said quietly. "None of us in her world mean no Poofs or Peregrines. And, as she said, with their travel schedule, they can't have a pet." He cleared his throat. "We're asking her to get attached—to the animals, to all of us—and then she's going to go back and we'll all be gone."

Everyone was quiet for a few long moments. And, as I looked at all these animals who were staring at me lovingly, and then at the men around me, I realized something shocking—I liked it here.

I liked it here enough to stay.

CHAPTER 43

HOWEVER, liking it here or not, we had jobs to do. And the one I knew I could handle best was up first. Cleared my throat. "We'll worry about that when we have to. Right now, Jeff and I need to get some rest."

Len and Kyle eyed us suspiciously. "What's going on?" Len asked. "Or, let me rephrase. What are you up to that the Secret Service isn't going to like?"

"Funny you should ask," Malcolm said. "Need you two to sleep up here tonight."

Kyle nudged Len. "Pay up."

Len sighed, pulled out his wallet, and gave Kyle a $20. "I just figured New Kitty would be less inclined to go off half-cocked."

"Hey, I think I resent that on behalf of my Cosmic Alternate."

"But, trust us, you can't deny it." Len said with a laugh. "Okay, let us know what the cover story needs to be if anyone from the Secret Service notices you're gone. Though I think Kyle and I should go, too, wherever it is."

Malcolm shook his head. "The Whites will be here babysitting, but I still want someone trained in protection and surveillance to be with Jamie."

Len and Kyle both looked shocked and pleased, but then

both put on Serious Faces and nodded. Clearly they looked up to Malcolm, and from what I'd seen and he'd told me, they probably had every reason to.

"What about Charles?" Richard asked.

"He should come too." Everyone looked at me.

"Why?" Martini asked.

"Because he was with me when I found what I'm looking for."

Martini shook his head. "No, 'he' wasn't."

"I know, but seriously, I think he needs to come with us." And not only because Paris was a droolingly romantic city. But there was that. Wasn't sure it was going to be safe for me to be wandering Paris with just Martini. And Malcolm and Richard. Okay, it was an excuse. But whatever.

"The smaller the team the better," Malcolm said. "However, he's a far better liar than our Vice President, so it may help to have him along."

"I'll discuss it with him," Richard said. "Discreetly."

Semi-plan of action decided, Len and Kyle headed for what appeared to be guest rooms, and the others left our apartment. Well, the other people. All but a few of the animals stuck around. Went into our bedroom to find Jamie and discovered why there were so many cat trees in it—they were loaded with Poofs.

Jamie's room was attached to ours. "Why is she still in a nursery?" I asked Martini.

"Empaths need to go into isolation periodically. The more powerful the empath, the harder we can push ourselves, meaning the harder we crash." He led me through her room to another room. It was very white, and seemed sort of soothing, if you ignored all the needles and such that were in evidence. "The Embassy has its own empathic isolation chamber because my Aunt Terry, Christopher's mother, was empathic. Because my talent came out very early, I ended up living here, with Aunt Terry, so she could help me. She was my second mother and she . . . understood me like no one else ever did. At least until I met Kitty."

"Where is she? I haven't met her yet."

Martini was quiet for a long moment. "She's dead. She died when we were ten years old."

Turned and looked up at him. He didn't look like she'd died twenty-plus years ago. He looked like she'd died last week.

Didn't think about it, I just hugged him. "I'm so sorry. I know exactly what it's like to lose your mother."

He hugged me back. "Yeah, I know. You understand that better than . . . my Kitty does. She tries, but, thankfully, she doesn't know."

Managed not to say that she'd know by now. Wondered how she'd take it, and hoped she'd handle it better than I had. Then again, she had Mom to come home to here.

Martini cleared his throat. "Anyway, my mother did her best with me and Christopher after . . . Aunt Terry died. Not as well as any of us would have liked, but it's finally all behind us now. Due in large part to Kitty. And Amy."

"Still can't believe Amy's not a total bitch in this world."

He chuckled. "Bitch is in the eyes of the beholder, baby." He kissed my head. "Let's get out of here. This is the nicest isolation chamber we have anywhere in the world, but it's still a place Jamie and I have to go when we've overdone it."

"Is it horrible for you, isolation?"

"No. Not nearly as bad as non-empaths think it is. It's a soothing, safe haven for empaths. But it's still the place you go because you have to, not because you want to."

"Unless you collapse fast, like in seconds—and in that case, I'd expect to see an isolation chamber every few feet—why do you need to keep Jamie in the nursery?"

"I guess we haven't thought about it," he said as we left the room and went back into Jamie's. It was a nice room, and she wasn't in a crib—there was a queen-sized bed in there. But that made the room look ridiculous, in that sense. "It's easier to move the Poof Condos into her room this way, too. Yes, because they all sleep with her. Though the dogs sleep with us." The way he said it, got the impression he'd be happier without the sounds of dogs snoring at night.

"She's still a toddler, but you've got her in an adult bed and it's obvious she's far more advanced than the average child. She deserves her own room, where she can have her privacy. And so you can have yours."

Jamie beamed at me. "I know which room I want, Mommy!" She jumped up and ran out. We followed her. She went to the room right next to ours. It was almost as big as the master bedroom, with both a bathroom and walk-in closet attached, but basically had nothing in it.

"Wow, you guys don't really understand how to utilize space, do you?"

Martini shrugged. "It hasn't been necessary. Two of the rooms down the hall are our official guest rooms. We haven't needed to pay attention to most of the spare bedrooms."

"Well, let's pay attention now. Jamie, what do you want in your room?"

"Oh, I'll tell the Elves what I want, Mommy."

"The Elves?" This was a new one. Couldn't wait to see what was going to appear.

Martini chuckled. "That's what Kitty calls the Operations Team. But you have to run what you want by Mommy, Jamie."

She looked at me. "*This* Mommy?" She sounded hopeful. And as if she was fully aware I wasn't her actual mother in this universe.

Martini sighed. "Yes. You seem to think this isn't Mommy."

"Oh, she is, Daddy," she said in a very Dutiful Daughter tone. "But at the same time, she isn't." She beamed at me. "That's okay, Mommy. I love it that you're here!"

"Thank you, sweetheart. Now, let's get your room all set up exactly how you want it. What colors do you want?" My bet, based on the colors that had been in the nursery, was pink. But it would be interesting to see if that was "her" color or if it was being forced on her.

"Pink and white! But mostly pink. Did you know there are a *lot* of shades of pink? Uncle Pierre says that he's learned that there are many because of me. Can I have a lot of pinks?"

"It's always good to learn." Bingo. Pink was Jamie's favorite color. My Jamie didn't have a favorite anything, other than her mirrors. Shoved that sadness away and focused on the Jamie in front of me. "And it's your room, sweetheart. You can have it whatever colors you want." Looked at Martini. "Uh, I'm somehow certain that Jamie and I are not going to have to race out to Home Depot and choose paint and such. So, how do we make this work?"

"Just sort of share with the room what you want. The Operations Team will hear it. We're wired for sound, so to speak."

Speaking of sounds the music had stopped. A while ago. Decided Walter must have assumed I'd gone to sleep, or someone else in the Embassy had requested silence or a different set of tunes or something. I'd worry about it later.

While Jamie prattled away describing her perfect room—which did not include a set of three-way mirrors, which I found a complete relief—Martini made dinner for us. He was a great cook and seemed to like it, proving that my CA continued to have good taste in men, even if she'd picked Martini over Charles somehow.

Dinner done, Jamie dragged me into her new room while Martini stacked the dishes in the sink for the Operations Team to clean. Apparently, they really were like elves. Hoped they were paid well.

We walked in and I gasped. The entire room was changed, just as Jamie had described it. Her bed was moved, too. It's hard to move a queen-sized bed from one room to another without the people in the same apartment noticing it, but the Operations Team had managed it.

All the Poof Condos were in Jamie's room, still filled with Poofs. So were all the dog beds. There were also some small, raised hammocks near the dog beds. Jamie's closet was full and her bathroom was all set up, too. And the rooms didn't smell like fresh paint. There was a faint smell of strawberries, but not paint.

"Is it time for bed yet?" Jamie asked eagerly.

"Sure," Martini said. "Mommy and I need to sleep soon. But I thought you were going to sleep with us tonight, Jamie-Kat."

"Oh, I'll do that tomorrow night. I need to sleep in my own new room tonight!"

Was about to ask what the hammocks were for when the rest of the animals joined us. The dogs trotted to their beds, the cats joined the Poofs in Condo City. And the Peregrines hopped up into their hammocks. There weren't two dozen of them in here though, for which I was grateful.

"Where do the other Peregrines sleep?"

"With their people," Jamie said. "Lola always sleeps with me, and Bruno does, too, if he's not watching you, Mommy. But I get to sleep with whoever's not on duty, too. Uncle Pierre has Sonny and Cher sleep with me most of the time, and Len and Kyle usually want Barney and Betty and Fred and Wilma with me, too."

"Don't they need the Peregrines to protect them?"

"Oh, yes, but they have Poofies and Poofies are great protection, too, Mommy."

Decided not to argue about what alien beasties were where. Jamie had the lion's share of the Embassy animals and if that made her happy, then that was good enough for me. Besides, Len and Kyle were just down the hall tonight.

To my great joy, they had a nighttime ritual. We had one with Charlie and Max but had given up with our Jamie. This Jamie got songs sung to her every night, a quick bedtime story, and then lots of hugs and kisses, for her and Mous-Mous, since she insisted. Kissing the Poof wasn't a hardship—they were soft and really adorable.

This routine was what I'd always thought we'd do with our little girl, and it was a joy to get to experience it for real, not just in a daydream that wasn't coming true.

Jamie happily tucked into her bed in her own special and

perfect new room, Martini and I headed for ours. Checked. The nursery was back to being a nursery. A white nursery. Complete with a crib and a lot of baby-type things.

"Are you guys expecting number two?"

"No, we're not. Not yet. Why?"

Pointed to the nursery. "The Operations Elves seem to be leaving you a rather broad hint."

He grinned at me. "Well, a man can hope, right?" He cocked his head and seemed to be studying me.

"What?"

Martini gave me a funny smile—tender and amused and wistful somehow all at the same time. "I promise that I'm not going to let anything happen to you. And that includes untoward advances from me. If you want me to sleep on the sofa, I will. But I'm capable of being in bed with you and not doing anything that will make you uncomfortable."

"In case anyone not in the know somehow shows up, you sleeping elsewhere would indicate we were fighting, and that's the last thing I think we need. So, sure. I can handle it. I think."

He grinned. "Well, I realize I'm completely irresistible to human females, but I'll be sure to save you from yourself and keep it totally platonic."

"You are *so* suave, Mister Smooth Operator. How *do* the ladies resist?"

Martini laughed. "I think we're about to find out."

CHAPTER 44

DID MY BEST not to think about Charles, and so was able to get into the white T-shirt and blue pajama bottoms Martini said were standard issue for sleepwear. Jamie had been in the little girl version of this. Aliens were kind of weird, but at least they chose unisex options for going to bed.

We discussed it. Both of us were used to sleeping next to our spouse. I had nights where Charles was gone, but Martini basically never did. Decided to trust him—apparently I could merely scream "com on" or for the Operations Elves if he stopped being a gentleman and help would show up. Besides, we needed to get to sleep and get some rest, not spend hours fretting about intimacy.

I turned my back to his side, my neck and head on his impressive bicep, and snuggled up against him. It was different than being next to Charles, but it wasn't uncomfortable. He wrapped his arm around me and held onto my shoulder. A few little adjustment moves, and we were set. The two Poofs joined us, snuggled next to my chest.

Bruno was in the room, too. He settled on one of the pillows, watching. He made eye contact with me, nodded, and winked slowly. "Uh, I think Bruno just told me you were okay, I didn't need to worry, and that he'd claw you up if you tried anything I didn't want."

"He probably did." Martini kissed the back of my head. "He's protective. Rightly so."

"Hey, can we listen to music to fall asleep to?"

"Sure, what do you want?"

"How about Jack Johnson?"

"Ah, Kitty, my Kitty, hates his music. I don't think we have any of it."

Managed not to say anything derogatory about her taste. "Uh, okay. What about Amadhia? She has to have her stuff."

"Never heard of that artist. Com on!"

"Yes, Mister Vice President?"

"Walter, can you get all of Amadhia's records loaded into the sound system somehow?"

"Searching . . . ah, I'm sorry, but there's no such recording artist listed. Anywhere."

"What? Really?"

Martini hugged me. "Shhh," he said quietly. "You're positive, Walter?"

"Yes. I've searched every database and outlet. No one listed by that name is a recording artist. I tried a variety of spellings, too, and searched internationally."

"Okay, Walter, thanks for trying. Com off."

The white noise that was quietly in the background when the com was on ceased. "I don't understand. She has the most beautiful voice—better than Enya or Florence or Adele or any of them. She's my favorite female singer. I can't believe Amadhia's not here."

"She may be in this universe, but she may not be a singer in this universe. Or at least, may not have a recording career." He hugged me again. "I'm sorry. You want me to have Walter load in Jack Johnson?"

"No, not if my CA hates him. He's the coolest guy, by the way."

"I'm sure he is. Kitty says he puts her to sleep."

"And yet she doesn't have his music."

He chuckled. "I usually find other ways to tire her out. Anyone else you can think of you'd like to listen to?"

Pondered. "Jewel, I guess. She *has* Jewel, right? Jewel *is* a recording artist here?"

"Yes. And yeah, Kitty uses her to sleep to a lot. Hang on." He rolled over, fiddled with something, and the sounds of "Foolish Games" started. "Huh." Martini went to the door, opened then shut it. Sugarfoot jumped up onto the bed. "He wants to sleep with you tonight."

"Works for me." We snuggled back up the way we had been, alien animals included, and Sugarfoot settled himself at our heads. With cat and Poofs purring quietly, Peregrine watching, and Jewel singing, I fell asleep.

The sounds of Panic! At The Disco's "New Perspective" woke me up. We both groaned, but managed to roll out of bed. I showered first since Martini was going to be able to get ready at hyperspeed.

The same clothes as I'd put on the evening before were waiting for me, though it was obvious they'd been cleaned while we slept. "Fine," I said quietly. "If this is the only look you want me in, I'll go with it. Thanks for all you did for Jamie, by the way. Her room looks amazing."

The purse was waiting for me on top of the hamper. Zipped up the hoodie, grabbed the purse, and headed out. Martini was out of his shower, towel wrapped around his waist. Yeah, it was easy to see why my CA had fallen for this guy—the term "hardbody" had been created to describe him. Muscled but not overly done like a bodybuilder, just the right amount of hair on his chest to be manly without being a total rug, and a tantalizing Happy Trail running over a perfect six-pack and leading down to where my eyes did *not* need to go.

"I'll, ah, meet you outside." Zipped out of the room as fast as I could. It was one thing to have what had amounted to a platonic sleepover. It was another to have all-out lust going for this guy.

Of course, because this was just how it worked around here, apparently, Charles was standing there as I exited the bedroom. I jumped and slammed the door behind me.

"Sorry," he said with a rueful smile. "Didn't mean to startle you. Richard said we were leaving at three in the morning and I didn't want to get left behind, since I was apparently the last man added to this team."

"It wasn't an insult." Hoped I wasn't looking totally like a cheating wife. Felt as though I probably was.

He noticed, of course. "It's okay." He stroked my cheek. "I'm not really your Chuckie and you're not really his Kitty, but it's awkward for all of us no matter what."

"You seem almost totally like my Charles. Only . . . you're sadder than he is."

He nodded. "I probably am." Charles turned and went to sit on the sofa. The others weren't here yet.

I joined him and took his hand. "I'm sorry. It must be very hard to be a widower so fast and so young."

"Yeah." He squeezed my hand. "And we'll make sure my counterpart doesn't have to face that, so don't worry. We'll all protect you."

"We're going stealth shopping in Paris and then to a diplomatic apology session in Canberra. I don't see a lot of danger in either one of those scenarios."

He chuckled. "You haven't been here that long. Just stay aware of your surroundings and make sure you're never out of reach of either Jeff or Richard."

"Why not you or Malcolm? Honestly, I'm used to running to you for protection."

He looked flattered. "Well, we don't have hyperspeed and superstrength. They do. That makes them better protectors. Buchanan and I will be there, too, but every human working with Centaurion has learned to keep near to an A-C as much as possible." He smiled. "But if you run to me for protection, believe me, I'll protect you."

"Just like always."

"Yeah." He squeezed my hand. "I guess the me in your world asked you to marry him better than I managed with the Kitty in this world."

"No idea. We were in Vegas, right after he sold his convenience stores to Circle K for a ton of money. He suggested getting married by an Elvis impersonator. I laughed, because I thought he was joking. He grabbed my hand, said he wasn't joking, at least about marrying me, and that he loved me and always had and always would, and went down on one knee. In the middle of the Bellagio. But we got married at the Mandalay Bay because that's where we were staying."

Charles looked a little ill. "So if I'd just had a few more seconds of boldness here, in this world, we'd be married."

"I suppose you would be." Had no idea what else to say. Apologizing for my CA picking a different and seemingly also awesome guy seemed wrong. But acting like I could totally understand her throwing Charles over for someone else was wrong, too.

"Yeah." He squeezed my hand. "I'm glad that I was man enough to tell the girl I loved that I did love her in another universe."

"Me too. I know you lost your wife here very early, but I know without asking that she loved you with all her heart."

"I loved her with all of mine, too." He looked utterly sad again.

"You'll find someone else."

He shook his head. "I don't know that I'm supposed to be . . . happy here. Maybe that's my role in this universe—to always be the guy who's alone."

Martini came out of the bedroom, moving us off of this heartbreaking and depressing subject. Martini eyed us and I let go of Charles' hand. "You up to this, Chuck?"

Charles nodded and stood up. "Yeah. Thanks. Where are the others?"

"Waiting for us in the basement. Uncle Richard thought it would be smarter." He went to the door and Christopher and Amy came in. Martini showed off Jamie's new digs while Charles woke up Len and Kyle.

"Jamie's room is beautiful," Amy said to me as she and Christopher took over the couch.

"Thanks. It's what she wanted, I didn't have a lot to do with it."

"You said yes to it," Amy said with a shrug. "That's a lot more than I guess you think."

"Are you saying that my Cosmic Alternate didn't want Jamie in her own room?"

"No. I just think it was kind of beyond time. I'm glad you recognized it, too." She smiled. "Our Kitty doesn't care about some of the 'regular girl' things the rest of us do."

"I guess. Well, gotta go. Thanks for babysitting." Turned and went to the door.

As I waited for Martini and Charles, heard Amy give a sad little sigh and also heard Christopher murmur to her. "It's not the same Amy," Charles said quietly as he and Martini joined me at the door. "Any more than you're the same Kitty."

"I know it's a lot to ask," Martini said softly, "but if you're able to, throw her a bone, baby."

"Oh, fine. Hey, Amy," I said in a louder voice, "if you see anything that Jamie missed in her room, or think of something you know she'd like or that my CA would like, would you have the Operations Team add it?"

She looked shocked and really happy. "Absolutely, Kitty! Have fun shopping!"

"Will do. Uh, anything you want from Paris?"

She shook her head. "No, I'm good."

Martini took one of my hands and Charles took the other. "Did you give her a hyperspeed pill?" he asked Martini.

"Yeah, with all her other pills. So you shouldn't get sick this time, baby." With that we headed off at a speed that made my head spin. We were downstairs in about a second and Richard and Malcolm were waiting for us.

I gave them a rough idea of where the shop was and Richard nodded. "I'm sure we can find the area with ease."

"Amy lived in Paris for several years," Charles said, as Richard fiddled with something I couldn't see. "And her father's facilities there hold some . . . bad memories for all of us. I mention this because I want to point out that she didn't tell you about this just now. Again, personal growth."

"Okay, I'll try to stop hating on her."

"Good," Martini said as he swung me up into his arms. "Because we need to focus all our energies on finding this mysterious shop that sells the only thing you think is going to fix things with the Aussies."

Richard went first, then Malcolm, and Charles. Martini fiddled with the same thing I couldn't see, and then we stepped through, too.

It was farther from D.C. to Paris than from D.C. to New Mexico, and I could tell because the time I spent totally nauseated was longer. My face was buried tight in Martini's neck when my stomach finally stopped screaming at me.

He put me down and I looked around. Sure enough, it was daylight, and we were standing in an alleyway surrounded by what surely looked like Parisian architecture. The many signs nearby in French also confirmed we'd arrived where I'd wanted us to.

We were definitely in the area I was hoping to be. Sadly, the shop wasn't just sitting right there in front of me. It so figured. Turned around and looked. Nope, not on this little street.

"Let's start searching. I'll lead, you guys follow."

"Or," Richard said, "as we call it, routine."

CHAPTER 45

CAROLINE INSISTED on taking her car and Pierre insisted on taking his, meaning we were a small parade by the time we left. Chuckie had the kids and their stuff, Reader had Dad and his stuff, Caroline had Aunt Carla and *her* stuff, Pierre had all the rest of the luggage and foodstuffs, Buchanan had the arsenal and related spy stuff in the car with him, and I had Stripes riding shotgun. Stripes totally felt I'd gotten the better deal.

Was happy my animal communication skills were still working here in Bizarro World. I was grateful to Jamie for mentioning the cat, too, because I'd gotten really used to rolling with some kind of animal along for the ride. Wasn't sure if Jamie knew this, or just wanted a cat and knew there was a homeless one waiting for someone to notice him, but decided to enjoy the small wins as I got them.

Thankfully all the cars had GPS and Bluetooth in them. Not that I thought the streets would be different here than in my world, but they could be, and if the Israeli Embassy wasn't where I thought it would be that could be more than awkward—it could be dangerous for everyone I was trying to protect.

Based on his skills and willingness to shoot first, Buchanan was bringing up the rear. Reader was in the lead. And

I was sort of floating along, sometimes on the side, sometimes out in front, occasionally in the rear with Buchanan. Hadn't had to do this kind of work a lot in my time with Centaurion but it was amazing how helpful TV and the movies were as training for my actual life experience.

Though Stripes and I were totally ready, nothing interesting happened on the drive. This was good, because hopefully it meant that Cliff and LaRue hadn't caught on or Raul wasn't late checking in. Had my doubts that things could be that smooth, but maybe I had better luck in Bizarro World.

Fortunately, the Israeli Embassy was right where I expected it to be. They headed us into underground parking, and our cars were checked carefully for bombs. Thought they were going to fill Buchanan full of holes when they found the arsenal, but Chuckie and Oren managed to calm that situation down.

Stripes settled himself into my purse. He was heavier than Poofs by a lot, but not by as much as he should have been—the cat needed some fattening up. He looked good in the Coach bag, though, I had to admit.

Leah introduced us to everyone and I gave up on remembering names immediately. Some were the same people I knew from my world, which was great, but the Israeli ambassador was different, which potentially wasn't. But he was gracious and shared that anything Angela Katt's family needed was A-okay with Israel.

Dad seemed happy in here, so that was one for the win column. They had enough spare rooms right now that we could all fit, as long as Reader and Buchanan bunked with Jakob and Oren. So Dad and Pierre were in one room, Aunt Carla and Caroline were in another, and Chuckie, the kids, Stripes, and I were in the third. Dad and the others were sharing a connected bathroom, but we had one in our slightly larger room. This embassy wasn't up to American Centaurion standards, but for Bizarro World it was great.

Leah was a cat lover, so all was good in that respect. She had food, both wet and dry, and a litter box in the bathroom for Stripes all set up. He chowed down, purring the entire time. "You going to keep him?" she asked as the kids petted him while he ate.

"Gently, kids. And, I don't know. I hope we can. But our travel schedule isn't great for pets."

"If he's housebroken, he could stay here when you're in Australia."

"Really? You'd share Stripes Ownership?" Stripes stopped eating, mouth full, and looked over at me. "Sorry. You'll let Stripes hang out with you when I'm not around?"

She laughed. "Yes. I know that cats aren't actually owned. *They* own *us*."

Stripes gave us both a friendly purr and went back to the business of eating.

Once he was done and snoozing on the nice cat bed Leah had acquired from somewhere, so did we. And the Israelis had pulled out all the stops. We had a lovely dinner, complete with Jewish specialties, some of which were like other Middle Eastern or Mediterranean specialties but better, because they were like my mother, father, or Nana Sadie made them.

I was ready to head off after this to find Cliff and, hopefully, kill him, but Pierre put his foot down. "You had an accident where by the grace of God you all survived, and then we had those horrible people attack us. You're all staying here, where it's actually safe, and sleeping. Save the world tomorrow."

"We never argue with Peter when he's right," Reader said with a grin.

Chuckie nodded, and so did Buchanan. "Rest, safe rest, would be advisable," Buchanan said.

"Then it's settled," Chuckie said. "Let's get the kids into bed," he said to me, specifically.

"Aww, do we have to?" Max asked. "It's so cool here!"

Oren grinned. "Let us show the kids around for a little bit first."

"Well . . ." Chuckie said.

"Pleeeeeeease?" all three kids said in unison. Jamie in-cluded. Her brothers shot her pleased glances.

Her asking was what I was sure convinced Chuckie. "Okay. *If* your mother says it's okay."

Looked at the time. "I do, but no more than an hour, and then it's all the bedtime stuff and right to sleep. Got it?"

The kids agreed that they were fine with that plan, Oren assured us that he'd keep an eye on the time, and they scampered off. Several of the people I'd met and a few I hadn't went with them. "Mossad," Leah said quietly to me. "Your children are very safe."

"Thanks. So, can the adults get a tour, too? Or at least web access? We're trying to find some other . . . allies."

She nodded. "We weren't joking—your gift of those four assassins has given you unlimited credit with our government." She leaned over and spoke quietly to Jakob, who nodded and got up and spoke to the ambassador. Who, after a few moments, nodded as well. "You're in," Leah said. "Shall we?"

Chuckie, Reader, Buchanan, and I excused ourselves. Pierre heaved a dramatic sigh, but Dad, Aunt Carla, and Caroline were in happy, animated discussions with the people around them and didn't seem to notice or care that we were leaving. Felt the love.

The Israeli embassy had their Super Spy Lab in the basement, too. Several normal layers of passwords and doors later, we were inside. It looked like any other mini command center I'd ever seen—lots of computer terminals, a couple big screens, personnel intently doing work or scurrying about.

"I want to discuss backup," Chuckie said to Jakob. "Because, based on everything that happened today, we think we've identified a C.I.A. mole."

"I want to search the web. I wasn't using it as an excuse. I'm looking for people."

"I'll help Kitty," Reader said. "You two handle things with Jakob." Chuckie and Buchanan went off with Jakob, while Leah took us to a couple of free computer terminals.

She got us online. "No one can trace your searches. And yes, I'm sure." Jakob called for her and she sighed. "Holler if you need me." Then she trotted off to the others.

"Who are you looking for?" I asked Reader as I started putting in names again.

"Your people, Cliff Goodman, all his aliases, and that woman. Using her two aliases to see if I can figure out what name she started life with. Who are you looking for?"

"Um, one person at a time, I'll tell you that."

"Hey, not my fault all your friends have really common, generic names, girlfriend."

Considered this while I ran through my Human Roster in my mind. "You know, what are the odds that LaRue's real name is something like Mary Smith? Something dull, boring, and common? She's extremely vain and also extremely brilliant."

"Well, the best anagram program around shares that unless her real name is Emeraude Stoner, she didn't create either of her names that we know of based on her original name. However, other than wondering what boring name she might have started with as a way to fall asleep, this seems like a dead end."

"Figures. I have a couple that aren't common, at least not here, but I can't find them."

"Give it to me and I'll try."

"Olga Dalca. She's older, probably in her sixties or seventies. In my world she's the wife of the Romanian ambassador." And my Oracle. If Olga was here, I had a shot of finding Cliff, because she'd know what was going on and I was sure she'd handle the idea of the multiverse calmly. She probably already knew it existed. "The other is Mona Nejem. She's the Bahraini Ambassadress in my world."

"Sorry," Reader said quietly a minute or so later. "I think I found your Olga. Was she KGB in her younger days?"

"Yeah, she was."

"She was caught spying and executed, along with Andrei Dalca and Zoya Darnell." He cleared his throat. "Ah, Israel is the country who caught and executed them. This happened near the end of the Cold War, by the way. So decades ago."

"Oh." Didn't know what else to say. No Oracle. No Chernobog, either, then. But also, no Adrianna. This world was missing so many people I cared about it was hard not to get depressed. Of course, Jeff wasn't here to be affected by it, so if I wanted to be down, I could be, darn it. But I preferred action to wallowing. "What about Mona?"

"She's not in an embassy, anywhere in the world. If she's here, she's still in Bahrain."

No help there, then. Mona the diplomat's wife I could get help from. Mona the Bahraini citizen wouldn't trust me, and I couldn't blame her. And no Mona meant trying to find Khalid would be an even worse dead end. Probably emphasis on "dead."

We kept on searching while the others continued to powwow. Had no idea why it was taking them so long, but it was taking me and Reader even longer, so they could strategize and fret as much as they wanted.

"How about Herman Melville?"

"Dead authors are magically alive in your universe?"

"No, his parents were literary. He's a police officer in D.C. Part of the K-Nine squad." I was typing as I was talking, and D.C.'s roster came up. No Melville. No one I recognized at all. Even the dogs didn't look right, though it was hard to be sure with German Shepherds. But I knew Prince well, and Prince wasn't in the pictures. "But he's not a K-Nine cop here."

"Hmmm . . . looks like he might have joined the military. This him?"

Checked it out. Sure enough, it was. "Yes! That's him. And that's Prince, his dog, too. Is there a picture of their unit?" Reader tossed up some pics. "Yes, that's all of them. Well, not all of these guys are familiar, but most of them are. Great, they're good help to have. Where are they stationed?"

"Arlington," Reader said quietly. "The entire squadron was wiped out by suicide bombers when they were doing a search for civilian casualties in Kandahar."

My throat was tight. "Dogs too?"

"Dogs too. Buried with their handlers, though. So there's that."

"Yeah." We were quiet for a minute while I did my best not to cry and Reader waited for me to lose it. Got it under control. Barely, but there. "War, what is it good for?"

"Absolutely nothing."

"Say it again. So why are we all always fighting?"

"Don't know. The prevailing thought is that aliens would come and show us a better way."

"Aliens came and were instantly turned into something to fight over."

"People are people, babe. That's all I've got for you."

We went back to searching. Found Mr. Joel Oliver easily. He was a hugely respected journalist and was in the Middle East, covering the war. Sure, we could contact him, but if he wasn't The Crazy Conspiracy Reporter here, then he either wouldn't believe us or we'd ruin his reputation. Shared this with Reader, who agreed.

"Leave the ones with good lives alone, girlfriend. It's a good motto to stick to. Huh."

"What?"

"Your Tim is around our age?"

"Yeah. Why?"

"Look over here, is this him?"

Leaned over to see a picture of a cute, grinning guy I recognized. Hair was styled a little differently, and he was in a blue shirt and contrasting blue tie, but otherwise, he looked the same. "Yes! That's him!"

"Really."

"Why do you sound so down about this? He's alive isn't he?"

Reader sighed. "Oh yes, he's alive. I found him by accident. He's just won an award, which is why he popped when I did a new search."

"Super, an award for what?"

"He's the best kindergarten and first grade combined teacher in Los Angeles."

CHAPTER 46

LET THAT SIT ON THE AIR for a moment. "Tim is a teacher? Of little kids?"

"Yep." Reader was clearly trying to control his Inner Hyena. "I can see why you want to find him—he can teach the kids while we race off to fight evil."

"But . . . he's my Megalomaniac Lad."

"No, Kitty," he said gently, laughter gone. "He's a grade school teacher. A popular one, too. Great at his job. Let's not ruin this life he seems very happy with by swooping in and saying, 'Hi, we're C.I.A. and our friend from another universe swears she needs help only you can provide.' It sets a bad precedent. Oh, and he's married."

"To Alicia?"

"No. His wife is another teacher, named Lori. She won for best fifth grade teacher in Los Angeles. Basically, they're the SoCal K-through-Twelve Power Couple. But superheroes they aren't. I'm sorry."

My flyboys and K-9 pals were all dead, along with my mother, my Oracle, and my Superhacker. Stryker was a successful author but not a government hacker and the rest of Hacker International remained completely off-grid. Len and Kyle were in the NFL, Mona was probably in Bahrain, MJO was a respected war correspondent, and Tim was teaching

school and had never met Alicia. There was no point in my
looking for her now.

No hybrids could be here, so looking for Erika Gower was
out, especially since I didn't know what her maiden name
had been. Irving Weisman was a science nerd and hated
action—if I needed brains I had Chuckie, so leaving Irving
alone sounded like a kindness.

Contacting humans we'd worked with for one mission
wasn't worthwhile. Looking for enemies seemed stupid, and
more work than we might have time for. Same again for my
Washington Wife colleagues. Finding Vance might be helpful, but he wasn't a fighter. Same with any and all politicians.
Well, maybe not one.

"Found Tito Hernandez yet?" I asked while I did a search
for Evander Horn.

"Yeah, I think I have. He's a doctor in Las Vegas. Looks
happy. I think this is another one to leave alone."

"Unless we're injured in Sin City, yeah. Have you found
my master assassins yet?"

"Nope. If they exist, I think they're off-grid."

"Figures." My search actually produced results. Par for
this course, they were depressing results. Horn had died in
the car accident that, in my world, had caused burns over
75% of his body. Considered one of the worst highway accidents of the past decades, everyone involved had died. But in
my world, Horn had saved most of these people.

Depressed as hell, I forged on. Realized I hadn't looked
for one person. Wasn't sure why I'd forgotten him—the ultimate nature of our relationship, I guess.

"See if you can find Brian Dwyer. He went to high school
with me and Charles, Amy, and Sheila." I'd found Sheila
simply by asking Chuckie about her. Happily, she was still
married to Roger and they had four kids and lived where they
did in my world and we were still friends. One person un-
changed.

Per Caroline, my sorority sisters were all fine, though
some of them had different jobs or were married when they

weren't in my world or vice versa. But none of them were butt kickers in this or any other world, as far as I could extrapolate.

Reader cleared his throat. "Hang on a second." He got up and went to Chuckie. They spoke for a few seconds, then Chuckie raced over to me.

"Who are you trying to find, Kitty?"

"Brian Dwyer."

"Why are you hunting down your ex-boyfriend from high school?" He sounded both worried and jealous.

"Because in my world he got over me and is married to an A-C. He's also an astronaut. But he works with us all the time and seriously, I'm running out of people. Everyone I know is either dead, unfindable, or doing jobs that are so far from butt kicking as to be ridiculous to hope they could help."

"Ah."

"Oh, God, is Brian dead, too?"

"Not . . . exactly." Chuckie squatted down so we were more face-to-face. "Brian didn't handle you and I getting married well. Amy was just insulting. Brian kind of . . . went nuts."

"Why?"

He sighed. "He'd sworn to you that he was going to do something to impress you and then he'd win you back."

"Oh, yeah. Mom remembered that speech. Me, not so much. Still, we didn't get married right out of high school or something."

"No, we didn't. But we got married right after I made several millions of dollars. Brian insisted that you'd only married me for my money and kept on bugging you to leave me for him. And by 'bugging' I mean we had to get a restraining order."

"I cannot believe that I'm such a femme fatale."

He grinned. "You are to some of us, at least. Anyway, he was following us like some people follow the Grateful Dead. He had to be stopped."

"You said he wasn't dead!"

"He's not. He's in a mental institution. Angela was able to have him evaluated."

"How so? You can't just shove someone into a mental hospital without cause."

"There was cause. He attacked me. Fortunately, just me—you and the kids were nowhere around."

"Oh, my God. Did he hurt you?"

"No. I was already a trained C.I.A. agent by that time. He got a beatdown from me, but only enough to get him to stop and under control. He's doing well, though—I check on him periodically."

"Why? I mean, that's nice of you, as long as checking means making sure he's okay, not giving him shock treatments, but why bother?"

He stroked my cheek. "I understand how he felt. It was how I felt every day until we went to Vegas and you said 'yes.' I didn't snap because you were always my best friend. But Brian didn't have that."

"I dated plenty of guys who didn't think twice when we broke up."

"And you dated a couple who felt you were their entire world. I was the lucky one, and Brian wasn't. Anyway, he's improving. They had me visit him in person the last time I went and he handled it well. He may be able to be released. But not right now. He'd be willing to break out if you asked him to, but seeing you isn't what Brian needs."

"In so many ways, Bizarro World sucks. I wish I could bring you guys back with me."

He kissed my forehead. "I'm married to you in this world and we have three beautiful children. No matter what, Kitty, I wouldn't be willing to trade that for anything."

Leaned against him for a bit. "At least some of you are the same, or close enough."

"Yeah. You okay?"

"Yeah." Straightened up. "Go back to the powwow. I'll get you if I think of some other ex I want to look up."

He sauntered back to the other men and I turned back to the computer screen. Brian had been obsessed with me in my world, but he'd channeled that into becoming awesome and then, thankfully, into being a great husband to Serene, his perfect match in obsessiveness, and as a wonderful father to Patrick. But then, in my world, I hadn't married Chuckie. And aliens existed.

Reader came back and sat at his terminal. "Sorry, Kitty."

"It's okay. Um, is my Uncle Mort still in the Marines and still alive?"

"He is, I don't even have to do a search. But he's on the ground in Afghanistan running a classified mission for the Corps. Can't drag him into this."

"Bummer. Uncle Mort's so good at saving the day." He might not have an issue believing in the multiverse, either. Could try for Colonel Franklin or Captain Morgan, or heck, even Colonel Hamlin. But if by some miracle they weren't dead and we guessed wrong and they thought I was crazy, that would end badly for everyone. "Do you guys know Burton Falk?"

"Yeah, he was part of Buchanan's team. He's dead now."

That was it. I was out of humans I could think of and was almost afraid to try to come up with more. God forbid I search for my Secret Service detail—couldn't handle knowing if they'd all died, and if they were alive, well, I wasn't the wife of a politician here, so why would they help me?

"Why are so many people I care about dead in this world?"

"I don't know. No aliens, I guess."

Yeah, that was coming to be my conclusion, too. We lost human agents in my universe, of course. In fact, we'd lost one in my first days of finding out aliens were on the planet. However, before I could pursue that line of thinking, Leah called to us. "Kitty, James, we need you."

We got up and joined the others who were clustered around one of the bigger screens, which looked like it had a satellite map of D.C. up. "What's going on?"

Chuckie put his arm around me. "Now I'm glad you took the cat along." His voice was grim and he was shaking.

"What happened? What's wrong?"

Buchanan pointed to a portion of the map. It was zoomed in on just one street. The street where Chuckie and Other Me lived. The street was still there. Their beautiful house, on the other hand, was smoking ash.

CHAPTER 47

"SO, THEY DIDN'T FOLLOW US, but we sure got the hell out just in time." For whatever reason, all I could think of was that Jamie's mirrors were gone. Hopefully she didn't require magic mirrors in order to see the other universes, because if she did, we were now out of luck.

"Thank God you got Jamie to leave without a fight," Chuckie said quietly. "I think we got to safety because we moved faster than they expected us to."

Buchanan nodded. "Based on your normal patterns, you'd have still been there, dealing with Jamie when this happened."

Wondered if Jamie had left without a fight and told me to take the cat because she'd seen this coming. She hadn't acted afraid, nor had she said anything, so maybe not. And if not, that meant that Cliff had given the order to blow the house up after we were gone. "Would Cliff know you'd call Mossad for help?"

"Maybe," Reader said, voice tight. "But does that mean we're putting all of you in danger?" he asked Jakob.

"Possibly, but we're used to it. I doubt that he's going to make a move against you while you're here—starting a war doesn't sound like it's in the interests of the Corporation."

Didn't agree but also didn't want to sleep in the bushes by

the Lincoln Memorial, so I didn't argue. "I can't believe that all your things are . . . gone."

"Our things," Chuckie said gently. "And it's okay, baby. The things that mattered are here. Most of our mementos and pictures are in Australia anyway."

"Do you think he's going to destroy that house, too?"

"I hope not." Chuckie hugged me again. "I'm not sure what to tell the kids. Or your father."

"The truth. We got out just in time. The kids already know someone really wants to kill us. So does Dad. Were the neighbors hurt?"

"Doesn't look like it," Leah said.

"One small favor. Okay, it's been that hour we told the kids they were getting. I need to get upstairs and get them into bed. You coming with or do you want to stay down here and strategize?"

"We'll monitor your other home," Leah said.

"What about your parents?" I asked Chuckie. In my world, A-Cs would be getting them to safety right now.

"We have them under surveillance," Leah said. "As well as your home in Australia. Our agents are aware that the C.I.A. has a mole and that mole is trying to destroy rival agents. We can get your parents if you want us to, though."

"They've been sitting ducks for years," Chuckie said. "But I don't like the idea that we just leave them there and hope for the best. On the other hand, freaking them out over nothing can lead to a variety of issues, not the least of which being that they have no idea what it is I'm really doing."

"I have an extended family that could be destroyed, too."

"I don't want to sound cavalier about our families, since my parents are also cluelessly sitting at home believing all I do is model, but I think the best way we protect everyone is to stop Goodman."

"James has an excellent point. So, do we tell the kids tonight or tomorrow?"

"Tomorrow," Chuckie said firmly. "They won't sleep if

they know their home has been destroyed, and no one else with us will, either."

It was decided that Reader and Chuckie would stay down-stairs and go over potential familial targets while I went and handled the kids.

Oren turned out to be the best babysitter in the world. He had the kids in their nightclothes and their teeth brushed be-fore I got there. Told him there were things he needed to get caught up on downstairs, then tucked the kids into one of the two queen-sized beds in this room.

"Glad you're all small enough to fit, but no kicking or shoving. Share the bed nicely and equally."

"We will," Charlie said earnestly. "Where's Daddy?"

"Working. You're stuck with me."

"Do you give goodnight kisses?" Jamie asked. Both boys stared at her, in shock as near as I could tell.

"I sure do." Gave her a tummy tickle and a kiss. She squealed with laughter.

Gave the two boys a hug and kiss. "Stop looking sur-prised," I whispered to them as I hugged them both at the same time.

The kids settled down. "Can we listen to music?" Charlie asked.

"Sure." Dug through the purse to find the iPod. There was a nice stereo dock in the room and I plugged it in. "Who do you want to hear?"

"Jack Johnson!" Max said.

Managed not to ask if he was serious, but only just. Jack Johnson had been on the radio when I'd switched places, and, per Caroline, Other Me loved his snoozer tunes. No worries. Snoozer tunes were what was called for right now anyway. Got it going and the kids snuggled down. Couldn't bear to focus on the music, so I focused on getting undressed and ready for bed.

Apparently I wore a lot of nighties in this world. Most of them were not appropriate to sleep in the same room with the kids, let alone with a man who wasn't my real husband. Kept the T-shirt I was wearing on and found a pair of soft cotton shorts and went with that.

Decided I was exhausted and lay down on the other bed. Stripes left his bed and snuggled with me. Jack Johnson worked his magic—I was out like a light.

Woke up briefly when Chuckie came in. He changed quietly, kissed each of his sleeping children, then slipped into bed next to me. He sighed quietly but didn't touch me. Felt bad. Reached over and stroked his hair. "It'll all work out. I promise."

He took my hand, kissed it, then moved it gently back onto the cat. "Thanks, Kitty. It's just been a hell of a day."

"It has. Get some sleep. I expect tomorrow to be worse."

He leaned over, kissed my cheek, then rolled onto his side, so we were back-to-back. Jack Johnson was still crooning away and I heard Chuckie's breathing go rhythmic fast. Relaxed and went back to sleep myself.

This time I had a vivid dream. We were facing off against Cliff and LaRue and they killed Chuckie and Reader and Buchanan. Disintegrated them. They couldn't get me, I was too fast, but they killed everyone—Dad, Caroline, Aunt Carla, the kids, the Israelis—until it was just them and me.

Cliff's face broke open and the Fugly of My Nightmares appeared. Mephistopheles was big and red, but I didn't smell his breath in the dream, so that was one small favor. "Why are you visiting me in my sleep again?"

"Because I like you."

"And you don't like the current Mastermind?"

"No. For many reasons."

"Okay. Not gonna lie, it's weird having you showing up and hanging out in my head, but at the same time, at least you're *from* my universe."

He nodded. "We were joined once. And that means we will be joined forever."

"Lucky me."

"Some would think so."

"So, why are you here, other than to put the finishing touches on my 'everyone's gonna die' nightmare?"

"You have the power I had when I arrived on your world. You can use yours the same as I did, you know."

"Except I'm not going to, and you know that."

"I do. However, you are still acting as if you are in your own world. You are as alone as Superman here. But a frontal attack is not always effective. Sometimes, when you're the only one with the power, you have to use it. Alone. With great power comes great responsibility."

"Pulling out the comics clichés much?"

"You comprehend them so much better than other options."

"True enough. But even Superman has a team, and Spidey does, too. I get no help? No backup? No sidekick? No mascot?"

"A mascot and a sidekick are acceptable. But they must *know* they are the mascot and sidekick." He smiled at me. It remained a combo of nice and horrifying. Focused on the nice. "You have been given an opportunity I took away from you. Don't waste it." He patted my head and, with that, he was gone.

Woke up yet again. This time, there was no reason, other than, you know, a nightmare and a Fugly Advice Session. Got out of bed quietly and checked on everyone, just in case. All sleeping soundly. Stripes woke up and came with me to investigate.

Sure, we were supposedly in a secure facility, but things were turned upside down here. Slipped my jeans and Converse back on, grabbed the hoodie, and slunk to the door. Stripes came with me. "You don't want to go fast with me. I'll be right back, promise," I whispered to him. Then I carefully opened the door and stepped out of the room.

Nothing and no one in the hallway. Zipped off at hyperspeed and checked on the others. Everyone was fine. Checked out the entire embassy, what I could access anyway. All fine,

most asleep, some on guard duty, but I moved past them at
hyperspeed so they didn't see me.

Got back to our room in less than thirty seconds. Stripes
wasn't at the door, though. He was sitting in my purse.

The problem with this safety check was that I was wide
awake. Wide awake, revved up, and contemplating what my
nightmare had told me. Looked at Stripes. He blinked slowly,
got out of my purse, and trotted to his food.

While he ate, I wrote Chuckie a quick note so that he
wouldn't panic if he got up before I was back. Double-
checked that the Glock with its single clip was in my purse.
Hadn't had the brains to grab more clips, but if I thought
about what Chuckie had said earlier and Mephistopheles had
said in my dream, I was a superhero. I was Wonder Woman.
Well, really, still Wolverine with Boobs. But either way, I
could kick butt and take names in a way that no one else on
this Earth could. I didn't need backup or the cavalry. I *was*
the cavalry.

Made sure I had hair spray in here, because, hey, you
never could tell. Took the iPod, too, and happily found that
Other Me carried portable speakers, just like I did. Tossed
whatever else had worked in the past in there, because why
not?

Stripes finished when I did and sauntered over to the purse
and jumped in. He was taking the role of Approved Mascot,
thank you very much. Decided not to argue—cats could yowl
to wake the dead and I knew without asking that Stripes was
going to raise hell if I didn't take him with me.

Kissed Chuckie on his forehead, did the same with the
three kids, and then Stripes and I slipped out of the room
again.

Hyperspeed meant I was able to get in and out of a door
so fast that it wouldn't trip an alarm system. The downside of
doing this was that I couldn't take one of the cars—they were
in the underground garage and I couldn't access it or get a car
out without waking the entire embassy.

My original plan had been to figure out where Cliff was

headquartered and use Raul's car to take us there, giving us the potential of camouflage and surprise. Since the house had been blown up, it was clear that wasn't going to work. Any of us driving up in Raul's car would just indicate it was time to shoot to kill.

No worries. I was used to discarding plans, after all, and if it was just me, I didn't actually need a car. And per Mephistopheles, it needed to be just me. And, frankly, I'd do anything to avoid seeing my latest nightmare come true.

But that meant I was going to have to use hyperspeed for everything. Again, no worries. So many people I loved were dead here, it was easy to get the rage going. It was an impotent rage, focused generally, but it was enough. Did a running jump and cleared the fencing easily. Go me.

Stripes meowed softly as we trotted off down the street. He felt he was superhero material and that he could take the hyperspeed. And if he did toss his kibble, he'd do it outside of the purse.

"You rock, Stripes. Plenty of barfing area where we're headed."

Fortunately, I knew these parts of D.C. well enough to not get lost as I headed us to the Lincoln Memorial. Got there fast—not as fast as Jeff, definitely not as fast as Christopher, but darned well up to Top Field Agent status.

Would have gone to the bushes first, but things were so different that I wanted to check something. Went up to the Memorial itself and stopped running. Stripes showed that he was the Cat of the Ages because he only hacked a little and really didn't throw up. And he'd just eaten, too. I was impressed.

Happily, the Memorial looked the same—same words, same sad, tired Lincoln looking down on me. I was about to leave and go handle what I'd come here to do, when I heard a man's voice, talking softly.

"I just don't know, sir. They say you're a hero if you're the only one who survives, but I don't feel heroic. I feel sad and tired and useless. And this new assignment . . . it's not what a hero does, sir. It's . . . cushy and a reward. But it's a reward I don't want. And it's a reward I don't trust, either."

Crept around to see who was talking to whom. The guy talking wasn't speaking to anyone I could spot. Then I realized he was talking to the Memorial, to Lincoln.

The speaker was a slender guy a little younger than me with strawberry blond hair, dressed in Navy dress whites. He wasn't smiling, but I knew who he was. Gave an involuntary gasp.

He heard me gasp and spun. "Who's there?" His hand was on his gun, but he hadn't pulled it yet.

"Just me." I stepped out, hands up in front of me. "I heard you talking and just wanted to know who else was here."

"Ah." He relaxed. And now looked embarrassed. "I was just . . . I needed to talk to someone who would . . . understand."

"I hear you. And I feel exactly the same way." Sat down on the top step.

He came and sat with me. "What brings you out to visit our nation's greatest president, ma'am?"

"I just discovered . . . many people I care about are dead or gone or very different. I'm normally a pretty cheerful person, but discovering people I love are gone, some long ago now, just . . . hurts."

"I understand."

"Yeah, I think you do." Mephistopheles had said I'd been given an opportunity he'd taken away. Now I knew what he meant. And, as they said, nothing ventured, no one to say you were totally mental, right?

"Have we met, ma'am?" he asked.

"Sort of. It's a long story. Something of an unbelievable story."

He chuckled. "I don't report to my new duty until oh-nine-hundred, ma'am."

"Call me Kitty. And, tell me, do you prefer to be called William, Will, or Bill, or should I go for formal and call you Lieutenant Cox?"

CHAPTER 48

I HADN'T BEEN IN PARIS for a while. I loved this city, and a part of me wished we could stay here longer. However, we had a mission, and it needed to be completed as soon as possible so that Jamie woke up with her parents there with her.

Martini caught up to me. "We can do this via hyperspeed if you want. You can lead, I provide the speed."

"Okay, that makes sense."

Richard took hold of Charles and Malcolm and nodded to us. "Lead on, just remember that we don't need to go at supersonic speed, Jeffrey."

"Wouldn't want you straining, Uncle Richard, don't worry." With that, we zipped off.

We were still going fast, but it was, somehow, slower than the other times Martini had used hyperspeed. We ran through the entire area a couple of times and I had to stop. "I'm sorry. I can handle going that fast now, thanks to whatever pill you gave me. But I can't *see* at that speed, not clearly enough to spot something I'm pulling up from memory. But I think I spotted where to start."

"Then it was worth it," Martini said. He kept hold of my hand. We were out in public, and that meant there was always a chance for photographers, so this was smart.

We wandered a little bit, but while I spotted some shops that were familiar, and some that were clearly new in the last couple of years, I wasn't finding the specific shop I needed. And we needed it, because if Singh had already checked everywhere online, then we only had this one shot.

"You sure it's this one item that's the key?" Martini asked me as we wound through some tiny side streets.

"Yes. I can't tell you why so much, other than that, in my world, Margie loved it. It was truly a one-of-a-kind item."

"From eight years ago. It's either been reproduced or it could be gone, you know."

"Reproduced it hasn't been. Per Raj, who did a thorough search. Gone? Yes, it could be, but I'm not willing to give up without trying."

He squeezed my hand. "That's my girl."

We rounded a corner when I heard something—a woman singing, not in French but in English. Her voice was familiar and I headed us toward the sound. As we got closer I recognized the tune and the lyrics. She was singing the Psychedelic Furs' "Heartbreak Beat." And I was positive I recognized her voice.

We ended up at a small café that was, for whatever reason, inside a tiny courtyard off the main street. The woman singing was handing plates of food to customers. She was slender and had a heart-shaped face I knew well. Her curly brown hair was pulled back, she was in a black dress with a white apron, and it wasn't clear if she was the owner or the waitress, but she was definitely working at this café.

"Why are we here?" Martini asked quietly. "And why are you so excited?"

"Hush." Waited until she finished. The patrons clapped and so did I. Then I went up to her. "Amadhia, what are you doing working here?"

She gave me a very pleasant smile, but looked confused. "I'm sorry, I think you've mixed me up with someone else. My name is Emily."

"Yes, but your stage name is Amadhia."

She shook her head. "You must indeed have me confused with someone else. I'm not on stage. Would you like to have breakfast? You're tourists from America, yes?"

"Yes, we are. And, I'm sorry, you just remind me of someone I know. And, uh, sure, let's have some breakfast."

She led us to a table while the men with me gave me looks that said they thought I was both crazy and wasting time. Once we were seated and looking at menus, Martini leaned over. "I know who you think she is, but *she* doesn't think she's that person. We need to find what you're looking for, not 'discover' a new vocal talent."

"Okay, but she's local and may know the shop I'm looking for. Besides, I'm hungry, and I'll bet the rest of you are, too."

"I confess to being a bit peckish, Jeffrey," Richard said. "Besides, my partner tends to be correct."

Martini sighed. "Women's intuition. Right." He smiled at me. "Yours is rarely wrong. So, fine, I'm hungry, too."

We ordered and ate. The food was delicious and Amadhia was an excellent waitress. She might say she was Emily, and she was, but to me she was always going to be Amadhia—I'd spent too long thinking of her that way to change now.

She also continued to sing when she delivered meals and bussed tables. I didn't recognize the song she was singing as she cleared our plates, but I was pretty sure she was singing in Catalan and I asked her about it.

"It's 'El Cant dels Ocells,' 'The Song of the Birds' in English," she explained.

"It was lovely. Do you own this restaurant?"

"My grandparents do. They'd immigrated to America just before World War Two, but missed France and came back here. My parents stayed in America, but after college I came to visit and stayed."

"Can't blame you. When did they come back, recently?"

"Oh no," she said with a tinkling laugh. "Once my father had married my mother and they had to move to California for work, my grandparents came home. They've been here for thirty years."

"Here, in this location?"

"Oh yes. We live above the café."

Meaning that if the shop I was looking for existed, Amadhia's grandparents would be likely to know. "Would you or they know of a shop that was here around eight years ago?"

"Possibly." She went off, singing a different song. "Ave Maria" in French, if I was going to guess.

"That was abrupt," Charles said.

"She'll be back."

Sure enough, Amadhia returned shortly with an older woman, also dressed in black with a white apron. Same curly hair, though the older woman's was white, same slim figure, same heart-shaped face. "My grandmother, Marie, might be able to help."

Marie nodded. "What shop are you looking for, my dear?"

"I can't remember the name, or even where it was, other than somewhere in this area. It was a little gift shop that had very unusual pieces, all done by local artists. The proprietor was a woman about your age, but her hair was dark brown and she was more plump than you are. I think the shop was in an enclosed block, but I haven't been able to find it. I can just remember that the block had a sort of Art Deco feel."

Marie looked thoughtful. "It could be you're looking for Celeste. Her shop was in *Le passage du Prado*, but she moved a few years ago because the Prado was in disrepair."

Disappointment washed over me. "Oh." Despite what I'd said to the political bigwigs, I didn't have a Plan B. And now I'd dragged everyone on a wild goose chase for no good reason.

Marie patted my shoulder. "Don't look so sad, my dear. Celeste moved, but she's still in this neighborhood. But that's why you can't find her shop—her shop doesn't look the same and it's not in the same place." She looked around. The last of the breakfast crowd had left so we were the only patrons at the moment. "Emily, take them to Celeste's. They'll get lost, otherwise."

"Happy to, grandmamma." Amadhia kissed her grandmother's cheek as Richard paid the bill and left a generous tip. Both women beamed at him and he gave them the Silver Fox Smile in return. Richard was absolutely a ladies' man of the highest order.

He offered his arm to Amadhia. "If I may escort your granddaughter?" he asked Marie.

She laughed. "Absolutely." She smiled at all of the men with me, then gave me a wink. "Such handsome men you journey with. You're obviously a woman of good taste, which is why you remember Celeste's shop. She only carries one-of-a-kind items."

"I hope the item I'm looking for is still there." Tried not to sound worried. Failed, if Marie's expression of commiseration was any clue.

Marie took my hand and patted it. "If not, you will find something else just perfect. I promise."

Didn't think about it, just hugged her. "Thank you. And thank you for lending us your granddaughter for a little while."

"Oh, she's young and should have an adventure now and then."

With that we left, Richard and Amadhia leading the way. Which was a very twisty, turny way.

"Who considers shopping an adventure?" Martini asked quietly.

"Many people," Charles said with a laugh.

Malcolm shook his head. "There's something . . . odd going on."

"Odd dangerous?" Martini sounded on guard and protective.

"We'll find out," Malcolm replied.

We wandered some more, turning here and there, going down some steps and up some others. Couldn't speak for the others, but there was no way I was going to be able to find the café again, let alone figure out where in Paris we actually were.

"Are we going to end up in Narnia, Oz, or Hogwarts?" I asked.

Amadhia heard me and smiled at me over her shoulder. "Maybe." We turned down a tiny alleyway and she stopped in front of three doors—one at the end of the alley, and two facing each other on either side. "Or perhaps we're going somewhere even more magical." She opened the door at the end of the alley and went inside.

The men all looked at me. "Think it's safe?" Charles asked.

"I think we came a long way to find out. And what's life without a little risk or excitement?" So saying, I followed Amadhia inside.

CHAPTER 49

THE SHOP WASN'T WELL LIT, and even though we'd been blocked from direct sunlight most of the way here, it still took a couple of seconds for my eyes to adjust.

I could hear Amadhia speaking to someone in French and as the men joined me I was able to take a look around. Relief flooded me—this was the right place.

The shop looked almost as it had eight years ago, when we'd found it on our honeymoon. The structure was different, of course, but the merchandise wasn't. There were paintings and artworks of all kinds everywhere—on the walls, on the ground, and hanging from the ceiling. Glass cases held jewelry and breakable collectibles. The shop was chock-full but somehow didn't seem ridiculously crowded.

When we'd visited before we'd wanted to buy the entire shop, but Charles had limited us to three things, one of which I'd given to Margie. Of the other two, one was in our home in Australia and the other in our home in D.C. Grabbed Charles. "Remember this place? I wanted to buy the entire shop but you managed to stop me."

He removed my hand gently. "No, Kitty, I don't."

"Oh. Right. Sorry. Got swept back to the past for a moment."

Amadhia brought a woman I recognized over. She was

older than when we'd first met, but she was definitely the proprietress who had helped us before. Managed to remind myself that she wouldn't remember me any more than the Charles here would remember her.

"I hear you were searching for me," Celeste said. "But I don't remember you."

"I was in your former location and it was a long time ago."

"I pride myself on remembering all my customers." Celeste sounded just slightly suspicious.

Richard stepped in and gave her a shot of the Silver Fox Smile. "The passage of time changes the young far more than the rest of us, madame."

Celeste laughed. "True enough, monsieur. True enough. Now, look around and see what you must have."

Everyone with me had seen my sketch, and while I was tempted to pull it out and show it to Celeste, that would make her even more suspicious, and we didn't need to create another international incident while trying to solve the first one.

So, we all wandered and searched. Other than trying to ensure that we got back to D.C. in time, this wasn't a hardship. As I had eight years ago, I still wanted to buy most of what was in this shop.

Amadhia joined me. "What are you searching for?"

"Something I saw here years ago and didn't buy." Well, I hadn't bought it in this universe. Spotted something familiar. Sure, it wasn't what I was looking for, but it was very like one of the other items I'd bought years ago.

"Oh, that's a beautiful mask," Amadhia said. "Is that what you're looking for?"

"Not exactly." The mask wasn't meant to be worn, at least I didn't think so. It was meant to be displayed as art. The mask was a sun and moon design, half the sun on the left, half of the moon on the right, with a crown of stars. It was hand carved out of a single piece of wood and hand painted. None of this was unusual, other than how the artist had created the carvings. I'd never seen any sun and moon design quite like this, which was part of the point of getting a unique piece of art.

Tried to put it back, but I just couldn't. Sure, we had one in D.C., but we didn't have one in *this* D.C. And it was so beautiful.

Martini came over and took the mask out of my hands. "We'll take this, and we're still looking," he said to Celeste. He smiled at me. "Get whatever you want. Even if it's more than you think you should. We can afford it," he added with a grin.

"Okay." Didn't need to tell me twice. Apparently Martini was looser with the purse strings than Charles was. Worked for me.

"Do you collect masks?" Celeste asked as she joined me and Amadhia.

"Not really. I mean, I like them, but we're more . . . appreciators of the eclectic than collectors, per se."

She nodded. "What else are you looking for? Something special?"

"Uh, yeah, actually, I am. I'm looking for something decorative in crystal, possibly glass or acrylic, something clear. But it needs to be unusual, too."

"How unusual?"

Considered the design. "Hoping for something that makes you think of the galaxy or universe or similar. Something that would hang on a wall. But not a painting."

She chuckled. "No small request. But . . . I think . . ." She wandered off. They seemed to do that a lot around here.

Kept on perusing. Charles was looking at something and I went over to where he was, Amadhia trailing me. "Whatcha looking at?"

"This music box. It's so . . . unusual."

Unusual it was. The main piece was a golden sun. The planets, Pluto included, were attached to it. Charles turned the key and as the music played, the sun turned slowly while the planets circled their star, accurately. I recognized the tune but checked to be sure—it was Mozart's Symphony #41 In C, K 551, "Jupiter," the first movement, Allegro Vivace.

It was also familiar. "Let's get it, too," I said quietly, as Martini came over.

"Like yours in Australia?" he asked softly. I nodded and he took it out of Charles' hands. "Nice pieces you're picking."

"Yes, they are," Charles agreed. He gave me a quick smile. "Nice to know we still like the same things."

The conversation was suddenly awkward, and I noted Amadhia noting this. But Celeste returned. "I believe I have something you may want." She indicated we should follow her, so we did, to the back of the store. "I've had it for years—it's never moved, and that's always surprised me. It's one of my favorites. Sadly, the artist who made it passed away a few years ago, so there can never be another just like it or even close. I keep on waiting for the right person to fall in love with it."

Richard and Malcolm were already there, admiring the piece. It was small, about the size of a grapefruit, and based on the intricacies, smaller than it had any right to be. Somehow, the artist had captured the feeling of the universe within the delicate threads of crystal that created a flat yet three-dimensional piece of art. My throat caught.

"That's it," I whispered. "That's exactly it."

"We'll take it," Martini said. "And we need it wrapped as carefully as possible."

Celeste beamed. "At last. I almost hate to part with it, but your taste clearly runs to the heavens, and this is the perfect choice."

She bustled off and Martini followed her, presumably to hand over wads of cash. I was excited and sad at the same time. There was only this one piece here, and there would never be another. In my world, the artist was still alive. I knew this because we'd found his work in a gallery on a trip to Paris. "I wonder if us buying this years ago made the difference."

Hadn't meant to say that aloud, and was instantly sorry I had, because Amadhia caught it. She touched my arm and moved us away from the others. "You are not . . . from here, are you?"

"What do you mean?" Wondered if Martini could pick up my panic. Hoped so.

"You're aliens, or at least some of you are, but that's not what I mean. You, you yourself, seem just slightly . . . out of place. You believe I'm someone else, and I can tell you still think I'm the person you know. You know of Celeste's shop and the items you've found—you were searching not for 'something' but for *them*, specifically. You found old friends, not new ones."

"Ah . . ." Had no idea of what to say at this point.

She smiled. "It's alright. I would never betray you."

"Why not?"

"Who doesn't want to experience magic at least once in their lives? And this is magic, isn't it?"

It was stupid, but I couldn't help myself. "In a way. You're meant to be a singer, internationally known, beloved by millions. You have the most beautiful voice . . . I can't understand why you haven't been signed to a recording contract."

"I'm not a . . . bold person."

Thought about something Charles had said earlier. "It only takes a few seconds of boldness to change your life." As I said this, I heard music. Rock music, being played live. It would start, then stop, and it was clear there were musicians nearby who were practicing. I grabbed Amadhia's hand. "We'll be right back," I called to the men. Then I led her to the alleyway.

CHAPTER 50

THE MUSIC WAS COMING from the door to our left when we exited, and I opened the door and dragged Amadhia after me. It was a recording studio, and the receptionist tried to stop us. Chose to pretend I didn't speak or understand French.

The music was happening upstairs, so I ignored her and dragged Amadhia after me. "International superstar," I shouted over my shoulder as we zipped past.

"Look, I can't sing these lyrics," a man said from where we were heading. "At least, not all of them. I'm a drummer first, man, and a guitarist, not a lead singer."

"Come on, Aaron," a different man said. "Work with me."

"I'm trying to. I need a female singer and everyone you've brought to audition is horrible. I need a hit, this song will be a hit, but not if I don't have the right person to harmonize with."

"I've got who you need," I said as we rounded the corner. It wasn't a large studio, and I didn't recognize anyone in it, but most of them looked American. "She can sing anything. Voice like an angel. And all that."

Everyone in the room gaped at me, Amadhia included. There were several people in the room, many with musical instruments, but the one who had to be Aaron was around my age and bearded, sitting in the recording booth holding a guitar.

The receptionist ran up, apologizing in French. Charles, Richard, and Malcolm were right behind her. Assumed Martini was still handling our purchases.

"This is her manager." I pointed to Charles. He managed James' career, after all. At least in my world. And spies or not, James had a fantastic career. "Her name is Amadhia." Turned to her. "I know you think you're Emily," I said in a low voice, "but if you want magic, be Amadhia and sing something, anything."

She cleared her throat and sang U2's "All I Want Is You." After a few shocked moments of silence, there were appreciative nods. Then the musicians in the room started playing along with her, Aaron included. By halfway through, Aaron had started singing along with her, harmonizing beautifully. By the time she was done she and Aaron were doing call and response with each other. And when they finished, everyone applauded.

Amadhia flushed but she bowed. "You're hired," Aaron said. "I want her, and only her."

Charles handed him a business card. "Send contracts here." He pulled Amadhia aside and gave her a card as well. "Sign nothing, agree to nothing. Feel free to sing, but don't give them a contract for anything."

She nodded. "I won't." She looked around. "Is this real?"

"God, I hope so," Aaron said. "Because we're going to number one if I have you on the record, Amadhia."

She flung her arms around me. "You have a friend for life," she whispered to me. "Wherever you are and I am, I'll be there for you."

Several men in Armani suits appeared. Charles spoke to them, then turned back to the rest of the room. "They'll be here to make sure none of you try to take advantage of our singer."

"We don't cross the Mob," an older man who'd been the one telling Aaron to work with him said. "Especially not when they bring us recording gold."

"We're not the Mob," I whispered to Amadhia.

She laughed. "I know," she whispered back. "You're something much better and much more amazing."

Aaron dragged Amadhia into the recording booth, excitedly talking about what songs he wanted her to sing solo, which one he was doing solo, and which ones they were going to do as duets.

"Good job," Martini said quietly from behind me, as he moved me out of the studio. "You just like saving people, don't you?" He took my hand and led me downstairs.

I looked up at him. "It's usually worth it."

He nodded. "I've had agents take the purchases so we don't have to worry about them. We need to head back, too, before someone realizes who just brokered this particular musical deal."

Heard footsteps on the stairs behind us, and turned to see Aaron there. "I have no idea what you two are doing here, but thank you. For what it's worth, I already was, but from now on I'll *always* be pro-alien."

"We'd appreciate your not mentioning who we are," I told him. "We're not exactly supposed to be here." Took the plunge. "But she's my friend and I just want her to have her chance."

He grinned. "No one would believe it if I told them and I'm sure your people will deny it. But from one very grateful registered voter, thanks for looking out for the little guys, and gals. We'll send the first press recording to you, if your offices will accept it."

"They will," Martini said. He handed Aaron a card. "Send it there."

"Front row tickets and backstage passes for our tour, promise." Aaron said as he bounded back upstairs. "Hey, I want to do 'Uncertain' with her. It's gonna be huge!"

Martini took my hand and we headed all the way downstairs. "Should we get the others?"

"Uncle Richard and Buchanan will stay with Chuck so he has backup. We're heading to the Metro. There's a gate there." He looked a little wistful. "It's one of our favorite places."

"To have sex, you mean."

He grinned. "Yeah, I do. Not that I'm taking you there for that. I just want your little musical matchmaking experiment to work out. And I think she needs Chuck watching over what's going on right now."

"And it's distracting him, in a good way, isn't it?"

Martini nodded. "Whether you want to call her Emily or Amadhia, she needs someone ensuring they don't use her and rob her blind. And Chuck knows business."

"He does." Felt a slight pang of jealousy, but shoved it aside. "Let's get home. Jamie's going to be waking up soon and I want to be sure we're there. Oh, and I want to make a stop along the way."

"Why?"

Shrugged. "I usually get the kids some little thing from every trip. I realize this isn't an official trip, but still, why break the pattern?"

Martini squeezed my hand. "You're a great mother."

"Let's see if Jamie agrees with that, shall we?"

The run to the Metro was interesting. I was getting better at seeing while we were racing along at hyperspeed. It was easier because I wasn't trying to find anything, just look at everything around us.

We went to the Gare du Nord station. Martini had us go to regular human speed out of sight of anyone, near a gift shop. I picked out something for Jamie, we paid cash—somehow Martini had euros—and then we raced off to the bathroom. The men's bathroom.

"Why are we here?" I hissed to him as we waited for the place to sort of empty out. We'd already dashed in and out several times—apparently there was one special stall and it was in use.

"Gates are in bathrooms. It helps us blend in and arrive and leave without a lot of notice."

"But I'm a girl, that's the men's room, and you all said the gates were in airports."

"They are. Every airport. But we have them elsewhere, and major train stations and bus stations and so forth are logical locations. We have gates everywhere it makes sense, honestly, which is more places than you'd imagine."

"The maintenance costs must be astronomical."

"Our Operations Team is exceptional. Hang on." We dashed in again.

We were now the only ones in the bathroom, other than whoever was in the one stall we needed. I bent down to look at the feet of who was stalling, and to make sure there really was someone in there, and straightened right up again. Tugged at Martini's hand, and he took the hint and ran us out of there.

"What is it?" he asked me as we reached our little hidey-hole.

"Get us out of here and call for a floater gate or take us to the airport. In fact, I choose airport. Now. Don't wait. But call Richard and have him and the others stay where they are."

Martini could talk on his phone while we were running, and he did so. "Uncle Richard wants to know why. So does Chuck. So do I."

"There was a dead body in the stall. With blood pooling. I think someone knows we're here and is trying to frame us for murder."

CHAPTER 51

COX JUMPED AND STARED at me. "What? How do you know my name?"

"In my world, your best friends told me they called you Bill."

"What friends would those be?"

"Jerry Tucker, Chip Walker, Matt Hughes, Joe Billings, and Randy Muir."

Cox went pale. "They're dead. Been dead for—"

"Years, yeah as I discovered yesterday."

"How could that be if they were supposedly your friends?"

"Remember that long story? It's kind of short. There isn't one universe, there are a multitude of them. In the one I'm from, aliens are on Earth and they're superpowered but basically pacifistic, so they're good guys. In fact, I'm married to one, and got some of the powers due to giving birth. But that's not important now."

"I can take you to a hospital, ma'am," he said earnestly.

"That's what I loved about you. In the short time I knew you, I mean. You always called me ma'am. Everyone calls me Kitty, by the way and again. But it's okay that you call me ma'am, though you can use Kitty whenever you relax."

"We haven't met, ma'am."

"Not in person, no. I know you from a picture Jerry gave

me of the six of you, when you were all at Top Gun together. It's in my other world, like everything else. Like all of them. They're all alive in my universe."

"Well, that's good," he said in the tone used when dealing with a scary crazy street person.

Decided there were easier ways. "Hang on." Stood up and picked him up. With one hand. But nicely.

"Whoa! What the hell? Put me down!" I did. "Are you some kind of bodybuilder?"

Grabbed his hand. "Nope." Took off.

Ran us all over the mall, in and around every museum and monument, and stopped in front of the Jefferson Memorial. In about thirty seconds.

Cox fell to his knees and barfed. Stripes sniffed as if to suggest that Cox was an amateur. Had to admit, Stripes had it goin' on in terms of handling hyperspeed.

"During an alien invasion, Matt and Chip got shot down over this water," I said conversationally. "I saved them. Well, me and our team doctor, Tito. In my world, aliens are here and most of them are good guys and help us. Some of them aren't and of those that aren't, some of them are monsters like only Ray Harryhausen could have come up with. During the operation when I got involved with the gang from Alpha Centauri, the original fugly of everyone's nightmares, nick-named Mephistopheles, was leading a major offensive in the middle of the New Mexican desert. We called in for help."

"So?" Cox said, as he stopped barfing and got to his feet.

"So, among those who came to help us were six Top Gun Navy pilots. They were amazing. But . . . sometimes the monster wins the round."

Cox stared at me. "What happened?" he asked finally.

"Mephistopheles smashed your jet into the ground. You died instantly." Took a deep breath. "So while we spoke via the radio and you treated me as your superior officer, I never got to meet you in person. You were my first."

"First?"

"The first casualty under my command. And you never

forget your first, and I've never forgotten you. I didn't get to know you, but I did get to avenge you. I killed Mephistoph-eles."

"You saying I owe you?"

Shook my head. "Different universe." I took his hand and ran us back to the Lincoln Memorial—sure, we ran across the water, but if he was going to have to barf again, why not have a cool experience prior?

Reached Lincoln and sat on the top step while Cox retched. "So, I get it, you're an alien," he said as he recovered.

"No. Pay attention. I'm a human, who's—"

"Right, right. Married an alien, the kid did this to you. Why are you here?"

Oh well, no time like the present. "We have a Sith Lord active on our world. I was switched with the 'me' in this universe because the Sith Lord is also in this world and he's after 'my' husband in this world. I need to stop him here. And then get home and stop him there. But I'm here, and I think I'm here for more than just one save. I think I'm sup-posed to do what I've been doing since I discovered aliens were real and really on the planet."

He sat next to me. "You want to take the Sith Lord down and out."

"Right. We call him the Mastermind. He's not really a Sith. He's a human, actually. But it makes the explanation a little easier."

"Yeah." He shook his head. "You've got the powers, I can say that. Makes your story a little more . . . believable." He looked around. "Why did you come out here so late at night?"

"Early morning really, but who's counting? I had a night-mare. Most of the time when I dream it's not someone giving me hints, but sometimes it is. This was one of those times. I think everyone else I care about that's still miraculously alive in this universe is going to die if I don't do a commando raid without them."

"Doesn't sound wise to do that alone, ma'am."

"It's probably not. But . . ." Finally, the tears I'd been holding back showed up and rolled down my face. Stripes got out of my purse and into my lap. Cuddled him and tried not to make his fur all wet. "Everyone's dead. Or they're teaching grade school or something. My mother is dead, and I want to ask her what to do so badly. My whole team is down to three guys, all of whom I love and none of whom can I stand the idea, let alone the reality, of losing."

Cox pulled out a handkerchief and gave it to me.

Sniffled as I wiped my eyes. "Thanks. Well, Mossad will help, but three of them are friends of mine in my own world. And I don't want more people I like to end up dead here."

"Why are you taking the cat along?"

"He said I could have a sidekick and a mascot."

"He? The cat talked to you?"

Decided not to answer this one honestly. I'd save the Dr. Doolittle news for later. "No, Mephistopheles. He seems to enjoy visiting me in my sleep."

"Really. You sure you didn't just hit your head or something?"

"Oh, I did, right before I rode the tornado here and wound up in Oz and all that, but A-Cs also have enhanced healing and I got that, too. Think of me as Wolverine with Boobs, but without claws, and you'll be right."

"The cat covers the claws part."

Stripes purred that Cox wasn't so dumb.

"Yeah."

Cox cleared his throat. "I'm the lone survivor from my unit. No one from my Top Gun class is alive anymore. My dad died while I was deployed. Hit-and-run drunk driver. They never found the person who killed him. I got sent home on extended leave because I'm a decorated war hero and my mom was dying. Cancer a thing in your world?"

"Yeah, we haven't cured it yet."

"Well, it's still a thing here, too. Though I don't think my mom wanted to fight anymore, not without my dad. Only child, so no siblings, and we were never close with the ex-

tended family. And, to thank me for my service and my sacrifices, I've been assigned to a TDY that attaches me to the
C.I.A."

"TDY?"

"Temporary Duty."

"Ah. You looking forward to it?"

"No. Not at all."

"Who are you going to report to?"

"Some guy named Clifford Goodman."

Stared at him. "Say what?"

"Why did you just get freaked out? Oh. No way! Is he
your Sith Lord?"

"Got it in one."

"You have proof?"

"Dude, of course not. That would make things far too
freaking easy. I'd like to get some before I take him out, of
course, because I like to be really sure. However, in my experience, the bad guys love to monologue while they have
you or an innocent at gunpoint, and that's when you tend to
get all the damn proof you need."

"Bet if you had an inside man who's cool under fire and
smart enough to know when to duck and when to shoot it
would help you out."

"Couldn't hurt. But there's lots of risk, not the least of
which is being killed. Or, much worse for someone like you,
being branded traitor."

"You're not a traitor if you save the world. Even if the
world thinks you're a traitor when you save it."

"I like how you think. The Sidekick role is still open."

"Not anymore." He stood up and helped me up. Then he
hit attention and saluted me. "Lieutenant Commander William Cox reporting for duty, ma'am."

CHAPTER 52

SALUTED BACK. "We're informal around here, Bill. Call me Kitty."

He grinned. "Absolutely, Kitty ma'am."

I laughed. "Ah, the start of a beautiful friendship." Stripes yowled softly. "You're cat approved, but we don't have a lot of planning time. The positive is that if you're being assigned to Cliff as a special post, then he's going to show up to meet with you. In addition to his other sterling qualities, Cliff is a mole in the C.I.A. because he's now the head of the Corporation, better known as the Cuban Mob. He's ordered hits on my mother and all of her extended team."

"Which is down to those three guys you don't want to lose?"

"Yes. But I never want to lose one of my side. As I learned early, though, what I want isn't what I always get. So, let's remember that while I want to take Cliff down, I don't want you to die to do it."

Cox gave me a small smile. "I appreciate that, ma'am. The best commanders don't want to sacrifice their troops willingly."

"Batman doesn't leave Robin and Megalomaniac Girl here doesn't leave Megalomaniac Lad, regardless of his universe of origin. Though I don't think I can give up hope and give you Tim's name for reals."

"Really? That's your superhero name?"

"Sadly, it's incredibly accurate. There isn't a crazed mad scientist or cackling evil overlord I can't make a love connection with. My original Megalomaniac Lad, in this world, is teaching kindergarteners and doing fabulously with it, ergo, he's not really available. I have high hopes for you, though, Bill, because you made the leap for why Cliff's name freaked me out without missing a beat."

Cox grinned. "Always good to impress your superiors right away."

"Super, Lunatic Lad. Let's strategize, because that's probably wise, since it was also suggested that a frontal attack wasn't a good idea."

"Excuse me, Lunatic Lad?"

"It's that or Megalomaniac Lad Version Two Point O. Or Evil Genius Lad, Bonkers Lad, Crazed Bond Villain Lad, or similar."

"Huh. Lunatic Lad it is, then. Just don't share that name with anyone I know personally." Cox looked thoughtful. "Outright assassination's out, right?"

"Right. There's a 'me' in this universe—we're pretty sure she's switched places with me and is in my world, handling things, God willing. But she has to come back here, just like I have to go back there, at least I hope so. And that means she can't come back to discover I've turned her into an assassin."

"Plus the people you're trying to protect would be affected, especially since you have no proof that this Cliff's done anything wrong."

"Correct. I just have no idea of what to do. I'm fine with sneaking around, I just don't know where to do it. I mean, other than at C.I.A. headquarters."

"He's not running his operation from there. But he's also not going to trust me on the first day. Probably not for a long time—my record wouldn't indicate that I was willing to become a traitor."

"Why are you being assigned to him, anyway?"

"I honestly have no idea, ma'am. It's supposed to be a

perk, a cushy post where I can just show up and not have to do much every day, while at the same time getting a lot of face time with important people."

"Huh. You have a smartphone? I do, supposedly, but it's Other Me's phone and I forgot to ask what the security code was, so I can't actually use it."

Cox laughed as he pulled out his phone. "Who are we calling or what do you want to look up?"

"Let's find out all we can on Clifford Goodman. I think he's originally from Florida." Sure Chuckie, Reader, and Buchanan had done their research, but I didn't have it, and besides, what Cox and I might find could be different, or mean something to us that it didn't to them.

Cox fiddled with his phone while I petted Stripes. "You hoping to handle things tomorrow, or, rather, later today, ma'am?"

"Oh, the sooner the better, yeah. I mean, I'd go murder this guy in his sleep, but I know that'll just mean that he has a backup plan in place that destroys even more people or turns power over to some giant Axis of Evil. This guy is a great chess player. Though not as good as my chess player."

Thought about this. I could beat Chuckie at chess. Not all the time, of course, but often enough. So, did that mean I just needed to challenge Cliff to a chess game, as if I were challenging Death?

Posed this question to Cox, who snorted. "He'd just cheat, ma'am. Someone like this, who's a traitor to his country and on a vendetta as well? He's not going to play fair in any way, shape, or form."

Pondered this most likely accurate assessment. Then remembered why I'd come to the Lincoln Memorial in the first place. "I think I know how he's not playing fair. Or how we can cheat, depending."

"Good, 'cause the internet's giving me nothing beyond the bland and obvious on our Potential Mastermind."

"Then let's just see if aliens were on Earth long, long ago, in all our universes." Put Stripes back into my purse and trot-

ted down the stairs at regular human speeds, Cox coming
with me.

Went around to the side of the building. The foliage
looked the same as how it was in my world. So far, so good.
Hunted around in the dark—A-Cs had better vision than humans and improved night vision as well. But it was still
pretty damn dark out.

Cox produced a penlight. "Always prepared, ma'am."

"You rock, Bill." Took the penlight and kept on searching.
Found what I was looking for in a short while. The entrance
to the underground tunnels. Put my purse over my neck, just
in case, took Cox's hand in my free one, and headed down
into the dark.

"How did this get here?" Cox whispered as we walked
down the slope.

"Put here ages ago by aliens. The Z'Porrah. They look
like dino-birds and have nasty attitudes. Earth's far out
distance-wise in terms of the galaxy—I think they and other
aliens were using Earth as their experimentation station, or
maybe even their zoo. The Z'Porrah and the Ancients weren't
friends—think of the Ancients like shape-shifting galactic
missionaries. But they were pro-humans or at least apes—or,
based on the A-C system, anything willing to walk upright
and on two legs—and the Z'Porrah basically hate our guts.
Both races have affected Earth's evolution, and the Ancients
for sure affected the Alpha Centauri system as well."

"So there's really a lot of intelligent life out there?"

"More than you can imagine, honestly. Fortunately or not,
depending on your viewpoint, none of them are here right
now. In my world, the Ancients crash-landed in Roswell in
the nineteen-fifties."

"We have those rumors, too, ma'am."

"In my world, they're real. But per the guy who's my husband in this world, the idea that aliens have visited us here is
just a hoax." We were no longer going down, and the path
was flat. It was also familiar. The tunnel looked exactly as it
did in my own world. Meaning that somewhere in here were

Z'Porrah power cubes. If I could figure out how to get one, we'd be golden. However, it had taken a cube to get into the dead zone rooms during Operation Destruction, and I had no real hopes it would be different here and now.

"How many universes are there?" Cox pulled me out of my power cube coveting.

"More than I think we can comprehend. If my physics or astrophysics or whatever is right, anytime there's a significant change, it creates a new universe. If you consider how many different populated worlds there are, it quickly becomes impossible to count. Infinite variety and free will means infinite potential. However, the significant change in my universe seems to be that the Ancients tried to visit again, and they didn't make a return trip here."

"Or they did and they didn't crash."

Stopped walking, pointed the light at the wall so it reflected, and stared at him. "What do you mean?"

He shrugged. "The movies suggest it all the time. That if an alien actually showed up here, the government wouldn't extend the olive branch of friendship and peace, they'd capture it and study it forever."

"It's like that on my world, too. Or it was. The A-Cs are powerful enough that the governments let them move in, in exchange for scientific and technological help and so forth. But even so, we don't go to human hospitals if we can help it." And before we were outed, an alien being admitted to a human hospital was a terrifying idea, for more than just the fact that it would prove aliens were on Earth.

"Is our technology less advanced than yours? In this world, I mean."

"No, not really. Huh, I see where you're going with that question. I know for a fact that there are things we have that are A-C created at their cores. And they're here, too." We went back to walking. "You don't have parasites."

"Sure we do. Tons of 'em."

"No, I mean from outer space. Parasitic superbeings. Interstellar jellyfish things that turn mammals into monsters.

So does that mean that Mephistopheles didn't destroy his solar system in this universe? Or that Alpha Four never figured out how to put up an ozone shield and so the parasites attacked that system?" Shuddered. "That would mean they're all . . . dead or monsters. At least monsters as we and they would see it."

"I point to that cell phone you can't unlock, ma'am, and say that, if in your world you *know* it's got alien tech in it, then it's got alien tech in it here, too."

"So, which aliens came here? And where are they now? I'm the only person who's got superpowers so far as anyone I've run into knows."

"How many people have you asked? You're hiding, right? I mean, you told me, but that's because of our connection, such as it was, in your world. And you've probably had to tell some others since you, what, did a body switch?"

"Nope, we changed universes, more like how it happens in Star Trek and Bizarro World—like we went through some cosmic portal and stepped out into each other's worlds. At least, that's how it was for me. I'm just spitballing on how it was for her." But I hoped it had been the same, because there were three little kids here who shouldn't grow up without their mother. "But yeah, I'm not announcing I'm a superhero."

"Because you know what'll happen to you."

"Well, that and I also don't want our enemies to know what I can do. But there aren't aliens on this world."

"How do you know?"

"There's a, for lack of a better description, Universe Wheel. I can see it, sometimes, sort of see all the many versions of me in all those worlds, and I kind of know what they know, while at the same time I don't. But I get the general gist. And the main general gist I've gotten, in addition to who I'm married to in each of these worlds, is that there's only one world where I know that aliens exist and are on the planet—mine."

"I think the key word in that sentence is 'I.' You not know-

ing they're here doesn't mean they *aren't* here. It just means
you don't know about it."

The thought that Jeff could be here, on this planet, was
exciting. But what if he was married to someone else? It
would be likely. However, I could see people moving at hyperspeed and I hadn't. So, if A-Cs were here, what would
they be doing? Not saving us from being run off the road,
that was for sure. But then again, that wasn't their job in my
world—why would it be their job here?

Realized that I wanted, desperately wanted, the A-Cs to be
here, on this Earth. I wanted it almost as much as I wanted to
protect everyone, stop Cliff and LaRue permanently, and go
home.

We were walking, not running, in part so that I wouldn't
have to make Cox sick for no reason, in part to conserve my
strength, and in part because in my world there was someplace close by I figured we needed to find or at least verify as
being there. As we rounded a corner, Cox grabbed the light,
turned it off, and shoved us up against the wall.

Spotted what he already had—there was light shining out
of a room up ahead of us. And I was pretty sure that said
room was one I was familiar with and had actually been hoping to find. The secret lab and the final resting place of Gaultier's Army of Hot Zombies.

CHAPTER 53

OF COURSE, Gaultier was supposedly a great guy in this world. But LaRue was the same as ever. So the odds were in favor of my not liking what was behind Door Number One.

"Could be bad," I whispered in Cox's ear.

"In for a penny, in for a pound, ma'am."

"Yep. I'll lead." So saying, I kept a hold of Cox and we edged along the wall. Looked for traps or tripwires. Didn't spot any. Hoped that meant there weren't any, versus my just being too lame to see them.

Made it to the door without issue. Listened at it—heard what could have been someone working quietly or could have been nothing. The door was firmly shut. So I either had to try the handle and let whoever was in there know someone was trying to get in, or I had to just break the door down, which didn't say "nice person coming through" on the off chance whoever was inside was a good guy, or at least neutral.

While I pondered options, Stripes jumped out of my purse. He went to the door and started meowing in an extremely pitiful manner. I went to grab him, but Cox grabbed me and pulled me back. "Let him work," he whispered.

Sure enough, the door opened a bit. "Who's there?" The voice was familiar, and as Stripes meowed again, the door opened wider, and a man stepped out to pick up the cat, I got a good look at him. "Come here, kitty. Are you lost? You look hungry."

"Alfred?"

He froze halfway toward Stripes, then spun toward me. "Who are you?"

Before I could answer, a ball of fluff jumped out of his pocket and went large and very toothily in charge. It was growling softly, but I knew it could growl a whole lot louder. Cox, to his great credit, neither screamed, ran, nor wet himself. Stripes didn't, either, but he jumped up onto my shoulder and hissed.

"Harlie, it's me. It's Kitty. It's okay, Stripes. Harlie is a good Poof, it's just protecting Alfred."

The Poof gave a confused growl. "I don't know you," Alfred said. He sounded unlike what I was used to in that he didn't sound happy, funny, charming, or in charge. He sounded frightened.

It was time to talk quickly before Harlie decided snackage was the better part of valor. "Alfred, there's a multiverse out there. I'm in the wrong universe. In mine, all your people live on Earth, and I'm married to your son, Jeffrey. You're my father-in-law. Due to a lot of factors, when I had your granddaughter, Jamie, I got A-C powers in a kind of feedback loop. I can run at hyperspeed, am stronger than most humans, have fast regeneration, and have most of the other bells and whistles, too. We also have Harlie with us, along with an absolute tonnage of other Poofs. I'm trying to fix things here and get home. And I think I need your help."

"How did you find me?" Alfred asked, still sounding frightened and suspicious.

"We have these tunnels in my world, too. They were created by the Z'Porrah. The Z'Porrah aren't our friends but we can still use what they riddled our planet with if we can find them. There's a lot more, but, um, could you please ask Harlie to relax? I don't want to become Poof Chow before I can save the day. And all that."

Alfred patted the Poof and it relaxed, but it remained large. "You . . . you said I had a son?"

"Yeah. You and Lucinda have five daughters and then Jeff, who's the baby of the family. He's the most powerful empath in the galaxy, possibly the universe. Well, my universe. I have no idea how powerful he is in this one."

Tears rolled down Alfred's face. "Lucinda is alive where you come from?"

Got the proverbial bad feeling in my stomach. "Um, yeah, yeah she is. Can you call Harlie off and can we come in? I'll fill you in and then I think you need to fill me in. Because I'm just spitballing here, but it sounds like things are very different in this universe than they are in mine."

He nodded. "Your military escort?"

"Lieutenant Commander William Cox, sir, U.S. Navy. I'm on Kitty's side. And I think that means we're on your side, too."

"And this is Stripes. He just joined the team a little before Cox did, which is why I don't have him fattened up to fighting weight yet."

Alfred nodded again. "Come in. I have food for the cat, if it's hungry."

We trotted inside and Alfred closed and locked the door behind us. Was glad I hadn't tried opening it or breaking it down.

The room was similar to the one in my world in that the equipment in it was clearly decades old. It was also highly functional and, in some ways, highly advanced. In other ways it was highly irregular—there were things I was pretty sure were coffee cans and similar attached to power tubes and so forth. Alfred was the rare A-C male who had strong science, technology, mathematics, and medical aptitude. And it was clear from the setup that he had all of his aptitudes going full bore here.

The door that in my world led into the Meat Locker of Horror here led into an apartment. Had the distinct feeling that this apartment had been created over time—nothing

matched and everything seemed cast off, as if Alfred had
scrounged it from somewhere. And yet, there were cell
phones and such in this world.

In full light Alfred looked even less like what I was used
to. In my world there was no way anyone could mistake Jeff
as anything but Alfred's son. Here, however, it would take
convincing. Alfred was still a tall, broad-shouldered man, but
he was sort of stooped, much thinner than I was used to, and
he had a scared and furtive demeanor. And he seemed overwhelmingly sad. I'd just seen this with Dad, but Alfred's sadness radiated off of him, as if it was his overriding and
possibly only emotion.

I couldn't help it, I hugged him. "What happened to you?"

"It's a long story."

"We have time, sir," Cox said. "And I think we need your
story as much as you need ours. Fate of the world could de-
pend on it."

Alfred sighed. "It always does, doesn't it?" Harlie went
down to small but stayed perched on Alfred's shoulder. Harlie
totally did not trust us yet. Alfred gave the Poof and Stripes
both some meat. Cat and Poof jumped off their particular
shoulders and the animals eyed each other. They ate with one
eye open, so to speak. "Can I offer you two anything?"

"Only if you'll be offended if we say no."

He managed a weak smile. "No, that's fine." He led us
into his apartment and sat on the edge of his bed. There was
a small loveseat and Cox and I sat on that. "I don't know
where to begin."

"In my world, Ronald Yates was exiled here. Is he still on
Alpha Four in this world?"

Alfred looked shocked. "No. He's dead."

"Well, he's dead in my world because I killed him." Alfred
looked freaked out. Went on quickly. "He was like a Renais-
sance Man for Evil in my universe. From your expression, I
take it he was a good guy on your world?"

"Yes," Alfred's voice shook. "He was a religious
leader . . ." He took a deep breath. "I fell in love with his

daughter, Lucinda, and my cousin, Terry, fell in love with her brother, Richard. They were a different religion than the rest of us on our world, and my family forbade the marriages."

"Because you were part of the Royal Family and you, specifically, were heir to the throne."

He nodded. "Ronald was making headway—those of his religion were always considered lower citizens. But they had such strong scientific aptitude . . ."

"The ozone shield didn't stop the parasites?"

"I have no idea what you're talking about. How could an ozone shield stop a parasite?"

"I don't mean little bugs, or microbes. I mean Jellyfish From Space. You didn't have those?"

"No, nothing like that was on our planet. And we didn't create an ozone shield. The Exonerates wanted to, but they were overruled by my father."

"Adolphus?"

"You know of him?"

"We've met." Contemplated what to say. "Um, he attacked me and the Poofs ate him."

"Really?" Alfred sounded shocked. "The Poofs turned on him?"

"Ah, yeah, yeah they did." So if there were no parasites, there was a good chance this meant that Mephistopheles hadn't blown up his solar system in this universe. Which was a good thing. But the way things were going, had a feeling this was going to be the lone item in the win column. "So, the Exonerates are what Ronald's religion is called?"

He shot me a suspicious look. "Why wouldn't you know that?"

"It's literally never come up. Richard just refers to it as 'their' religion." And me, being Ms. Observant and Interested, had never asked what they called themselves when they were *on* Alpha Four. I was batting a thousand in terms of paying attention. Apparently my other sterling qualities had won Jeff over, because my interest in so many normal person things was clearly not up to snuff.

"Richard? He's alive?"

"Yes and wow. I want the rest of your story, right now. Please and thank you."

"Ronald was making headway with our people, and the Exonerates were becoming more integrated into society. But my father felt that was an insult to our proud way of life. Our religion isn't based on mercy or forgiveness."

"Right, you toe the line or you go to Hell, correct?"

"Correct. But the line being toed is determined by the king. And if your king is bad, and my father certainly was, then the people are led to do terrible things. My father, he . . . he had Ronald murdered."

"And he managed it? Because in my world, he tried twice and Yates survived each one. Those incidents were part of what turned him to the Dark Side."

"No," Alfred said quietly. "The first attempt worked. It was during the Exonerates' most holy day of the year. There were so many killed . . . Ronald and all his family weren't the only ones slaughtered."

Let that one sit on the air for a moment. "So, Richard and Lucinda and Gladys?"

"Richard and Lucinda, yes. I don't know a Gladys."

"Okay, you not knowing Gladys makes sense. She was the daughter from Yates' second marriage."

"Ronald was only married once. And his wife died that day, too." Tears filled Alfred's eyes. "Terry . . . Terry was empathic. She was already in love with Richard and Lucinda was her dear friend. So she felt their deaths, and the deaths of all the others. She couldn't handle the pain, the overload. She died that day, too, in mental and physical agony. In my arms."

"Alfred . . . I'm so sorry." So, all the bad guys who wanted to hurt me and Jamie to get to Jeff all had the right idea for how to destroy him. I had to get home to be sure none of them ever succeeded. But first I had to fix what I could here.

Alfred's eyes flashed. "I started a rebellion, right then. And I might have been able to sway the people. But my father was too crazed with power."

The reality dawned. "You're who they banished. That's why you're here. They sent you to Earth because it was far, far away, but close enough that they could keep an eye on you, and you looked like us."

"But I am not one of you."

"Just like Superman," Cox said quietly.

Alfred nodded. "But I'm not a superhero. I'm a scientist. And everyone I loved was murdered or stripped away from me." Harlie bounded over and jumped into Alfred's lap. "All but one. They couldn't stop Harlie from coming with me. We're both alone here together, but at least we have each other."

No Lucinda, White, or Terry meant no Jeff and no Christopher. And all the others in the Martini clan were gone, too, wiped out before they could begin. I was here, and because I was, so was Jamie, but that was it. "What about Stanley Gower?"

"Stanley was executed for treason—he wasn't as close to the throne as I, so he was made the example of what would happen to anyone who tried to follow in my footsteps."

"Charming, but so like your father." My throat was tight. "We have an enemy that's trying to do the same thing to my mother—to get rid of all those who supported her, and all her bloodline. He's killed her, and pretty much everyone else, other than three guys from her team and my father. In my world he's bent on Total World Domination, and we're pretty sure he wants that here, too. That's who we're trying to stop."

Stripes sauntered in, rubbed up against Alfred, then jumped into my lap and started purring.

"I don't know what I can do. I can give you weapons, I suppose. I provide things to the governments, things they need. I tinker, to keep my mind active. When I create something new, something helpful or fun, I let them know. I get paid in bearer bonds, they get what they want."

"And they don't know where you live?" The last thing we needed was government interference.

Alfred shook his head. "I make arrangements through a

variety of scientists I sought out. They handle things, discreetly when necessary."

"You have some of the scientific community working as your fences?"

"In essence. They know they can't find me and that I can escape if they try to capture me. Besides, I let them claim credit for certain inventions, so it's in their best interests to continue to help me. They'd rather get the credit or their finder's fee than stop my ideas from coming. And if I were betrayed, no more ideas, and none for any of them, specifically."

Knowing human nature, that made sense. Mostly. "But what if one of them decides turning you in is more worthwhile financially?"

He shrugged. "They have no idea what I can really do, so they have no defenses against hyperspeed or increased strength. They all just think I'm an eccentric genius and they humor me because what I provide makes that humoring worthwhile."

"Don't they try to find you, just out of curiosity?"

"They may. But in all this time no one's found these tunnels, and since I enter them at hyperspeed, no one can see me doing so. *I* wouldn't have found the tunnels without Harlie. Harlie found them when we first got here—we use them to get all over the world. I have underground safe rooms like this one all over by now. They can't find me—nothing on Earth can penetrate whatever is lining these tunnels—and I want to keep it that way. If they knew I was an alien . . ." He shuddered.

"We won't let them know, sir." Cox cleared his throat. "I've lost everyone here who mattered to me. In a small way, sir, I do understand what you're going through. But some things are still worth fighting for. And saving innocent people from someone like your father is one of them. You were right to try to fight. I understand why you didn't once you arrived here. But right now, sir? You're not alone anymore. At least, you don't have to be."

"You lost your family, son?" Alfred asked.

Cox nodded. "My parents and all my friends. I'm an only child. I understand feeling alone. But if we don't help her," he nodded toward me, "then all the sacrifices become worth nothing. She's come from another universe to try to save what she can of our world. I'd say that's worth revving up the fighting spirit for."

Alfred stroked Harlie, clearly thinking. "If you will tell me about your world, about my family there," he said finally, "then I'll give you whatever help I can."

"I'll be glad to. Even if you don't want to help us, I want to tell you about the life another you is living, because it's a good life, filled with love and success and happiness. It's the life you deserved here that was taken from you, but for whatever comfort it's worth, that better life is out there, and you're living it to its fullest."

Alfred smiled, a real smile for the first time since we'd met him. "That sounds like a gift, a true gift, and one I'll treasure forever."

CHAPTER 54

MARTINI AND I RACED OFF to Charles de Gaulle air-port. This time when we went into the men's room I made him check under the stall door right away. We zipped right out again, never slowing down to anything resembling slow.

"There's another dead body in there," he said, voice tight, as we left the airport as fast as we'd come. "And I'm sure it's one of our Secret Service men. That's too much of a coincidence."

"We call it a frame-up where I come from."

"We call it that here, too. But who the hell could be framing us? I mean, who knows that we were coming here?"

"Well, half of the Embassy, basically."

"They're all trustworthy. And I say that based on the fact that Chuck has everyone swept and searched for emotional overlays and the like regularly and randomly, and there isn't a human without an emotional overlay or blocker on them who can lie to me."

Tried really hard not to think of the one human who was fooling and lying to Martini and Charles both on a regular basis, but there wasn't any music around for me to focus on.

Martini headed us into a deserted alleyway in an industrial area and stopped. "The Mastermind is a human and you're sure that he's lying to me on a regular basis. Just tell me this—is it Chuck?"

"What the hell? Are you high?"

"We're deadly allergic to alcohol and we don't do drugs as a rule, so no."

"No. The Mastermind hates Charles. Chuckie, sorry. Both, really, in my world and yours. And Malcolm and I both confirmed that to you already. Why are you even asking this?"

"Because you're thinking of him, of Chuck."

"Because the Mastermind is fooling him and you both. And therefore he's fooling everyone else."

Martini stared at me. "Oh. God." He looked pale. "I hope I'm wrong, but I know I'm not."

"Crap. Did you just read my mind or my emotions?"

"No, actually. I just thought about what you said. There's really only one person who Chuck fully trusts aside from Kitty, and that would mean only one person who could, therefore, fool him." He swallowed. "And the Secret Service reports up to him. And that means if one of them did some kind of random check, then they'd discover we weren't in our rooms, badger Christopher, Amy, Len, and Kyle, and they'd tell them where we went, because we trust those people. We're not telling them about *you*, but telling them about our mission to save the day? They'd tell them that."

"Does the Secret Service just randomly drop into your bedroom?"

"They do if Cliff Goodman tells them to. He's the Mastermind, isn't he?"

There was no way I was going to hide this from Martini, not when he was asking me directly. And I could tell he'd gotten confirmation from my emotions or mind before I answered. "Yes. And, Jeff, if we let him know that we know, he's going to destroy everyone."

Martini ran his hand through his hair. "And, per everyone, your Cosmic Alternate in particular, I can't lie. At all. I'd grab an emotional blocker, only he'll read my face and actions, won't he?"

"Yeah, I'm pretty sure he will. So, what do we do?"

"I have no idea. At all. This is usually the time when my

Kitty comes up with some insane plan that usually means some or all of us, me in particular, almost die, and yet we manage to survive, most of us, anyway, and then she saves the day." He looked at me hopefully. "So, whatcha got?"

Now wasn't the time to say that I had nada. Now was the time to Cowgirl Up and accept that if my CA could do it, then it stood to reason that I could do it, too. Whatever "it" was or was going to be.

"Gimme a mo. Need to ponder."

For whatever reason, me saying this made Martini relax. "Take your time. Well, not a lot of time, but no rush." He looked expectant. Remembered that they were used to my CA thinking aloud. Decided to throw the poor man a bone.

"Okay, so we can't tell Chuckie, because he will just try to kill Goodman, and even if he succeeds, we lose because he gets killed or goes to prison."

"Right. No telling Chuck is rule one."

"So, we need to not use his name anymore and go back to what you've been calling him—the Mastermind." Martini nodded. "We need to figure out why the Mastermind doesn't want us making things right with Australia."

"Why—oh. Got it. You have a fix, and if someone got one of those in the know at the Embassy to talk, they'd be focused on explaining how you have this great fix that will solve everything to explain why we snuck out."

"Yeah. Dead bodies suggest that someone wants to ensure we can't fix things up with Australia quickly or easily, so there must be a reason the Mastermind wants this political unrest to go on."

"Anti-alien sentiments going strong would be my guess. Get us on the run enough, and we ask Alpha Four to let us come home."

"Sounds right to me. Where did you send the gifts, the ones we bought? Back to the Embassy?" Tried not to ask that with dread in my voice. Failed, if Martini chuckling was any indication.

"I sent them to Sydney Base, just in case. Figured it was

safer for them to be within an A-C facility than in the Embassy. And no one will give them to anyone but you or me—I made that order clear."

"And you used to be Head of Field, right? So it's like you're the retired president or head of the military for all of them. They'll listen to you even over James, won't they?"

"Depends on the order, but in this case, no one's going to override my order unless you and I are dead."

"Let's avoid that outcome. So, okay, the gifts went elsewhere, thank God. Did you tell anyone at the Embassy about this decision?"

He grimaced. "I did. I told Christopher so he could back us up if necessary."

"They're being harangued by Cliff, either in person or via the Secret Service, and so, yeah, Christopher says things are fine and the gifts are in Oz, what's the big freaking deal."

"Sounds about right." Martini stiffened. "He's with Jamie!"

Grabbed his arm just before he took off. *"Stop!"*

He froze. "Why? He's got our daughter."

"No. If he's there he's in a room full of people who are there *only* to protect Jamie. That man's been around your daughter for as long as you've known him. He's not going to take her, not where anyone could see, not until he's either set up to win and take the prize right then, or until his hand is forced. You rampaging in will force his hand. Beside, I'm betting your plethora of animals aren't going to let anyone near her."

"Yeah. Why haven't the Poofs or Peregrines killed him off yet? They're supposed to guard us."

"Why does a dog not bite the friend of yours the dog hates? Because you, the owner, like that friend and tell the dog to behave."

"But the Poofs think independently."

"Do they? You all told me my CA has Doctor Doolittle skills. And if Charles trusts or hates someone, I trust him. Surely she's the same way with Chuckie."

"She is. That's what you and Buchanan determined, isn't it?"

"Yeah. If he could fool Chuckie, then he's fooling my CA, and that means the rest of you are being fooled. But this is us rehashing what we know. The animals are just that—animals. Stop expecting them to think like people. They don't, and why they have or haven't done something to the Mastermind isn't our issue right now. What I want to know is how in the world he could have gotten to the bathrooms we'd be using. I mean, how would he know?"

"We have A-Cs who are . . . traitors."

"Are they here? In France? Following us?"

He shook his head. "I don't know. We've caught some of them. But not all."

"Why didn't we take a floater gate?"

"I wanted to stay under the radar. Using a floater requires coordination with the Dome. Using a regular gate doesn't."

"That's it. The Mastermind knows your playbook, and he's a master chess player. So he figured out your moves, and put something in your way to incriminate you. I wonder if the other dead person is anyone you know."

"I don't think it's safe to go back to Gare du Nord. But . . ." Martini grabbed my hand and we were off again. This time we went to the Orly airport, and, as per usual, visited one of the men's rooms.

Martini took a long look under the Special Stall and then raced us back to the alleyway we'd been to before. Now he looked grim and ill, both. Wasn't his best look, but that could be said for everyone. Was sure I was going to match this look in a moment.

"Who is it and how were they killed? I can tell you know them by your totally-not-able-to-lie expression of horror."

He swallowed hard. "The two I saw . . . both their throats were slit. Based on the blood you said you saw pooling at the first gate, the first one's throat was likely slit as well. And . . . this third man is another from your Secret Service detail."

CHAPTER 55

I **DIDN'T KNOW ANY OF THE MEN** on my detail, but I knew my CA did. And it didn't matter. These men had jobs where they willingly put their lives on the line. To be murdered by some brilliant lunatic they reported up to in order to make his take over the world plans work better was obscene.

"He sent them after us."

"Or they went once they realized we were gone." Martini ran his hand through his hair again. "But, it makes no sense. Why go to these three locations? We were in a group, it's not like we'd normally split up."

"Well, first off, we don't know that there aren't more bodies littered throughout the Paris transportation system's men's rooms. And from what I've seen, you guys split up all the time. But let's err on the side of ridiculous optimism and assume that they went to the three gates you'd be most likely to pick."

"Yeah," Martini said slowly. "We normally use the Metro gate because of where it's located, but there are other main Metro stations we use as well. And du Gaulle is the airport of choice, Orly would almost always be second, but there are other airports available as well."

"Then there are either more dead Secret Service agents in the other obvious places or the Mastermind just figured one of those three places would work. The problem is that while Chuckie, Richard, and Malcolm actually have airtight alibis, you and I now do not."

Martini stiffened. "He can't know about that."

"What do you mean?"

"I mean the Mastermind cannot know that you ran into someone you know in your universe that we absolutely did not know in this one. You finding Amadhia altered both what we did and where we went, and how long we took, too. And it's why Chuck and the others have that airtight alibi. Because they're with Amadhia, in a recording studio with a bunch of musicians, not with us."

Considered this. I hadn't seen Malcolm unless he'd wanted me to see him, and he told me he was probably shadowing me in my universe, too, and while he felt familiar, I didn't know him in my world, meaning he was really good at not being seen. "Is throat slitting an A-C thing?"

"No, but the C.I.A. loves it. He's not trying to frame you and me, is he? He's trying to frame either Chuck or Buchanan."

"Call Malcolm, we need to talk to him."

Martini nodded, pulled out his phone, and dialed. "Hi, where are you? Great. Stay there. Don't leave. Make sure all three of you stay with those people until we tell you otherwise. Yeah, putting you onto speaker."

"What's going on?" Malcolm asked. We filled him in quickly. "Ah. I've been made. It happened during what Missus Chief calls Operation Infiltration. When . . ."

"When Naomi was killed," Martini said quietly to me. "Got it," he said toward the phone. "So, this is being done to frame you, isn't it?"

"I think so. I've done my best not to be noticed by the Mastermind, but—"

"I know who it is," Martini said. "Not Kitty's fault, by the way, I figured it out based on what's going on. But yeah, if I was trying to take over, I'd want you out of the way. Because I know what the Mastermind wants is Kitty dead."

"Go to the Eiffel Tower, and go now," Malcolm said. "Get to the top and make out. Make sure you're seen."

"What?" we both said in unison.

"You have to have an alibi for when the agents were murdered. We have one. You don't. You were supposedly going home. But, hey, it's Paris, it's romance, you two went to the Left Bank, walked along the Seine, and then went to the top of the Tower. Get over there, make it work. People will buy it if you weren't seen near the bathrooms."

"We bought a present for Jamie at the Metro."

Malcolm cursed. "I paid cash," Martini said. "And we really weren't in there a long time."

"We stopped to get her a prezzie, I saw a poster of the Eiffel Tower, went into a pout about us being in the most romantic city in the world and only working, we then went to the Left Bank, walked along the river, and then went to the Tower."

"That works," Malcolm said.

"I called on our secured lines," Martini added. "We just need to somehow ensure that no one at Centaurion gives Homeland Security or any other agency this information."

Malcolm laughed. "They won't. Reader hates all the Alphabet Agencies and doesn't like them in our business. We're fine. Now, get off the phone and get your alibi in place. And I mean it, you need to make out and make it real, or we're all incriminated in some way and the Mastermind knows we're on to him."

We hung up, Martini grabbed my hand, and we took off again. "We won't have been seen at the right times."

"No, I think we can make it work." He zipped us by a popular coffeehouse on the Left Bank side close to the Tower. We went into the back alley, stopped hyperspeeding, and left, arms around each other, strolling along as if we'd been so for quite a while. "I'm following your CA's game plan. Let's ensure we're seen, looking relaxed and casual."

"Works for me."

We went in and waited in line to order. "Enjoying our

romantic side trip?" he asked me in a normal voice, meaning those around us could hear him.

"Oh yes. Walking along La Rive Gauche was wonderful and so romantic. I can't wait to go to the top of the Eiffel Tower."

He nuzzled me. "I'll make it worth your time."

I giggled. "I know you will."

We got cafés au lait and then left the coffeehouse. The grounds around the Eiffel Tower were beautiful, even at the end of winter, and we strolled through them, arms around each other, sipping coffee and talking about nothing of consequence other than how fun it was to be playing hooky in Paris.

While we wandered, I did my best to think if we'd left fingerprints anywhere. Only at the gift shop in the Metro. The bathrooms were the kind with open main doors, and we hadn't touched the stalls. This was all good.

Prepping to make out with a man who wasn't actually my husband wasn't. However, this wasn't adultery so much as spycraft. And since I'd just found out that my husband was apparently a spy, there was always the possibility that he'd had to make out with some glamorous female agent or asset. And even if he hadn't, it wasn't as though I was looking forward to making out with Martini.

Blithely lying to myself and prattling about Paris, we reached the Tower. Thankfully it was open every day, and we were well past opening time. We got tickets and instead of going up in the elevators, we took the stairs.

"You up to this?" Martini asked me quietly.

"Sure, I'm in shape." I hoped.

He squeezed my hand. "I'll help, don't worry."

We trotted up the stairs, all seven hundred plus of them. Martini used hyperspeed when we weren't near anyone else, and sometimes just to give us a little boost. It helped, and I wasn't completely exhausted by the time we reached the top. And we'd been seen by a lot of people.

The view from the top of the Tower was amazing, as always. Charles and I had come here, of course, on our honeymoon. And we'd made out up here, too, also of course. Figured that Martini and my CA had, as well, since from what I'd picked up, they'd been to Paris more than once.

We were up high, it was February, the air was cold, and I wasn't dressed warmly enough. Started shivering the moment I recovered from the stairs.

Martini opened his suit jacket and pulled me in close to him. "Let me keep you warm, baby." He wrapped the jacket and his arms around me and I snuggled into his chest.

He was warm and his heartbeats were soothing, and I relaxed against him and snuggled closer, wrapping my arms around his waist, while he held me just a little tighter.

This was a great option—we looked incredibly romantic, intimate, and relaxed with each other—all without sucking face. I realized Martini must have been having the same adultery issues and worries that I was, had realized this was an option before I had, and had taken appropriate action.

Looked up at him. "You really are the greatest guy in the world, you know that?"

He smiled slowly. "I never get tired of hearing you say that, baby."

Our gazes were locked and I was reminded again of how easily I could believe my CA had fallen, and fallen hard, for this man. He wasn't trying to be sexy and romantic, he just managed it naturally.

What might have happened next was anyone's guess, but we were both saved by the ringtone. Martini sighed, let go of me with one arm, and dug his phone out. Not the same phone he'd used to call Malcolm, meaning this was probably a call from someone who wasn't in the A-C Special Phone System.

"Hello? Yeah." He moved us away to a part of the platform where no one else was. "Yes, we snuck out because Kitty didn't want this shopping trip to become a media circus. Still in Paris. At the Eiffel Tower. Because the French don't care what we do, and Kitty wanted to have an hour where we just felt like a happy, married couple, not the current black sheep of the political stratosphere."

He rolled his eyes. "Yes, I know, we've been bad. Again. Harangue me when we're home. What? No, we didn't tell them to follow us, why would we? We have our own protection and, again, it's hard to be stealthy while being trailed by your people."

His eyes narrowed, but he kept his tone the same. "Yes, as a matter of fact, I do know exactly where he is, and has been. He's with Richard and Chuck and a room full of musicians. It's a long story. One I don't want to tell you over the phone. Yes, I can get you the address, but I have to get off the phone to do so. I'll text it to you. You want us to wait here or take a gate back? Got it." He hung up and sent a text.

"Who was that?"

"Hang on." His phone beeped, he grunted, then sent another text.

"Waiting impatiently here."

"Just had to make sure I got that done. My caller was none other than Cliff Goodman. Asking me if I knew the whereabouts of all the men assigned to your Secret Service night detail."

CHAPTER 56

"**W**OW. He decided to cover all the bases, didn't he?"

"We're going to find out. He didn't tell me why he was trying to find them, by the way. And he didn't sound like he was trying to get me to incriminate either myself or you. It's clearly an attempt to frame Buchanan. He's normally not with us so much as tailing us from the shadows."

"You sounded fine, by the way. I had to ask who it was because it didn't sound like someone you wanted to kill."

"One small favor, but I'll take it. It's easier over the phone. No bet for how I'm going to do when we actually see him face-to-face."

"We'll worry about that when we get there. You know, in the next few minutes. So, now what do we do?"

"Cliff wants us to use a floater gate to get home right away."

"Meaning he doesn't want us to see what's at the other gates."

"That's my bet, yeah." He dialed the phone. "Hey James, sorry to wake you. Oh? Well, yeah, sorry about that, too. We need a floater. Not on my mark yet. I think it would make more sense for us to get down to the bottom of the Eiffel Tower first. Yes, I'll send you a text when we're ready. Thanks." He hung up.

"You used the tapped line for those texts and that call."

"Regardless of your universe of origin, we just can't put anything past you, can we, baby? Yes. Cliff expected me to get him an address and call James. Nothing says 'we have our own phones you have no access to' like me making that call or sending that text from another line. James will know something's up—we only use the tapped phones if we have to, meaning he's on alert."

"So, elevator or stairs to get down?"

"Honestly, based on the waiting line for the elevators, the stairs are going to be fastest."

"Oh good. I need the exercise."

Martini chuckled, took my hand, and we started down the many hundreds of steps. Going down was always faster than going up, and again he used hyperspeed to move us more quickly when we had sections where we were alone.

Reached the bottom and Martini and I strolled off, still not looking as if we had a care in the world. Reached some heavy foliage in the park around the Tower and then he sent a text to James.

A shimmering in the air appeared before us, Martini swung me up into his arms, I buried my face in his neck, and he stepped us through.

The trip back was just as nauseating as the trip to Paris had been. Only this time I had food and drink in my stomach. Managed not to throw up, possibly because of the hyperspeeding medicine, but only just.

We landed in our apartment, which was loaded with people, including Goodman. However, nausea had given me an idea for at least a short term way to avoid Goodman. "We'll let you yell at us later, we need to check on Jamie."

Martini didn't even put me down, he just nodded and zipped us into her room. She was awake, with most of the animals on the bed with her. "Mommy, Daddy, did you have a fun trip?"

Martini put me down. "We sure did. And we brought you a present."

She looked surprised. "Really?"

Pulled it out of my purse. "Really." It was a soft stuffed striped pink cat that said "Paris, Je T'aime" in a heart on its chest. "I know it's not the same as having real kitties, but—" But it was cute and the only pink thing the gift shop had carried.

She took it from me and hugged it. "It's so pretty!" She showed it to all the animals, who sniffed it obligingly while giving me betrayed looks. Then Jamie bounded up and gave me and Martini kisses. "Thank you so much, Mommy and Daddy! I'm going to name him Stripes!"

"Great name. Let's get you dressed, Jamie-Kat," Martini said. "Mommy and Daddy have to go to work."

She frowned. "Couldn't Mommy and I go to the zoo today?"

"Actually, I think we're going to Australia today, Jamie. And you're coming with us."

"Oh, okay, Mommy! Can we go to the zoo in Australia?"

"If we have time, absolutely."

"Yay!" Jamie trotted off to her bathroom, still holding her stuffed cat.

"You stay and help her get ready," I said to Martini. "I'll handle the others. That keeps you away from certain people longer."

He grinned. "I love how you think. And Jamie really loves that toy, by the way, she wasn't pretending."

"She has lots of toys that I've seen, I'm just glad she likes this one."

He nodded. "We usually don't bring her back anything when we go on, ah, trips like we just did."

"Ah." Considered all that had happened. "You probably don't have time."

He chuckled. "That's frequently true, yeah." He kissed my cheek then followed Jamie to the bathroom.

Looked at the animals, who were still looking at me as if I was a traitor. "Having stuffed animals doesn't make anyone love the real animals any less, you know." They weren't appeased. "It's pink. None of you are pink. That's why she's so excited."

The animals chose to allow this to mollify them, and I steeled myself for the next round of madness and subterfuge. Hoped I could manage it without Martini or Malcolm around to help me.

Stepped out of the room to a sea of frowny faces. In addition to My Favorite Mastermind and those who'd been in the room when we'd left, Singh, James, Paul, Crawford, Lorraine, Claudia, and Serene had piled in. Decided pretending I had no idea of what was actually going on was in everyone's best interests. "Look, I know we were bad, but we found what I know will smooth things over with the PM couple. So, we snuck out. It's not the end of the world."

"It is for eight of your Secret Service detail," Goodman said.

"What? You can't fire those guys. It's not their fault!"

He shook his head. "No, Kitty, that's not what I mean. They went after you two—each one went to a different gate where we figured you might be. And . . ." He looked upset. I was impressed. He really was a good actor.

"And what? What happened?"

"They're all dead," Amy said, sounding horrified. Everyone in the room looked horrified, which wasn't a surprise. "Someone slit their throats."

"Oh my God. That's horrible. Who? Why?"

Goodman took a deep breath. "Frankly, the only suspect we have is someone you're not going to like."

"He thinks Buchanan did it," Christopher snapped. "However, I don't believe it."

Points to Christopher. "I don't, either, in no small part because Malcolm was with us the entire time. He wouldn't let us leave without being right there with us, Richard, and Chuckie the whole time. As far as I know, he's still with Richard and Chuckie and several other people. Malcolm was never out of our sight until Jeff and I went to the Metro station. We got Jamie a present, and then," I shrugged, "well, I just wanted to, you know, have a little time where no one was yelling at me."

And points to me, because no one in the room, Goodman included, looked like they didn't believe my story. Which was, essentially, true, so go team.

"We've confirmed with my dad that Buchanan, and Reynolds, were basically never out of his sight. Neither one of them have hyperspeed, so there's no way they did some side trip, and before you try to suggest it, my dad didn't, either." Christopher was snarling. Had the distinct impression he didn't like Goodman. Good. It would make revealing the truth, when the time came, a tiny bit easier.

"There's no way Richard would do something like this," Paul said. "Ever."

"Neither would Reynolds," Crawford added. "And, frankly, Buchanan wouldn't kill anyone who wasn't a threat to Kitty or Jamie." The Three Beauty Queens nodded their agreement.

"I think it was the Mastermind," Amy said. "It sounds just like him. He must have been trying to do something against Jeff and Kitty and wanted their Secret Service detail out of the way."

My jaw dropped. I hadn't credited Amy with anything like this level of ability to think. "You think so?" I managed.

She nodded. So did everyone else, including Goodman. "Actually . . . that makes sense." He looked ill. "But that means . . ."

"What?" I asked. Wanted to see where he was going with it.

"The only being able to kill eight people at different locations basically at the same time would be an A-C."

The whole room gasped. I didn't, but I managed to slap a look of worry on my face.

I was, frankly, hella impressed. In one minute Goodman had managed to take an utter frame-up failure and turn it into something that was now going to have every person in the room suspecting every A-C on the planet. No wonder everyone was having trouble figuring out who the Mastermind was—he was manipulating every success *and* every failure to his advantage.

"Okay," I said slowly. "But five minutes ago you were convinced it was Malcolm. He's not an A-C. How would he have done those eight murders?"

Goodman nodded. "That's a good question, Kitty. What I'd kind of assumed was that Buchanan had followed you and Jeff and lain in wait for whoever was coming after you. Killed one, realized others weren't coming, and then gated to the other obvious gates in Paris to take care of the others."

"Ignoring the entire 'why in the world would he do that' question, *how* would he, since he's not an A-C?"

Goodman looked sheepish. "I guess I didn't think it through."

Meaning he'd hoped to make the frame-up so convincing that no one would ask the obvious questions until it was too late—like after Malcolm had been shot dead for "resisting arrest" or similar.

"In this country, we demand a little thing called proof," James said.

"And we want proof before you accuse anyone else of this heinous crime," Singh said. His voice wasn't soothing—it was quite crisp and official. Had a feeling he wasn't happy with anyone right now. Considering he was in charge of PR, could feel his pain.

"Kitty's question's the key one, though," Crawford added.

"A smarter way of doing it would be to kill them here," Amy suggested. "You know, kill them right *at* the gate, then shove them through to their respective locations."

"Wow, you've given that a lot of thought?" I asked because it seemed amazingly logical and also a likely answer for how the agents had been killed. Pondered how someone would do that quickly without any of the victims, especially victims two through eight, suspecting. A disguised piano wire at neck height would do it, especially if the killer was able to manipulate the gates quickly. Which again indicated an A-C. Decided to keep this theory to myself for now.

She blushed. "Sort of. There are so many people trying to kill us so often, I've tried to come up with all the ways they could, so that we can counter them."

"Well done."

She brightened up. "Thanks, Kitty!"

"The love in the room is nice," Goodman said dryly, "but I have eight dead Secret Service agents and no clue for who the culprit is, other than that he or she is either an A-C and/ or lives in the Embassy. And, that means I actually have to hold all of you for questioning, because Amy's explanation makes logical sense."

Crap. He'd once again turned the tables and gotten exactly what he wanted. Only more so.

CHAPTER 57

IT WAS A GOOD THING I was a fast talker and Alfred,
being an A-C, could hear at hyperspeed, because there was
a lot of ground to cover. By the time I was done, I was hoarse
and he was both happier and sadder than he'd been before.
But he was also angry. And, as I'd been learning for the past
few years, anger could be a very good, powerful, and moti-
vating emotion.

"Whatever I can do to help you stop this madman, I'll do.
And I'll do what I can to help you get back home afterward.
Your world sounds . . . so much better than this one."

"It is in some ways." Looked at Cox and Stripes and
thought about Charlie and Max. "And in some ways this one
is better. But what I want is to ensure that the Mastermind
doesn't get to do to Earth what your father did to Alpha
Four."

"Are you advocating murdering him?" Alfred asked.

"I'm fairly sure that before we have that option he's going
to have a weapon pointed at people we care about, or innocents, or both, and we're not going to have that particular
moral quandary. I *am* advocating not letting him or LaRue
live long enough to create the cloning process that I'm sure
they're working on."

"Incarceration isn't an option?" Alfred didn't sound hopeful so much as he seemed to be checking off boxes in his head.

"No. The problem every government has, that plays right into the League of Evil Geniuses' hands, is that when you have a brilliant mind in captivity, you want to get what you can from said mind. But that just means the bad guys are creating escape plans, takeover plans, and turn-the-tables plans. And they win more often than not, in part because there are always evil people scattered throughout every government and they can smell their own."

"So a straight fight is likely out," Alfred said.

"Yes, and more than that, we don't want either you or me landing in their hands, because the moment Cliff or LaRue realize that, for this world, we're superheroes, they will do all the things you're afraid the various Earth governments will do to you, only more so, with a great deal of horrific glee, and as drawn out and painfully as possible."

Alfred shuddered. "Let's not allow that to happen."

"We need a plan," Cox said. "Beyond terrifying Alfred. Because I'm supposed to report to my new post in a couple of hours, and I don't know if I should or not."

"Until we know where Cliff and LaRue are holed up, we have an entire world to search. And, hyperspeed and the tunnels or not, Alfred and I can't search all of Earth in a couple of hours. Without gate technology, I'm not sure that we can safely get off the continent."

Harlie mewled. "Hush," Alfred said gently.

"No, go on, Harlie."

"Excuse me?" Cox said.

"Oh, right. I left out one specific superpower I have. I'm kind of Doctor Doolittle."

"In addition to being Wolverine?"

"Yeah. But that's not important now. I mean, it is, because Harlie thinks it can find where Cliff hides out."

"How?" Cox asked flatly. "And I'm asking because if you have these things in your world, why haven't they found your Mastermind already and dealt with him?"

"They're not really from . . . around here. And by that I mean they aren't from Alpha Four, either. Alfred, you probably don't know this, but the Poofs are from the Black Hole Universe. And therefore they have abilities we don't. But their original owner is a Free Will Fanatic, to put it mildly. And in order for an individual to have free will, other individuals can't do everything for our first individual, or they're taking said free will away."

Both men stared at me. "That seems like a tenuous reason," Alfred said finally.

"Well, there's more to it. In my world, just killing the Mastermind won't solve anything. Remember that cloning stuff I told you about? Kill him, they just make a new one and Leventhal Reid takes over again. We may have blown up their facility, but I guarantee they're back in action somewhere else, because Reid and LaRue got away." Couldn't repress the shudder. "I'll take our current Mastermind over Reid. I'll take anyone over Reid."

"Let's get back to what the Poof said," Cox suggested. "How could it find someone Alfred's never seen?"

"Well, Harlie could go with you to meet Cliff."

"Yes, but that won't solve it," Alfred said. "You said yourself you have no idea how long you'll be here before whatever put you here will send you home. You have a small commando force, if we can even call three people and two animals that. We can't afford to take our time—we may not have much of it left."

"I'm open to suggestions, Alfred. You're the scientific genius, not me. I'm Megalomaniac Girl, not Science Woman."

Alfred cocked his head at me. "Okay. Then . . . if you were this person, in this world, with all the restrictions humans have—in other words, the world you *thought* you were in before you met . . . my son—where would you base your secret stronghold?"

"Great question. Gimme a mo and lemme ponder. Okay, so Cliff has to show up at Langley on a regular basis. So while a country like Belarus sounds all promising and such, as does the country of Corporation origin, otherwise known as Cuba, somewhere outside of the U.S. seems unwieldy and therefore unlikely."

"I thought you said you were going to ponder," Alfred said politely.

"Oh, sorry. This is how I ponder. Out loud. So you all get to share in the wonder that is my mental process. Full transparency, that's me. Some people pay money for this opportunity."

"Your universe must be starved for entertainment, ma'am."

"Careful, Bill. Stripes can take over the sidekick role and reduce you to mascot in a New York Minute. And while New York seems like a great choice, I doubt that Cliff's holed up there—it's just too crowded and space is at too much of a premium. And neither he nor Reid had the Corporation's resources until recently."

"Millions of people all on top of each other means that you're more likely to be spotted somehow," Alfred agreed.

"Right. So, somewhere with more, if not space, then privacy, and fewer potential prying eyes. Cliff has to have a residence in D.C., but he's in the C.I.A., so there's no way that he's leaving clues here for his coworkers to discover. But Chuckie, known here as Charles, has two homes, on either side of the world. Presumably because he's using the jet-setting lifestyle as his main cover."

"Makes sense, if the Current Sidekick is allowed to chime in on the 'pondering session,' ma'am."

"Chime away, Lunatic Lad."

"I'm reporting into a division that is publicly facing, meaning that Goodman is unlikely to be doing the same kind of covert or clandestine ops that Chuckie known here as Charles is."

"Sarcasm is so unbefitting an officer and a gentleman, Bill."

"But you've made it an art form, ma'am, and I just want to represent."

"Fine, fine. And you're right, so that means that Cliff can't go too far afield whenever he wants to visit his Secret Lair of Evil, meaning he's probably chosen it on the East Coast somewhere. And he has to be somewhere that it's easy for him to deal with the Corporation's employees, both here and in Cuba."

Stopped and ran that sentence back in my head. "Oh. Wow. And I'll give myself the 'duh' on this one because Chuckie here known as Charles and Jeff aren't here to do it for me. He's freaking based out of Florida, isn't he?"

"Miami would be my guess, ma'am. He's from there originally, as was Leventhal Reid. Miami's got a huge Cuban population, and a ton of crime."

Considered this. "Miami is the obvious choice, right? So why does it feel wrong to me?"

"So, not Miami?" Cox asked. "Just to be sure that in the moment we've found the obvious answer you immediately think it's wrong."

"I have more experience with this kind of crap. And I don't think Miami's right."

"Where then, and why not?" Alfred asked. "Because I'm with William—it seems like the most convenient choice."

"Extremely convenient," Cox said, sitting up straight. "So if I'm following Kitty's logic, he won't be based in Miami because it *is* obvious. He's smarter than that, right?"

"Right, because the first place you're going to look for whoever's running the Corporation is Miami, right?" Both men nodded. "But Cliff is a master chess player. And you don't win by being obvious, unless it's a feint that you're using to fool your opponent." Looked at Alfred. "This universe is closer to mine than I'd originally thought. So why wouldn't things be here that are there?"

"I'm not following you, I'm sorry," Alfred said.

"And it's only about five or six hours from where they live in my world to Miami. And there's plenty of ocean around that area and, once you're a little south of the Cape, there's an Air Force Base, which he could access with his C.I.A. credentials without issue."

"I'm with Alfred, ma'am. Not following you at all now."

"Well, guys it's like this—because I truly understand Ironic Justice, I'm betting I know exactly where Cliff's very large and very private estate happens to be."

CHAPTER 58

"A ND, as a sort of side benefit, you, Alfred, can see where your counterpart lives."

"If you say so." Alfred didn't sound convinced. "We can get to Florida fairly quickly, though, so it's worth it to look."

"I don't know that I can handle the hyperspeed that long, sir, and trooper though he is, I doubt the cat can, either."

"Oh, we're not going to be running," Alfred said. He stood. "However, you two should eat something before we go."

"I could probably find the will to force something down," I admitted.

Cox nodded. "I have nothing in my stomach and am finally at a point where eating doesn't sound horrible."

Alfred whipped up a rather nice couple of sandwiches using hyperspeed, and provided more food for Stripes and Harlie as well. Cox, the animals, and I all munched while Alfred bustled about, muttering to himself.

"You should eat, too, sir," Cox said.

"Oh, I already did. Hyperspeed, son, it's good for everything."

"You know, Alfred, the A-Cs on my world have to be taught from birth how to do things at human speeds. How did you learn?"

"Necessity is the mother of invention, Kitty."

"And panic is the father of ability. Yeah, right there with you."

"Is everyone done eating?" Nods and purrs to the affirmative were given. "Excellent. And now that you've eaten, both you and Stripes shouldn't have any issues with hyperspeed for at least a week, William."

"How so? I tossed an entire day's worth of food up when Kitty showed me what she could do earlier."

"I've created a powder that allows mammals to deal with supersonic speeds without issue. Originally created for NASA and various high-speed sports. I gave some to Kitty, too, because we're going to be going at supersonic speeds. You all just ingested it with your food, and don't worry, there are no side effects."

"I remain incredibly impressed." Tito had created Hyperspeed Dramamine on my world, it made sense that Alfred had done the same here.

"It's always nice to be appreciated. Now, let's get going." He handed me and Cox a set of facemasks each. They were similar to gas masks, but a lot less creepy. "Put those on, they'll protect your eyes and let you breathe normally." He produced similar for Stripes, who obliged and allowed the contraption to be affixed to his head. "Good kitty," Alfred said. "Such a brave boy."

"You have masks for cats just lying about?"

"Oh no," he said with a chuckle. "I put this one together while you were eating. Hyperspeed, you know."

I hadn't really noticed, but then I'd been focused on eating, so Alfred could have put an elephant together and I'd have missed it. "Gotcha. Doesn't Harlie need a mask?" I asked as Alfred put a mask on as well.

"No, Harlie has no issues with how we're going to travel. Earpieces in, we need to stay connected."

These were similar to what the bad guys wore in *The Matrix*, only they went into both ears and attached behind our heads, hooking into the masks, with a small transmitter connected to the tubes and masks sitting at the back of our heads. I could still hear everyone—in fact, I could hear more than just us, but it wasn't painful. Was glad I didn't care what my hair was going to look like once we took this gear off. However, we were essentially unrecognizable with this stuff on.

Completing our War Ensembles, Alfred handed each of us a ball of what appeared to be really slick black Silly Putty. "Smash them onto your chests."

Cox and I did so, and were instantly enveloped in a slick, lightweight bodysuit that went up to our necks, and covered everything else on our bodies, while still going over our clothes. Was glad I'd put my purse down before I'd gotten "dressed," but once we were suited up, I put it back over my neck.

The Coach bag wasn't nearly as incognito as what I usually carried, however. Alfred frowned at it, and put a tiny speck of the Super Silly Putty on the purse. It was covered the same way the rest of us were, and it now resembled the purse I was used to. I was good with this.

"What about Stripes?" Alfred was clearly prepping us for battle and I didn't want Stripes to have less protection than the rest of us.

"I can put this onto him as well, if he's willing."

Stripes meowed. "He wants to know what happens if he has an itch or the need to wash."

"He can scratch through the body armor, but I don't recommend licking it."

Stripes considered his options and meowed at me. "He's willing to give it a shot if you can take it off of him if he can't stand it."

"Yes, I can. It's easy to remove—you just peel it off."

Cox gave it a shot. "Not peeling for me, sir."

"Oh, well, you have to start at the neck and go down, William." Alfred said this as if it were totally obvious. Was glad Cox had taken one for the team and given it a try before I had.

Cox did as instructed and the suit rolled down. He let go and it slid back up into place. "Impressive, sir. What does it do?"

"It will protect us from the elements, including going faster than hyperspeed. It also repels projectiles. It can't stop all of them, but it's similar to Kevlar. Only the next iteration."

"The military and police force could use something like this," Cox said.

"In due time," Alfred said, concentrating on getting the suit onto Stripes.

"Meaning you sold them Kevlar already but you're not sure that you can trust the world with this improvement."

Alfred shot a smile at me. "Yes, exactly."

Looked at Cox. "Protecting Alfred and keeping him out of our enemies' hands is Job One."

"I agree, ma'am."

"Alright, we're all set." Alfred sounded pleased and just a little bit excited. Stripes looked like a Nightmare Cat, but then, the rest of us looked like Nightmare People, so that fit. Picked the cat up and put him into my purse, and Harlie mewed at Alfred and jumped into the purse to join him. "That's fine," Alfred said with a chuckle. "You can ride in fancy comfort all you want, Harlie."

With that Alfred ushered us out, turned out all the lights, and locked the door behind us.

The masks had an infrared capability in the goggles, and probably some other extras. I could see as clearly as if the tunnels were lit with thousand-watt light bulbs, even though Alfred's lab hadn't seemed any brighter than it had before I'd put the goggles on.

Alfred zipped off at hyperspeed. I grabbed Cox and followed. We stopped shortly and Cox and Stripes both didn't even gag. We were at a wall, but when Alfred pushed against it in a pattern that looked random but clearly wasn't it opened up to reveal a large, perfectly square room.

"I know what this is. It's a Z'Porrah Power Cube room. Or it was." This room was filled with books. More books than the Library of Congress or the Library at Alexandria. Possibly put together.

Alfred went in and we followed him. It was a maze in

here, with shelf after shelf loaded with books. Some shelves moved to reveal more shelves and different paths. Decided this wasn't my kind of room and stayed very close to Alfred.

Alfred moved a few shelves in a very deliberate way that said "combination" to me—similarly to how Reader had moved the wine bottles in the cellar of Chuckie's now-destroyed house. "If you say so. They're all over the world—in every branch of the tunnel system. And some areas have more than one. However, there was nothing in these rooms when I found them. The doors were open and the rooms were empty."

"Huh." Thought about something Cox had said earlier as another shelf of books appeared. Alfred moved this one and took something from behind it, then put the shelf back. "So, maybe you're right, Bill. The Ancients didn't crash when they came here. On my world they died because they didn't wear spacesuits, though."

"How stupid are these so-called intelligent life forms, ma'am?"

"They're shape-shifters, remember. In my world, a Z'Porrah power cube is what we're pretty sure brought down the Ancient's spaceship."

"Well," Alfred said, as we headed back through the Maze of Books, "maybe in this world they were able to avoid the attack. And in doing so, that would have given them more time to study the atmosphere and make adjustments."

"That makes sense, actually. I have to figure the Ancients could and therefore would go after the power cubes, because they're weapons—the Z'Porrah were going to activate them to destroy the world when they came back to my world. But the Ancients are on our side, and they'd survived an attack, meaning they'd want to get rid of the Z'Porrah Weapons of Mass Destruction. Leaving the doors open was probably their way of saying 'nanner nanner' to any Z'Porrah that might drop by to check on things."

"Well, they've been lifesaving for me. I installed a door in the first one I found, where you found me. I didn't even explore much until I was safely set up there. Once I did . . ." Alfred shrugged. "Let's just say that I have all the storage and safe houses I'm going to ever need."

We left this room and he closed the wall. There was no way to tell that any part of the wall was a door. Alfred took off again and again we followed. Zigged and zagged a bit, then he stopped again. Once again, he pressed on the wall and once again it opened onto another perfectly square room.

Only this room definitely had something extra inside.

CHAPTER 59

THE ROOM LOOKED LIKE what I could only think of
as a futuristic motorcycle showroom. Only the motorcy-
cles were a little wider than the ones I was used to, and they
had running boards where the foot pegs would have been.

Cox whistled. "Can those go as fast as they look, sir?"

"Faster," Alfred said with some pride in his voice. He
went to one, sat on it, and pressed a button. A clear, oval
bubble went around the bike and rider. "It's a metallized plas-
ticine. Repels projectiles, protects the tires from punctures,
makes supersonic speeds easier and crashes far less fatal.
And it runs on self-sustaining batteries."

"It's like *Robotech*. And the laser shields we have in my
world. Don't give this to anyone." It was far too easy for me
to imagine this in a war setting, and while it would be great
to protect our own soldiers, it would inevitably be used by
the enemy, too. And even though we seemed stuck with it,
escalation rarely seemed to be the answer. However, Alfred
was basically the War Division all by himself. It was kind of
nice that he was sharing the credit with all the Dazzlers back
home. Of course, he had nothing else to do here as near as I
could tell, other than hide and tinker.

"No, I'm not planning on it. But they help me get around.
I have these placed in rooms all over—I keep several in each

one because while the batteries do recharge themselves, they need to charge when they're not used regularly, and I never want to be without an escape."

"I hear that. So, in my world, A-Cs can't use equipment like cars or planes because their reflexes are too good and they'll destroy the machinery. How did you get around that?"

He grinned. "Those are human-created machines. These were created by me, for me. You should be okay, but William may need some help." He pushed the button and his shield turned off. Alfred trotted over to a case against the far wall of the Futuristic Vehicle Showroom and grabbed two things that looked like robotic gauntlets.

"What are those?"

"Robotic gauntlets." Score one for me. "I made them in case I ever . . . found a friend I could trust." Tried not to let my heart hurt for Alfred. Failed. Utterly. "William, with these on your forearms, you'll be able to control the bike if necessary."

"If necessary?" Cox asked.

"I'll have your bikes programmed to go where Kitty tells us we're going. You shouldn't have to steer or control anything." Alfred shrugged. "But in case of a problem, the gauntlets are a failsafe. They'll allow you to stop the bike, if nothing else."

"Really don't let those fall into anyone else's hands." Was now sincerely worried about going on this raid because if we failed, Cliff got everything he'd ever need to take over this world quickly and easily. And everything he'd need to kill the people in this world I loved. Decided he'd get this stuff and/or Alfred over my dead body.

"Sir, are you sure you should come with us?" Clearly Cox had come to the same conclusions I had.

"Yes," Alfred said firmly. "You're going to need me, I'm sure. And if they do have advanced tech, someone has to be with you who can dismantle or destroy it, safely and effectively."

Couldn't argue. Jeff might not be in this world, but Alfred

was Jeff's father, and Jeff didn't hide from danger. And apparently, with a little bit of moral support, Alfred didn't hide, either.

"Before we take off, what, if anything, do I tell my superiors?" Cox asked, as Alfred showed us how to work our Supersonic Speeders. The gist was "let the bike do the work" and "this is the off switch in case something malfunctions."

"I want to tell you to call in sick, but I'm not sure how that works in the military."

"In the military it doesn't work at all, ma'am. However, I'm reporting into the C.I.A. right now."

"I'd call in," Alfred said. "Tell them you had a celebratory dinner and got food poisoning. Apologize profusely, but indicate that you're not going to report in for at least a day, maybe two."

Checked my watch. Jeff had gotten it for me. Shoved away the pang of fear that I'd never see him again. "It's just about dawn. If you call in now and say you've been throwing up all night, they should buy it."

"Can a call get through from here?"

"Not really. Let's do a test run and go back to the Memorial entrance. That's where you two came in, isn't it?"

"Yes, not through the golf course entrance."

"Those are the only two entrances for the D.C. area," Alfred confirmed. "We'll go slowly until you two get used to using the Speeders."

We walked the bikes out of the showroom, Alfred closed and did whatever to lock this room, then we mounted up and started off. Slowly, for these things, was at about what I called the slow hyperspeed rate. Fast enough that the human eye would still miss you, not so fast that you couldn't focus on a specific thing with human eyesight.

We had limited control over how fast we went—Alfred had programmed that for this leg of the journey—though the control dial for speed was easy to spot. So was the control to remove the autopilot. Frankly, all the controls on the speeders were more easily and obviously spotted than on any A-C "improved" vehicle I'd ever seen in my own universe.

Alfred had programmed the bikes to go about halfway up the tunnel slope that led up to the Lincoln Memorial entrance, and that's where we went. Then Cox made his call using a burner phone Alfred provided.

Cox sounded completely believable as someone who hadn't slept and was sick as a dog when he left his message, so we congratulated ourselves on what we hoped was a successful ruse, then Alfred programmed the speeders' GPS systems with a new set of coordinates.

Was really glad we had the shields as we took off, heading toward what I hoped was Florida, because we were going much faster than before. It was a relief that wind resistance on our bodies was basically nonexistent, because it would have been hard to stay on the speeder otherwise.

We zipped along and I couldn't have told anyone where we were in the tunnels, let alone where we were in relation to the world above, even if everyone's life had depended upon it. Sort of wished I'd brought Chuckie along—he'd have memorized everything already and have formulated a variety of escape routes as well.

Reader would have taken the bike off autopilot and mastered the speeder within five minutes. Buchanan probably would have, as well. And they were trained operatives. None of my little commando team was really prepped to handle whatever we were going to find in Florida, not even me, really.

However, we were doing this so that I wouldn't have to watch any or all of the actually trained guys die, so I stopped whining to myself.

The trip was scary and fun at the same time, racing through these underground tunnels faster than I'd ever gone before, other than when Christopher was pulling me along at his Super Flash Speed Level.

We stopped after we'd been going about an hour. Alfred turned off his shields and dismounted, and Cox and I followed suit,. Alfred opened a door to what turned out to be another Future Vehicles Showroom and had us change speeders. "Always pays to have the freshest batteries when you're about to tackle the hardest part of your journey," he said cheerfully. Had the distinct impression that this was the most fun Alfred had had since well before he'd been banished here.

The next leg of our journey was short. "We're under Cape Canaveral," Alfred told us when we stopped. "We'll need to go up and go the rest of the way on the surface, because I have no idea where Kitty wants us to go."

"And I have less than no guess while we're underground. But is it safe to just leave the speeders here?"

"They work on the surface, too. Though I've only used them there at night."

"It's early morning now," Cox pointed out. "I'm worried that we'll be seen on these, and that's only going to fuel some bizarre rumors, dangerous speculation, or, worse, indicate to powers that be that Alfred has new toys they're going to want."

"What Bill said, ad infinitum. While I'd love to use these aboveground, I'm really concerned about someone else, anyone else, getting their paws on them." Thought about this. "But I think I can find Martini Manor on a map and show it to you. Maybe you can, I don't know, figure out where in the tunnels they'd be?"

"I could, but it doesn't matter. There are only a few entrances and this is the only one in this part of Florida. Trust me—I've been here for decades—there isn't a portion of this tunnel system I haven't examined and searched. But we need to conserve our strength, and if where we're headed is too far away, we're going to be at a distinct disadvantage."

"Well, if we knew exactly where we were going, Alfred could just program our GPS systems," Cox suggested.

"What about things like people, cars, buildings, and wildlife?"

"Oh, I can send avoidance directives within the GPS program," Alfred said cheerily. "Kitty, can you truly show me where we're going on a map?"

"If someone pulls up Google Maps for me, yes, I can."

Alfred cocked his head at me. "Why can't you do it yourself?"

"It's not really her phone and she's locked out of it," Cox explained.

"May I?" Alfred put out his hand. Gave him the cell phone. His fingers worked at a blur and he handed it back to me. "There you go. Opened. The combination is zero-eight-zero-one."

Thought about this. Chuckie and I had gone to Vegas at the end of July the year he'd proposed and I hadn't realized he wasn't kidding. "Oh. I bet that's their anniversary. I can remember that." I hoped.

We walked the speeders up the slope for this entrance and stopped when I had full bars. Pulled up the map and found Martini Manor on it. Per what I could see, it was pretty much the same—three gigantic houses—giant, supergiant, and colossal—sitting in the middle of a fenced estate. The look screamed Drug Lord, something I wisely chose not to mention to Alfred here and made a mental note to never mention to anyone in my own universe, either.

Alfred loaded the maps into our GPS systems, which now displayed the path. "It'll tell you when to turn, too, not that you'll need to do anything, since you'll be on autopilot. And it will match the speed you're going, so you're told in an appropriate manner."

"This you should share. Because current GPS needs some serious help."

"I'll keep it in mind. Shall we?"

"Once more into the breach and all that."

"Kitty, you lead, I'll bring up the rear," Cox said. "That way, we have Alfred protected."

"Works for me. Let's make our own lane and roll."

"Wow, you sound so 'street' when you say that."

"Just keepin' it gangsta throughout the multiverse, Bill."

CHAPTER 60

MARTINI WALKED OUT of Jamie's bedroom. "Except that Kitty and I are going to Australia, with Jamie, because we're actually not suspects, and if you think you're going to accuse my three-year-old daughter of being a murderer, I'm going to kill you with my bare hands."

If I hadn't been married to a man I loved with all my heart, and if I hadn't known that Martini loved my CA in the exact same way, I'd have literally told him I was his forever for this. He'd managed to ensure that we could get out of here and come up with an explanation for why he might be acting angry with Goodman at the same time. And I loved good looks and all that, but there was really nothing better than a brilliant mind. And Martini might not be up to Charles' standards, but he was damned close.

"In fact," Martini went on, "Chuck, Buchanan, and Richard aren't suspects, either. So the six of us are going to go to Australia. Today. We're not going to fly. We're going to take a gate and the world is just going to have to deal with that. The Operations Team has us packed, and I asked them to pack for the other three as well."

"You need protection," Goodman said.

Martini shrugged. "Per your well-made point, which, yes, I heard, every member of the Secret Service who was in the

Embassy is also a suspect. Alpha Team, on the other hand, weren't in the Embassy until, I imagine, you called them in, and yes, I'm certain Walter can prove that. So, Alpha Team will accompany us as well." He looked at James. "Right, Commander Reader?"

"Correct. Alpha Team is prepped and ready to accompany you, Mister Vice President." Both men had their In Charge voices on.

Goodman sighed. "You like to make it really difficult for anyone to protect you, don't you?"

"Frankly, it seems like we need to protect our protectors, not the other way around."

Everyone looked at me. "That's true," Amy said slowly. She looked at Len and Kyle. "You two need to be careful. Because you could be targets."

Figured they were, right after Malcolm. Meaning I wanted them with us, if I could manage it. Frankly, I wanted the entire Embassy staff with us if possible, even Amy, because they were all probably targets. "Seriously, Len, Kyle, Amy and Christopher were all here, in our apartment, babysitting Jamie while we were gone. Unless you're going to accuse the four of them of collusion, I think they can alibi each other."

"That's true," Amy said. "We were all here, and no one left for any reason."

"Your words may not be good enough," Goodman said, sounding worried.

"Actually, Missus Vice President Chief," Walter said over the com, "I can verify that no one other than the five of you used our Embassy gate for anything prior to the Secret Service agents requesting transfers to the various gates in Paris. And the five of you only used it once, to go to Paris."

Goodman shook his head. "That's great, but I have to have proof."

"Isn't this kind of data proof? Look at Walter's records, that's part of what law enforcement does, isn't it?"

"Records can be tampered with," Goodman pointed out. "Who calibrated the gates for the Secret Service?"

"I did, Mister Goodman," Walter verified.

"Suspect," Goodman said without missing a beat.

"So, you're now accusing Walter of having killed those Secret Service agents? I'd love to hear what his motive could possibly be. Frankly, I'd like to have someone come up with a motive for *any* of us to kill any of those people."

"I as well," Singh said. "Because right now, all I can come up with is a hate crime, or an attempted assassination of the Vice President and his wife that these brave agents managed to foil while losing their lives in the process."

He was good. Realized he'd already formulated our most likely response. It was both a good one and probably far more accurate than anything else we'd come up with.

"What do the Paris police say?" Martini asked. "Where do they think the agents were killed?"

"I'm in contact with them," James said. "And with Interpol. Both agencies feel the agents were murdered on French soil. Meaning no one who can be confirmed to have been inside the Embassy at the time of their murders can be considered a likely suspect."

"And now we have another international incident," Goodman pointed out.

"We do, but unless we want to get pissed off at France, it was *our* people who were murdered, not theirs. We should be helping the police and Interpol with their investigation, but I don't see how locking down our Embassy personnel actually does that. If it were me, I'd be looking at our enemies, not our allies."

"Speaking of hate crimes, Club Fifty-One certainly has enough members that they could have done this," Amy pointed out.

"Same with the Al Dejahl Terrorists," Lorraine said. "And the Church of Intolerance, as Kitty calls it, can't be overlooked either."

"Bottom line, we have a lot of enemies," Claudia pointed out.

"And it's relatively easy to spot which bathrooms have a

gate in them, after all," Amy added. "Once you know that little red mark at the very back of the stall indicates a gate, you can stake it out easily."

"How did they know you were in Paris?" Goodman asked.

"No idea. Maybe someone spotted us. We weren't trying to hide because we weren't doing anything illegal. The only people we were trying to avoid were those same people who were murdered, and we didn't want them with us only to prevent a media circus."

"Look, we're going to Australia," Martini said, voice filled with authority. "I want Len and Kyle with us, for their protection and ours. Alpha Team is coming to protect us, which is, newsflash, their job. You want to fight me on this one? I'll call the President. I guarantee Vince wants Australia handled far more than he wants to lock us down so you can create another problem for his office to have to solve."

Goodman sighed. "You're right, Jeff. I'm sorry. We're on the same side. I just don't want to do something that will cause even more problems down the road."

"Then help figure out who killed your men," I suggested. Should be easy, since I knew he'd either done it or assigned someone to the task. "Head to Paris and help Interpol." Or, in other words, get the hell out of my house. Hoped that didn't show on my face, but under the circumstances, it wouldn't matter—we were all mad at Goodman for an obvious reason.

He shook his head. "They don't want us doing that, I can guarantee it."

"True enough," James said. He'd been texting the entire time, and he waved his phone at Goodman. "They've asked us to stand by but to remain out of it until they ask for assistance. I agree with Kitty—let them do their jobs. Jeff, I think I want Christopher and Amy going along with you and Kitty."

"No," Christopher said. "Amy and I need to stay here. I want Raj with Kitty, not me."

Singh nodded and so did Martini. "I agree. We need our PR Minister with us, for obvious reasons, and we want someone who's handled our military actions here in charge. That's

Christopher, helped by Kevin Lewis." He looked at me. Had no idea why. "Baby, as the Ambassador you're going to have to make that official."

"Oh, right. Make it so. Raj is with us, and while we're gone, Christopher's in charge and Kevin's his right hand and you're all to keep us posted at all times."

"Good enough." Martini looked pointedly at Goodman. "Cliff, I'm sorry, but under the circumstances, you've just accused every one of us of murder. Take off and handle things from your offices. We'll get over it, but right now, no one here likes you much. Trust me."

Goodman gave us all a rueful smile. "I understand. Part of my job, the cruddy part, but a part nonetheless. And it's not meant personally toward any of you, believe me. I'll go, but you have to take your Secret Service detail with you. Period."

"No problem," I said quickly. "Glad to have them along, in part because hopefully we can ensure no one murders the rest of them."

"Escort him out," Martini said to Len and Kyle. "And make sure he's not hurt or attacked while you're doing it."

They nodded and flanked Goodman, who grinned. "Thanks. I appreciate the care and protection."

"Oh, believe me," Martini said with a smile, "we don't want some crazed stranger or anti-alien lunatic killing you, Cliff."

"I'll go, too," Singh said, presumably to ensure that there was an A-C with Len and Kyle. I wholeheartedly agreed with this plan.

"Thanks, Jeff. Kitty, everyone. Watch your backs." With that, Goodman left, Singh leading the way, Len and Kyle bringing up the rear.

"Walter, make sure that they're all okay. I realize they're just going downstairs, but it's been a creepy day."

"Yes, ma'am, Missus Vice President Chief. I've called his office for a car to pick up Mister Goodman. It's outside. Pierre has already verified that it's the right person driving."

"Good man."

"Let us know when Goodman's not on the premises anymore," Christopher said.

"Yes, sir."

"Why?" I asked him.

"Because I know who the A-C is who murdered all those agents."

CHAPTER 61

WE WERE ALL QUIET for a few long moments. "Mister Goodman is in his car and gone."

"Thanks, Walter. Wait for the others to get back," Martini added quietly. Christopher nodded.

The three were back quickly—assumed Singh had used hyperspeed. "Embassy is secure, Mister Vice President."

"Thanks, Walter."

Singh put up his hand, pulled out some small blinking object, and disappeared. He was back momentarily. "We swept for bugs on the way back," Singh said. "Found none. And I just checked everywhere here, we're clean. Nice change on Jamie's room," he said to me. "It's about time."

"Whatever, as long as she likes it. I want to know who the traitor is."

"Me too," Martini said. "Only, Christopher, I assume you think it's who I think it is, right?"

Christopher nodded. "Stephanie."

Looked around the room. Okay, no one here who didn't know that I didn't know. "Who's Stephanie?"

"Our niece," Martini said sadly. "She turned traitor a while ago."

"Long story we need to fill Kitty in on immediately," Serene said, and I noted that she had an In Charge voice, too. I hadn't heard it before. "Leave that to me and Raj. The rest of you, get us prepped and get the Secret Service prepped. I want Richard and the others back here before we go to Australia, because I don't trust that they're not targets, too."

Crawford sent a text. "Sending agents from Euro Base to pick them up and bring them back here."

"Are we sure we don't want to fly?" Singh asked.

Having just flown from Australia to the U.S., I had the answer. "Not just no, but hell no. Those gates may make me sick, but we're not going to die because of turbulence or get shot down or whatever."

The others nodded. "I agree with Kitty," James said. "Regardless of how 'alien' that makes us appear. We're officially under attack, again, and that means we need to minimize our exposure. Air travel is not on the list of options right now. Besides, based on the time differences, we can take our time and be ready and take a gate and still get there in Australia's morning, versus losing an entire day on an airplane."

This settled it, Walter and the com turned off, and everyone scattered to ask the Operations Team to pack for them. Nice setup. Of course, I had Peter to do that, but still, he actually had to take time, versus just snapping his fingers.

Serene and Singh sat me down on the couch. "High-level is this," she said without preamble. "Jeff has five older sisters. The eldest, Sylvia, was married to Clarence Valentino. Most of Jeff's brothers-in-law are jealous of him and Christopher to the point of treason, and Clarence led the way. He was first working with our former Diplomatic Corps, who were discovered to be traitors. Then he joined up with LaRue Demorte Gaultier and Ronaldo Al Dejahl and left our part of the galaxy with them in tow. They came back with the Z'Porrah, an ancient alien race, to destroy us. We foiled the invasion, though not without help, and thought Clarence was dead. But the Mastermind found him and he joined that team, or, rather, he joined the head guy on the overall team, since we know they all are or were in league with the Mastermind. Kitty killed Clarence, but not before he turned his and Sylvia's eldest, Stephanie, against us."

"She's confirmed to be with the Mastermind," Singh added. "So if we had an A-C attacking your agents, it's pretty much a sure bet that it was her."

"Makes sense. The pertinent question is how they knew we were gone and where to find us."

"That's easy," Singh said. "The Secret Service checked in on you about an hour after you'd left. If you'd found what you needed quickly you might have been back." He gave me a chiding look.

"That whole romantic interlude thing was a ruse to fool the Mastermind. Jeff and I found the bodies, or at least we found three of them, which is why we put that ruse into action. So stop blaming us for this—this was going to happen regardless of how long we did or didn't take in Paris."

They both looked shocked. "Why didn't you tell us?"

"Because we could tell it was set up to frame us or Malcolm or both."

Serene stared at me for a few long seconds. "There's only one logical reason for why you didn't tell us that before now." Her expression went to horrified. "No," she whispered. "Really?"

Singh jerked. "Oh. Oh no. No wonder . . ." He looked ill. "We've told him all our moves, and he's in so tightly with—"

"Crap, stop guessing! Malcolm's going to kill me. None of you guys can lie."

Serene and Singh exchanged an amused glance. "Well, as to that," he said, "some of us have troubadour talent. It's the ability to sway and to act and so forth. And you know what acting actually is?"

"Oh, wow, yeah. It's pretending in a believable fashion."

"Exactly," Serene said. "We have an, ah, group. That only our Kitty knows about. We function in a protective fashion."

"Oh my God, you're running the A-C spy organization."

They both looked pleased. "Well done," Singh said. "And yes, we are. Someone has to. We've been trying to determine who the Mastermind is, of course, just as everyone else has been. But we've come up short. However, I know Mister Buchanan knows who it is."

"He does. It's why the Mastermind was trying to frame him. And why he doesn't want any of you knowing."

"We're different, I can promise you that," Serene said. "So, to confirm, it's Cliff Goodman, isn't it?"

"Malcolm is going to be so freaking mad at me."

Serene smiled brightly. "Hey, Jeff. Kitty's worried that Malcolm is going to be mad." She didn't sound in charge. She, frankly, sounded like a total ditz, and I saw Singh alter his expression so he looked amused and slightly worried, but nowhere near the intense he'd been just seconds ago. I stopped worrying about either one of them giving anything away to Goodman.

"No," Martini said as he joined us. "He won't be. I guessed, you two guessed, we can't be faulted for thinking. We're going to handle Australia and get back and handle the Mastermind."

Singh shook his head. "We need proof, Jeff. And if Mister Buchanan had it, he'd have shared it already."

"Yes, that's the issue. And, frankly, if Goodman didn't kill the agents—and it sounds like none of you think he actually did—then us finding Stephanie would only get her caught. Because I'm just betting that she's become a fanatic, especially since my Cosmic Alternate killed her father."

"Yeah," Martini said sadly. "She hates us all with a passion that I can't figure out how we'd overcome."

"Then we don't. We have to make sure we don't give away that we know who the Mastermind is and we have to find proof of some crime, any crime, that will allow us to get him convicted in a court of law."

"It's more than that," Serene said. "There are the clones to consider."

"Oh. Great. I can't wait."

"We mentioned them, briefly," she said. "They've cloned LaRue Demorte and Leventhal Reid. They're tightly tied to the Mastermind. And from what we know, they have their minds backed up into a database that allows them to recreate new clones with the sum knowledge of all their prior clones. Each and every time."

"Well, that just sucks, doesn't it? So, we have to actually destroy more than this version of the Mastermind, don't we?"

They all nodded. "And that is and remains the problem," Singh said. "Though knowing who the third person in the Unholy Trinity is helps dramatically."

"Supposedly." Martini ran his hand through his hair. "We need to avoid him as much as possible, and we really need to be sure no one lets Chuck figure out who it is."

"And we need to get to Australia and attempt to save that particular day."

"But not yet," Singh said. "We have hours before we need to go—it's the middle of the night in Australia right now. You two should get some rest, you've had a busy few hours and we need you both to be at your best."

"And we don't have a confirmed appointment time with the Prime Minister yet, either," Serene said. "Though James is working on it, coordinating with the President's Press Secretary."

"I don't want to take that Strauss woman with us. She can fly."

"She's not our enemy," Martini said mildly.

"She's not your friend, either, and I don't care what you get from her emotionally. She's a bitch and I don't want her with us."

"I'll tell James and let him handle it," Singh said soothingly.

Decided to let it drop. If Strauss came along, I'd be watching her. Closely. "So, what will I wear? The usual stuff you all do?"

"No," Martini said. "The Operations Team has your outfits hanging up in the closet. They'll be packed once we're ready to go. And don't worry—they apparently consulted with Akiko."

"Who?"

"The fashion designer on retainer with us," Serene answered. "She's great, you love her stuff. She's aware that you tend to, ah, get a little disheveled."

"Yeah, using today as an example, why any of you go out in anything other than jeans and combat boots is beyond me."

Martini grinned. "We like to live on the edge."

Stood up and headed to the bedroom. "Well then, I'll check out what I'm going to wear to dazzle the Aussies before I nap. Let's just hope it's something I can run in."

"Oh," Serene said, "it will be. Akiko knows you."

"I think I should resent that on behalf of both myself and my CA."

"You can resent it," Singh said with a laugh. "But, trust us, you can't deny it."

CHAPTER 62

THE OUTFITS LOOKED GREAT. Wondered if this designer existed in my world and made a note to find out when I got home. If I got home.

Shoved that worry aside. There was nothing I could do about that right now and, frankly, the people here needed me. "Fix the problems, then you can worry about getting home, right?" Shoved the fact that I was getting attached to them, really attached, aside as well.

This Akiko was good at comfortable fashion that looked great. It was summer in Australia, so this outfit was layered. An iced blue sleeveless sheath dress was overlaid by a wrap-around shimmering iced blue sweater dress that had long sleeves and a slightly longer hem length.

Low-heeled neutral boots and a matching scarf were there for this side of the world; low-heeled neutral pumps and a cute, floppy, wide-brimmed blue sunhat rounded out the summertime outfit.

Tried them on separately and together—looked great all three ways, and when wearing the layers it was impossible to tell that I had another outfit on underneath the sweater dress.

As I hung them back up, it seemed clear that Akiko had expected us to go to Australia via plane. Had a moment's worry about our gate plan, but the turbulence from only a few days ago was still—despite everything else that had gone on—a vivid memory. And while James might be piloting here just as he did for us, I didn't relish the idea of a repeat of the Flight From Hell.

As I contemplated if I should just wear the summertime outfit alone when we went to Oz, one of the little furballs bounded into the closet and joined me. "Hello there. What's your name?"

It mewed at me. I wasn't sure, but it didn't appear to have a name. Len had said that the Poofs attached to whoever named them. Supposedly Poofikins was "mine" but it wasn't, not really. It belonged to my CA. And it had been so long since I'd had a pet.

Put my hand out. "So, Gershom, what do you think I should wear?" The Poof jumped onto my hand and purred. "Both, huh? You like your name?" More purrs. "Good. Because I am indeed a stranger in a strange, strange land."

The Poof jumped onto my shoulder and nuzzled my neck. My neck was my main erogenous zone, but happily when the kids and now the Poof were snuggling there it didn't trigger anything other than feelings of happiness. "I wish I could take you home with me. Charlie and Max would love you so much. And my Jamie might even stop looking in her mirrors because of you. I bet we could sneak you through customs and avoid quarantine, too."

The Poof mewed at me. Had no idea what it was saying, but I chose to believe it wanted to come to my world with me, too. Which was ridiculous, since it had only just become "mine," if it even was mine for real. The Poof purred and rubbed against me some more and I stroked its fur.

Felt something near my leg and looked down. The Peregrine, Bruno, was standing there. Bent down and gave him a gentle scratch between his wings. "There you go, big guy. You know, where the heck were you when we were in Paris?"

He warbled, fluffed his feathers, scratched the rug, and did a head bob thing. He was guarding Jamie, because she was the focus of the Mastermind's plans, and we weren't the ones who'd been in danger.

"Wow. I almost hate to say that I understand you. I don't have this freaky Doctor Doolittle skill at home."

Bruno flapped his wings. I had no pets at home, so how would I know?

"Wow. I'm having a conversation with an Alien Attack Peacock. That would be a great name for a rock band, you know that?"

Bruno gave me a look I could only think of as snide.

"Well, I think it'd be a cool name. Okay, so are you gracing us with your presence for the next leg of this journey?"

Bruno indicated that Australia was lovely at this time of year and he'd always wanted to see Sydney and Canberra.

"How the heck does she handle this communication without seriously wondering if she's crazy?"

Bruno cawed. I was fairly sure he was laughing.

Decided not to press on about either my CA's sanity or my own. Figured I should check one thing before I left the closet. "Uh, I'm not sure if you're here, but thanks again and, ah, is there anything else you think I might need to have with me? Just in case and all that?"

Several clips filled with bullets appeared on top of the hamper. "Huh. Uh, she carries a gun?" Thought about it. Of course she carried a gun. Dug through the purse—sure enough, she had a Glock .23. Went to check if the clip was full or not and had the surprise of my life. "Whoa! What the hell? Is there a safety on this thing?"

"What?" Martini said, coming in to join me. "Oh, you can shoot?" He sounded relieved.

"Yeah, Charles made me learn. I even have this model. But why is there a safety on this thing?"

"All guns have safeties."

"Glocks don't. Well, not external ones."

He shrugged. "In this universe, Glocks have safeties."

"What a world. What a world. Okay, well, I guess I'd better get used to that." Put the clips into the purse, then left the closet, many clips the richer and with another "it's so different" moment. Go me. "So let's take a nap. After we feed Jamie and get her settled down with something fun to do."

"Ah," Martini looked uncomfortable. "I already took her and all the pets to daycare and gave her breakfast there while you were talking to Raj and Serene. She'll be with Denise and the other kids until we're ready to leave. Denise will make sure she gets an early nap."

Chose not to ask how he'd gotten all those animals out without my noticing because I assumed he'd used hyperspeed or I'd just been totally unobservant. Both were very possible.

"You know, I get that you're really busy people and all that, and I'm sure whoever you have handling daycare is awesome, but still, it's clear Jamie would like more attention."

"Is it?" Martini looked panicked and worried.

"Well, either that child lives to go to the zoo, or she hasn't been taken in a really long time."

"Kitty and I took her there a couple weeks ago."

"Huh. Then she must love it."

"She likes it just fine, but she has her own personal zoo here." He ran his hand through his hair. "Honestly, I think she just wants to spend time with *you*. Because, ah, you're, ah, new. I mean, she loves her mother, it's not that. But you're . . ."

"Different yet the same." Considered this. "Maybe it's the same with my kids. I'd bet my CA isn't going to assign them field trip reports."

Martini laughed. "Hardly. She's more likely to take them to the shooting range."

"After what happened to send me here and what's going on in this world, I can get behind that idea." Maybe, when I got home, I'd suggest a family trip to the shooting range. And maybe Charles wouldn't flip out about it. Hey, it could happen.

The com came on. "Excuse me, Mister and Missus Vice

President Chief. Commander Reader says he needs to talk to you right away."

"Why is that, Walter?" Martini asked.

"Because we appear to have a problem with the team in Paris."

CHAPTER 63

IT WAS PROBABLY STUPID, but I'd really checked out the speeder's controls on the trips though the tunnels. I flipped off the autopilot, revved the engine, and put the pedal to the metal.

If the speeders had been fun in the tunnels, it was nothing compared to what they were like out on the surface. It was all I could do not to shout "Yee-hawwwww" every time we zipped around people, animals, cars, and buildings like they were not only standing still but going backward.

The only thing I could compare it to was the speeder scene in *Return of the Jedi*, but this was better because I was doing the riding and driving instead of just watching it.

I'd been worried about hitting things like birds, animals, or foliage—let alone cars and buildings—but the GPS system was really advanced, and I was warned in plenty of time to make adjustments. Sure, the warnings were nanoseconds before I reached the obstacles, but my reflexes were more than up to the task. It was exhilarating to be able to go this fast and control it, to zoom around a butterfly as easily as a building. For the first time, I really understood what Christopher was trying to train me to be able to do.

Fortunately or not, depending on your perspective, we reached the outskirts of Martini Manor quickly. As was typical for this kind of compound, there was a high stone wall that surrounded the property, and there were a lot of trees and such on both sides of this wall.

"You did well with the speeder," Alfred said. "It was a bit reckless of you to take control yourself, of course."

"That ride is now in my Top Five Most Fun Things I've Done, Ever list. Besides, your GPS program is beyond amazing."

"Unlike you, ma'am, I was happy just enjoying the ride."

"Really? You fly jets for a living. I'd have thought you'd have done the same as me, honestly."

Cox grinned. "I'll be happy to train on these puppies, but until then? I've never been much for the idea of going splat."

Stashed the speeders in an area thick with bushes. "You sure no one's going to come along and jack these?" I asked Alfred.

He pushed a button on each bike and they disappeared. "I doubt it."

"Wow, you know, I thought the invisibility shield and such came from the Ancient's technology, not from you."

"It's a simple process utilizing light refraction, Kitty."

Just like they used at the Crash Site Dome in my world. There would be no Dome here, so bringing it up was pointless. "You say tomato, I say blah, blah, blah, but okay. So, what's our plan?"

Everyone, cat and Poof included, stared at me. "Ah, I thought that was your bailiwick, ma'am," Cox said finally.

"Always the way. Okay, we need to determine how much and how deadly the security systems are that are guarding this place. Then we go over the wall, get inside, and see what's what."

"That's it?" Cox asked. "That's your entire plan?"

"Well, the general outline, yeah."

"We are gonna die." Cox turned to Alfred. "Tell me you have something up your sleeve, sir. So to speak."

Alfred shrugged. "We're essentially superpowered for this world, son. It's not that bad a plan."

"Hyperspeed can handle most issues, though to show willing and support Bill's concerns, I don't know that we can handle a direct hit of anything strong like a laser or a death ray."

"Please tell me you were just using 'death ray' as an example, not because you know Goodman has one on hand."

"I have no idea what this world's Mastermind has in the ways of Bond Villain weaponry, Bill, but I've got to assume our Masked Avenger has something that gives him the edge against all the many assassins and such he has working for him."

"We can't handle a direct laser hit normally, but the bodysuits will help. Try not to get in the way of a death ray, son, that's my advice."

"And good advice it is, too, Alfred. Harlie, Poof of the Multiverse, I believe you're up."

"Harlie?" Alfred sounded worried now. Figured. Of course, I didn't want Stripes doing recon if I could help it, either, so I felt his pain.

"Poofs have amazing abilities, as you well know. Harlie, can you please safely and carefully do Alfred, Kitty, and Bill a huge solid and determine where it's safe for all of us to enter this property and its various dwellings? We want to find the secret lair, but honestly, we also want to be sure that Cliff Goodman and LaRue of Death are hanging out here and that we're not actually at the residence of Florida's most successful drug lord."

Harlie mewled. Right, it had no idea who Cliff actually was, and less of a clue about LaRue. "Lunatic Lad, use your mad internet skills and see if you can whip up a picture of our man of the hour for Harlie to take a look at." It was definitely easier to roll an offensive back home, possibly because everyone was trained back home. And possibly because the Poofs had been involved in the madness that was my life for a lot longer than the Harlie that was here.

"How do I get my phone out of the bodysuit?"

Dug through my purse and gave him my phone. "I'm sure you heard the code."

"Yes, ma'am." Cox tapped some buttons.

"It takes forever to get the internet around here."

"It's faster in your world?" Alfred asked, scientific interest radiating.

"Yeah, a *lot* faster."

"I apologize for the lack of speed in our sad little corner of the multiverse, ma'am, but I have the picture now." He showed it to Harlie, who mewed.

"Bill, I'll hurt you later. Harlie's got it. Go forth and find out if we're even close to being in the right place, will you? Oh, and be a careful Poof—we want no casualties on our team, and that includes our team's furred members."

The Poof purred at me and disappeared. Meanwhile, I considered the fact that the goggles we were wearing were hella impressive. "Alfred, can I make these work like binoculars?"

"Yes, and microscopes if needed. You just have to concentrate. The transformer at the base of your skull is capturing your brainwaves and transmitting what you're thinking to the goggles and the earpieces."

"Amazing. Terrifying if in the wrong hands, but still, amazing. Okay, then I'm going to climb this giant tree and see what I can see, both near and far, I guess."

Stripes meowed at me and jumped out of my purse and onto the tree trunk. He scrambled up into the branches.

"He can get his claws out?" Cox asked.

"Yes, they're a part of him so they're covered by the suit, but their sharpness still works."

"Alfred, you're amazing."

"Thank you, Kitty. What does your cat say?"

"Hopefully something more interesting than what the fox says. Stripes, what do you see?"

Stripes scrambled down to share that he saw a whole lot of nothing. As he was sharing this with me, Harlie returned. Cat and Poof did a lot of sharing, all of which said that this place, though furnished and impeccably clean, appeared completely deserted.

Shared this with the others. "So, does that mean we're in the wrong place?" Cox asked.

"No place this gigantic and well maintained is uninhabited, at least no place like this that doesn't have a For Sale sign somewhere around the property. Hang on."

Did a run around the place at hyperspeed. There were no For Sale signs anywhere, and there wasn't a weed in evidence, either.

Returned to the others. "It's not for sale and someone's paying a fantastic gardener to keep it up. But if I were a criminal mastermind who didn't want anyone to know who I was, maybe I wouldn't have my henchmen here, but rather at my pad in Miami where everyone else thinks I am."

Harlie jumped up and down, then disappeared again. "Where is Harlie going?" Alfred asked, sounding worried.

"To check out Miami. Trust me, Harlie will be back soon." I hoped. "I found the main gate and the back gate. The back gate might be the best place for us to go in, but I'm not sure. There's no surveillance that I saw or Harlie found, which is odd for anyplace, let alone someplace as big as this."

"Are we sure there isn't any underground entrance?" Cox asked.

Alfred and I stared at him. "Lunatic Lad, I'm so glad you're here. We were focused on the fact that the tunnels don't have an entrance here, but if Cliff knew about them, Alfred wouldn't be happily hiding out there, trust me. But the tunnels are deeper than any human would dig. A-Cs and, apparently, other aliens, like to burrow far down into the ground, but most humans don't."

"Harlie didn't find anything," Alfred pointed out.

"Harlie hasn't been trained in this universe like in mine. And we sent the Poof to look for surveillance and traps, not for the entrance to secret labs." Looked around and realized Stripes wasn't nearby. In fact, I couldn't see him. "Crap, where did my cat go? Now isn't a great time for him to use the litter box or demand his own special kind of independence."

"Should we call for him?" Cox asked.

"Only if we want to give away that we're here. I mean, the place appears deserted, but if they're just using the same light refraction technique that Alfred is for the speeders, then we're kind of screwed."

"Harlie would have seen through that," Alfred said, as Stripes came bounding back and jumped into my arms.

Hugged him. "There you are! Kitty was so worried."

Stripes purred and meowed. He was, justifiably, pleased with himself.

"What's he saying?" Cox asked.

"He's found the way in. Haven't you, my best cat in the world?"

"Good," a man said from behind us. "Then you can lead the way."

CHAPTER 64

WE ALL JUMPED and spun to see, if not the last person I was expecting, certainly someone I wasn't prepared for. A rather handsome Latin man in a nice business suit was standing there, and, of course, he had a gun trained on us. He also wasn't alone—there were six men with him, all dressed like commandos. They too, naturally, had guns trained on us. Always the way.

"Esteban Cantu?"

His turn to jump. "How do you know me?"

"Ah . . . it's a really long story. What are you doing here?"

"What agency are you with?"

"You have the guns, you go first." Presumably our bizarre garb was giving him the impression we were working for one of the Alphabet Agencies in some way. That hopefully meant no one was going to shoot us. Yet.

He flipped out his badge. "C.I.A., Department of the Inspector General."

"Oh, you're with Internal Affairs." That, hopefully, was a good thing.

"Yes. Your turn."

"We're, ah—"

"With the U.S. Navy, sir," Cox said crisply. "Office of

Internal Affairs. Undercover. I'd pull out my badge, but I'm not certain your men won't try to shoot me if I do."

"What the hell is the military doing with this level of tech? And a cat? At least, I think it's a cat—it's hard to tell the way you're all disguised. Seriously, why a cat?"

"Experimental. Trained to go where dogs can't." Really hoped that Harlie wouldn't return right now. Explaining Stripes might work. Explaining the Poof wouldn't. "We aren't disguised, we're in experimental bodysuits. We weren't told there were other operatives here."

"Neither were we." Cantu sounded suspicious. Could not blame him. He was going to demand proof of what Cox had said we were, and the moment he didn't get it, we were arrested or worse.

Alfred stepped forward and took off his mask. "I can show you proof that we're with the agency we say we are, but I'd like to ensure that I'm not shot down while I do so."

Cantu nodded. "Just don't try anything funny."

"Oh, absolutely not." Alfred walked over to where we had the speeders parked and uncloaked one.

Cantu jumped again, indicating that he couldn't have been watching us all that long. "What the hell?"

"It's just a light refraction cover, no big deal, the Navy's been using them for years. Let the man get our stuff so you can stop pointing guns at us." I had no idea of what Alfred could possibly do, but I really hoped it was something effective.

"Sure it has," Cantu muttered.

"So, while we wait in this sorta Mexican standoff, who are you after?"

"You tell me. And while you do, remove your masks so we can see that you are whoever your IDs say you are."

Had no idea if taking off our masks was a good or a bad idea. Decided going with something of the truth might be wise. Put Stripes down between my feet. "Look, my name is Katherine Katt-Reynolds." Took off my mask and hoped I didn't look too disheveled. Cox followed my lead. He looked a little messy but not too bad, meaning I probably looked like I'd been in a tornado. "My mother was Angela Katt, formerly of the C.I.A., just like you. So, tell me—are you investigating the man who murdered her and most of her team, or are you trying to help him finish the job?"

Cantu jerked. "You're not in covert ops."

"No, but I'm working with the Navy because they're willing to help me find out who just blew up one of my family's homes."

Cantu nodded. "We were advised."

"That our house was blown up or that we were still alive?"

"Both. Your husband advised me early this morning that he and his partner, along with another operative, were the targets of a variety of assassination attempts, culminating in your house being destroyed. Which is why we're here."

"So, where do you stand in relation to my husband?"

"I'm his boss since your mother was killed."

Interesting. Chuckie hadn't mentioned this. Of course, I hadn't mentioned Cantu, either. In my world, Cantu was an oily bastard who'd been working with our enemies. He'd accidentally shot LaRue in the head instead of me, and he'd been murdered by the Mastermind before he could give anything away. He didn't seem like a bad guy in this world, but I had no real way of knowing, since I couldn't exactly call Chuckie to get his impressions of his boss right now. "So, you're the reason we came in from Australia so we could almost be killed several times over?"

"No. I'm the one who's investigating why your husband and his partner were given orders to return to the States that seemed to come from the Inspector General's office but, in point of fact, did not."

"What have you so far determined?"

"Why are you at this particular estate?" Cantu countered.

Gave up. "We're trying to find where the headquarters for the head of the Corporation, as in the Cuban Mob, is located. We're pretty sure it's here. So, why are you here?"

"Because we're trying to find out what's happened to the

head of the Office of Public Affairs. He was supposed to be in D.C. to welcome a Navy officer assigned to him in a PR move. The Naval officer called in sick, but no one's heard from Clifford Goodman since yesterday morning."

"I was that officer," Cox said. "Sent in undercover, as we said, because we suspect Goodman of treason. However, we had reason to believe that Goodman has moved up his time-table, hence, why we're here."

Alfred returned and handed Cantu three badges. "Here you go."

Cantu studied them. "Huh. I'm amazed, but these look legit. So, you're both consultants with the Navy?"

"Yes. The Navy was very supportive. I believe my uncle, Mortimer Katt, may have had something to do with that." I was amazed. Cox and Alfred were lying like they'd been born to it. Cox and I being able to lie like wet rugs was one thing. But I wasn't used to the majority of A-Cs being able to lie at all, let alone this well. Either Alfred had been practicing as long as he'd been on Earth—always a real possibility—or he was a natural Liar. Had no idea which to hope for, so set-tled for trying not to think about it right now.

"I'm sure he did. Though why he'd want you in the line of fire, I have no idea. Fine, you check out. We have jurisdiction here, however."

"Do we seriously have to argue about who gets to go first? I mean, dude, you didn't know how to get in without being seen any more than we did. Our scout figured it out. I say that makes us partners, at least."

"Right. Because you know that your trained undercover cat has found the way in."

"Do I stand here insulting your commandos? No, I do not. I don't say, 'oh, why do we need six guys decked out like Rambo?' No, instead I say, let's work together to stop this creep before he kills anyone else. You know, like my husband and children."

"Fine." Cantu put his gun away and motioned for the com-mandos to do the same. "As I said before, you can lead us in."

"We need to put our masks back on first. And, ah, we need help." Looked at Alfred. Who looked at Cantu.

Who sighed. "Sure, go ahead, Doctor Martini. God forbid we'd be able to see your faces for longer than five minutes."

"I'm flattered, but when you have nice tech from the Navy you use nice tech from the Navy."

Alfred helped Cox and me back into our masks and ensured that everything was back where it was supposed to be. "How did you do it?" I asked him in a very soft whisper.

"I like to be prepared for every emergency, especially when I leave the tunnels," he replied in kind. "The speeders have everything any Bond car has—those movies have been wonderfully inspiring. I hacked into the Navy's database, altered some records, and had the badges print out using the speeder's three-D printer. That's what took me so long."

"Oh. Good plan. And nice accessory on the speeder." What else did one say? Alfred was clearly identifying with Q from MI6 and qualified for the Genius Mad Scientist Club at the same time. Nice to have one of them on our side for once.

Cox and I re-dressed, so to speak, Cantu gave us our IDs back. "Maybe you should put these in your purse," he said.

"Is sarcasm one of the services Internal Affairs offers?"

"Around here, yes, it is. So, Missus Reynolds, where are we going?"

It was weird to be called Mrs. Reynolds, but at the same time, it was kind of nice to have someone talking to me the way White normally did. Didn't let it make me comfortable or complacent, however. Cantu might be a good guy here, or he might be tricking us, big time.

But there was really only one way to find out. "Stripes, lead the way, please and thank you."

He meowed, swished his body-suited tail at us, and sauntered off toward the back of the property. The rest of us followed.

CHAPTER 65

STRIPES STOPPED at a tree that looked like most of the other trees around here. I wasn't much of a girl for tree and plant identification, so I had no real guess for what it was. An oak, maybe. Something with lots of branches and also lots of leaves, end of winter or not. Then again, winter in Florida was a lot like winter in Arizona—a lot nicer than most everywhere else.

This tree was about fifty feet from the wall, and about a hundred away from the back gate. Stripes walked to the side that faced away from the complex and sat down.

"It's a tree," Cantu said. "Are we supposed to climb it?"

"Stripes isn't climbing it, so no." Looked around. Stripes felt that the entrance was obvious. He wasn't trying to be coy, but I wasn't seeing it.

"No," Cox said. "He's sitting." He picked Stripes up and handed him to me. "Huh. What's wrong with this picture?"

"Nothing. The ground looks normal. Covered with leaves and such, but otherwise, normal. Only . . . the tree has all its leaves, and the leaves on the ground don't match those on the tree." Gave Stripes a nuzzle, weird masks and all. "Who's a clever boy, then? Who's gonna show the K-Nine squads what for? *You* are."

Cantu made a gagging face while Cox felt around where

the leaves were and Stripes purred up a storm. "I see why you're the feline wrangler," Cantu said as Cox found was he was looking for and lifted up an old-fashioned trapdoor.

"I'm ignoring you, Esteban. And, it's nice to see the criminal element holding onto the old ways, isn't it? Traditions are important, after all."

"It's dark down there," Cox pointed out.

"And this, Esteban, is where the Navy says, 'oh, let's let the C.I.A. feel good about themselves and lead the way.' So, you know, go for it. We'll be right behind you."

The commandos gave me "what a girl" looks. I didn't care, and now wasn't the time to prove my independence or show that women could do anything as well as or better than men. Because what I wanted to prove was that someone else was going first, so that if there were tripwires and such, they'd spot and neutralize them before my team could get hurt.

Four commandos went first, then Cox, me, Alfred, Cantu, and the last two commandos brought up the rear. There was a stairway, made of concrete, not wood, meaning it was in good repair. It was also something I didn't want to fall and hit my head on. Once in a lifetime was enough for me.

The commandos had come almost as well equipped as my team had, so they had infrared goggles, which they put on before starting down. Cantu did as well. So while it was dark, it wasn't terrible.

The stairs went down what I guessed was about a floor and a half, and then we were on a pathway. Based on where the stairs had faced and the straightness of the path, we were heading right under the complex.

As we walked—and no tripwires were set off or anything—the suggestion that this was going far too well reared its head. I'd never been involved in a Mission or Operation that hadn't had some awful snag or two along the way. But so far, this one was going swimmingly. Meaning that something was really, really wrong.

"Be prepared," I said softly. "Because I think we're walking into a trap."

Cox, who was in front of me, nodded and slowed down. Alfred was behind me, and he got up closer. I was carrying Stripes, who I put into my purse, just in case. Wasn't sure if the others had heard me, or if the transistor system Alfred had on our team meant only they had heard my warning.

My brain nudged. Something Cantu had said was off. Had Cox stop walking and moved Alfred between the two of us. "Esteban, you said my husband called you this morning," I said softly.

He motioned the two other commandos to go on around us. "Yes," he replied in kind.

"What, exactly, did he say to you?"

"Why?"

"Humor me."

"He said that he had proof that Cliff Goodman was a mole and had been trying to kill him and his family. He described everything that had happened. I've been investigating your mother's death for the past two and a half years—along with the deaths of most of her team. I know we have a mole, I just don't know who it is definitively. Frankly, I suspected one of your mother's team for quite a while."

Interesting. Because, barring something appearing to Chuckie in his sleep, we had no proof at all that Cliff was a traitor. We could determine that he was, but proving this was why Buchanan hadn't solved everyone's problems already. "Malcolm Buchanan was your suspect, right?"

"Right."

"He's not the mole."

"Yes, based on other evidence I've found, it appears Buchanan was being set up to be the fall guy. I've found some discrepancies in Goodman's records recently, and I've been pursuing those. Charles' confirmation helped, but I've had my sights on Goodman for the past few weeks."

"Did Charles tell you where he and the others are?"

"No, he said everyone was in a very safe place. Why?"

"Did he, by any chance, mention that I wasn't with him?"

"No," Cantu said slowly. "He didn't. But if you were on an op, he wouldn't."

Except that, if Chuckie trusted Cantu, he'd have told him that his wife was missing. The note I'd left for Chuckie just said I was going to follow up a lead from my side of things and that I'd be back sometime in the day and to wait for me to return before they left the Israelis. In this or any other world, I had to figure that, if Chuckie was calling his boss to share that Cliff was a murderous traitor, he'd mention that he had no idea where his wife was and that she could be in danger. Of course, there could be another reason, as well.

"Did you talk to Charles directly?"

"Yes, I did."

"Did he sound normal?"

"No, he sounded stressed, but who could blame him?"

Chuckie didn't do stressed, as a rule. He'd learned too young to never let anyone see him sweat. I found it almost impossible to believe that he'd let his boss know he was freaked out, especially if he'd called from the safety of the Israeli Embassy. The only times I'd heard him freaked out in this world had been when the kids and I were in danger.

"Did he mention assassins or Israelis or anything of that nature?"

"Yes, on the assassins. He said you'd been run off the road, four people had attacked at your home but they'd been subdued, and that your house had been blown up. There was no mention that the assassins were Israelis."

"They weren't Israeli, they were with the Corporation." So he'd left out some key activities. There were two potential reasons why. One was that Chuckie didn't trust Cantu or had never called him and Cantu was making all of this up. Or someone was forcing Chuckie to call Cantu, to get Cantu into a position to be killed.

"Did you ask what he'd done with the assassins who attacked?"

"I didn't have time. We don't have long conversations

when we have operatives in danger and out in the cold. He gave me the gist, I told him to head in to Langley where I have a team waiting to protect him and the others."

"So, how did you know to come down here? Have you tracked Cliff to this location?"

"No. Charles told me about this location and said it was where I could find Goodman."

And there it was, because there was no way that Chuckie would know about this place. My team was here because we were following what I'd call a hunch, what Mom would call my gut, and what Jeff would call my feminine intuition. But Chuckie had no knowledge of any of this. So, if he'd told Cantu to come here, it was because someone had forced him to. And that meant that Cantu wasn't a bad guy, but was a target. Made sense—if he'd been investigating what he'd said he was, then he would be someone Cliff would need to get out of the way along with the remains of my mother's team.

"Call your guys back," I said urgently. "This is a trap."

To his great credit, Cantu didn't argue. But as he tapped on his watch I heard a sound I was very familiar with—guns being fired.

Grabbed Cantu and Alfred, who grabbed Cox. We both took off running, toward the sounds of battle.

CHAPTER 66

"TELL JAMES we'll be right there," Martini said. "Wherever his there is."

"Alpha Team is coming back to you," Walter shared.

I went to the door and got it just as James was knocking. "Nice timing, girlfriend," he said with a grin. "Do I call you that in your world?"

"You do, as a matter of fact. So don't stop here."

"Duly noted." He, Paul, Serene, Singh, and Crawford came in. I wasn't sure that Singh was officially on Alpha Team, but based on what he and Serene had told me, assumed she wanted him around to hear whatever so the A-C C.I.A. would have all the intel. Couldn't argue with the logic.

"Where are Lorraine and Claudia?"

"Taking their kids to daycare," Serene said. "My husband is taking Patrick. Oh! You probably don't know—I'm married to Brian."

"Brian?"

"Brian Dwyer. Your old high school boyfriend."

"Oh. That's great, go you guys." I hadn't given Brian any thought for quite a while. For a variety of reasons, our having to get a restraining order against him being just one of them. "Ah, is he, um . . . mentally stable?" Because if he wasn't, wanted to ensure we didn't have a reunion in this world. Ever.

James started laughing. "I see he was obsessive in your world, too?"

"Yeah. To, uh, an unhealthy degree. But if he's married to Serene, then he's in far better shape here." I sincerely hoped.

"Yes. I was kind of the unhinged one when we met."

"Our enemies were drugging her," Martini said. "Club Fifty-One is an anti-alien organization, and they slipped Serene a lot of a drug we call Surcenthumain and my Kitty accurately calls the Superpowers Drug. They gave it to me, too. And . . . to Christopher."

"It's made the three of us more talented than normal," Serene said. "And it made Jamie and Patrick . . . much more talented."

Stared at them. "You know, you're all acting like Jamie is the focus, but if your son is like her, why isn't he under the same guard as Jamie is?"

"He is," Paul said. "Believe me, all the hybrid children are under guard. It's one of the reasons we're so happy that Denise Lewis is running the daycare program. The children are here when they're not with their parents or other guardians, and the Embassy is very well protected."

Thought about Charlie, Max, and my Jamie, who had none of this protection. Supposedly they had my CA guarding them, though, so that had to be good. She wouldn't ignore the boys just because she only had Jamie in her own world, would she?

Felt a hand on my neck. "Relax," Martini said quietly, as he massaged gently. "She'd die before she'd let anything happen to your children. Or your husband and friends. They're all hers, too, never forget that, because I promise you she won't."

Took a deep breath, let it out, and did my best to stop worrying. "Okay, so you said there was a problem with the team in Paris. Are they all okay?"

"Yeah, I didn't mean for Walter to panic you," James said.

"But Reynolds doesn't want to leave the singer you found there alone."

My immediate reaction was one I wasn't proud of—jealousy. Which was ridiculous. Shoved the jealousy away—if he liked her that was fine. He wasn't my husband here. And if he just felt protective of the person I'd essentially made him manage, well, that was okay, too. It wasn't like I wanted anything bad to happen to my favorite female recording artist, especially since she hadn't even gotten started on her career in this world yet.

"Tell him to bring her along," Martini said. Everyone gave him looks that said they feared he'd lost his mind. Martini sighed. "She knows we're unusual, and the guy she's recording with knows we're aliens—he recognized me and Kitty. So, bring her along. Her grandmother said she needed an adventure. So, she'll get one."

"You're sure?" James asked.

"I think we have a potential hostage both Kitty and Chuck are going to care about, and by now, Richard and Buchanan probably will, too. Let's keep her safe, and that means with us."

"And who knows, maybe the PM couple will like her singing."

"I meant to just bring her to the Embassy, baby."

"Yeah, but . . . let's see how she handles it. If she's cool with coming and with what's going on, let's bring her."

"Why?" Paul asked.

I shrugged. "She's something the Mastermind can't predict. Sure, maybe he can extrapolate now that he knows something about her. But she's an unknown, even more than I am. And . . . I just think we should take her with us."

"We ignore Kitty's feminine intuition to our detriment," Martini said. "So, fine. Let's see how she handles the gates, and if she can deal with it, she's part of the auxiliary team. Oh, and if Chuck wants the male singer to come along, too, bring him. Why risk losing a registered voter who likes us?"

Alpha Team took off and we headed into the bedroom. "We're both napping?"

"Yeah, we need it." Martini kicked his shoes off and took off his jacket and tie, then lay down on the bed. "I'll change before we go, but this way it should be less uncomfortable for you."

"You're really an awesome guy, you know that?" Took off my shoes and climbed up onto the bed next to him. Put my back against his side and my head on his arm, we shifted a bit, and then both relaxed. "You going to be able to sleep?"

"Yeah. All of our agents are trained to sleep whenever we can. I'll be out fast. How about you?"

"Mother of three, learned fast to nap when the kidlets napped or were at a friend's house, so yeah."

He kissed the back of my head. "Great. Then let's power nap."

Martini wasn't kidding, he was asleep fast. I might not have managed it, because everything going on had my brain actively spinning, but Gershom appeared and snuggled between my chest and Martini's arm, purring softly, and as I buried my face in its soft fur, I fell asleep, too.

We were all awakened by a knocking at our door. Martini groaned but I was trained to go from dead sleep to wide awake if I heard one of the kids, so I bounded up and went to get the door.

A gorgeous black Beauty Queen was standing there. Was fairly sure I'd met her at the gigantic briefing session but couldn't swear to it, nor could I remember her name. Thought she might be Paul's sister, though. She gave me a beaming smile. "Wakey wakey. I'm your personalized wakeup call."

"Ah, thanks?"

"Abigail, what are you doing here?" Martini asked drowsily as he joined us.

"Seriously, I'm here to wake you guys up. Walter's coordinating things with Alpha Team, the Office of the President, and the Office of the Australian Prime Minister as well as with Sydney Base and James doesn't want his focus disturbed. So, you're up, my work here is done."

"Thanks?"

She laughed. "You have no idea who I am, do you?"

"Ah . . ."

Abigail came inside but stayed near the door. "I'm Paul's youngest sister." She stopped smiling. "His only sister now. And he's now my only brother."

"Oh, so you're Charles', sorry, Chuckie's sister-in-law?"

"Yeah. Speaking of which, pretty girl you found in Paris. I have hopes."

"Hopes?"

"For her and Chuck. To get together. You wake up kind of slowly, don't you?"

"I guess so." The jealousy came back. Kicked it to the curb. He was allowed to have a love life, and based on what everyone, including Charles himself had said, he'd been terribly depressed and lonely. I wasn't here to become his wife in this world. I was here to fix things, and if he and Amadhia hit it off, well, that was fixing things.

"Well, the guy with her is a cutie, too."

"Oh, Aaron came along, after all?"

"Yeah. He's all jazzed about the two of them premiering their partnership for the Vice President and the Prime Minister both."

"Glad he's embraced the plan."

Abigail laughed. "He's like Jeff's biggest fan now, so I say we keep him. Anyway, you two get dressed and ready. I think we're going to Sydney Base first, then to the capitol. I'll get Jamie from daycare so you two don't have to worry about that. Just expect us back soon."

Abigail trotted off and Martini and I went back to our bedroom. "I feel like I haven't had nearly enough sleep, but Mister Clock says that we've slept for a good five hours."

"It's the time zone changes. It's hard on the body, no matter how much you do it. We should probably shower again, just in case."

"Is that your way of saying I didn't use enough deodorant earlier?"

He grinned. "You smell like roses, baby."

"Wow, you *can* lie a little, can't you?"

As before, I showered first. Made it a point to ensure that my hair was dry, in a ponytail, and back up in a banana clip before I left the bathroom. Wanted to avoid seeing Martini in nothing but a towel again. Well, that wasn't true—I desperately wanted to see him naked. I was just smart enough to know that doing so wasn't going to be good for anyone, me especially.

As I came out of the bathroom with my robe wrapped around me I noted that there were three rolling bags at the foot of the bed. Two were clearly a His and Hers set, in black. The third was a cute Hello Kitty bag that basically screamed that it was Jamie's. "This seems like a small amount to make it through a full trip to the other side of the world."

"Like Abigail said, we'll be stopping at Sydney Base first, and that's where we'll be sleeping as well. While it's nice to hope that we'll fix everything in an hour, there's no guarantee, and if we're lucky and the Prime Minister forgives us and goes so far as to ask us to stick around a bit, we'll want to have our personal things close by. The Operations Team will take care of anything we need when we're at the Base, but it just helps to have essentials with us, just in case."

"Works for me."

I got dressed with Gershom assisting me. Put on both layers—just in case, and besides, I really liked the way the sweater dress looked.

Fortunately for me, as soon as I was dressed and had my purse hooked onto my rolling bag, there was another knock at the door. Fortunately, because Martini was once again coming out of the bathroom with just a towel wrapped around his waist.

And once again, all I could think about was what he'd look like if he dropped the towel.

CHAPTER 67

SCURRIED OFF like the Hounds of Hell, or at least the Hounds of Inappropriate Lust, were at my heels, to find Abigail and Jamie at the door. They were accompanied by five guys in Armani. Four of them had one dog each, and one had the Feline Winnebago. Inappropriate Lust was shoved aside for Jamie and the Pet Parade.

"Mommy, can the pets all come with us?" Jamie asked as Abigail handed her to me and they all came inside and headed for the living room.

Abigail shook her head violently, as did the five agents, where Jamie couldn't see. "Ah, I don't think that's a good idea, Jamie-Kat."

"Poofs and Peregrines are okay," Abigail said quickly.

"Yes, but the dogs and cats aren't allowed into Australia without waiting a very long time in cages, all alone. They'll be much happier and safer staying here."

"Okay, Mommy," Jamie said with a sigh, as she squirmed out of my arms.

She gave each dog a hug and kiss, opened the Winnebago, took out each cat, and gave them a hug and a kiss, too. The animals seemed appreciative. Gave the dogs and cats pets, to ensure that I didn't seem off to anyone.

Some of the Poofs got out of the Winnebago. Those that

didn't got hugs and kisses from Jamie, too, and pets from me. Then Abigail nodded to the agents, and they took the dogs and cats down the hall and into what Martini had said were guest bedrooms.

"Why not just let them sleep in our rooms like they always do?" I asked Abigail.

"And leave the pets all alone?" Jamie gasped. "Mommy, they'd be too lonely and they'd cry and cry."

"Or, as we call it, howl and caterwaul," Abigail said dryly. "All day and all night. Trust me, taking care of your animals is an assigned duty. Happily, we've found a couple of sets of agents who have become dog and cat lovers."

The remaining Poofs, who were amassed on the living room furniture, all looked at me expectantly. "Ah . . . do they *all* come with us?"

"If they're invited, Mommy, yes they do."

"Okay, then any Poofs," felt a feathery nudge against my leg, "and Peregrines who want to experience the adventure of travel, come on down." There were now no Poofs in evidence, but my purse felt slightly heavier and I looked inside. There was a lot of condensed fluff in there now. Decided not to care. Felt something soft rub against my neck, then Gershom mewled at me and jumped into the purse as well. "Have Poofs, will travel."

"Auntie Abigail, are you coming with us?" Jamie asked.

"No, I'm not. I'm staying here with Doreen and keeping the Embassy running." She winked at me. "Someone has to do their jobs while the rest of you are off gallivanting."

My memory did me a solid and shared that she meant Doreen Weisman, who was the only truly trained diplomat on staff. I hadn't met her, and I couldn't remember if she knew I wasn't the Kitty they all expected or not. Decided that if she wasn't coming along it didn't matter.

"Just heard from James," Martini said as he came out of the bedroom, fully dressed and carrying all three bags. "We're leaving from the Zoo."

"Oh, enjoy that," Abigail said. "You're going to miss Boggy, though. She's across the street, visiting Olga."

"Boggy? Olga?"

"We told you about them—Boggy is Chernobog the Ultimate. The best hacker in the world, basically. She's on our side now. And Olga's the wife of the Romanian Ambassador and your good friend."

"Impressive. And I don't remember this at all."

"Long stories," Martini said quickly. "And ones you don't want right now, trust me. Just know that you're the one who brought Chernobog over onto our side and that Olga's never wrong, if you can figure out what she's telling you. Which you usually can."

"Go my Cosmic Alternate."

"Right." Abigail hugged me. "And go you, too. You'll do great. Call us if you need anything, we'll have someone up and ready twenty-four seven until you guys are all back." She left the apartment with us, but took the stairs.

"You don't mean we're leaving from where the animals are and where Jamie supposedly wants to go, do you?" I asked Martini as I picked Jamie up and we headed for the elevator. If the Peregrines were along, they were in their Invisible Mode, but I had a feeling more than just Bruno were coming with.

"No. We bought the other building on this block, and have a raised, covered walkway that connects them. It's where Hacker International, as your Cosmic Alternate calls them, live and work. And, ah, you need to be prepared."

"For what?"

"For Stryker Dane."

"Stryker's here? That's great!"

"Ah, yeah. Great. Per Chuck, and based on your descriptions of the Stryker in your world, you're not going to be able to handle how he looks in this world."

"Oh my God. Did he have an accident or something?"

"Ah. No. Just . . . try to control whatever reaction you

have, okay? And we have not told them what's going on, so you literally have to act normal, normal for my Kitty, around them."

"What is that normal?"

"Sarcasm and one-upmanship."

"Oh. So how it was with Eddy when I first met him. Gotcha."

"Probably exactly like that," Martini muttered.

We got out of the elevator on the second floor and the others joined us, rolling suitcases in hand, Secret Service agents included. Meaning we had a lot of people. Wanted to ask if we always rolled with this much of an entourage, then realized that no one seemed fazed, so of course they did.

Christopher and Amy were there, too, presumably to see us off. Len and Kyle took the luggage from Martini as we headed down the hallway. Had no idea what to say to the agents. "I'm so sorry about what happened," was all I could come up with.

"Those are the risks," Evalyne said briskly. "We would really appreciate you two not trying to escape from us in the future, however." She sounded unhappy with us, not that this was a surprise.

"They weren't after them," Kyle said. "Think about it. They're after the people protecting them, but not them. At least, not this time."

"Seems like it," Phoebe said. "However, our jobs are to protect the three of you. And Mister Reynolds as well."

"Where are they, by the way?"

"Waiting for us in the Zoo," Crawford said. "Reynolds is giving the hackers some directions and Richard and Buchanan are there to ensure that the recording artists you've added to the team don't get into trouble or break something."

The walkway was impressive. When I looked outside I saw protestors. Managed not to ask what was going on, only because I could see some of the signs. They were protesting that aliens were on the planet and that Martini was in public office.

"People like that," Evalyne said softly to me, "are part of what we're supposed to protect you from."

"Who protects the protectors, though? It's a two-way street. If we can protect you, we should."

She sighed. "We appreciate that sentiment, Kitty. But if you hadn't left in the middle of the night—"

"Eight of your peers might be alive. I know."

"Kyle's right," Len said. "Why were they sent to eight different gates? That screams setup to me. And I know it screams setup to all of you, too, Kitty especially."

People around me stiffened, Evalyne and Phoebe in particular. "Mister Goodman sent them to their locations," Phoebe said. "To cover all the bases . . ."

This wasn't good. These people weren't stupid, and they were all about to figure out what some of us knew already. But that just meant Goodman was going to catch on and put whatever his Doomsday Plan was into action.

Evalyne looked at me, and then looked at Martini. "Cut the chatter," she said, using her In Charge voice. "We'll discuss this when we're all at Sydney Base."

We were across the walkway and in a large room that had what appeared to be a bank of bathroom stalls against one wall, a gigantic, industrial kitchen at the far end, an elevator, two stairwells, and nothing else in it.

"No," Martini said. "We'll discuss it now." He jerked his head at Singh. "Search them."

Singh nodded, pulled out his bug finder, and ran it over every one of the Secret Service agents. "They're all clean. No bugs, no trackers, no emotional blockers or overlays."

"Great." Martini took a deep breath. "You all know we feel that we have a Mastermind who's running all the actions against us." Everyone nodded. "Well, we've determined who that is."

"Cliff Goodman," Evalyne said, voice like ice.

Martini nodded. "We think your coworkers were murdered in an attempt to frame Malcolm Buchanan and get him out of the way. It didn't work, but only because we figured out what was going on in time."

"How could he have done that?" one of the male agents whose name I hadn't been told or hadn't caught asked. "And why?"

"Why?" Singh asked. "Why does anyone betray their country and the people who trust them? Money, power, influence."

"And more," Martini said. "Since we've arrived on this planet, people have tried to control us to use us for their own ends, not for the reasons we came here—to protect and help our adopted world."

Everyone looked at me. No, not at me—at Jamie. I held her a little more tightly. "They want Jamie." We shouldn't be talking about this in front of her, but I had no idea how to stop this conversation.

Jamie hugged me. "It's okay, Mommy."

"It's not if one of you is working for Goodman, instead of working for the good of your country," Singh said.

"No." Everyone looked at me again. "I don't want people working for the good of their country. I want people around us who are working for what's right and decent. People who don't want a crazed madman to take a little girl and use her in ways I honestly don't even want to imagine. I want those kinds of people around us. You can do a lot of evil under the guise of doing good for your country. We want people around us who won't use those excuses to betray us, kill us, or use us."

"Kitty's right," Serene said. "If you're not with us, you're against us. Plain and simple."

"In other words," I said, "choose your side."

"And," Martini added, "choose it now."

CHAPTER 68

EVALYNE AND PHOEBE exchanged a look. "With you," Evalyne said, as they both stepped across the invisible line Singh had created when he'd searched the agents. "For all the reasons you named and one more—the agents who were murdered were our friends, and I'll be damned if I'm going to help the man who intentionally sent them to their deaths."

The other agents stepped across, one by one. The first one, the one who'd asked why Goodman would have done what he did, was the last man standing on the other side. "I want proof, not speculation, before I make the decision to betray my official orders."

"This is the Vice President of the United States," Phoebe said. "He overrules someone at Homeland Security."

"It's a legitimate request," Martini said. "But, we have no proof. Only the connection of events taken to their logical conclusion. I know you're new to the team, Sam, but we want to get the proof you want. Will you help us?"

The agent relaxed. In fact, he'd relaxed when Martini said that we had no proof. "Sure."

It was one thing to trust. But if your entire demand in order to give that trust was proof, relaxing when the confirmation of no proof was given was a contrary reaction. Malcolm wasn't

here. I wasn't sure if anyone else would listen to me. But had
to give it a shot. "Stop him, he's working for Goodman."

Everyone gaped at me. Everyone other than Christopher.
He moved faster than I could blink, grabbed Sam's arms, and
pulled them behind his back. Sam struggled, but he wasn't
going anywhere. "What the hell? Is this how you killed
everyone else?"

"Note that he thinks we killed those agents. Or else he's
spouting the party line. But he's not on our side."

"He didn't show as having any bugs or overlays," Singh
said, sounding uncertain.

"And I didn't feel anything wrong from him beyond suspicion and some fear," Martini added.

"If he's focused on fooling you, maybe he can."

"Or he swallowed an emotional overlay," Amy suggested.
"I don't think the detectors can tell if one of those things is
ingested."

"Good point. Search him again, please," Martini asked
Christopher. "The old fashioned way, this time."

Len and Kyle held the agent while Christopher frisked
him. "Nothing."

"Let's see his wallet," Crawford said. "And any other papers he might have on him. Just in case."

Christopher looked through the wallet at hyperspeed. At
least I assumed so, because I couldn't see anything his hands
were doing, but suddenly he had a card in one hand and a
seriously pissed expression. "It's a Club Fifty-One member-
ship card." He handed it to Martini. Who looked ready to kill.
Couldn't blame him.

"The only people who have those are our enemies," Martini said, voice like ice.

"We pointedly screened for anti-alien sentiments," Phoebe
said.

"Clearly not well enough," James said. "I'd like Christopher to go through the rest of your wallets, badges, and similar. That's not exactly a request, by the way," he added with
a smile that was a lot more feral than cover boy.

"Agreed," Evalyne said, as she produced her wallet. The others followed suit.

Christopher took just a few seconds. "No one else has anything anti-us on their person." He smiled at me. Nice to know he knew how. "Good catch, Kitty."

"It's what I'm here for." Literally, as near as I could tell.

Christopher gave everyone back their things, then Evalyne produced handcuffs and cuffed the agent. "What do we do with him? Until we have the proof we lack, I can't turn him over to Homeland Security."

"We have holding cells at Dulce," Singh said.

"I wouldn't send him there." Everyone looked at me. Heaved a sigh. "That just puts an enemy into the center of your operations. He needs to be locked up, I'll give you that, but not where, should he escape, he can cause more havoc."

"It's a good point," Martini said. "We have no idea what Sam's training or mission might actually be."

"Let's hope that no one else swallowed one of those things, because Amy's suggestion sounds right." Waited. Saying something nice about Amy didn't kill me. Amazing.

"We haven't, but all you have is our word," Evalyne said. The other agents nodded. Most of them looked seriously upset, but not with us, so that was a nice change.

"I think we can trust them," Martini said to me quietly. "Especially since I can feel all of them, and their emotions switched in a way the emotional blockers and enhancers don't seem able to mimic. The rest of them have been with us for months and have never done anything but be incredibly loyal and put up with us."

"One small favor. I'll take it."

"Where are we going to stash him?" Serene asked. "Like Jeff said, Kitty has a good point, but we normally use Dulce's incarceration facilities."

Felt something feathery nudge my leg and looked down. Bruno looked at me and winked slowly. "Ah, why don't we tie him up and leave him here, under Peregrine guard?"

"That works," Christopher said. "Kevin and I will keep

him and the birds with us. The Peregrines will claw him up if he manages to get free."

Bruno indicated that he'd been going to Australia because of Sam, and that he and the rest of the flock looked forward to clawing Sam up if he didn't cooperate with the authorities. Worked for me, but I decided not to share this information with anyone else.

"We can do some interrogation, too," Amy added. She didn't sound like the questioning would be pleasant.

Plan agreed to, Christopher and Amy decided they'd take the prisoner off instead of seeing us all the way to whatever gate we were going to. Kevin Lewis joined them before we all separated. I'd sort of met him during the gigantic info dump that everyone seemed to think I'd managed to memorize, but now that I saw him up close and personal I realized he was someone I knew in my world—he'd been over to my parents' house when I was younger. He was a gorgeous black guy with at least as much charisma as Martini.

"I'll advise Angela," he said once the situation was explained. "If she wants to take him, we'll let the P.T.C.U. enjoy themselves. Until then, we'll handle it. You guys go off and be diplomatic."

Kevin then helped Christopher with the prisoner—Sam hadn't been too much for Christopher, but got the feeling they were muscling him around to prep him for a Good Cop/Bad Cop/Amy Cop routine. Worked for me.

The rest of us got into the elevator. In shifts. Because there were a lot of people in the entourage. Each elevator shift had an A-C in it, presumably because no one felt too confident in the Secret Service all of a sudden.

Martini, Jamie, and I were in the first group to go up, but that just meant that we got to hang out and wait for the others to join us. Nothing untoward happened, which was a nice change of pace.

"Remember," Martini said to me in a low voice as we waited outside a door that said Computer Center, "you have to control your reactions."

"Yeah, yeah, yeah." Had no idea why he was acting weird about Stryker, but I'd handle it, whatever it was.

The last part of our group arrived and Martini opened the door. We entered what appeared to be a very large, very high-tech computer center, just like the door had indicated. It was a little reminiscent of the Bat Cave at the Science Center, but it wasn't bustling with gorgeous people.

Well, that wasn't quite accurate. Charles, Richard, and Malcolm were in here, so handsome to gorgeous was covered. There were also two people in the room who were clearly A-Cs, a man and a woman, and they looked like they were siblings, too, and clearly a part of the Gorgeous Contingent. Amadhia and Aaron were also here, having an animated conversation with Richard and Malcolm, and helping to support the Good-Looking Human side of the house.

The others, however, were not the most impressive specimens of manhood ever seen. I vaguely remembered who most of them were—Charles and I had met them at Stryker's place a few times. But I hadn't given any of them any thought in years, possibly because Stryker and Charles never mentioned them these days.

However, as a guy with unkempt but still somehow nice hair, manboobs, an unkempt and unattractive beard, dirty shorts and an even dirtier Star Trek T-shirt turned around, I now understood why Charles had been worried and Martini had spent so much time prepping me.

This wasn't the Stryker I knew. Well, that wasn't quite true. This was indeed the Stryker I'd *known*. I just thought I'd gotten rid of him eight years ago.

CHAPTER 69

AT HYPERSPEED it didn't take us too long to reach the commandos. They were pinned down at the end of this long corridor, on either side of a concrete doorway. We chose the side with the two commandos, versus four, and got out of the way.

"Who's shooting at you?" I asked the commando nearest me.

"Not who, what."

Risked a look to see an impressively large Gatling gun surrounded by smaller versions, all shooting at the doorway, apparently without anyone there to fire them.

"Is anyone hit?" Cantu asked.

"No, sir. We got out of the way just in time."

Considered this. During Operation Sherlock, Clarence had set up a set of guns to "shoot" us, but they were filled with blanks because Raul the Pissed Off Assassin wanted to kill us personally. Perhaps that wasn't either Clarence's or Raul's move, but Cliff's.

Maybe these guns were loaded with real bullets. But I couldn't think of a better early warning system that doubled as a way for your enemies to use up all of their ammo than this. But there was really only one way to find out.

Took my purse off and took Stripes out of it. Dug through to find a package of tissues. That'd do the trick. Sure I could use Other Me's wallet, but that seemed wrong, somehow.

Tossed the pack of tissues up high into the doorway. It fell down, with nothing hitting it.

"Stop wasting ammo!" The commandos ignored me. Figured. "Esteban, tell them to stop shooting."

"Just because your tissues weren't hit means nothing," he replied.

"Some men deserve what happens to them." Ran out at hyperspeed. Nothing hit or even winged me, not because I was going fast but because there was nothing to be hit with.

Got behind the guns to discover there was a projector there. Turned it off. Immediately the guns stopped firing and disappeared. Took a good look at the wall by the doorway—it was wired for sound. Looked up. Sure enough, this room had a high, sloping ceiling, and there was a grate, about two stories up, give or take.

Everyone else poked their heads into the doorway. "Well, now that you've wasted your ammo *and* let the bad guys know we're here, who wants to apologize for not stopping when I said so?"

Cox brought my purse over. "I would, ma'am, but I listened to you."

"How did you know?" Cantu asked. "This was realistic enough to fool men who've been in war."

"I kind of know this particular bad guy's playbook. Not all of it, mind you, but some of it." Enough of it to know that we'd just begun the gauntlet.

The others joined me, and as Stripes jumped onto my shoulder and the last commando crossed the threshold, a grate dropped from the doorway. The commandos tried to move it, but it wasn't budging.

Went over and pulled. "Alfred, need you." He came over and together we were able to rip the grate off. Tossed it to the side and turned around to see the commandos and Cantu staring at us openmouthed. "These suits are da bomb. Speaking of bombs, expect anything and everything a Bond villain might throw at us to be here in some way, shape, or form."

"Are you sure?" Alfred asked me.

"Dude, did you not just see that grate drop after, and only after, the last person who was on the walkway walked through the doorway? That means the concrete has some kind of pressure plates or they're observing us now, since our friends The Battle-Experienced Commandos alerted whoever to the fact that we're here."

"But Harlie found no one," Alfred said quietly.

"Yeah, well, your Poof is not trained like my Poofs. I didn't tell Harlie to look underground." And with Algar's Free Will Manifesto having been drilled into them, had to figure that the Poof wasn't necessarily as clear on what to look for and share as mine. Also, the Poofs tended to be really picky about specifics.

Alfred looked around. "Where do we go from here? This just looks like a round room."

It did. A very bland, very nothing round room. There was nothing on the concrete floor, nothing on the concrete walls other than the sound equipment by the doorway, and the only thing in the room was the projector, which was behind a small, curved, concrete sorta-wall that was only about waist high on me. However, there had been a lot of effort put into making this room, so I really doubted that it was the dead end it appeared to be.

"Let's start tapping the walls," I said to the room in general. "There's a secret door around here somewhere. Could be in the floor, too."

The commandos just stared at me. Decided I didn't like them. At all.

Went over to Cantu. "Okay, your guys just let our enemy know we're coming. I'm giving you this opportunity to let me lead the team."

The commandos snorted or muttered. Clearly they weren't

open to a woman being in charge, or else they somehow thought they hadn't mishandled the situation.

Cantu picked it up, not that it was hard to miss. "Let's check for secret doors in the walls and floors." The commandos instantly started tapping on things. Decided I might just have to hate them.

Cantu took my elbow and moved me away from his team. "Clearly you know what's going on, but these men aren't going to listen to you. I'd suggest you go over what you want to do with me, and I'll pass it along in a way they'll understand."

"They speak English, so that means they understand me. *You* mean they want their instructions coming from someone with a penis. And yeah, um, no. That doesn't work for me, because we're heading into a very dangerous situation and I'd like to ensure that my team and I get out of it alive. And leadership by committee surely doesn't work, and you're not actually my boss, so you can't get away with this particular glass ceiling. By the way, I assume my husband, children, and friends are already hostages, and I really don't want them harmed, either."

"So you think that Charles called me under duress?"

"I don't think, I know. He and the others had no idea this was Cliff Goodman's hideout—if they'd known, they'd have already handled this. Better than your commandos, by the way. The only way he could have told you to come here was if he was told where to tell you to come."

Cantu looked pissed. "That's why you wanted to know what he said, exactly. You were trying to figure out if he was passing along some kind of clue or warning to me."

"He was. He sounded scared and stressed. Charles doesn't do scared or stressed." Unless some bastard had a gun to his children's heads, which is what I figured was going on. "And if you were his boss, you should know that."

Cantu sighed. "I am his boss. And I'll give you that I should have noticed. I was just . . ." He shrugged and looked embarrassed. "I was just worried about my team and excited that I had a solid lead. I didn't pay attention."

"Right. Like you didn't pay attention at the doorway."

"It was very realistic gunfire. Very much like at the Farm."

"True." The Farm was the C.I.A.'s training center. Had to figure that if I'd been discussing this situation with Chuckie, Reader, or Buchanan, none of them would have compared what was going on to their training camp. In part because their time in training camp would have been years ago, and they'd certainly seen a lot more action since then.

Looked at how Cantu was dressed. Unlike the commandos, he was in a suit and nice shoes. The infrared goggles looked completely out of place on his head. And, as I looked around the room, Cantu looked completely out of place here.

I was so used to working with highly trained and efficient people who literally lived to be in suits that it hadn't dawned on me until this exact moment that Cantu was dressed completely inappropriately for bringing down a drug lord or an Evil Mastermind. He was dressed to take a meeting.

Internal Affairs tended not to be out in the field—they were the investigative branch, but that meant they spent most of their time investigating their own people, usually through paper trails and such.

Basically, Cantu was a desk jockey, hoping to bring down the Mole of Moles. In other words, he was the last guy who should be leading this team, and also likely the first one who was going to die. He wasn't James Bond or another Double-O—Chuckie, Reader, and Buchanan fit those positions. He wasn't even Q or M. He was the guy who Bond, Q, and M ignored until the day was saved and Her Majesty's Secret Service was back on top.

And he was the boss of the three men I was trying to save, and the only one who was going to be believed if things got as hairy as I knew they were going to.

Alfred chose this moment to call me over; Cox was already with him. I dutifully trotted over, reminding myself that, so far, pop culture had never let me down. Alfred had his mask off and was holding something that looked like a cell phone with some extras. "What do you have there, Q?"

Alfred beamed. "I do love those books and movies, Dou-ble-O-Seven."

"Glad to oblige and even gladder that you're not a sexist idiot."

"Does that make me Moneypenny, ma'am?"

"Works for me, Bill." Stripes meowed. "Stripes says that to him I'll always be Catwoman. I'm good with that, too. Now that the superspy and superhero names are all set, what's up and in your hand?" Looked a little closer. "And where did you score that duffel bag?"

"I ran back to the speeders and got more equipment. I figure we're going to need it. This is an advanced smartphone with extended reach capabilities—it can send and receive through metal and concrete—a three-D printer, and several other very useful programs. I'm scanning the rocks to see if I can spot the door or doors. I have to have my mask off to see the data on this screen, though—just one of those things I haven't perfected yet. By the way, I also did a search and it's not good on the Israelis," Alfred added in a low voice. "Their embassy was attacked early this morning—from what I can tell, just an hour or so after you'd left."

I'd been expecting this. But it didn't make my stomach clench any less. "Are they listing casualties?"

"Not yet."

"We know your husband's alive," Cox said. "And I have to figure your kids are, too. Probably the others as well. No reason to tell Cantu to come down here if they're all dead—why help out your enemy in that way?"

"I agree, Lunatic Lad. I'm certain Cliff has some of them—hopefully all of them. But saving them is going to be harder because of who we're stuck working with."

"Those are paid commandos," Cox said derisively.

"You're sure?"

"Yes, ma'am. Heard them talking. They don't think they were paid enough to, and I quote, 'have to listen to some chick carting around some weird cat who thinks she knows what she's doing.' Needless to say, I'm not impressed."

"Charming. But I think I know how to handle them. So, Alfred-Q, what's the status on how we get out of this room and move on?"

"Interesting." He went over to the only thing in this room—the curved little wall. "I'm positive there's a mechanism of some kind in this. But I can't see how to trigger it."

"And I already checked this area, and I couldn't find anything," Cox said.

The commandos were done and complaining that there were no doors and that this was a colossal waste of time. Cantu wasn't telling them to shut up and stop whining. Figured I was going to have to get tough and soon. But first, time to test a theory.

"Everyone, be ready to move."

Then I lifted up the projector.

CHAPTER 70

CONVENIENTLY, my team was with me, so when the curved wall and its surrounding floor started to move, both men grabbed one of my arms, just in case. Our part of the floor started to sink as we turned, thankfully slowly, in a clockwise direction.

"Better hurry up and come along if you're coming," I called to Cantu. Figured the commandos could do whatever.

"Follow them!" Cantu barked, as he trotted over and jumped down to join us. Cox caught and steadied him.

The commandos followed, but none of my team bothered to try to steady them. A couple of them bounced off the wall, but no one seemed hurt.

"How did you know?" Cantu asked.

"When all other options have been eliminated, the last choice, no matter how bizarre or right out of the movies it may seem, is the only option. Plus, I have a rule—I always go with the crazy. So far, it's never let me down." Handed the projector to Cox. "I think if we put that down we go back up." He nodded.

Turned to the nearest commando. "So, I understand you boys don't like following a female leader."

"No offense," he said, with offense definitely in his tone.

"Huh. You have some big guns and such there. Can I hold one?"

He sniggered, pulled a weapon I knew to be extremely heavy, and handed it to me. "Sure."

"Awesome." Took the gun without any issue. All the commandos looked shocked. "Yeah, I'm a lot stronger than I look. And you're a bunch of misogynistic assholes." Slammed the butt of this gun into the commando's stomach. He buckled. Held the gun in my right hand, grabbed him by his throat with my left hand, and practiced Commando Bowling by tossing him at his buddies as hard as I possibly could.

"Wow, got a strike. Left handed, too. I've still got it."

"Uh, why did you do that?" Cantu asked nervously.

Considered my options. Pulled off my mask and shot him a look I hoped was channeling Mom's most intimidating stare. My hair looking crazy bad could, in this instance, only help. Based on the way Cantu backed up, it worked.

"Because I am in charge and every asshole on this platform had better accept that, right now, or I'm going to beat the crap out of them and throw them up into that room we were just in, so that they don't endanger me and my far more awesome team. *Capisce?*"

The commandos nodded as they slowly got to their feet. "You take that suit off and try to tell us what to do," the one whose gun I had muttered.

Went over to him. "I would, but I'm not as stupid as you." Used my fist to give him an uppercut. He went down and out. "My team, strip him of all his gear. Do it fast."

The other commandos looked like they wanted to intervene. Pointed the big gun at them. "Try me. I'm pissed, and you're not my boys. Frankly, you're hired guns, meaning that the next person to offer you more money gets your loyalty. I have no idea what the C.I.A.'s paying these days, but I'll just bet it's not what a Bond Villain can cough up."

Missed Jeff something fierce. He'd have been able to tell what these guys were feeling and know if their entire plan was to get Cantu inside, hand him over to Cliff, and then take a bigger payday.

However, having spent the last several years with people who truly could not lie, I'd gotten exceptionally adept at spotting signs and tells—hanging with A-Cs was a master class in this, and considering how often the people around me passed little signs back and forth, I was an expert at spotting the most minute of reactions. And all the signs and tells were there. I'd hit their nail right on their heads—they were planning to turn as fast as the money came in.

"All done," Alfred said.

It wasn't a large room, and my guys were near the commandos. Literally right on cue four of them grabbed Cox and Alfred.

"Now, let's talk," the fifth one said, as he produced a gun and pointed it at me.

"Oh, blah, blah, blah. Let's not and say we did, okay?" I was mad as hell, and just wasn't going to take it anymore.

Stripes was pissed, too. He leaped for the commando's face while I hit the forearm holding the gun down and away. Felt and heard the satisfactory sound of bone breaking. As Stripes landed, I slammed my foot up and into the guy's groin. As he crumpled, cat still going to town, I tossed my big gun up in the air, jumped up to grab the faces of the two commandos holding Cox, and slammed them back into the wall, hard. As they both went down, did the same with the two holding Alfred. Caught the gun as it came down and pointed it at the guy Stripes was mauling.

"Good kitty, come to Mommy." Stripes hissed one last time, then jumped back onto my shoulder. "Yo, dude, I want some answers, and I want them now." He groaned. I stepped on his foot. Hard. He yelped. "There we go. Who are you working for?"

"No one," he managed. "I mean, we're working for him," he nodded toward Cantu, "but we were going to see if the drug lord was open to paying us more."

Looked at Cantu. "You told them you were after a drug lord?"

He nodded. "I had to go outside of the Agency because I truly don't know who we can trust anymore. It's easier to get mercenaries to go after drug lords than Agency moles."

"My God. You know, when this is over, you really need to have a session with Charles, James, and Malcolm, especially Malcolm, wherein you spend a lot of time listening and learning and they spend a lot of time telling you how to actually survive in the field." Turned to Alfred. "You have zip ties and duct tape in your bag of Q Tricks?"

He nodded proudly. "I do. Duct tape is the best thing this planet has ever invented."

"Really, that's not one of yours?"

"No, but it's one of my favorite things." He produced a big role of tape and a handful of zip ties.

"You rock. Okay, my boys, strip 'em and tie 'em up. I want them all down to their skivvies and said skivvies searched. These are people I'm generously not going to kill," looked at my lone conscious commando, "though I really want to, but we don't want them having a hope of getting free."

Alfred did the stripping at hyperspeed, Cox did the tying up. Being the Sidekick, he also got stuck with the Skivvy Check, but since he was still wearing his weird mask, I couldn't see his expression. His reactions said that this was potentially the most unpleasant thing he'd had to do in a long time. Probably was.

"Alfred, am I right in that you want to keep your mask off to see what's on your Screen O' Wonder?"

"Yes but, under the circumstances, I think I'll put it on just in case."

"Wise man." Put my mask back on as well. "Esteban, you're kind of screwed in the protective department. However, we now have a lot of Kevlar for you to choose from. Find the stuff that fits you the best and put it on. Now. Oh, and that's an order, not a suggestion."

Proving he was far smarter than his hired muscle, Cantu did as requested. He found a vest and got it on just as the slowest hidden elevator in the world stopped moving. Had a feeling all of this was setup so that Cliff could have his killer sharks with lasers all primed and ready.

But instead, what we were treated to was another hallway. This one had a light at the end. Figured it was going to be a freight train. "Okay, Esteban, if they have Kevlar pants, you want those as well."

"Just the vests," Cox shared. "What do we do with all their weapons?"

"Carry what we can, empty all chambers, take any extra ammo with us."

"I can carry it," Alfred said to Cox. "I have room in my bag."

"It's going to be pretty heavy," Cox said uncertainly.

"I'll let you know if it's too much for me," Alfred replied.

"Take any and all knives, because I truly don't want these guys getting free." Picked up the projector from where Cox had put it down and examined it. Looked like a regular projector. Put it in the doorway so that, should this elevator try to go up, we'd at least have a shot of hearing the projector get destroyed as an early alert.

Cox handed me a plethora of knives. "I have all I can carry and Alfred's bag is full."

"Wow, Esteban, at least you're getting your money's worth in terms of weaponry." Stashed the knives in my purse. I still had the big gun because I liked it. Maybe I'd even fire it, though I was enjoying using it as a blunt instrument.

"So," Cantu said, "what do we do now?"

"I love a man who can learn. Now we creep down the hallway, weapons at the ready, looking for traps and such, and expect to find bad things trying to kill us at the end. Or, as I like to call it, routine."

CHAPTER 71

"O KAY," Cantu said, "what I expected. Since you've in-capacitated the people I would have sent first, who's leading?"

"Me." Hey, none of the guys I worked with normally were here to shove me behind them, Jeff in particular. And the person with both hyperspeed and field experience should be going first anyway. "And I'm not going to apologize for in-capacitating our potential cannon fodder. They're less of a danger to us this way."

"I'm not arguing, and since you've broken right through that glass ceiling, lead on, Missus Reynolds."

We headed out me first with Stripes on my shoulder, my purse over my neck, and a gigantic gun in my hands. Then came Cantu, Cox, and Alfred bringing up the rear. Would have preferred Cox back there, but I still wasn't sure that we could trust Cantu, so wanted Cox keeping an eye on him.

Showing that I could be taught, I looked carefully for trip-wires and such as we moved forward at a snail's pace. Sure, I wanted to run in and save everyone, but I knew better. The Cliff here didn't know me, but he'd clearly memorized the Bond Villains' Guide to Wealth and Power and I didn't want to fall into the shark tank simply because I'd been too eager to engage.

Alfred's goggles were the greatest here. Not only could I see, but I could actually spot the areas on the walkway that had pressure plates on them without having to use Alfred's Super Duper Smarty-Pants Phone. Meaning the plates weren't as hidden as the elevator mechanism had been. Had no idea what this meant, so chose not to worry about it.

We were able to inch around or jump over all of the traps, though there were a couple where Cantu and Cox couldn't have done it without me and Alfred assisting. Hoped we wouldn't have to run back the way we'd come, because I wasn't sure I could spot and avoid these again, especially if I was going fast.

As we neared the doorway I could hear sounds. In addition to my improved hearing, the earpieces definitely made distant sounds easier to hear. So I could make out that people were talking.

Got a little closer and I could confirm the voices—Cliff, LaRue, and Chuckie. This boded, not that everything hadn't boded already.

Reached the point where I could hear clearly, which was conveniently right before another pressure plate, which was placed about twenty feet from the door. Put my hand up and everyone behind me stopped moving. The doorway was at one end of the next room, because all I could see was the wall on the left, which had nothing much to mark it as interesting, and the far wall, which had a lot of scientific-looking stuff, but nothing that I could identify. I couldn't see anyone, but I could indeed hear them.

"They're taking forever to get here," LaRue said. "Make one of them scream and maybe they'll hurry up."

"Leave my family alone," Chuckie snarled.

"Oh, Cantu and his men will be along shortly," Cliff said. He sounded incredibly smug. "And, really, Chuckie-boy, there's nothing you can do for yourself, let alone your adorable little moppets here. I'm just sorry that your wife was off having an affair behind your back and so is going to miss all this."

"Keep away from her, too," Chuckie said.

"Oh, we'll find her," LaRue said. "If you're lucky, we'll find her with her boyfriend and you can watch her choose saving him over you."

Wondered if they'd somehow found me and seen me meet up with Cox. However, from what Chuckie had said to me, it was clear that he and Other Me had some trust issues based on his secret career. So this was probably just the bad guys going for a weakness, not them having any clue about reality.

"You're both so full of shit," Buchanan said.

"You're just jealous that she's not screwing you," Cliff said.

"Can I give the kids some candy while you all argue?" a woman asked, with sarcasm dripping. Recognized who was speaking—Bernie. Meaning that Cliff and Company had attacked the Israelis to get their assassins back, and had scored my family and friends in the process.

Rage could be a bad thing if uncontrolled, but I'd learned that it was my friend. The more enraged I was, the more my A-C talents worked exactly as I wanted them to. Christopher had spent a lot of time working with me on being able to bring up the skills when I wasn't mad, but he'd never had to help me when Rage was riding along as my copilot. And Rage was now with me in full force.

"You're a mean, ugly lady," Jamie said defiantly. "Our mommy's going to come and make you sorry."

"This is a bad time for you to act like a normal kid," Bernie snapped. Heard the sound of someone getting slapped and then heard Jamie start to cry softly. "I say we kill this little bitch first. I'd like to kill someone or something, after what they did to us. And she does look just like her mother, so that would be extra satisfying."

"Stop hurting my sister, you big bully!" Max shouted. This earned him a slap, too, but he didn't cry.

"You're going to be sorry," Charlie said defiantly. I could tell he was terrified, but he was still being brave. Was so proud of all three of them. "You can hit me all you want but you're still going to lose." Yet another slap. If I thought I'd hated Bernie before, it was nothing compared to how I hated her now.

"Leave my children alone," Chuckie said, and I could tell his teeth were gritted. "You want to hurt someone? Hurt me, not helpless children."

Heard the unmistakable sound of someone being punched in the gut. "How was that?" This was from Raul. At least, I thought it was Raul. He sounded kind of slurred and as if his teeth were gritted even more than Chuckie's.

"You're *so* brave," Reader said.

"No, just returning the favors you gave us earlier," another man said. Was positive it was Lopez. Heard another punch being handed out and heard Reader shout. It was a *kiai* though, so hopefully that meant he wasn't badly hurt.

"Can I hit the other one, just to make it fair?" Sanchez asked as I heard Buchanan make the "ooof" sound associated with getting punched in the gut. Goody, the Evil Gang was all here. And, just possibly, they didn't have any hostages other than those I'd heard.

How Dad, Aunt Carla, Caroline, and Pierre, let alone everyone else, had escaped capture I had no idea. Chose to believe they'd escaped, as opposed to the alternative, which was that they'd already been killed in the attack. Rage said that it was going to focus on the latter option, just because it made Rage want to sing the song of its people. And that song sounded a lot like *Kill 'Em All*, which was also a great album from Metallica. Shared with Rage that I felt we should both "Seek and Destroy." Rage gave me a high five.

"Stop playing around," Cliff said, sounding bored. "Plenty of time for that later. We need everyone here so that we can finish this once and for all with no loose ends. We're ready to roll out my master plan, so I want to be sure that all the t's are crossed and all the i's are dotted."

"The woman, she's not normal," Lopez said. "You can't forget about her."

"Oh, we haven't," LaRue said. "But, really, she's the least

of our worries right now. However, you can check and see what's going on with our visitors. It's taking them far too long to show up."

"Nothing's been triggered," Cliff said. "Stop worrying. They're probably just trying to figure out where to go, since there's all of one way."

Realized what Cliff's weakness was—he'd spent too long being the smartest. He had the person he viewed as his only rival captured and essentially helpless, and that was making him sloppy.

However, this was a chess game. And the thing I'd learned about chess was that even when your opponent seemed overconfident, it could actually be a ruse to make you foolhardy.

So it could easily be that Cliff knew we were in the hall and was baiting us. Because Lopez didn't come to the doorway. Meaning the assassins had told them about me and what I'd done to them. Meaning that all the boyfriend crap was to bait me into racing in there to protest that I was a good, faithful wife.

There had been a grate in the first room, too, high up to investigate. However, there could easily have been a camera up there, meaning that Cliff knew that all of us were here. And he also knew we were weaponized in some way.

But all the assassins really knew was that I was hella strong. And while Alfred had used hyperspeed while we were in the room, what it would show on camera is him suddenly having a duffel where he'd had nothing before. Meaning that Cliff might think we possessed some sort of super attractor or had had the duffel camouflaged.

In this world, there were no superheroes, after all. Just Alfred, who'd spent decades hiding, and me. They didn't know what hyperspeed was, because humans couldn't see someone going as fast as the two of us could. And there was no way any human would be able to see me going at Full Rage Level. And since Bernie had slapped Jamie, I'd gone well beyond that level of rage.

Put the big gun down carefully, took Stripes off my shoulder, and handed him carefully to Cox. "There's a pressure plate two steps away," I said in the softest whisper I could. Cox and Alfred both nodded. Cantu opened his mouth and I put my hand over it. "Beyond that I'm not sure. Stay here and don't come in unless it's obvious that I need you."

Really wanted to hear some music. Didn't think I could take the time to dig out the iPod. But Alfred had said the transmitters worked via our brainwaves. Concentrated. For this kind of battle, I wanted the song I'd used when I'd taken out the former Diplomatic Corps in the Parisian dungeon.

The sounds of Tina Turner's "Steel Claw" started up. Amazing. No wonder Alfred had every patent in his name in our world—he was a freaking miracle worker.

Picked up my big gun. Then, Tina rocking in my ears, I took a deep breath, jumped over the pressure plate, and kicked my hyperspeed up to eleven.

CHAPTER 72

MANAGED TO KEEP my jaw from dropping, but only just. "What's up, Kitty?" Stryker asked. "You look like you've seen a ghost."

The Ghost of Bad Fashions and Worse Hygiene Past, but managed not to say that, either. "Just been a long day." That was certainly true.

"We're in a hurry," Martini said.

Stryker rolled his eyes. "When aren't you?"

"Don't mouth off to him like that," I snapped. One of the guys, who was wearing sunglasses, jerked and swiveled his head toward me. Right, that was Yuri Stanislav and he was indeed blind. He also looked a little freaked out.

"You're in a mood," Stryker said, shooting me a baleful look. "Still a little sensitive about screwing things up with Australia?"

"You'll fix it," one of the other guys, who faded memory told me was Ravi Gaekwad, said. The Beauty Queen was sitting on his desk and it appeared they were an item. No accounting for taste, but whatever. At least Ravi looked normal. Looked at Stryker again. Ravi looked incredibly good by comparison.

"Thanks. We need to get moving," I said to Martini, in part to avoid staring at Stryker. He hadn't looked like this for years now, not since I'd convinced him that a bestselling author should take a modicum of care with his personal hygiene and wardrobe.

To see that what I considered First Iteration Stryker was apparently Only Iteration Stryker in this world was unsettling at best and horrifying at worst. And the hope that maybe he wasn't an author here was dashed by looking at the shelf above his head—where all twelve books in the *Taken Away* series were prominently and proudly displayed.

"Right." Martini hustled us over to what looked like a big computer server but which, when the front was opened, turned out to be empty. Martini fiddled with something I couldn't see and I realized there was a gate inside. Clever. Why they had to hide it in their own building was beyond me, but like so many things alien, I just went with "whatever."

"We're set for a noon meeting, meaning they're going to let you guys break bread with them," James said. "This is good. But we're pretty sure they expect us to blow it again. Plan for press to be there in full force."

"We'll handle it." I would have defended our plan, such as it was, but I was too busy eavesdropping on the guys Martini said my CA called Hacker International. They were speaking softly, but I caught the gist—Yuri thought I sounded wrong. And he wanted to call Tito in to check and see if I was an android.

The other four were readying to tackle me in an effort to ensure that I couldn't harm anyone or steal Jamie. Which was rather heroic, all things considered. However, it would mean that, in order to explain what was really going on, we'd have to tell even more people what *was* going on, and I knew that wasn't in anyone's best interests.

Yuri hadn't reacted to the first thing I'd said. He'd reacted when I'd told Stryker not to be rude to Martini. Meaning that it wasn't the sound of my voice but the words I was saying or the tone I'd used, or both, that had made Yuri react.

Time to go back to high school, which Charles and I had been in when he'd first found Stryker. "What are the five of you whispering about like you're in grade school?" I asked as I went over to them. "You'd better not be watching porn on our time."

"Ah, Kitty," Yuri said. "Why don't you let us hold Jamie for a minute?"

"Because I don't trust any of you not to drop her on her head. Seriously, what's up with all of you?"

"Sounds like Kitty to me," Stryker muttered.

"Yuri might be right," a small Chinese guy who I was fairly sure was named Henry Wu said nervously.

"I don't know," Ravi sounded worried. "Might be her. Might not be."

"Oh my God, seriously? This is what the powwow is about? It's me. I had a concussion in case you didn't register that. Sorry if I'm not making your days with witty banter right now. We're in the middle of a crisis."

"When aren't you?" the tall black guy, who memory shared was Big George Lecroix, asked. "But, just to make everyone feel comfortable, what do you call us?"

"You mean besides my favorite idiots? Hacker International."

Big George shrugged. "Works for me."

"Great," James said, coming over. "While we'll have several hours to kill before your luncheon, let's kill them in Australia, shall we?" He put his hand on my back and steered me back to Martini. "Now, if we can start going through and actually get to Sydney Base, that would make everyone, the President and myself in particular, happy."

"We're ready, James." Martini indicated that the others should start walking through. Which they did. The slow fade was unsettling to watch, so I didn't.

"Do we carry Jamie through?" I asked him quietly.

"Yep. I'll be carrying both of you." He grinned and kissed the top of my head. "You never have to go through a gate alone unless I'm not around, baby." Noting Yuri noting this exchange.

It took what seemed like forever but really was only about

two minutes for everyone else and all the luggage to go through. Evalyne and Phoebe wanted to go last, but Martini overruled them.

"Are they trustworthy?" I jerked my head toward the hackers. If they were the same as or better than I remembered, then these were probably the best hackers in the world right now, meaning they were extremely smart in a lot of ways. Ways that might help me.

"Your CA thinks so, yeah."

"Yuri suspects. I think I can keep them from blowing my cover, if it's okay."

He sighed. "Make it fast."

Handed Jamie to her father and went over to the hackers. "Yuri's right," I said softly. "But I'm not an android. I'm in Bizarro World, and your Kitty's changed places with me. I don't know how to get back and I'm not sure that she does, either. Can you work on that while we're in Australia?"

"I knew it!" Yuri said triumphantly. The others looked interested and freaked out in about equal measures. But none of them looked like they didn't believe me, and that was good.

"Keep it down and keep it to yourselves. And, see what you can come up with for inter-universe exchanges." Refrained from mentioning anything about their clothing or personal grooming choices and hightailed it back to Martini.

He gave Jamie back to me and swung me up into his arms. Held her tightly and leaned my face into him, and away we went.

If the transfer from D.C. to Paris had sucked, the transfer from D.C. to Sydney was a million times worse. It took all I had not to throw up, but just when I thought there was going to be nothing I could do to stop from barfing, we stopped and hit solid ground.

Opened my eyes as Martini put me down and took Jamie from me quickly. "We're close to a bathroom," he said quietly.

Shook my head. "I think I can manage it. You'd think I'd get used to it, wouldn't you?"

He patted my back gently. "Some things make the gate transfers harder."

Before I could ask what those things were, the others were around us. "Let's get everyone into housing," James said briskly. "We may not be here for more than a few hours, but let's be comfortable in that time. Everyone take about thirty minutes to settle in and then we'll regroup and go over strategy."

Sydney Base looked a lot like what I'd seen of the Science Center, only smaller, as far I could tell. Australian A-Cs were just as gorgeous as the rest, so that was nice and normal.

Housing in a Base wasn't like at the Embassy, at least not what I'd seen of the Embassy. We were put into what was basically a really nice hotel room. Thankfully, we had two beds in the room—one king, one full. Had to figure the Operations Team had set this up especially for us, but I appreciated it.

There was a knock at the door. "Enter," Martini said. The door whooshed open.

"Wow, how very *Star Trek*."

"It's nice, isn't it?" Richard asked as he came in. "I'm right next door and since it took me all of two minutes to unpack, I was hoping I could steal Jamie and show her around the Base. I don't believe she's been here before."

"Yay! Can I go with Uncle Richard, Mommy? Can I?"

Looked at Martini who grinned. "Sure, why not?"

"It's okay with Daddy, so it's okay with me. Be good, have fun, and remember that we're going to have lunch with important people so don't eat anything to spoil your appetite." Jamie hugged and kissed us, then Richard took her hand and led her out, Mous-Mous on her shoulder.

"Uh, is everyone around us?" I asked as I unpacked Jamie's bag.

Martini shrugged. "Should be. But, don't worry—Chuck's in a single room. And he's not in love or even romantically interested in Amadhia, by the way."

"Huh?"

"I felt your jealousy. He just thinks the same as I do—if we leave her alone right now we leave her vulnerable to attack. Probably the same with Aaron, especially since he's now firmly on our side. Amadhia and Aaron have single rooms. They're not romantically interested in each other, either. Both of them are just too excited about the fantastic day and grand adventure they're having to focus on romance with anyone."

"Oh. Uh, good. I guess."

He ran his hand through his hair. "I know you'd rather be with him than me, especially when we sleep. Chuck, I mean, not Aaron."

"Yeah, I figured." Thought about it. "But no. Neither one of you are really my husband. Yes, there's a part of me that wants to take care of him, but honestly, this isn't my world."

Martini looked surprised. "You've been struggling with this whenever he's nearby and whenever it's seemed like he was focused on another woman. What's changed your outlook?"

"Stryker Dane and what you said about Amadhia."

"Come again?"

"Seeing Stryker just brought home to me how different it is here. I like it here, and I like all of you, but this isn't the world I'm from. If I'm forced to stay here, then we'll figure out what the heck to do. But right now, I'm working on the assumption that once we solve the problems with Australia, I'm going to be zapped home."

"Okay, what did you mean about what I said about Amadhia?"

"Her great adventure. This is *my* great adventure. And, honestly, it's been scary and exciting and even romantic, and I think my being here will help all of you. But, even with Mom here, this world is missing something I'm not willing to live without."

He smiled gently at me. "Your children."

I nodded. "I'm sure my CA is doing a great job with them, but they aren't hers, they're *mine*, and they need *me*. And it's been wonderful to see what Jamie could be like, but my Jamie needs my help, not for me to skip off with the perfect version of her. I need to help her become the best she can be, however much or little that might be. And her brothers need to know that I've missed them and they can't know that until I go home and tell them so."

He hugged me. "I promise, we'll get you home."

"I'll hold you to that. Now, let's get unpacked and then figure out how to ensure that we compliment instead of insult our hosts."

Martini grinned. "First time for everything."

CHAPTER 73

THE LESS SAID about the several hours of stress that we went through to prep for meeting the PM couple and not blowing it this time the better. Getting to see video replays of what had happened was a special extra. The call from Strauss bawling us out on speakerphone for going without her was the most fun, and only a few people reprimanded me when I hung up on her mid-rant.

Our luncheon was confirmed, however, and Martini, Jamie, and I went back to our room to freshen up. I'd kept the sweater dress on, just in case, but happily I hadn't spilled anything on myself and the sheath dress didn't even look wrinkled. Jamie looked adorable in a pink and black ensemble, and Martini looked great like he always did.

Martini had me take the dress off so he could apply sunscreen to my arms and such. I was wearing a bra and panties that showed less than a swimsuit, and I sunburned in three point two minutes, so decided to let this lack of modesty be overruled by common sense. Chose not to wear makeup—I wasn't a makeup wearer on a regular basis, and the idea of getting lipstick on this outfit was terrifying.

Zipped back up into my dress and assembled like a picture-perfect VP family, albeit one covered in sunscreen, we went to the level where the main gates were. Apparently

A-C Bases went down more than they went up. Refrained from asking if they had groundhog in their DNA and instead just chalked it up to another "aliens are weird" moment.

The plan was to take a gate to the Canberra airport and then take a limo from there. Martini wasn't happy about this, but he was overruled by everyone else.

Well, really, it wasn't a limo—it was limos, plural. Because there were a lot more than just the three of us. As per usual for the A-Cs, we were rolling with an entourage.

In addition to the three of us, Alpha Team was coming along as were Charles, Malcolm, Len, Kyle, and, thankfully, Richard and, of course, Singh. No one said it out loud, but it was clear that everyone was hoping that Richard and Singh would do most of the talking, Charles in particular. Pointedly didn't allow this to hurt my feelings. Much.

Amadhia and Aaron were also along for the ride, because my "let them sing a song or something" idea was taken as a great Plan B. Both of them were basically acting like kids at Disneyland for the first time, but hopefully their excitement and enthusiasm would wow the PM couple. Thankfully, they hadn't objected at all to being dressed like every other male or female A-C. Jamie and I were essentially the only spots of color in our entire group. Which meant Jamie and I were exceptionally good targets should someone want to shoot at us. Chose not to point this out, since I had to figure this had occurred to someone else aside from myself.

We also had a plethora of random guys in suits, which I was told were Field agents who were functioning as A-C Secret Service. And, of course, our massive actual Secret Service contingent. Basically, we looked like the best-dressed and best-looking invading army of penguins ever.

Because of how nicely everyone was decked out and the brevity of the gate trip from Sydney to Canberra, Martini was encouraged to carry only Jamie through the gate. Chose to show I was a big girl, in part because Aaron and Amadhia couldn't wait to try the gates and I wasn't going to let them show me up.

Field agents and some of the Secret Service went through first. I was sandwiched between Crawford and Martini, which was okay, because if I threw up, I figured Crawford might forgive me for it.

Crawford did the horrible slow fade thing and then it was my turn. "You can do it, baby," Martini said softly from behind me.

Nodded, took a deep breath, and stepped through.

It had been bad enough being held. Walking through on my own meant I felt the entire transfer. I made the mistake of keeping my eyes open, meaning not only did I see nothing-ness in front of me, but I could see the world literally rushing by me in my peripheral vision. No wonder my CA never went through this alone or without her face buried in Marti-ni's neck.

But in less than two seconds my lead foot hit terra firma and the horrible feeling of the world racing past me at faster than hyperspeed ended a moment later. I gagged, but didn't throw up, and Crawford was waiting for me, to help me stay up and move me out of the way.

"Hang in there, Kitty," he said nicely. "Hopefully that's the worst today has to offer."

"Gaack. Sorry. Yeah, a girl can dream, right?"

Making me green, well, greener with envy, Amadhia and Aaron both had no issues with the gate. They both thought it was the coolest thing ever and chattered about how they had to write a song about the experience. Apparently they were musical soul mates and literally loved each other's ideas all the time. Hoped the honeymoon phase would last a long time.

To their credit, when they saw how sick I looked, Amadhia hugged me and Aaron offered me a peppermint. Accepted both, both of which made me feel somewhat better.

We'd landed in the middle of a Qantas Airlines executive lounge that had been cleared for us, which was nice and, per my entire lifetime's experience, typically Australian. It was going to be unsettling, meeting Aussies who were angry with me and mine. I was used to my family being greeted like the Prodigal Reynolds Clan whenever we came back to Sydney and Canberra. To have people I loved not know me and not like me was going to be harder to handle than the gate transfer.

Entourage assembled, we headed for ground transportation. Apparently the A-Cs had their own worldwide fleet of limos, and, as we went to the area where dignitaries and celebrities got to go—in other words, where the average person and the paparazzi couldn't—saw at least a dozen gray limos waiting. The entourage heading for them without hesitation indicated these were our sweet rides.

Martini, Jamie, Charles, Richard, Singh, and I were ushered into the back of one limo together. Len booted the driver and Kyle took shotgun. We weren't the lead car, but one a few back. Was surprised that neither Malcolm nor the Secret Service were with us. Looked around—Malcolm and the Secret Service were getting into impressive-looking black SUVs. "We're going to look like a parade. Or a funeral."

"Let's stick with parade," Charles said.

"Do you live here? I mean part time."

He nodded. "I do. I used to have a place in Sydney but once the A-Cs were outed, so was I, so I gave up my cover home in Sydney and now I have a nice flat in the Forrest suburb of Canberra."

"Oh, we looked there. Decided to stay in Sydney and just fly into Canberra when we needed to. Our house is in Darling Point."

Charles whistled. "Nice location."

"You felt we deserved the best. Besides, it's not like you're suffering in Forrest."

He grinned. "No argument."

Singh sighed. "You two need to stop that and stop it now."

Shot a guilty look up at Martini. "Sorry."

He shrugged. "All they're doing is talking about real estate, Raj. However, Kitty, remember that we don't have a home here."

"Right, we live at the Embassy. Why there and not the Naval Observatory?"

"Due to the anti-alien groups we have all over, we felt it was safer for the Vice President to remain in the Embassy," Singh said. "And as you're still the Ambassador, it made sense that way as well."

"Is that normal? To have the wife of the VP remain as an ambassador?"

"When the king of a solar system that has faster-than-light travel and many different kinds of impressive battle cruisers says he's watching to be sure his relatives aren't being abused, certain allowances are made," Richard said with a twinkle.

"Especially when those battle cruisers saved the planet from other aliens who weren't so nice," Charles added.

Decided I'd better change the subject before they all went into Information Overload Mode. Especially because I'd just remembered something. "Uh, did we actually bring the gift along?"

"Yes," Singh said with a smile. He knocked on the glass partition and it lowered. "Kitty needs reassurance. And keep the glass down." Kyle passed a nicely wrapped box back, which Singh handed to me. "It's wrapped very well, so even if you drop it, the contents shouldn't break."

"Thanks for that vote of confidence." Put the package into my purse. "So, we're heading to the Lodge?"

"Yes," Singh confirmed.

"We're really obvious. Is no one even the teensiest bit worried about someone, ah, choosing to make a statement?"

Richard shook his head. "You and Jeffrey are still incredibly popular with the general populace."

"Yeah, Kitty," Len said. "Take a look out the window."

Did so, and saw there were some people with signs along the side of the road. "Martini for PM!" "Aliens not Costello," and "Aliens Speaking For Us All" seemed to be the main slogans.

Martini groaned. "This isn't going to help us with the actual Prime Minister, is it?"

"Probably not, but if we can find a way to turn it into a joke, Tony might get over it."

"And that, baby, is why we're looking to you to save the day."

"But no pressure."

Richard chuckled. "Don't worry, Katherine—around here, you saving the day is just routine."

CHAPTER 74

IN MY WORLD, the Lodge was a sore point with everyone—
it needed renovations and they were, of course, taking far
longer and costing much more than planned.

Apparently having aliens on the planet made many things
go much more smoothly, and one of the favors that the A-Cs
had done for Australia was help renovate the Lodge. However, that had been a couple years prior, right after the world
got to find out lots of aliens existed all over, so the gratitude
was long gone.

Sadly, the nearer we got to the Lodge, the more people
with signs there were. But these weren't nice signs. The anti-
alien protestors had chosen to camp out closer to the Lodge,
for obvious political reasons.

However, our massive fleet of limos and burly SUVs kept
them back, and no one threw anything, so all things considered, it wasn't nearly as bad as it could have been.

Jamie had been quiet for most of the trip and I hugged her.
"Are you okay, sweetie-pie?"

She looked up at me and she looked worried. "Mommy, if
you had to stay here, would that make you sad?"

"I honestly don't know. I love being with you, and Nona
Angela. But I miss my family."

"But Daddy and I could be your family." Jamie sounded worried.

I hugged her again. "And if that's what has to happened, then we'll make it work. But this isn't something you should be worried about right now, okay?"

"Okay." But she sounded doubtful.

Martini looked worried, too. "What is it?" I asked him quietly.

He shook his head. "Not sure. But you're right, it's something to worry about later."

We reached the entry gate and went through. So far, so good. There was plenty of parking, and we pulled in. But no one got out of the car. Everyone seemed on edge until the last vehicle was through and the gates were closed. Then, I felt all the men in the car relax.

Secret Service and our Field agents got out of the SUVs and fanned out. Only when Evalyne and Phoebe came to our car were we allowed out, and Len and Kyle got out first, then opened the doors to help us out. This was being done for every limo that I could see.

Once out, I carried Jamie and Martini kept his arm around me, while Evalyne took the lead, with Len and Kyle on either side of us and Phoebe behind. Charles, Richard, and Singh had similar coverage—Secret Service in front and back, Field agents on the side.

I should have felt safe like this. But I didn't feel safe at all. I felt like the most exposed target in the world. Not because I saw any danger, but because everyone was acting as if we were one second away from someone tossing a bomb at us.

However, we made it into the Lodge without issue.

We were greeted by staff, taken through part of the Lodge, and then taken outside again and led to a lovely patio area, complete with set tables. Apparently we were going to eat outside.

This boded for a variety of reasons, sunburn being only one of them. While there were umbrellas over tables, every seat left for us was in direct sunlight somehow. That screamed planning, not accident. Was thankful Akiko had given me that lovely sunhat, which I put on. Sadly, there was no hat for Jamie, meaning I was going to have to try to shield her as best I could or have her sit under the table within ten minutes.

What boded even more was that the press was here, complete with a lot of cameras. Sure, this was a big deal, but it seemed set up to make us look bad—or keep us on our best behavior. But press around meant that there was no way to actually relax and be real people. Everyone would be forced to be a politician all the time. The only positive was that I saw no video cameras, meaning they'd get stills only. So one small favor.

But we did the paws shake, brief though it was, cameras flashing. "It's nice to see you under better conditions," I said to Margie, who flashed the briefest smile ever and didn't reply. Okay, they were really pissed.

Having seen the footage, I understood some of it. But the rest had to be because their people currently thought Martini and I were the greatest. Or else they were really happy to buckle to the anti-alien contingent. This wasn't like the Tony and Margie I knew, but things were different here.

We made some idle chitchat for a while that didn't address any of the issues. Any time Martini or I tried to apologize, we were ignored or the conversation shifted away to the lovely weather or how cold it was or wasn't in D.C. at this time of year.

The food was set up as a buffet, which was casual but awkward considering how everyone was dressed. Well, awkward for me and Jamie, anyway. Everyone else was apparently used to dressing formally every day of their lives.

After fifteen minutes of awkward and uncomfortable chatting, during which neither Tony nor Margie smiled even once, they suggested we all eat. They sent us through the buffet line first, supposedly to be polite. But of course that meant we were going to look like pigs in the many photos being snapped. Fine, whatever. Got a small plate of food for me and for Jamie. Martini was still in the food line, chatting with the waitstaff, all of whom seemed to enjoy speaking with him, marking them as non-politicians.

I went back to our seats in the sun, but Jamie had spotted the dessert table and like any other little child, had headed for it. A waiter gave her a gigantic piece of cake, and she came back with it, all excited. "Mommy, look! It's a pink cake!"

"Very pretty, and I'm sure it'll be delicious, but you have to eat your lunch first."

"Okay," she said cheerfully as she went to set the cake on the table. Only, she was three and the table was high and she missed. And I missed catching the plate as it went down, right onto her.

The cake went all over her dress. Jamie looked up, round-eyed and horrified, tears already there. And the cameras snapped like crazy.

"Well," Tony said. "I see like mother and father, just like daughter."

Jamie burst into tears. "I didn't mean to spill on my pretty dress!"

I hugged her tightly, regardless of the fact that cake would get on my pretty dress, too, and kissed her head. "It's okay, baby. Clothes can be cleaned, and there's always more cake somewhere." I picked her up and handed her to the nearest person in my entourage, who happened to be Evalyne.

"Cyclone is on the move," Evalyne said urgently into her lapel. "All hands."

"Yeah, call in everyone. I'm about to create a true political event." I marched over to the press. "Give me the film."

They all kept on taking pictures. "Freedom of the press, my Sheila," one said.

"Yeah? That's fine. Insult me and my husband all you want. But our daughter is a little girl. You don't get to humiliate her for being a child, nor do you get to share her pictures with the world, so she can be a target for every nutjob out there. Now, give me the film. Or I'll make you give it to me."

"The PM asked us here," another reporter said. "We're free to do what we want."

"Indeed." Spun on my heel and went back to our table. "You two disappoint me. And more than that, you disappoint your entire country."

"I beg your pardon?" Tony asked.

"My husband is a fledgling politician. You know that. You're not. You should be helping him learn how to deal with bad situations with grace. Instead, your tender feelers are hurt because your constituents looked at our mishap from the other day as a great way to make fun of you. You want to do the same to us? Fine. But you do not get to harm a little girl for fun or pathetic revenge." Turned to Margie. "You have three girls. How *dare* you allow this to happen to someone else's daughter, with your permission, with your *blessing?* And to think I spent time trying to find a gift that would show how badly we felt and how much we valued your friendship. Well, screw *that*."

"You already flipped me off—" Tony started.

But I'd realized why my CA had done what she'd done. "Oh, bull. I saw some older men making that sign and I thought it was your way of doing V for Victory. Clearly it wasn't. But, just so you know, *this* is how you flip someone off in American."

With that, I flipped him the bird. With both hands.

CHAPTER 75

I WAS IN THE ROOM in a nanosecond. In fact, I was going so fast I wasn't on the floor—I was on the wall. And then I was on the ceiling, to avoid trampling the equipment. Not that I wasn't willing to destroy it—I just didn't want to destroy something we were going to end up needing.

The positive of this speed was that I was going to be hard to spot and harder to hit. The negative was that it was still harder for me to see the stationary objects in the room than it would be for an A-C.

So, the first part of my rescue consisted of me running around the room several times. Sure, it only took a couple of seconds, but I felt like an idiot. At least I hadn't shouted "cowabunga" or "yippee-ki-yay mofos" or similar.

Thankfully, they really and truly weren't prepped for hyperspeed, because there were no nets, tripwires, rods, or baseball bats set up for me to run into. Thanked the powers that be for the favor and did my best to pay attention to the layout.

This place was textbook Bond Villain Lair. The room was a long, large rectangle, with all sorts of machines, torture devices, and cases, refrigerated and regular, that seemed to hold viruses or body parts or, in the case of one, Cliff's trophies from his amateur softball league. I was going too fast to be sure, and figured I'd leave the categorization of all the crap to Alfred, since he was likely to know what it all was and actually enjoy the task.

Completing the look, the room also had a nice "In Case of Fire" box with a fire extinguisher and an ax. So Cliff was practicing fire safety. A responsible Supervillain, how refreshing.

The prisoners, aka my family and friends, were strapped onto what looked like metal autopsy body trays, cranked up at forty-five degree angles, presumably so they could see the ongoing and upcoming torture but not get free easily. The straps looked both sturdy and efficiently locked, going by the fact that the men were struggling but barely moving. All six of them were wearing nightclothes of some kind.

The kids were on one side of a nasty-looking machine that Cliff was literally stroking, and the men were on the other. There were just the six of them in here, along with Dr. No, Ms. Crazypants, and the Assassination Squad.

The Assassination Squad looked like they'd had a bad night, which I was fine with. Happily, Raul's jaw appeared to be wired shut, indicating that I'd indeed broken said jaw and also explaining why he'd sounded funny when he was talking. Even though the Israelis had been all nice and given him medical attention, I knew without asking that he was probably a little bitter about this turn of events.

Wished Buchanan and I had just killed all four of them when we'd had the easy chance to do so and prayed the others at the Israeli Embassy were somehow safe. But I didn't have time to think about anyone not in this room.

As I ran around the ceiling for a while, I focused on the machine. A cube about six by six feet made out of four-inch metal pipes made up the framework. There was a large, round, golden metal ball that really resembled a giant cartoon bomb in the middle. And there were pipes running from each section of the frame into the metal ball, so that it was supported and held in the center of the cube.

Per what Alfred had said, I could get down to a microscopic level using the goggles. I didn't want to see the atoms, though. I wanted to see what was going on inside that golden sphere. A roiling ball of white-hot energy circled what looked like a blinking cube. But this was all I could spot, and I couldn't look at it too long because it was blinding. Whatever was in there, it wasn't good.

There was a bank of TV monitors along the wall behind the prisoners, showing various places in the compound. One was clearly in the tree that had the secret entrance. So they'd seen us coming right then. There was also a view of the concrete room where the projector had been, and of the start of the Underground Path of Potential Doom. The other cameras were focused on exterior and interior shots of the houses and such in the compound.

All this room was missing was the wall of water and/or lava, and the pool with sharks. However, what it lacked in sharks it made up for in alligators.

There was an alligator enclosure against the far wall, next to the stairway that I presumed went up to the ground level. The enclosure was complete with a whole little herd of gators in it. Checked using Alfred's Super Shades—yep, those were real alligators, not animatronic fakes. Didn't figure I'd luck into seeing Alliflash or Gigantagator here, but one never knew. Was careful not to run on the Gator Glass, just in case.

The bad guys were clearly expecting company. LaRue had a gun right out of a *Justice League Unlimited* episode—a six-shooter that really had six separate mini guns that radiated out from the main gun via flexible metal arms. And Cliff appeared to be getting off on whatever that machine was. They weren't cackling, but I assumed that was because they hadn't seen me yet or were saving it for when my team came into the room. Or they'd gotten tired of cackling at the prisoners and were taking a short cackle break before starting up again.

By comparison, the four assassins looked sane and normal. If, you know, I didn't note that Bernie had guns pointed at Max and Charlie's heads, and that Sanchez, Lopez, and

Raul were doing the same with Buchanan, Reader, and Chuckie, respectively. This was in addition to LaRue's super six-gun, which a quick Super Shades check confirmed was real and likely working. By comparison, Jamie was in the least immediate danger because she was only covered by LaRue. This hour's textbook definition of damning with faint praise.

In my world, the Mastermind wasn't a baroque supervillain. Clever and evil, yes, but while Marling and Gaultier had had a lot of aspects of this behavior, the Mastermind—whether he was Yates, Reid, or Cliff—was just a cold, brilliant, vicious bastard.

But that might be because Yates had been an A-C and, combined with Mephistopheles or not, Bad Guy of Bad Guys or not, A-Cs were, at their cores, formal conformists. Could imagine what Yates would have to say about this particular setup, and the term "cutting insult" didn't begin to cover it. And if he saw this, Mephistopheles would hurt himself laughing.

This didn't mean it was any less dangerous. But it did mean that Cliff had given in to something that, in my world, LaRue had in spades but he'd kept at bay—vanity. And vanity could always be played upon.

Did one more pass around the room and this time I raced up the stairs, just to see what was up there. The ginormous, 6-car garage with one SUV in it was what was up there, but no more assassins and no hired goons, either. No tripwires or bombs, either. This was good news, because it was going to be a lot easier to get out this way than back through the Underground Path of Potential Doom. You know, relatively speaking.

Back down into the Secret Sanctum Insanitorium. Nothing much had changed. However, my return rattled the gator glass, just a little. But it was enough, if every bad guy head in the room turning toward the sound was any indication. Always the way.

"I know you're in here," Cliff called cheerfully. "And

while you might be fast enough to save one of them, I don't think you're fast enough to save all of them."

Sadly, because of how close the guns were to everyone's faces and heads, Cliff was probably right. But Mom was a great teacher, and along with her "never drop your weapon" advice, she'd also mentioned that if the enemy didn't know where you actually were, then it behooved you to continue to keep them in the dark. Kept on moving.

"If I'm jostled even a little I pull the trigger," LaRue said nastily. "And then you can watch them all die." She smirked. "But they're not really yours, are they? So what will you care?"

She was baiting me. Probably. But if she knew I wasn't the real Kitty from this universe, what else did she know? And how did she know it?

"Or you can stay hidden," Cliff said, "and just watch us kill everyone."

Right on cue, Cantu came in through the doorway at the other end of the room, gun at the ready. Heaved an internal sigh. Had I not told him to wait in the dark corridor unless it seemed like I needed help? Surely my lack of screaming was a clue that I still had things in hand. Cantu was proving why I hated working with men who hadn't caught on that women were at least as competent as they were.

Naturally by the time he'd fully entered the room LaRue's weird guns were extended and floating in front of the face of each of the prisoners, basically right at their noses. All guns in assassin hands were cocked. And Cliff was swinging a part of his favorite machine toward Cantu, who wisely froze.

"We'll kill him," Cliff said conversationally. "Unless you turn off your invisibility device and show yourself."

So they'd taken the hyperspeed to indicate an invisibility machine of some kind. And that meant Cliff was saying that, as a human, I couldn't save everyone. Good. Not that even Christopher would have a shot of saving everyone at once in this situation, based on where the guns were in relation to the prisoners. But the less the bad guys knew I could do, the better.

"Clifford Goodman, you're under arrest for treason." Had to give it to Cantu—he didn't sound scared.

"That's nice, Esteban," Cliff said genially. "Do you know what I have here?"

"No idea," Cantu said.

"It's a death ray."

Cantu snorted. "Seriously?" He was speaking for both of us.

"Oh, very seriously. It's a disintegrator, a laser with enough power to dissipate quite a lot of matter. A human being's worth isn't even close to its full ability. Would you like a demonstration?" Cliff's voice was like honey.

"No, I wouldn't," Cantu said. "I'd like you to surrender and give yourselves up so that I don't have to use excessive force."

"You and what army?" LaRue asked with a laugh.

Decided I should take that as a cue. And considered a key fact—the prisoners were raised off the floor. But the bad guys were standing. And if there was one thing I liked, it was the classics.

Ran to the gator's window and did a flying bicycle kick feet first right into the glass.

Results were immediate. And interesting. Not necessarily in a good way.

CHAPTER 76

AS THE GLASS SHATTERED, the gators, sensing something interesting happening, headed toward their new door. The assassins, sensing a much more immediate threat than six captured prisoners and one desk jockey with a gun, started shooting at the oncoming alligators.

And I slammed into the other wall, feet first. And stopped.

This was more than jarring, and I'd probably need to see a chiropractor when I got home, but accelerated healing meant that my spine and joints settled themselves back into place quickly.

Fortunately, increased strength meant I could extract myself from the wall I'd jammed myself into reasonably quickly. Once free of the wall, I had to dodge bullets, but even the ones I couldn't dodge didn't do much. Alfred's Super Kevlar was amazing—the bullets just bounced off. They stung when they hit, but I'd take feeling like someone was throwing pebbles at me really hard over leaking blood from a hundred different orifices. And most of the bullets were being sent at the gators anyway, who were getting seriously pissed about being shot at and therefore charging.

One was near Cliff, who swung the nozzle of his Death Ray toward it and hit the button. A blinding light flashed, and then the gator was no more. He did this to all the rest of the gators. The machine was quite exact and all the zapping took very little time. There were tiny piles of dust where the gators had been, but that was all. Felt everyone in the room get very still.

"You will stop hiding," Cliff said, presumably to me, "you will put that gun down, and you will come here, or I will turn this on again." He aimed the nozzle at Charlie. Who winced but didn't cry. Max and Jamie just looked terrified and angry, but they didn't make any noise. Awesome kids. The men were also thankfully silent.

In this case, decided dropping the big gun was the way to go. Tossed it to the edge of the gator enclosure, right by the broken glass. "Sure, okay. Turn that on me, though, not on the kids."

Cliff shrugged. "Since you insist. Oh, and Esteban, in case you didn't notice. Raul's got his gun pointed at you. He won't miss. Don't try anything heroic. And you others who are hiding in the hall—I want you in here, too. Or the kid dies."

Alfred and Cox stepped into the room, Cox holding Stripes.

"Take those ridiculous masks off," LaRue ordered. The men obliged. "Off the stupid animal, too." Cox took Stripe's mask off. Stripes hissed at LaRue but not for the obvious reasons. He didn't think she smelled right. LaRue turned back to me. "Mask. Off. Now."

"My hair's kind of a mess. I'd like to keep it on." At least as long as I could. Was trying to figure out where the off switch was on Cliff's Death Ray machine or if there was anything I could do to it that wouldn't hurt everyone in the room I cared about. Sadly, I wasn't Alfred. I wasn't Chuckie, either. There were many things in there, but they were just so many weird, moving parts to me.

"Take the mask off or say goodbye to the little boy," Cliff said as he swung the Death Ray back at Charlie.

Took the mask off, though I kept it in my hand. Sadly, this meant that I no longer heard Tina Turner in the background. On the other hand, Cliff was ensuring I could stay enraged, so that was good. "Okay. Again, stop threatening a little kid. You want to threaten? Threaten me."

Cliff turned the nozzle back my way. "If you insist."

"I do." I was tensed to leap and run and I kept Rage right there in front of me. Hoped I would be fast enough to escape the Death Ray but avoiding finding out was my preferred plan.

"Where are you from?" LaRue asked.

"Arizona." Well, this was true.

"That's not what I mean and you know it," she snapped. "Where are you from? And when?"

"I have no idea what you mean."

"You're not from around here. And the tech you're using, it's not from around here, either. So, when and/or where are you from?"

So they thought I was a time traveler? Maybe that would help. Had no idea how, but hope liked to spring eternal. Mercifully, no one was looking at Alfred, though he was doing well with keeping his expression neutral. "No idea what you mean." Get her talking, figure out what to do.

"Don't worry. We're going to use your DNA, and hers," she nodded toward Jamie. "You'll ensure that we can live forever."

This boded. "That's impossible."

"Hardly," Cliff said. He sounded smug and excited. "Cloning isn't even a new process. But adding in special genetics makes it work so much better."

Damn. They were talking about cloning themselves. Could not allow that to happen here. This world had no defenses against them. "So, you want to clone me over and over again? I get why, I mean, 'cause I'm awesome and all, but still, it seems a little pointless."

LaRue laughed one of those low, nasty laughs. She was really good at them, in any universe. The assassins, picking up a cue, all sniggered along. LaRue shot them a look and they shut up. "I've been waiting a long time for someone like you."

"How do you mean? Someone who isn't impressed with your crap? I cannot have been the first."

"No, you idiot. A genetic leap. Or a visitor from another planet, or another, future time. You're one of those."

Ah. So they didn't know who I was, just that, somehow, I could do things that were unheard of on this planet. Hence why they thought I was an alien or a time traveler. She hadn't included Alfred, Cox, or even Stripes in this, meaning they were thinking everything we had and were doing was from me. It was a small favor, but I was willing to take it.

"It's a nice compliment, but I have no idea what you're talking about."

"You can go invisible and make other things invisible," Bernie spat out. "And you have increased strength."

"Oh. That. Well, it's a long story. But, LaRue, I'm more interested in your story."

"Really?" She sounded mildly surprised.

"Why do you care about her?" Cliff asked. He sounded just a teensy bit peeved. "I'm the one who created the Death Ray."

Vanity. His weakness was absolutely vanity. And hers probably was, too. One didn't become a Bond Supervillain with without a hell of a lot of vanity egging you on, after all.

"Are you? I'm not so sure. I mean, usually—and LaRue and even Bernie can probably back me up on this—men like to take the credit for what women create and think up." Madeline Cartwright had certainly felt this way, and since I wasn't in the best position to bargain, it was time to channel Cartwright and see what I could come up with.

"LaRue assisted," Cliff said.

Her eyes narrowed. "I more than assisted. You're not a scientist."

"It's my design, and my plan," Cliff said airily. But then, LaRue was looking at me, not him, so he couldn't see her expression. If he'd seen her expression, he might have apologized.

"And Cliff's vendetta, too," I added helpfully.

LaRue looked confused. "What do you mean?"

"I mean, why in the world do you care about hurting any-one in this room? I get why Cliff's upset—my mother killed his father-figure and that can get a person into a *Kill Bill* kind of mindset." I was certainly in said mindset, for example. And, sure, Chuckie had said he'd actually killed Reid. But now was *not* the time to remind anyone with a weapon about that. "But no one here has done anything to you, LaRue. I don't think anyone here other than me knows who you are."

"Who am I?" she asked with a smirk.

"You're the brains of the operation, the power behind the throne, and the person who should probably rightfully be called the Mastermind."

LaRue smiled. A small, funny, proud little smile. "You're much more insightful than you seem." Sent a mental thank you to Cartwright, wherever she was.

"Oh, please," Cliff said derisively. "LaRue is my partner, yes, but I'm the one in charge. And I can see what you're do-ing. You're trying to drive a wedge between us. Well, it won't work. LaRue is more than my partner, she's my woman."

"That's what men like to say when they're taking credit for your ideas, isn't it?" I said in a "just girls" tone.

"Where are you from?" LaRue asked me, fairly nicely. "Seriously, I want to know."

My brain nudged. She was asking this too much. She did want to know, but her attitude no longer seemed supercilious, or even curious. She sounded just a tiny bit hopeful. And Stripes felt she didn't smell right, and he wasn't passing judgment on her perfume.

When Cartwright and I had been chatting, we'd gotten along, because we'd actually understood each other. In my world, LaRue had been an adversary for as long as I'd known her—Amy's father's mistress wasn't going to be my buddy. But here, we'd never crossed paths. So, in that sense, this was a fresh relationship.

My father had always instructed me that when you were asked a question you didn't know how or didn't want to an-swer, it was more than acceptable to answer that question with another question. It was sound advice that had served me well.

"Where are *you* from?"

LaRue's eyes widened just a bit. "Far away. And you?"

"Second star to the right and straight on 'til morning."

"Ah. I'm from farther than that."

And she hadn't read the classics while she'd been here. Which was interesting. Alfred was a stranded alien, and he'd read and watched everything, as near as I could tell. Algar was the same—per my King of the Elves, there wasn't a book, movie, record, or TV show he'd missed. But LaRue appeared to have no idea I was quoting from *Peter Pan*. Which showed an amazing lack of interest in the arts of this world. And art reflected and affected society, which was part of why Alfred and Algar had paid attention to Earth's art.

In my world, when LaRue had left Alpha Four in a stolen starship, she'd headed to parts unknown and had returned with the Z'Porrah, who were enemies of mankind. They were also enemies of the Ancients. And yet, they'd come across the galaxy to help LaRue, who certainly looked like a human, try to take over Earth. And LaRue's hair had still been the same dyed color when she returned as it had been when she'd left.

Chuckie was the Conspiracy King and he'd trained me well. And, per Sherlock Holmes and my "uncle," Peter the Dingo Dog, when you removed all the other possibilities, the one that remained, no matter how bizarre, was the truth.

There could be many reasons why LaRue smelled wrong to an Earth animal. And there were a lot of good and bad reasons to clone. But there was one reason that made sense for both—she wasn't a human or an A-C, and if you had no one else to mate with, cloning was your only option to continue your race.

"It's hard to be the last of your kind, isn't it?"

She got a funny look on her face. "Some still exist."

Took my best guess. "At the galactic core, sure, maybe. If they haven't died out by now. And on Beta Twelve. But they mingled in centuries ago, they aren't pure."

"No, they're not."

Managed not to high five myself. Time for my next guess. "Did you come in the nineteen-fifties? You look way too young to have been here that long."

The compliment worked. LaRue shot me a friendly smile. "We age differently than humans, but no. I was on the team that followed up when those sent here on the mission you're referring to didn't check in at the planned time."

"Did they stay here?"

She shook her head. "No. Frankly, they were just late to contact the Home World. However, my mission was already launched." She shrugged. "I was the communications officer and I didn't feel any need to share that we'd been recalled."

"So, when you came here, did you decide to change sides, or were you always a Z'Porrah spy?" Had my guess, of course, but it was better to have her confirm or deny.

LaRue shrugged. "I have more in common with the Z'Porrah than my own people."

I was batting a thousand. If only we weren't all still in extremely grave danger I'd preen. Hopefully there'd be time for that later. Hopefully we'd get a later. "We call your people the Ancients where I come from. Is that the name you use for yourselves?"

"No, but it's not pronounceable for most other races. It means 'people,' though. And Ancients is a good name for them." Now she sounded bitter.

"What did they do to you? That made you change sides, I mean."

"That's enough," Cliff snarled at me. He looked at LaRue. "You're an alien? And you never told me?"

LaRue shrugged and turned away from me. "You never asked." Their attention was focused on each other and the assassins' shocked attention was focused on them. I'd never have a better chance.

Sent a request up to whoever might be listening for this effort to go a lot better than the last one. Then I rolled.

CHAPTER 77

WELL, I rolled standing up.

Flipped myself into a standing forward roll and threw my helmet at Bernie's head. Kicked the gun down and out of LaRue's hand. Landed on the gun, hard, crouched down, and slammed my elbow up into Cliff's groin. As he buckled, grabbed the Death Ray nozzle and turned it back toward the machine itself. But I couldn't figure out how to trigger the ray. My helmet hit Bernie square in the face and slammed her back into the TV wall.

As all this went on, Cantu fired at Raul at the same time Raul fired at him. Wanted a Glock. Remembered I had knives my purse. Grabbed one in each hand. Stabbed a knife into Cliff's chest while I did a spinning low kick and knocked LaRue off her feet. At the same time, Alfred followed my lead and slammed his helmet into Raul's head, then ran, knives at the ready, and cut Chuckie, Reader, and Buchanan loose.

Cox and Stripes were also reacting, but they looked like they were moving in slow motion compared to Alfred and even slower compared to me because I was going so fast. Cox headed toward Cantu. The trajectory and size of Raul's bullet meant that Cox and Cantu both were going to be shot.

I was crouched down now as if I was in sprinter's blocks right before a race. Dropped the other knife and launched myself, aiming between Cox and Cantu, arms wide. Hit them both in their midsections and took them down as the bullet sailed harmlessly into the wall.

Well, sort of harmlessly. The bullet hit a machine, and that machine blew steam out, big time. This created the creepy atmosphere this entire scenario had so been missing.

Flipped into a crouch and took in what I could of the scene. Cantu had missed Raul and hit a TV screen. My men were engaging in hand-to-hand with the three male assassins. Stripes was on Bernie's face, yowling, clawing, and biting. Alfred had freed the kids and had them behind him. And LaRue was up, with the Death Ray nozzle in her hand. I was pretty sure she knew how to turn it on.

"You shouldn't have done that," she snarled. "I was willing to let you live."

"But only if I agreed to let you clone me." Stood up and moved nearer to the back of the Death Ray machine. If she was focused on me, she couldn't hit anyone else. Noted there was another pipe that attached in to the bottom of the frame and connected to the machines behind it. Had no idea what this meant for me in terms of stopping anything.

The men hadn't stopped fighting, but LaRue ignored them. Which was too bad, seeing as she missed Buchanan, Reader, and Chuckie all twist Sanchez, Lopez, and Raul's necks farther than necks were meant to twist, pretty much in unison. Wondered if they practiced that, or if Mom's team here had just been the gold medalists in the Synchronized Neck Breaking competition.

Bernie was still alive, however, and as she got up, screaming, she threw Stripes off of her. Who twisted midair, claws out, and landed on LaRue's head, yowling the cat version of "yippee-ki-yay mofo" at the top of his cat lungs.

I didn't hesitate. Ran forward and grabbed the Death Ray nozzle, too. LaRue was strong, but I was stronger. As Bernie tried to shoot at me, Buchanan repeated history, at least for me, grabbed Sanchez's gun, and shot Bernie in the head. I would have applauded, but my hands were full.

Cliff lurched up, knife still sticking out of his chest. "Kill . . . them all," he gasped out as he grabbed at me. "Do it now."

"Kitty, if the nozzle hits the thermal core, it will self-destruct," Alfred shouted.

"What?" As if I could tell where the thermal core was. "Alfred, get everyone up those stairs and out of here!"

"Slam the nozzle into the big round ball in the middle," Chuckie translated. Thanked God that in any and all universes he spoke Kitty.

Heard glass break and then a clanging sound and risked a look. Cox had broken the "In Case of Fire" case open, grabbed the ax, and was slamming it onto the pipe on the floor, the one that connected the Death Ray to the machines.

"No!" Cliff shouted, as he let go of me and ran around the Death Ray. He pulled the knife out of his chest as he bore down on Cox, who wasn't paying attention to anything but the pipe he was chopping.

"Bill!" I could not watch Cox die again, I just couldn't.

Cox, hearing me shout, swung around, ax in hand. The ax, thanks to its handle, was a lot longer than Cliff's arms. And, thanks to how Cox had been holding it and was spinning, the blade was at just the right height when it connected with Cliff's neck.

Apparently it hadn't been dulled by hitting the pipe.

"Whoa!" That was shouted by everyone who was watching, LaRue and myself included, as Cliff's head bounced off the machine and, this being my life, ricocheted into Cantu. Who, to his great credit, didn't scream. At least until he caught the head automatically. Then he screamed like a banshee as he threw it across the room and out onto the Underground Path of Potential Doom. Heard an explosion, meaning Cliff's head had landed on a pressure plate.

Alfred took all of this as a clear sign to finally listen to me and leave. He ran the kids upstairs and was back in a flash to grab Buchanan and Reader, who just managed to grab Chuckie. They all disappeared as well.

In this same time period of approximately two seconds, Cox neither screamed nor ran. He just spun around and slammed his now bloody ax back onto the pipe. Cliff's body landed against the wall with all the machines and sprayed blood on them. Things started to sound like they were shorting out and this distracted LaRue just a bit.

Took the opportunity and did what Alfred and Chuckie had told me to—I shoved the Death Ray nozzle against the metal sphere. Just as LaRue undistracted herself and activated the beam.

I let go and flipped the hyperspeed up to well past eleven. Grabbed Stripes by the scruff of his neck and pulled him off LaRue's head, spun, and ran for Cantu. Shoved Stripes at Cantu's chest while I grabbed his arm. The cat was smart, and dug his claws into Cantu's clothes. Based on the look of pain starting to come onto Cantu's face, Stripes probably had his claws in skin, too.

Didn't pause, because Cantu had proved that he had a good catching reflex, and that meant he was going to hold onto Stripes. Grabbed Cox in mid-swing. The impact caused him to let go of the ax. Would have looked to have seen where it went, but sprinters who looked behind them lost their races.

Ran us up the stairs faster than I could blink. Could have sworn I saw something fluffy going past me but turning to look was still not in the cards. No one was in the garage, which was good. I was faster than the SUV could ever be, so I kept on moving. A wall was broken out, meaning I had a good idea of where Alfred had run. Went that way, too.

Got outside and to the far wall as the ground under us rumbled. Ran us past the wall and to where I could see the rest of our group was as the ground started to crumble down in an implosion worthy of a Spielberg movie.

Stopped running when we reached the others and did a fast head count. All accounted for, cat included. Took Stripes from Cantu and cuddled him, then handed him to Cox. Spun around to see the entire complex go down as if it was being sucked into the bowels of the earth. Readied myself to grab everyone and run, but while the outer wall and the tree went down, the cave-in stopped well away from us.

Realized that the speeders were going to go down, too. Grabbed Alfred and took off. We reached the area they'd been in just in time. He hit something and they appeared. He grabbed one, I picked up two, and we ran them back, as the ground slipped away behind us almost as fast as we were running.

But not quite. Reached the others and put the speeders down. Alfred fiddled with them, but since the immediate danger was over, I took the opportunity, grabbed the kids, and checked them for injuries. Realized I was still moving at hyperspeed by the confused looks on their faces and the panicked look on Chuckie's.

Alfred put his hand on my shoulder. I could feel him slowing me down. "It's okay, Kitty," he said. "Everyone's here, everyone's alright."

Let myself slow down and hugged the kids tightly, but not too tight. Then got up and hugged Chuckie. After a long hug, let go and hugged Reader, then Buchanan. And then asked the question, praying the answer wouldn't make me cry. "What happened to everyone else at the embassy?"

"They're safe," Buchanan said. Let out the breath I hadn't realized I was holding. "The underground room we were in last night doubles as their bunker. Everyone got in and the doors locked in time."

"In time for what?"

"In time for the embassy to be bombed to bits," Reader said. "But your dad, Carla, Peter, and Caroline are all safe. They were inside the bunker."

"Why weren't the six of you inside said bunker?"

"Well, *I* was searching for you," Chuckie said. "As were some others." He looked at the boys. Charlie looked like he knew he was in trouble, but Max looked defiant.

"She was gone, and we couldn't leave her," Max said. "And Stripes was gone, too."

"I left a note."

"I was awakened by the sounds of bombs exploding," Chuckie said dryly. "I didn't stop to read. I had Jamie, and thought I had Charlie and Max. But when we got into the corridor, each one went a different way."

"Charlie ran into us," Reader said. "So we had Leah, Oren, and Jakob get the others downstairs. Charlie refused to go without his siblings, parents, and cat, and by refused I mean he thrashed and kicked."

"I'm sorry, Uncle James," Charlie said quietly.

Reader shot him the cover boy smile. "It's okay. Now. But by the time Buchanan had caught Max, we were blocked from the bunker by six well-armed commandos. We could let them take us or kill us. We let them take us."

"Which they did," Buchanan said. "We got to watch them turn the embassy to rubble and then we were all knocked out. I came to partway here, and I can guarantee we came here in a Sherpa." Opened my mouth. "It's a military aircraft used to transport personnel. I think it's probably housed at Patrick Air Force Base." Which tracked with my assumption that Cliff had used his C.I.A. clearance there.

"Hang on. Six commandos . . ." Looked at Cantu, who looked like he'd been hit in the gut. Really wished Jeff was here. I needed to know if this man was just remarkably stupid and/or unlucky, or if he was waiting to take over as the Mastermind.

"From what I could tell, you came in with them," Chuckie said. "We thought you'd been captured, too."

"Well, I'm happy they're buried in the rubble, but now, Esteban, that leaves us with a mystery."

"I had no idea," he said. He sounded pissed and horrified and as if he was telling the truth. But I needed to be sure.

"Is Cantu here your boss?" I asked Chuckie.

Who nodded. "Yes, he is. Goodman made me call him, to get him down here. I know why you're suspicious, Kitty, and I can't blame you. But Goodman was waiting to get Cantu down with us and kill all of us at one time."

"Why?" Cox asked.

"To get rid of all his enemies before he took over the world," Reader said. "Literally. Guy was as insane as a typical Bond villain."

"You called that one," Cox said to me.

"Who are you? Jeff?" Chuckie sounded pissed off and jealous.

"Wow, dude, no. This is Lieutenant Commander William Cox of the U.S. Navy. You need to get over the whole jealousy thing. Seriously, I know the bad guys were baiting you and all, but did you really think I'd left the embassy to go have a tryst?"

He heaved a sigh. "No, honestly, I didn't. I'm sorry."

"When she gets back, you two really need to work on this."

"She can't," Jamie said in a little voice. "The mad ladies said our house . . . our house was blown up?"

Picked her up and hugged her. "Yes, it was. Just like the embassy. I'm sorry. I know that means everyone's lost all their things. But the things that matter are the people and the animals. And as far as I know, we're all alright."

"But Mommy can't come home," Jamie said, lower lip trembling. "I can't see me now, and if I can't see me, I can't see her, and if I can't see her, I can't help."

The realization of what Jamie meant would have been more upsetting if I hadn't heard a sound I was really familiar with—the sound of a big gun being cocked.

Turned around slowly to see LaRue standing there somehow. With the gun I'd left in the alligator enclosure in her hands.

She looked like crap, but she was alive and apparently well. "The Z'Porrah were right," she said. "The only good naked ape is a dead naked ape."

I didn't think about it. I tossed Jamie toward Chuckie and ran straight for LaRue. She fired. And she hit me.

CHAPTER 78

MY MIDDLE FINGERS up and pointed right at the PM was, of course, photographic gold for the press. Not that it mattered at this point. I left the PM couple gaping at me and went back to the press. "You get one more chance. Give me the film. You can keep the shots of me flipping everyone off, but not of my daughter."

"Too bad, too sad," one shared.

"Uh huh."

I might not be an A-C. But my husband had ensured I could defend myself. I wasn't as skilled in Kung Fu as he was, but I was a brown belt. And it was time for the Fists of Fury.

Only Martini was there, and he put his hand on my shoulder. "No, baby. You take care of Jamie." His voice was a low and extremely dangerous. "It's up to me to protect our family."

"Yeah?" yet another member of the press said. "You'll commit political suicide over a few snaps, mate?"

"I've killed men for less, yeah." Martini shot them a smile that wasn't nice—it was feral. "Or are you all forgetting that my rank in Centaurion Division was as Commander? Of our entire military. You represent a threat to my child. Guess what I'm willing to do to protect her?"

"Stop it," Margie said as she came over, in a Mother Tone that brooked no argument. "Stop it now. All of it and all of you. Confiscate the cameras," she said to her staff and ours. "All of them. And take the press into a room for a debrief."

Our Field agents used hyperspeed and wrested every camera away within seconds. "Search them," Singh said, as he joined this party. "Assume they all have recording equipment on them."

The full patdowns were done, at hyperspeed. Many recording devices were indeed found. Martini took them all and crushed them between his hands, one at a time, while the photographers winced. Then he took the cameras and ripped them apart, again with his bare hands, crushing each piece. He did it at human speeds, too.

"Now," he snarled when he was finally done, "you can continue to piss me off, and I'll do this to your heads, or you can stay the hell away from my family."

"Here's a tip about America and Americans. We really just want to be left the hell alone and for everyone around us to just freaking get along. We try to stay out of your business, but everyone likes to call us in, because we're big and we make such a great target—someone to hate even if they happen to be solving a problem. But when you piss us off, really piss us off, we get *angry*. Sometimes it's a bad choice, and sometimes it's not, but that's how we *are*. We don't like getting angry with our friends. But we will. And if you're set on proving you're *not* our friends? Then we truly are willing to rain down fire upon you. You'd think the rest of the world would have caught onto this by now and stop kicking at us, but apparently you'd be wrong."

"You . . . you're a friend to the press," one of them tried.

"No," Richard said. "We're a friend to two reporters who happen to be focused on showing the truth. And, Jeffrey, I took the liberty of inviting them here. Mister Joel Oliver and Bruce Jenkins joined us during the attack on Jamie, and, once things are calmed down a bit, they'll be happy to report on how this summit meeting went."

Martini nodded. "Raj, I'd like you to handle the debriefing of the press corps."

"Absolutely." Singh jerked his head at the Field agents. "Let's go."

They hustled the press corps away. Decided now wasn't the time to ask what they were really going to do to them.

"What are you really going to do to them?" Margie asked. Okay, apparently now was the time.

"Give them another memory of how this went," Martini said. "Harmlessly. It's one of our abilities." He shot a cold stare at her. "One we only use in danger situations, when we can, to keep the populace calm and protected. We haven't used it on anyone in a long time, but I'm perfectly willing to in order to protect my family. You and your husband crossed a line I won't allow anyone to cross."

Margie nodded. "We did, you're right. And . . . we were wrong to do it."

"Not that this was the goal," Tony said as he joined us, "but now we both have things to apologize to each other for."

"You get to start," I snapped. "Because my accidentally flipping you off and our spilling coffee on you because I was falling down concrete stairs so I could crack my head open is a lot less threatening than what you did to our three-year-old daughter. And I'm truly pissed enough to never forgive you for it." With that, I spun on my heel again, grabbed my purse from where I'd left it under the table, and went to retrieve Jamie from Evalyne. Our Beauty Queen Contingent was with them.

Jamie was still crying and I took her and cuddled her. "I'm so sorry, Mommy," she wailed.

"Shhh, shhh, it's okay, baby. It is. Nothing that's happened is your fault."

"Yes, it *is*." She buried her face in my neck and cried more.

Serene, Lorraine, and Claudia huddled around us and moved us a little ways away. "I don't think the cake is why Jamie's crying," Serene said quietly. "All Field agents are either empaths or imageers. And the empaths are telling us that Jamie's upset over something else."

Considered what it could be. She'd been acting funny in the car. Got a bad feeling. "Jamie, something's gone wrong, hasn't it?" She nodded against my neck. "I'm not going to be leaving any time soon, am I?" She shook her head. Held her more tightly. "It's okay. Daddy and I will figure it out, I promise. It's not your job and it's not your responsibility."

"But it is," she sobbed. "And things went wrong and I can't talk to her at all . . ." She couldn't talk she was crying so hard.

My stomach clenched. Had a variety of guesses as to how things could have gone wrong. Most of them ended with the idea that my family in my world was dead. Or that my CA or my Jamie were. Because this Jamie had surely indicated that she'd been responsible in part for the Great Mommy Switch.

Martini joined us now. "Handle things," he said to the Beauty Queens. "The PM couple are now feeling like crap because Jamie's so upset. Use charm and support Richard until Raj comes back, then have Raj use charm."

The women scurried off. "Jamie, the 'her' you mean, is it my Jamie, from my universe?"

Jamie nodded. "I can always talk to her. Any time I want or she wants. But now . . . I can't," she wailed.

Martini put his arms around me and Jamie. "Jamie-Kat," he crooned softly, "it'll be okay. Daddy and Mommy will fix it. I know what you're afraid of, but there are many reasons for you not being able to talk to the Jamie in the world Mommy's from. And none of those reasons are your fault."

"But, but . . . what if Mommy can't come back? I didn't want her to be gone *forever!*"

Kissed Jamie's head. "I know, and neither does she. But she's me, and I wouldn't stop trying to get home, and neither will she. I know that she's going to fix it and get us back to how we're supposed to be. You just have to have faith, Jamie. That's all." Looked up at Martini. "I want my parents here, Mom especially, as fast as they can manage it."

He nodded and jerked his head. James came over. "Is Jamie okay?"

"She will be," Martini said. "Get Sol and Angela, Angela especially, here ASAP. Treat it as a top priority. I don't care if Angela is in a closed door meeting with Vince, I want her with us in five minutes or less."

"You got it." James shot me a comforting smile. "It'll be okay, Kitty." Then he moved off, phone up to his ear.

Martini and I rocked Jamie together, and in a few minutes she fell asleep, exhausted from crying. Probably for the best. I kept a hold of her—she was asleep on my shoulder and right now, I wasn't willing to let her go.

Tony and Margie were hovering nearby, and they both looked stricken and more than a little ashamed. "I'm so sorry," Tony said. "You were right, Kitty—we were behaving like children, not adults, and not like leaders of, pardon my national pride, the best country in the world."

"Let's go inside," Margie said. "I doubt that anyone feels like food right now."

"I could use a drink," I said dryly. Saw every A-C and human in the know look at me in wide-eyed panic. Right, A-Cs were deadly allergic to alcohol—that had been spoken of in the Info Meeting From Hell, and Martini had mentioned it, too. "Not that I can. So, I'll take a Coke, please and thank you, hold the rum."

Margie laughed. "We have that, and plenty of other non-alcoholic beverages as well. Some regional, which you may not have had before."

Managed not to say that I'd tried every regional soda Australia possessed, along with every other beverage they had, and definitely had my favorites. "Sounds great."

"Good," Tony said with a smile I knew was genuine. "Then, let's talk about how we're going to make what happened at the stadium into a joke we own. Then, I'd like some suggestions for how to get the Club Fifty-One contingent out of Australia for good."

Martini smiled as well. "Happy to talk about all of that.

The reporters my uncle invited will probably have a lot to add, on both counts."

"Then, it's a party," Tony said, as he clapped Martini on the back.

"But first," Margie said to me, "let's get the two of you cleaned up. I know I have a dress that will fit your daughter. And I think I can find something for you, as well."

I nodded and Martini kissed my cheek as he let go of me. "No matter your universe of origin, baby, you always manage to save the day somehow. Remember that."

Knew he was telling me not to give up hope. Just hoped he was right.

CHAPTER 79

MARGIE TOOK ME up to their private quarters. "Let's take care of you first, since your little one's still asleep."

Laid Jamie on the bed and she stayed asleep. Put my purse next to her, then risked a look in the mirror. Yeah, this dress needed dry cleaning. And a miracle.

Margie rummaged around in her closet. "Do you want to stick with blue?"

"I don't care. Someone cares, but I don't."

She laughed. "Yes, public life has its restrictions." She came out with several cute, sleeveless dresses. "I think these will fit you and should be complimentary to your figure and complexion."

"One can hope, right?"

Margie put them up to me and we both ultimately decided that the black and white one—with a white silhouette in front and back and black down the sides—was the likely winner. "It's a little formal for midday, but then your people are formal, so it fits."

Hoped the dress itself would fit—this style was attractive and slimming, and the fabric was comfortable.

She helped me out of the blue dress and while I got into the black and white one, which zipped on the side, Margie trotted off. She returned as I was checking my look in the

mirror with my blue dress in a nice bag in one hand and a
pretty, light pink little girl's dress in the other. It was a dress
I recognized.

"All three of my girls wore this," she said as she put the
bag next to my purse. "It was a present for our first daughter
and we've held onto it."

"Are you sure you want Jamie in something that's sort of
a family heirloom?" Tried to keep my tone neutral—in my
world Margie had given this dress to Jamie, not because
she'd ruined her own but because we were like family and
Jamie was the next little girl in line for it. "I mean, obviously,
we'll return it when we're home."

She shook her head. "If it fits her, keep it. Use it if you
have more little girls. Save it if you don't. I'll get it back from
you when my first granddaughter arrives." She smiled at me.
"Because that's what friends do for each other."

Didn't think about it, I just hugged her. "Thank you."

She hugged me back. "I'm sorry for all the hurt feelings
and upsets and everything else. Sorrier still that we didn't ask
how you were feeling—you took a nasty spill."

"I did," I said as we let go. "And I do have a concussion.
So, just in case I seem flaky or like I've forgotten things, it's
likely because of that." Had to work under the idea that Martini was right and sometime soon I was going to get zapped
back into my world. And that meant I had to set things up
right for my CA. "But I just want you to know how much this
means to me—us making up and hopefully becoming friends,
your generosity, and all that."

She smiled. "Being friends is much more pleasant than
being enemies, I agree. And, as a friend, if you have any Wife
of the Big Man questions, I'd be more than happy to help."

"Thank you. My mom is great, but she's not really a politician."

"Oh, she is in her own way. Exactly the way you were just
a little while ago. However, sometimes the softer touch is
needed, and I'm happy to help you with that where I can and
as you need it."

"Believe me, I'll take you up on that offer. And if it seems like I forgot, remind me that it's the concussion talking."

She laughed. "I will do."

"Oh, that reminds me." Went to my purse and took out the present. "We really did hunt for this. I hope you like it, but you're under no obligation to. And if you hate it, I won't be hurt. Much."

Margie laughed, sat on the edge of the bed, and opened the box. She stared at the crystal for a few long moments. "It's absolutely beautiful," she said finally. "I've never seen anything quite like it, so delicate but with so much . . . depth."

"Sadly, you won't again. It was a one-of-a-kind in the first place, and unfortunately, the artist has passed away."

"And you still gave it to me, despite everything." She put it down carefully in the box, got up, and hugged me again. "I'm going to hang it up in our home in Sydney, if that's alright with you. I can enjoy it more there."

"Wherever you want to hang it is fine with me." But I couldn't help but grin—Sydney was where this piece hung in my world.

Jamie woke up and I cuddled her. She wasn't crying now and didn't seem as desolate as she had been, which was a relief. Margie hugged her, too. "I'm sorry I was a mean lady. Can I make it up to you with a dress that's not as pretty as yours but that means much to me?"

Jamie nodded and I got her out of her dress and put it in our dirty clothes bag while Margie helped her into the other dress. "Look, Mommy! It fits me just right!"

"It does, baby, and you look absolutely beautiful, just like always."

Margie wet a washcloth and we wiped Jamie's face, then I combed her hair, and she was ready to go. "Are Grandma and Grandpa here?" she asked as we headed for the door, her carrying the dirty clothes, me with my purse, and Margie carefully holding her gift.

"They should be, yes."

"Yay! I can't wait to show them this dress!"

Sure enough, when we rejoined the others, Mom and Dad were there. They both hugged me and Jamie, then Dad picked her up and she started to prattle on about her dress and share cake sadness with him.

"Let's get another piece," Dad said. "I'll carry it and we'll be very careful." They wandered happily off.

The food had been brought inside—A-Cs around meant everything happened fast—and the large dining room was where everyone was now. Things seemed far more relaxed and informal than they had. The press corps was in attendance, without cameras, so most of them were being forced to take notes. Each one had at least one A-C with them, most had two.

The two journalists who were with Martini and Tony were the ones Richard had identified as Mr. Joel Oliver and Bruce Jenkins. Decided my not hanging out there was probably in everyone's best interests, since these guys knew my CA well.

Margie steered us toward the Beauty Queen Contingent, which was fine with me. We ended up with a girl's table, which was much more fun, and we were basically ignored by the press, which was wonderful.

Amadhia and Aaron did some songs, and they were well received. There was talk of them recording in Sydney, since they were here. Charles made arrangements to fly Aaron's band out, and Tony suggested a free concert as a way to show both countries were pals again. Calls and arrangements were made.

"Stay in Australia a few days," Margie said as the afternoon wound down and we were starting to make noises about leaving. "At least until the concert. Really see at least some of our country. We'll be happy to show you around or just let you investigate on your own."

"We'd like that." I would, for sure, and it seemed politically wise.

"Jeff isn't needed at home," Mom, who'd joined us at the Girl's Table an hour or so prior, said. "I think it might be good for all of you, kitten."

"Then we'll do that. We can stay at Sydney Base, we're already set up there."

"Wonderful!" Margie beamed. "I'll set up a few dinners and luncheons. Not too many, but enough so that you can really get to know the other movers and shakers here."

Plan agreed to, we headed for our massive fleet of vehicles. Mom and Dad went with me, Martini, Charles, and Jamie this time, though Len and Kyle were still driving.

Jamie fell asleep within a minute of being in the car, snuggled next to Dad.

"What did you get from Jamie?" Mom asked Martini.

"She thinks something's happened on . . . the other side." He took a deep breath. "And she's afraid that our Kitty will never be coming home."

Mom nodded. "I figured it was something like that when James called." She looked stricken for a moment, then turned to me. "How are you doing?"

"I'm not sure. I guess I don't believe there's no hope yet. The situation with Tony and Margie looked hopeless, but we worked it out. Maybe things just look bad there right now, but it'll all work out in the end."

Mom looked at Charles, then at Martini. "And, if you can't go home—if we wait a reasonable amount of time and you're still here, then what?"

"Then she divorces me and marries Chuck." Martini said this as if we'd all already discussed it and it was a done deal. Knew Len was listening because the car jerked a little.

"Excuse me?"

"You'll have to," he said. "Trust me."

"Ah, Jeff," Dad said, "looking at everyone's expressions in the car, we'd all like an explanation. I realize that this Kitty isn't 'yours' as we're all used to, but if she's going to remain here, then she's still our daughter, still Jamie's mother, and still your wife."

Martini sighed. "But this Kitty doesn't love me. She likes me and," he smiled at me, "she thinks I'm hot. But love? She loves Chuck."

"She loves me in another universe," Charles pointed out.

"But you're the same guy," Martini said patiently. "You've been in love with Kitty most of your life. And Naomi's gone. Maybe . . . maybe this Kitty is here to fix that."

Everyone stared at him. Charles shook his head. "Who are you, and what have you done with Jeff?"

Martini made the exasperation sound. "If this was *my* Kitty? I'd kill you before I let you have her. Unless she wanted you more than she wants me. And she does. And she's not my Kitty."

"Jeff, I realize you're being, like, the King of Chivalry, but I can't even imagine what this would do to your career. Or to those who don't know what's really going on. Or even those who do. I'm not saying that I'm in love with you, because I'm not. But this isn't my Charles, either, and you've both made that clear. I don't understand why you're so insistent that we don't even, well, try."

Martini sighed. "Because, in exactly nine months, the entire world will know that you and Chuck have been having that torrid affair all the papers say you are."

CHAPTER 80

"UH, EXCUSE ME?"

Martini heaved a bigger sigh. "Kitty, you're pregnant. Congratulations, by the way. No idea what the sex is yet, but I'll know in a few months."

The entire car was silent for a few very long seconds. "How do you know?" I asked finally.

"I told you I can read my Kitty's mind, right?"

"Yes. And you said that I'm enough like her that you can do it with me, too."

"Well, I can see her internally, if I'm concentrating hard enough. I tried, to see if I could maybe see her through you. Instead, I saw you. Inside you."

"You knew when our Kitty was pregnant with Jamie," Charles said. "She told me you knew almost immediately."

"Yes. It's a change, a big change, in a woman's body." He smiled at me. "But you came like that. So the baby that comes is going to be your child with Chuck, your Chuck. And it's likely to look like his child, not mine, because you're both humans."

"Human genetics rule the outside," Kyle said from the front seat. "A-C genetics rule the inside. For hybrids, I mean."

"Oh. Wow. Uh . . ." Looked at Mom. "I don't know what to do."

She nodded. "We do nothing right now, other than rejoice that you're not able to drink alcohol with the A-Cs anyway. We don't share that you're pregnant, we don't race to divorce court, and we don't admit that anything's wrong."

"For how long?" Martini asked. "I wouldn't be worried, but Jamie . . ."

"Jamie is a little girl," Mom said firmly. "A talented and amazing little girl, but a little girl nonetheless. As adults, we need to listen to her concerns, do what we can, but also accept that what seems like the end of the world to a child is not the same as the actual, real end of the world."

Dad smiled at me. "You saved the day here, so James tells me. When it looked like everything would be disastrous. I'm willing to have faith that our Kitty will do the same."

Leaned against Martini. "I hope you're all right."

Staying here wasn't the issue. Never seeing my children again was the issue. Not seeing my Charles again. Leaving Dad alone without me to take care of him. And so many other things.

We reached Sydney Base and went to our rooms. Mom and Dad were going to stay in Australia with us—the President agreed that ensuring our relationship with the PM couple remained strong was vital, and he also wanted Mom here to handle any issues with the actions Australia was going to take against Club 51.

"Do you want to get dinner in the commissary?" Martini asked me, after I'd changed out of Margie's dress and into the standard wear to match the Beauty Queens. Would have preferred jeans, but I had to represent while we were here officially as Mr. and Mrs. Vice President.

"Honestly? No. I'd like to go out. This is my city half the year."

He nodded. "Then we'll go out. You want Jamie with us or with your parents?"

"Whichever will make her feel the most normal."

"We'll leave her with your parents, then."

We checked with them and they were fine with keeping

Jamie. Who hugged me. "I do love you, Mommy, you know that, right?"

Hugged her tightly. "Yes, I do. And I love you, too. So very much. And if your real Mommy can't come back, then I'll do everything to be as much like her as I can be."

Jamie shook her head. "You just need to be you."

Kissed her head. "That's good advice for everyone, Jamie-Kat." Hugged her tightly again, then did the same with Mom and Dad before we left and headed to the ground level. Len and Kyle were waiting for us. "You two are coming?"

"You two are going by car, meaning Len's driving and I'm the muscle."

"And Mister Buchanan's lurking somewhere," Len added with a grin.

"Works for me."

We got in the car. "Want to see where you live?" Martini asked me softly.

"Yeah." Gave the address and directions to Len.

While we drove there, both Martini and I looked out the windows. "It's a beautiful city. I can see why you like living here."

"I like the people. So much."

"If you divorce me, I'm sure you two will end up here, just for the sake of convenience and to avoid the media frenzy."

Took his hand in mine. "Stop saying that. Stop assuming that she and I won't be able to go home."

He squeezed my hand but let it go. "I have to be prepared for the . . . worst."

"There's no guarantee the baby will look like Charles. Jamie is our third and she looks exactly like me."

"It will be easier for you, Chuck, me, and the child if you're married to him."

"Jamie needs her mother as well as her father."

"Joint custody."

"Wow, are you always this fatalistic? Dinner's going to be a blast."

He laughed. "Sorry. I'm just trying to accept that the life I thought I was going to have isn't going to really happen." He sighed. "Chuck's been dealing with this for a year and a half. I've tried to help him. But some of this kind of pain and acceptance you just have to go through alone."

"Maybe. But only if you insist on it."

We were quiet for the rest of the ride to our house. My house. Not our house. Didn't know how to think of it. Kyle put music on. The Neon Trees' "Living in Another World" came on. Refused to let tears come. Held out until Paul McCartney and Wings' "Just Another Day" hit the airwaves. But I blinked the tears away. Martini had been the one telling me to have hope. If he didn't have any, why should I?

More songs and more roads and finally we were on the street where I lived as Gerry Rafferty's "Baker Street" came on. But we didn't live on Baker Street. And we didn't live here, not in this world. However, this album was the one I listened to whenever I was down. For whatever reason, this album, more than any other, spoke to me when I needed it to.

"Gated community of one," Kyle said, whistling, as we idled, parked across the street. "Nice."

"You live in that embassy and you're impressed by this?"

He grinned at me over his shoulder. "I'm easily impressed by wealth, Kitty, what can I say?"

"You should have turned pro."

He laughed. "What we do with Centaurion and the C.I.A. is so much better. And so much more important."

"You want to get out?" Martini asked me.

"Maybe. But, Kyle, can we just hear this album, not a mix?"

"Sure, Kitty, whatever you want. Straight or mixed up within the album?"

"Oh, we can keep ourselves guessing a bit. Surprise me and mix the album up." Why not? Things were mixed up, after all.

The song ended and "Right Down the Line" began. Let Rafferty's soothing voice and music relax me. "I can't wait for Amadhia to record. Her voice can make everything right, even when it's all wrong."

Martini took my hand in his again. "You changed her life. And Aaron's. No matter what else you did, and you did a lot, you've made the difference in the lives of two people who deserved it."

"Most people deserve to be happy."

He kissed my cheek. "True. And you deserve to be happy, too."

"You're right. You and Charles both deserve to be happy, too. You know, he said that he thought his role in this world was maybe to be the guy who's never happy. I don't believe that. And I don't believe that you're supposed to take that role and be the unhappy person, either."

"There's only one you."

"No. Actually, there's at least two mes. And if there's really a multiverse out there, then there are probably a lot of mes. And a lot of yous."

"But we only know the life we have, baby." As he said this, "Stealin' Time" came on. Chose to take it as a sign. I wasn't going to be here for long, so I should enjoy the time with these people and this world that I had.

"True enough. Len, let's go. Use GPS or whatever and find us a nice restaurant."

"You don't want to pick?" Martini asked.

I smiled up at him. "No. I've never been here before."

CHAPTER 81

ALFRED'S SUIT took a licking and kept on ticking, even though these bullets felt more like rocks hitting me than pebbles.

I reached LaRue in a second, wrenched the gun away from her, tossed it, and tackled her all in another second. "You shape-shifted into something to survive that explosion."

"In a way." She sounded funny and she was glowing from the inside. "I shifted into something that was able to absorb the explosion." She grabbed me and held on. "It's going to destroy me. But I'm going to take you with me."

Better me than everyone else. We rolled and I was able to see that while the speeders were still there, no one else was. Hopefully this meant that Alfred had had them link up and he was getting them the hell away.

"So, you were always a traitor?"

"I was always willing to see the Z'Porrah's side in the evolutionary argument." LaRue wasn't fighting me, she was just holding me so tightly that all I could do was roll.

"They tried here with the dinosaurs and then, when that failed, the Ancients tried a more successful experiment with apes."

"The Ancients sent a bomb to destroy the Z'Porrah's experiments, as you call them, because they felt the Z'Porrah were raising an army."

I'd met the dino-birds, I could believe it. "Were they?"

"Yes, and why shouldn't they use this planet as they needed?"

"Nice to know we're the entire galaxy's dumping ground and experimental alien ant farm. But we're sentient and we're just not willing to put up with that crap anymore." Was doing my best to roll us near to the crater. "So you were always a traitor. Did you kill the others on your ship when you landed here?"

"Yes. I expected us to be shot down, but the weapons I was promised weren't here. They'd been stolen."

Go the Ancients. Presumably that 1950s mission had saved this Earth by removing the power cubes. Hoped they'd made it home okay. "Why aren't you shifting into something else?"

"I can't anymore." She was glowing more brightly. I had one shot.

Slammed my forehead into her face. She hadn't expected it, and her hold released a little. Did an escape move Tito had taught me and scrambled out of her reach.

She was on her knees and one hand. The other hand reached for me. "I will take you to what you call Hell with me."

Did a spinning back kick and sent her flying into the chasm. "Not today." As always, when the skills were exceptional and my execution perfect, there was absolutely no one around to witness. Watched her explode, to be damned sure this world was safe from her, then I ran for the speeders. As I did, a camouflaged plane rose up from a grove of trees in the distance. It was flying low. Jumped on a speeder and headed for it. Didn't activate the shield, though. Was glad I'd taken it off autopilot before, because it was my only hope.

Chuckie was leaning out the door on the side of the plane and I headed for him at a diagonal. Hoped he was braced, because I was only going to get one shot. As I just missed the wing I leaped up and the acceleration kept me moving forward.

The speeder went under the plane and Chuckie just managed to grab my extended arm. I hung there for a moment, each of us holding on, me looking up while he looked down. He tightened his grip, and I saw him say, "I will never let you go."

Then someone pulled him back and me up and I flew into him. He fell back and we knocked into Alfred and Buchanan, who had been holding Chuckie and pulling us up. We all went down, but I was inside the plane.

"Go now!" Charlie shouted. "Go! Go!"

The plane rose sharply and I realized Cox had to be the one flying. Figured Reader was in the cockpit with him, but this was a war zone, and that meant Cox would have taken the stick.

Buchanan got to his feet and struggled to close the door. Went to help him and saw the golden explosion take more of this area, including the three speeders, even the one I'd been riding. We got the door shut just in time, as the plane banked to the right and we rolled into Chuckie and Alfred again.

The shockwaves hit, and the turbulence was horrific. Chuckie threw himself on me and Buchanan did the same with Alfred, to keep us from flipping around. Thankfully the kids were buckled in against the right side of the plane, as was Cantu. Cantu was holding Stripes and Stripes was clearly holding onto Cantu. Cantu might need stiches later, but had to hand it to him for not crying like a baby.

For a long few seconds I thought we were going down. But we stayed airborne. Because in any universe, if I had a flyboy, he was the best flyboy there was.

Then the turbulence stopped, and we were just flying. The four of us got up from the floor of the plane and staggered to seats. Chuckie got me buckled in before he took care of himself.

"Meet Alfred," I said to Chuckie, who was on my left. "In my world, he's my father-in-law. In this world, he's alone."

Chuckie reached over me and shook Alfred's hand. "In this world, you're not alone any longer, sir. Welcome to our family."

Alfred grinned and for the first time he looked like the Alfred I knew. "Thank you, son." Then he patted my knee. "You did well, Double-O-Seven."

"You as well, Alfred-Q. Moneypenny represented well, too. And isn't it always the way? MI Six has to save the C.I.A.'s butt."

"But the C.I.A. rescued Bond at the end," Buchanan said with a laugh. "So we still matter."

Looked around at everyone. "Yes, yes you do."

"I wish I knew where Harlie was," Alfred said, sounding worried and sad.

Remembered the fluffy thing I'd run past when I was leaving the now-destroyed lab. Had a horrible feeling that fluffy thing had been the Poof.

"Ah, I'm sure Harlie's still in Miami," I lied.

Heard a mew, and the Poof appeared on Alfred's lap. "There you are! Thank goodness!" He picked Harlie up and cuddled the Poof. "Where have you been?"

Harlie looked at me and mewled again. Then it opened its mouth and hacked up a blinking cube.

Realized I should have recognized it when I'd managed to take that short look into the Death Ray. "It's a Z'Porrah power cube."

"I haven't seen one of those before," Alfred said.

"I know, that's why I thought they were all gone." Thought about it. "Maybe LaRue brought it with her. She was a Z'Porrah spy." And that would explain why, in my world, she'd been able to open the room under the Lincoln Memorial—she'd brought the key with her. And that meant that, in my world, this was the cube the Mastermind had.

"What do we do with it?" Cantu asked.

Considered my options. Decided that precedent had already been set. Handed it back to Harlie. "You keep this safe.

You'll know when it's needed, and I know no one will be able to make you give it to them."

Harlie purred at me, opened its jaws much wider than its size should allow, engulfed the cube, and swallowed. Then burped discreetly.

"Are you kidding?" Chuckie asked. "You let that, is that an animal, take something that powerful?"

"Yes, it is an animal. And yes, I let that animal eat that alien artifact. Be happy. Your world doesn't need it, trust me. At least not yet. Think of it as insurance." For Alfred and Harlie, as well as everyone else. "Now, where are we heading?"

"I'll check." Buchanan got up and went to the cockpit.

"How are we going to explain this?" Cantu asked.

"That's your job, Esteban," Chuckie said. "I can't speak for James or Malcolm, but I'm going to be officially resigning the moment we land."

Cantu looked stricken. "Why?"

"Why? My family almost died, several times over! It's one thing to be an operative when you're single. It's another to do so when you have family that can be used against you."

"Enemies are always around. And you've always been married with children as an operative." I patted his leg. "When Other Me gets back, just tell her the truth, finally. I guarantee she can handle it. Make this decision as a couple, as a family. Don't make this change without asking her."

"I agree with what your wife says," Cantu said. "Though I'm confused. Why are you talking about another you?"

Leaned back. The movement of the plane was making me sleepy. Chuckie put his arm around me and I leaned onto his shoulder. "That, Esteban, is a long story."

I fell asleep before I could tell it.

CHAPTER 82

LANDING WOKE ME UP, and I could swear that I was somehow hearing Gerry Rafferty's "Home and Dry" even though no music was playing. Not that Cox's landing wasn't textbook, but still, it jarred me awake. But not the kids. They were more used to air travel than I was.

The menfolk had decided on our story, and since it was basically the truth, Cantu told it. Cliff was a raging psychopath, an Agency mole, and the new head of the Corporation, and he had a vendetta against all of Angela Katt's family and former team, a vendetta that had led him to try to nuke Florida to show how much he hated everyone. Fallout had been contained, and no innocents or civilians had been harmed. Go team.

Reader had confirmed the "no one harmed" facts before we were off the plane, and Alfred, Cox, Stripes, and I got out of our special suits and stashed the Special Silly Putty and Alfred's Super Smartphone in my purse before we'd taxied to a gate. Which was good, since we had armed escorts who took us to the Pentagon, not Langley.

Alfred, being introduced as my uncle and a helpless hostage, and I, being the mother of three and also obviously a helpless hostage, were allowed to stay with the children, who were clearly helpless hostages and who would also probably need a ton of therapy the government was going to be paying for. None of us were searched. Being a helpless hostage had its benefits.

After a brief hour in quarantine, Stripes was allowed to be with us, too, especially because I said he was Jamie's therapy pet and she, smart thing that she was, started to sob and throw a tantrum until Therapy Cat Stripes was back with our family. Harlie, of course, was somewhere, either in Alfred's pocket or my purse or wherever the Poofs went when they disappeared.

The younger men, however, Cox included, were being questioned. For days.

Our little family group was treated well, and the time in one small room with two beds really bonded the boys with Alfred and Stripes with Jamie. We were questioned, but not a lot, and when we were we gave vague, incoherent, and ditzy replies. The kids were amazing at fooling the adults questioning us. Hoped Chuckie and Other Me were ready for when they hit the preteen and teenaged years.

A few days into our Not Really Incarceration, we were released into the care of the Israeli Ambassador, who was justifiably upset with America's allowing an insane home-grown terrorist to destroy his embassy and try to kill all his personnel and guests.

Aunt Carla came with him, and she was in her element. Realized I'd never seen her work before, but she was damned impressive. She had everyone at the Pentagon terrified, as near as I could tell. Profuse apologies for our Not Really Detainment were given, which Aunt Carla explained were nowhere near to being good enough. When she mentioned that her law firm would be in touch, I saw four-star generals go pale. Apparently Mom wasn't the only strong, intimidating woman in our family. Go Aunt Carla.

The Israelis had been put up in the Watergate, and we had three floors to ourselves. We enjoyed a nice reunion with Dad, Pierre, and Caroline, all of whom were smart enough to act like they knew who the hell Uncle Alfred was, with help from me and Aunt Carla, of course. Dad even wept with joy to see that his "adopted brother" was miraculously still alive.

The rest of those from the embassy were happy to see us, Leah, Oren, and Jakob especially. Israelis weren't afraid to show emotion, and a lot of tears, hugs, shouts, singing, dancing, and drinking ensued. It had been a long time since I'd had alcohol, but under the circumstances, I indulged. The less said about my arak hangover the better.

Had the fun task of bringing everyone in our extended family group up to speed on what had transpired. Because they were prepared, finding out that Alfred was an exiled alien didn't throw them nearly as much as I'd worried that it could. Aunt Carla was definitely giving it her all to show Alfred that he was a welcomed member of the family and he seemed flattered and more than a little interested. Aunt Carla did resemble Lucinda, in a way. Had no idea if they'd work out, but Alfred surely deserved a shot at happiness and, after this ordeal, I had a whole new appreciation for Aunt Carla.

Was the most worried about Cox, but apparently Alfred's hack of the Navy's databases had been extremely effective, and his being a part of Internal Affairs wasn't even questioned. Why the Navy had gotten involved at all was, but Cox just said I'd come to them for help and he'd felt it was the Navy's duty to assist. The Navy agreed—Cox was given a commendation. Proving he was no dummy, Cantu immediately requested Cox for his team on permanent assignment.

Which was quite a coup of an assignment, since Cantu had more than proved his ability to find the bad guys and lead his team to triumph, at least as far as anyone in authority knew. He was being given a new special position reporting directly to the President. I might even have suggested that he name his new team the Presidential Terrorism Control Unit.

Chuckie, Reader, and Buchanan were convinced to join Cantu's new team, at a nice increase in pay and rank. Chuckie held out the longest, meaning he got the best package and highest rank on the team, though he made sure that Reader and Buchanan were well taken care of. Alfred was also annexed as a special consultant. And so was Dad. Both of them seemed flattered and a little excited. For Alfred, this would give him purpose. And for Dad, I hoped it would give him something besides missing Mom to focus on.

During all of this I waited to get zapped back into my own world. But it didn't happen.

Jamie, Stripes, and I were alone, sitting on the king bed in our family's suite. There was a mirror in the room, but she wasn't looking at it. "You're done with mirrors, Jamie-Kat?"

She shook her head. "These aren't right."

"Ah." So the mirrors in D.C. had indeed been magic. Did my best to swallow the lump in my throat. Charlie, Max, and this Jamie getting to grow up, and with their father and family alive, was more important, wasn't it? "I'm sorry about those bad people destroying things that you treasured."

"Daddy says we'll get new things." She hugged Stripes who purred. He'd put on plenty of weight, all of it in muscle, as near as I could tell. "And you saved our kitty, Mommy, so, like you said, the important things are safe."

Wanted to suggest that we find other mirrors, but that wasn't fair. I couldn't put myself before Jamie, not even if it was a Jamie I hadn't technically given birth to. She needed to keep on looking at this world, not at all the other worlds.

Cleared my throat. "Daddy says we're going to be able to go home to Australia very soon."

Jamie looked at me, surprised. "But you said the bad people blew up our house."

"Well, they did. The house here, in Washington. Just like they did to the nice Israelis' embassy. But our house in Australia is fine—Leah checked. More than once."

She brightened up. "Oh. Then everything's okay."

Would have asked her what she meant, but Chuckie came in to tell us that, yes, we were going to be heading to Australia tomorrow. "Just having the plane triple-checked," he told me as he picked up Jamie and Stripes both. "I don't want to trust that Goodman didn't tamper with it."

"Sounds good. How are we going to handle Stripes?"

He grinned. "It's amazing how grateful the government is that we contained Goodman and that we aren't suing on behalf of the children . . . yet. Carla's found a loophole—as long as Stripes has his shots here, which the Pentagon already gave him when they first detained us, he's Jamie's assistance animal, and we'll be allowed to quarantine him in our home."

"Really?"

"Yeah. She contacted Doctor Marling and he's sent the medical paperwork necessary. As you said, we're rich. It's about time I used that to ensure that our family can have a pet." He stroked Stripes' head. "Especially one as brave as our big guy, here."

Stripes purred. He felt Chuckie was A-okay. Well, not as A-okay as me, Jamie, Charlie, Max, Cox, or Alfred, but right after.

"How is it going to work, you reporting to Esteban's new unit but us living in Australia?"

"Supersonic jets are amazing, and we now have a pilot who might be even better than James, and is certainly licensed to fly said supersonics. Bill's going to be staying with us, at least for a while. Esteban will have others on his team. We're going to handle one side of the world, the D.C. team will handle the other. Video conferencing should manage the rest."

"Who am I to argue?"

Chuckie put Jamie down. "You and Stripes go pester your brothers for a little bit, okay?"

She smiled up at him. "Okay, Daddy." She trotted out, lugging Stripes, who winked at me over her shoulder.

Chuckie stared after her. "I never thought we'd ever see this day. When she was . . . normal."

"It just took her realizing that she needed to help her own family more than everyone else's."

"Yeah. How are you doing, really?" Chuckie sat on the bed next to me. "I know we both expected you to . . . be home by now."

"Maybe this is where I'm supposed to be." I didn't want to believe that, not really. But if Jamie couldn't connect to my universe anymore, there might not be a choice.

He took my hand in his. "I know this is . . . hard. For both of us. I just want you to know that, if you can't go back, we'll figure it out. Even . . . even if it means you end up divorcing me. I've loved you all my life, but in all that life, I've only wanted you to be happy."

Looked up at him. "You really are the greatest guy, you know that?"

"Yeah. That and three-fifty will buy me a cup of coffee I get to drink alone."

"You said that to me before, in my world. When I was getting ready to marry Jeff. But this decision involves more than me. It will affect you, the kids, the family, and then some."

"I know. But . . ." He stood up. "You're not my wife. I know that, you know that. Hell, the entire family, including our new extended members, knows that. Esteban is being willfully dense about what you did, in part because he's smart enough to know that if he tries to say you or Alfred are, ah, exceptional you two will just disappear."

Thought about living in the tunnel system with Alfred. I never wanted to have to live there and I never wanted him to have to go back to living there, either.

"Look, I'm not saying that I don't want to go home. Jamie just . . . Jamie doesn't think she can get me back. So, if that's true, we need to know what we're going to do."

"I don't know, Kitty. I just don't know."

"Right before you pulled me onto the plane said you'd never let me go. Which me were you talking about?"

"Both of you. I won't let anything hurt you, if I can stop it." He rubbed the back of his neck. "But I miss my wife. So much. More because you're right here, because you're not really her. So close, and yet so very far. You know?"

"I know." Stood up and hugged him. "Then we'll worry

about it in Australia. I've never been. So I guess you're going to have to brief me."

He hugged me back. "I will. You'll love it. It's your kind of place."

"Guess I'll find out."

CHAPTER 83

TURNED OUT Cantu was coming with us to Australia, ostensibly to ensure that our setup would work and that he could have half his team across the world.

At first I thought it was because he didn't trust us, or wanted to get me onto the team as well or something. Then I realized it was because Caroline had taken vacation time, with Senator McMillan's blessing, so that she could come with us to recover from the "fun" few days we'd had. It was clear Cantu was smitten with her—not that I could blame him. But what shocked me was that Caroline seemed receptive. Well, he was handsome, and brave, and it couldn't hurt to have my BFF keeping an eye on Chuckie's boss.

Cox handled the piloting and Reader copiloted. Would have worried that Reader felt slighted, but he and Cox were getting along great. Wasn't sure if it was the start of a bromance or a romance, but either way, they were having fun hanging out together.

The flight was a long one, and I wasn't used to long flights any more. Though the Reynolds Family Jet was definitely the way to go. It put the A-C's jets to shame in the comfort and sleekness departments.

Slept some, played with the kids, played cards with Dad, Aunt Carla, and Alfred, ensured Stripes and Harlie were okay, and let Pierre fuss over all of us. Wondered if this was going to be my life now. If I could stop missing Jeff, my Jamie, Mom, and everyone else, it would be great here. But I couldn't.

Stryker Dane was waiting for us at the airport. At least, Chuckie insisted it was Stryker, and he greeted me like we'd known each other forever, so I accepted that this well-groomed, well-dressed, fit, confident guy was really the Stryker Dane I knew.

"You're back in time for the concert after all," he said as we piled into two stretch limos. "I didn't get rid of the tickets, just in case."

"Concert?"

"Amadhia," Chuckie said quickly. "Your favorite female recording artist."

Managed not to say that I'd never heard of her. "Oh, great! When is it?"

"Ah, tomorrow night. All ages. Whole family was planning to go to celebrate my being here on book tour. Well," Stryker looked around, "the whole family you went to the States with. The new additions may have to pass on the event."

"Kitty hit her head," Chuckie explained to Stryker. "She's having some memory issues."

"Oh, I'm sorry, kiddo." Stryker hugged me and kissed my forehead. "Don't worry, you'll remember her when you hear her. Voice of an angel, that's what you always say."

Stryker took meeting Uncle Alfred in stride, shared that it was about damn time we'd gotten the kids a pet, and generally acted exactly like you want the friend picking you up from the airport to act. Seriously had trouble associating this person with the Eddy Simms I knew.

The Reynolds home was fantastic. If the home in Colonial Village had been large and lovely, their home in Darling Point proved that things were indeed better Down Under. Managed not to say I was impressed with the house, grounds, and furnishings because I knew without asking that Other Me had chosen them.

We had almost no luggage, seeing as everything the family owned in the States had been blown up, cars included, and we hadn't overshopped during the few days of freedom the government had given us. Talk about starting over. There. Here, the place was furnished and closets filled as if no one had ever left.

Thankfully, Pierre showed everyone to their guest rooms, of which this house had plenty, while the kids scampered to their rooms. I followed the kids. Charlie and Max's room was similar to the one they'd had in America—still loaded with science, sports, and Lego stuff.

Jamie's room was almost an exact replica of her room in America. Complete with a three-way mirror. She raced to it and plopped right down in front of it, Stripes in her lap. My heart sank. She'd been so normal, as Chuckie had said. And now, this again.

But I went over to her, sat down behind her, and put her and the cat into my lap. "What do you see?" I asked softly.

She heaved a sigh of relief. "Everything." She smiled at me in the mirror. "It's going to be okay, Mommy. I promise."

I hugged her. "I know. But . . . you need to promise me something else."

"What?"

"You need to not spend all your time in front of these mirrors. I know that you saved everyone by bringing me here and sending your Other Mommy to my world. But your family needs you. Daddy needs to see his little girl smile at him. Your brothers need to be able to tease their little sister, and you need to be able to drive them crazy. For some kids, they can never have those things—it's not their choice, it's just how their brains are wired. But your brain isn't wired like that."

She shook her head. "But the other mes need me."

"I know they do. But you know what?"

"What?"

"You don't have to do it all. And you shouldn't do it all. If you can do it, then the others can do it, too. Maybe, one hour a week, you look in your mirrors. Make sure everyone's okay. But that's all."

"But what if they need me when I'm not looking?"

Hugged her again. "Baby, your family needs you all the time. They need you looking at *them*. Papa Sol needs you to keep him from missing Nana Angela so badly. Uncle Alfred needs you to remind him that in another world, you're his granddaughter. Aunt Carla needs you to remind everyone why we love her. And your Other Mommy needs you, so much, to be the little girl she gets to dote on. I know she wants to, and I know she hasn't been able to. Doesn't she deserve that?"

Jamie nodded. "But what if something happens when I'm not watching?"

"Then I'll handle it. Somehow. Just like I did here. Okay?"

"You promise?" She was looking at me in the mirror still.

Looked right back. "I promise."

"What if the only way I can send you back is if I look in the mirrors all the time?"

The hard question. The question I knew was coming as soon as I saw the mirrors, if I was honest with myself.

Took a deep breath and sent an apology to the cosmos. "Then I stay here. You're more important—you having a good life, as normal a life as someone as smart and wonderful as you are can have, is the most important thing to me. In every universe, you're my daughter, and in every universe I love you and want only the best for you. And if that means I can't go home to my universe, but you'll have a better life because of it? Then I'll stay here. Because that's what mothers who love their children do—they sacrifice for those children. And one day, when you have children of your own, you'll know exactly why I'm saying this."

Jamie smiled. "Then it will all be okay, Mommy."

She put Stripes down, got up, kissed me, picked Stripes up, and trotted out of the room.

"Okay," I said to myself in the mirror. Stared at myself for a while. And then I could see her. Not me, not Jamie—

Naomi. Both in front of me and somehow also in the reflection of every one of the multiverse images. As I'd known her, not as a superconsciousness, but as the beautiful Dazzler with ebony skin, kind eyes, and a smile that reminded me of Jeff's and Alfred's.

"We miss you," I said softly to the images in the mirror. "I know you can't come back. I wish you could. But thank you for watching over Jamie and Chuckie wherever and everywhere they are."

She smiled at me and blew me a kiss. Same smile, same kiss, repeated at the same time all over the multiverse. Then the mirrors went back to normal, and all I saw was me.

It wasn't an answer, but I felt a little better. No matter what, no matter where, Naomi was watching and doing what she could to protect those she loved. I got up and followed Jamie out of the room.

Met Chuckie in the hall. "Is Jamie—"

"We talked. She's going to look in her mirrors one hour a week. We'll want to police that. But she seemed to accept it."

"Did she . . . say if you could go home?"

I could tell him, tell him what I'd told her, tell him who I'd seen and what it might mean. But why?

"She isn't sure." Leaned up and kissed his cheek. "It'll be fine. One way or the other."

CHAPTER 84

WE'D BEEN IN AUSTRALIA for a good week, and I was still *in* Australia. Of course, I had no idea where in the world my Cosmic Alternate actually was, nor did I have any idea if we had to be in the exact same place at the exact same time in order to switch back. Refused to consider the idea that she or my Jamie were dead, and didn't allow Martini to bring it up, either.

On the plus side, we'd had a nice time seeing all the sights, including the Taronga Zoo, which Jamie loved. Martini and I were doing fine with the public displays of walking around holding hands, with our arms around each other, or nuzzling. Sure, the nuzzling was more about passing along information than smooching, but the average person on the street was fooled.

We'd also had a lot of political mover and shaker meetings, as Margie had promised. They were okay. The hardest part was pretending I didn't know people I'd been friends, frenemies, or enemies with for years. But I smiled and nodded and it seemed to do the trick.

I'd also spent a lot of time with my parents, Mom in particular. "When you get back, I want you to give your father a message," she said when it was just her and me alone. "Tell him that I love him throughout the multiverse, but if

I'm gone, he needs to find someone else who makes him happy."

"I'll try, Mom, but I don't know if he'll listen."

Mom stroked my cheek. "He will. Now."

"Do you think I'm going to go back or stay here?"

"Honestly? I don't know, kitten." She pulled me to her and hugged me tight. "But I love you in all the multiverse, too. You are my precious one and I'm proud of you every single moment of every single day. Don't ever forget that, for the rest of your life, whether you're here or there."

We hugged for what seemed like a long time. But it wasn't nearly long enough.

I'd also written out what had gone on, as much as I could, in the hopes that it would help my CA. And in the additional hopes that my CA would see them because we'd be back in our own worlds someday soon. Wrote notes for Jamie and Martini and Charles as well. And for Mom and Dad. And I spent a lot of time with Gershom. Had no idea what happened to a Poof when the person who named it disappeared. Maybe it would just be attached to my CA. Hoped that whatever happened, the Poof would be okay.

The night for Aaron and Amadhia's concert finally arrived. They'd been practicing all week and this was the last day we were going to be in Australia; Martini was needed back in the States, in part so it didn't seem like the VP was spending all his time hanging out and having fun.

It seemed mighty fast to get a venue and all the other things necessary to a live show set up and going in a week, but apparently when the PM wanted a thing done, that thing happened. At least if it was a concert to celebrate what great pals the U.S. and Australia were while raising money for charity at the same time. And it wasn't the largest venue, so that might have had something to do with the speedy setup.

The Operations Team had my clothes ready for me—jeans, Converse, an Aerosmith hoodie, and an Amadhia shirt, hot off whatever presses were used to make concert T-shirts. Charles had had shirts made with just Amadhia, just Aaron, and both

of them. "Thanks for the clothing choices and all your help," I
said to the hamper.

Jamie was being allowed to come along, since all her
babysitters were going to the concert, too. The humans who
weren't Centaurion agents were dressed casually. Everyone
else, Martini in particular, were in their suits.

We headed to the Big Top Auditorium. Amadhia and
Aaron were already there—I'd already told both of them to
break a leg hours earlier.

Our entourage made up a good portion of the attendees,
but much of the political hoi polloi were in attendance as
well, since this was a benefit concert to support those injured
during or at cricket matches—the way we'd turned the whole
incident at the stadium into a positive joke.

There were the usual opening speeches any kind of fund-
raiser seems required to have, and then the music started.
They opened with the Australian national anthem, and then
the Star Spangled Banner.

"Want to dance?" Martini asked me. "When the real music starts, I mean?"

"Sure." Hugged Jamie and gave her to Mom, then gave
my purse to Dad. "We're going to get up a little closer."

Mom laughed. "I'm so shocked."

Martini took my hand and as we got up nearer to the stage,
Amadhia spoke. "I want to dedicate this to Kitty, for making
our dreams come true." I heard the first notes and realized
this was the first song I'd ever heard the Amadhia in this
world singing—"Heartbreak Beat."

Couldn't help it—I squealed. Martini laughed and kissed
my cheek. "Enjoy this. You more than earned it."

Listened to her sing the lyrics, and really heard them, as I
danced along next to Martini. Couldn't help myself—I sang
along, too. Well, that's what you did at concerts.

Started to twirl with the chorus, and as I did, I felt something.

As if I was floating away.

CHAPTER 85

THE KIDS, Chuckie, Stryker, Reader, Cox, and I were
going to the Amadhia concert. Pierre had been supposed
to go, but he felt he'd had more than enough excitement recently, and he gave his ticket to Cox.

The night before I'd taken the time to write out what had
gone on, so Other Me would have a hope of understanding
what had happened and who the new people in her life were.
I'd also written notes to everyone here. This wasn't something I normally did, but in case I did get zapped back, I
wanted them to know how I felt about them.

Hugged everyone goodbye, even Cantu. Didn't want to
leave the house or the people for some reason. But the kids
were excited about the concert and, besides, I'd been thinking I'd be zapped home for so many days now that this was
probably just a reaction to the disappointment of still being
here. Even though part of me wasn't disappointed to still be
here.

I'd slept with him cuddled next to me the night before, but
I cuddled Stripes again for a good long while. "You'll always
be my cat," I whispered to him. "Whether we're together for
years more or just a day or two. But no matter what or where
I am, I need you to take care of Jamie, okay? I know you're
the cat for the job." Stripes purred at me. He wasn't worried.

"Mommy, we need to go," Jamie said as I finally put the cat down. "We can't be late."

I was in jeans, Converse, an Aerosmith hoodie, and an Amadhia T-shirt because, well, why not? Other Me certainly had a lot of them to choose from.

We were heading to someplace called the Big Top Auditorium, which had the kids excited. Per Stryker, it was a smaller venue, great for hearing and seeing a favorite artist up close. Amadhia rarely played venues this small anymore, so we were lucky to see her here and luckier to have tickets to the show.

Chuckie drove us in the family's big SUV. We went in with the rest of the excited crowd. It was an all-standing setup but we lucked out and got into an area near the front.

There were the usual delays, but finally Amadhia hit the stage, singing a song I didn't recognize but the crowd did, if their screams were any indication. After her first number was met with thunderous applause, she chatted up the crowd. She was sweet and gracious, looked almost elfin, and the crowd loved her.

Jamie tugged at my hand and I bent down. "I love you, Mommy. I'll take good care of Stripes, I promise. And everybody else, too."

"What?" As I said this I was surprised to recognize the opening beats of the next song—a cover of the Psychedelic Furs' "Heartbreak Beat."

"This is the right music now." Jamie hugged me. "You should dance with Mommy, Daddy," she said to Chuckie seriously but with great urgency.

Chuckie laughed. "If you insist, Jamie-Kat."

Stryker picked her up and Reader held Charlie's hand while Cox took Max's. "Go have a little fun, ma'am," Cox said, as he took my purse. "We'll hold down the fort."

"I'm not going more than a few feet away." But I did love this song, and I bobbed to the beat.

We moved off a little closer to the stage and as the chorus started I sang along with Amadhia. I mean, that's what you did at a concert, right?

Allowed myself to just enjoy the music. Let go of Chuckie's hand and started to twirl with the music.

And as I did, the song got louder, as if Amadhia was singing harmony with herself. And as if there was another me singing along too.

The right music. I reached out to touch Chuckie, but my hand went through him. And I floated away, the music still playing.

CHAPTER 86

I SPUN, as Amadhia sang. And Chuckie faded away.

While Amadhia sang, Martini floated away from me or I floated away from him. I wasn't sure which.

Wanted to tell them all I loved them and would miss them, but I couldn't. I wasn't sure where I was going, but I didn't want to forget where I'd been.

If I was going home, that was wonderful. But what if I didn't remember everyone? What if they didn't remember me?

I'll never see Stripes again. Or Cox. Or Charlie and Max.

I'll never see Mom again.

Should I try to stay? They needed me. I'd helped. I'd saved them, saved the world.

Should I try to go back? I could make it work. Maybe. But if I stayed, I'd never see Charlie or Max again.

But if I stayed, I'd never see Jeff again. Or the flyboys. Or

Mom. And all the rest of my friends and family. It was a heartbreak beat I was on. Lose one life, gain another. I couldn't have both.

I can't have both. Even if I want both. I have to choose. The heartbreak beat goes on.

Take care of them for me, like I took care of them for you.

Remember them for me, and I'll remember you for them.

It didn't just feel like love.

It was love. It still is.

Always remember.

Never forget.

CHAPTER 87

THE FEELING OF FLOATING stopped and I blinked. The song was over. Looked around. I was still here, still in the Big Top. I didn't know whether to laugh, cry, feel relieved, or feel cheated.

"Hey, I almost lost you there." A man took my hand in his. I knew the sound of his voice and the feel of his hand, and I spun toward him.

Charles smiled at me. "Ready to keep on dancing or do you want to go back with the others and dance with the kids?"

"Others? Kids?" Looked around. There were no gorgeous people in Armani suits in evidence, no politicians. It just looked like a typical casual Australian crowd.

"Kitty?" He looked worried. "Are you okay?"

"I might be. Have I been . . . odd . . . over the past couple of weeks?"

"Odder than you normally were? No."

"Huh. So you didn't notice anything off about me?"

He pulled me closer. "Are you okay? I'm not sure what you're trying to get me to say, especially not in a crowd. Are you trying to give me some kind of danger hint?"

"What do you do for a living?"

He sighed. "You know what I do."

"No, I don't. Well, I didn't. I do now. I'm pretty sure."

He stared at me. "How many weddings did we have?"

"Three. One in Vegas, one in France, and one in Australia. 'Cause someone wanted to make extra sure I wasn't going to change my mind."

"How long were you in labor with Max?"

"Two hours. He almost got delivered in the back of Peter's car."

He moved me and studied my wedding ring. Then he looked back at me and smiled slowly. "If I kiss you, really kiss you, what are you going to do?"

"Try me and find out."

He did. We made out while Amadhia sang her next song, whatever it was.

Charles ended our kiss slowly. "I thought I'd lost you forever."

"Me too. Are the kids here?"

"They are. And we have a lot to tell you about. But first off, we have several new residents and a cat."

"We got a cat?"

"Yeah, he's named Stripes. Jamie loves him."

"She does?"

"She does. You fixed her."

"You mean my Cosmic Alternate did."

"As far as we're all concerned now, you did it. And, I'll tell you what else you did while you were on vacation. Oh, and I work for the C.I.A. And I love you more than I can ever tell you, but I'm going to try to give you a good idea as soon as this concert's over and we're home in bed."

I laughed as we headed toward where I could see our family, arms around each other. "It *is* you. Oh, and I have news, too."

"Yeah? What?"

"We're pregnant. Number four is going to arrive nine months from a couple weeks ago, which was the last time we did the deed, right before all the cosmos broke loose."

"Isn't it too early to tell?"

"Not where I was."

"I'm going to not be jealous and just wait for the story."

"See? You're still the smartest man in every room."

Charles laughed and kissed me again as we reached the others. Stryker, my Stryker, was there, along with my James. And a cute young guy I'd never seen before who looked like he was in the military.

The kids squirmed out of the men's arms and ran to me and I held them for what definitely wasn't a long enough time. "I missed you all so much," I murmured.

"We missed you, too, Mommy," Charlie said.

"I missed you more," Max claimed.

"I'm sorry it took so long to bring you home, Mommy," Jamie said, sounding guilty.

Hugged them all more tightly. "It's all okay, and it all worked out, and we're together again and we will never, ever be apart."

Heard a soft mewling and all of a sudden, a cute ball of fluff was sitting on Jamie's head. "Gershom! You came with me!" The Poof purred, hopped onto my shoulder, nuzzled me, then disappeared. But it was here, with me. Meaning everything that had happened was all real and I'd have something with me to remind me of the world I'd gotten to visit.

Stood up and the young military guy gave me a funny smile. "Ma'am, my name is William Cox, but you can call me Bill. Or, if you feel like it, Lunatic Lad. Or Moneypenny. Though I prefer Bill."

"There's a story behind that, isn't there?"

He grinned. "There is. And we all can't wait to tell it to you."

CHAPTER 88

BLINKED. Thought I'd spun away from Chuckie but I was still here, in the Big Top Auditorium in Australia. Amadhia was still on stage. "Heartbreak Beat" had finished and she was doing another cover, this time with a dude singing harmony. Recognized it. Panic! At The Disco's "New Perspective." Liked the song. They did a fine cover of it.

Felt let down and kind of bittersweet. Thought I'd been going home, but apparently not. So, I'd be here a while longer. Okay. I could handle that. Sorta.

A man grabbed my hand. "Almost lost you." I knew the feel of his hand, and I knew his voice.

Spun to see Jeff standing there. "Um, am I awake?"

"I think so, yeah." His brow wrinkled. "Are you okay?"

"Pretty sure I am now." Jumped into his arms and kissed him.

"Whoa, whoa!" Jeff moved me away and put me down gently, without really kissing me back.

"Are you okay?" Put my hand onto his chest. Yep, he had two hearts. This was my Jeff. "Did you happen to, ah, miss me? At all? Over the past, oh, couple of weeks?" Hoped that was why he'd shoved me away, because he still thought I was Other Me. Tried to send an emotional clue, but he'd have his blocks up in a crowd this size, and besides, my emotions were extremely jumbled right now.

Jeff was studying me and I could tell he was concentrating. He looked closely at my wedding ring, then looked back at me and smiled slowly. "You're not pregnant."

"Nope. At least as far as I know."

He pulled me up into his arms and kissed me, for real this time. As I wrapped my legs around his waist, it felt like the first time, only different—better, because I hadn't been sure if I'd ever feel his kiss again. His lips were soft and demanding, his tongue owned mine, and, as he wrapped me up in his arms, I allowed myself to accept that this was real and that I was really home.

We made out through the entire song. And then the next couple as well. It was all I could do not to grind against him or rip his clothes off. But we were in a big crowd, so I managed to control myself. Barely.

Jeff ended our fantastic kiss slowly. "I missed you, baby. But just so you know, you saved the day and everything's fixed."

"You mean Other Me did that."

"I do. But as far as most of the world is concerned, it was all you."

What he'd said registered. "Was she pregnant?"

"Yes. It'll be their fourth."

"Yeah, I know. You know, if we hurried up, we could, um, catch up and maybe, you know, coordinate."

Jeff laughed. "I'm willing to try as much as possible, just to make you happy."

"As it should be. Now, I'd like to see our daughter and my mother. And then I want to see everyone else, especially the flyboys. And your dad."

"Oh? Why?"

"I have a story they're going to appreciate. Oh, and I need to get a really good three-way mirror set."

"Why?"

"I made a promise."

"To whom?"

"Mommy!" Saw Jamie in Mom's arms. But that was only for a second. She was out of Mom's arms and in mine in less than a moment. Hyperspeed, it was the greatest.

There were plenty of things I needed to tell everyone, like what had happened in the other world, and who our world's Mastermind really was. But for right now, the most important thing in the multiverse was to be with my family and friends, and in the one place in the multiverse I fit perfectly. In Jeff's arms.

Available May 2015,
the eleventh novel in the *Alien* series
from Gini Koch:

ALIEN SEPARATION

Read on for a sneak preview

REVENGE IS A DISH best served cold.

Yeah, I have no idea what that means, either. But it's what they say when you're ready to go after someone who's done their best to destroy you. I think it's supposed to mean that you should be levelheaded and calm while plotting your enemy's ultimate, untimely, and ugly demise.

Sound plan. Pity that I work better angry. But then again, I'm pretty angry. So we should be good here.

Of course, that's probably being far too optimistic.

Not sure what was more shocking—discovering that there's a multiverse out there and I'm representing in most of the zillion and one universes, or discovering the identity of the Mastermind.

Visiting another universe was kind of cool. Nice to see how the other half was living with basically no aliens on the planet. Not as well in some ways, just dandy in others. It was a "fun" vacation, if we define fun to mean spending a couple weeks unsure if I'd ever get home again or if I was going to spend the rest of my life in Oz, both literally and figuratively.

Coming home was better—always nice to have that "took a trip but boy it's great to sleep in my own bed and have great sex with my alien mega-sexy husband again" feeling.

But while I got to save the day for the other world, back

in mine, I'm not so sure how to manage it. The term "it's complicated" has never been more apt. And, as in the other world, a frontal attack is probably not the right plan.

A battle will be coming, though, one way or the other. Because it's time to take the bull by the horns and ram those horns right into the Mastermind's personal tenders. So to speak.

But at least I won't be fighting this battle with a small commando force. For this battle, I'm going to ensure I have an army. And, to quote one of my favorite 80s glam rockers, it's time to make the Mastermind Stand and Deliver. For I am a Woman of the Multiverse and I will not allow evil to continue its run unchecked.

Yeah, fine, fine. Let's go with what's been working all this time. Yo, Mastermind—just thought you should know that Megalomaniac Girl is back and she's madder and badder than ever. So watch your step, 'cause I'm coming for you.

*   *   *

Early morning and I are not best buds. I'm not a girl who sees any virtue in watching the sun rise. However, it was the morning after I'd come back from an unintended vacation, and my husband and I had spent the night wide awake and extremely active in the best sense of the words.

Now we were lying next to each other, relaxing in the afterglow of a night very well spent.

"I know who the Mastermind is." As post-coitus comments went, this was probably not going to go down as the World's Most Romantic Statement.

"Yeah?" Jeff rolled onto his side to face me, leaning on his hand. His other hand stroked my body. It was great to feel his hand on my skin—I'd spent the last couple of weeks wondering if that would ever happen again.

We had music on, and as Weezer's "My Best Friend" hit

our airwaves, I shifted likewise so we were face to face and I could also stroke Jeff's chest and such. And I could look at him. Considering I hadn't been sure I'd ever see his face again, it was nice to be here, like normal, as if nothing much had gone on.

We were in Sydney Base, and because of that, the standard nightlight glow was in the room, meaning we *could* see each other. Aliens, of which Jeff was definitely one, were different from humans in many ways, not all of them physical. As near as I could tell, no A-Cs liked to sleep in the extreme dark. I'd never asked why—and as I'd learned during my foray out of this world, I probably needed to be a bit more curious about many things.

However, since we'd moved into the American Centaurion Embassy in Washington, D.C., I'd gotten used to sleeping in the actual dark again. But this was kind of a nice retro moment. My first night discovering aliens were on the planet I'd spent in a room very like this one, half of it with Jeff. The best half.

I was willing to stay in bed with Jeff forever but, somewhat because I'd had a two week "vacation" in another universe, duty was calling in a loud and insistent manner. Also, Mr. Clock shared that it was six in the morning, and that meant that our daughter was going to be up in an hour, give or take.

"Yeah. Only . . . I don't know if I can tell you."

"Because you're worried I'll give away that I know because I can't lie, any more than the rest of the A-Cs can, right?"

"Right. You sound like you had this conversation already."

"I did. With you, in that sense."

"Oh. Other Me figured it out?" I'd switched universes with another version of me. Yeah, my life was just that kind of exciting. Hers was, too, now, come to think of it. Oh well, she was me. She'd roll with the punches.

"Pretty much."

"How? I mean, I realize I'm great at looking at accepted truths and quickly spotting the flaws and all that, but she couldn't have had a lot to go on."

"Oh, she didn't. But she had the one key piece of information we've never had. The same thing to go on I figure you discovered while you were in her universe—her Chuck hates the Mastermind's guts, with good reason."

Other Me was married to my best guy friend since high school, Charles Reynolds. Well, her universe's Charles Reynolds, at any rate. It had been instructive and interesting to see how my life might have been different. Hoped she'd enjoyed seeing how the other universe lived.

"Wow, yeah. So, you know who it is?"

Jeff nodded as "Bad Blood" by Ministry came on. "Almost the worst person it could be."

"Got that right. So, does Chuckie know?"

"No." Jeff sighed. "We've managed to keep it from him. For the all of about a week and a half that we've known. And only because we were frankly so busy and focused on fixing things with the Australian government and getting you and your Cosmic Alternate to switch back."

"Did Malcolm already know?" Malcolm Buchanan had Dr. Strange powers. At least as far as I was concerned. If he didn't want you to see him, you didn't see him. If he said it was so, it was probably so. Luckily for me, my mother had assigned him to be my bodyguard when we first got to D.C. She'd assigned the Buchanan in the other universe onto Other Me a lot sooner. Apparently things were dicey wherever I was. Go me.

"Yeah. Buchanan's known for what sounds like three years. But he has no actual proof. None of us here do."

"We had no proof, either, other than the fact that Cliff Goodman was that universe's Charles' lifelong enemy. And the fact that he tried to kill Other Me, their kids, Charles, James and Malcolm. He'd already . . ." Murdered my mother in that world. Along with the rest of her and Buchanan's teams, which included other people I knew and loved in this world.

"I know," Jeff said gently. "We figured it all out. Well, most of it. I'm sure we're both missing parts of the whole nightmare." He grinned. "And I know I don't have the full story of how you kicked butt and saved the day."

"You just assume I did that?" I hadn't really had time to brief everyone on what had happened, in part because Chuckie was here with the group that had come to fix things with Australia and I hadn't wanted to let anything slip.

Jeff kissed me, his typical awesome kiss. "Yeah, that's my default assumption," he said after his lips and tongue had owned mine for a good, long time, emphasis on good. "That you're going to do what has to be done, better than anyone else ever could."

"I could get used to this form of hero worship."

He laughed. "There's nothing wrong with accurate hero worship, baby."

Snuggled my face in between his awesome pecs and rubbed against his chest hair as the Veronicas sang "I Could Get Used To This". "Works for me. After all, I hero worship your bedroom and leadership skills, so we're even."

Jeff chuckled. "Always nice to be appreciated."

"Back atcha. So, what do we do? I don't know how to tell Chuckie that the guy he thinks is his best friend is the reason his wife is dead. He's normally laid back and able to roll with whatever's thrown at him, but I'm not willing to bet he'll be able to deal rationally under the circumstances."

Naomi Gower-Reynolds wasn't really dead in the technical, universal sense. She'd taken so much pure Surcenthumain—what we called the Superpowers Drug—in order to save Jamie and Chuckie from being destroyed by the Mastermind that she'd become something far more than human or alien. She'd become a superconsciousness. And she was never allowed to come back to Earth. Our Earth. However, she'd found a way around that rule by covering the protection of her beloved goddaughter and husband in every other universe they existed in. And I was the only one who knew this. Well, me, and my daughter Jamie. Daughters Jamie, I guess.

There was a multiverse out there, and I discovered that I'd seen it before. In the past, when I'd seen the Universe Wheel, I'd never remembered it when I'd woken up or come back to life or whatever. But now, after this trip, I remembered it all. And I was pretty sure I did because of Naomi's influence.

I existed in a large number of the universes out there, and in every one I was in, Jamie was there as well. Same birthdate for every Jamie throughout the multiverse, though her father was usually Chuckie, or James Reader. This was the only universe where Jeff was on Earth, so it was the only one with him as her father.

Jamie had learned how to communicate with her other selves. I wasn't sure if it was because my Jamie housed a superconsciousness in her mind now, since ACE had taken up residence there, or if she was just that highly talented. Probably both.

"None of us have a plan for that yet," Jeff admitted. "It needs to be broken to him gently, if that's at all possible."

"There's a slight possibility that I'm wrong about Cliff being the Mastermind in this universe. Very slight."

Jeff shook his head. "No, you're not. Too many pieces fit."

"Yeah, they fit to me, too. I don't know what to do. Other than get a three-way mirror pronto."

The Jamie I'd spent time with in the other universe was also special—she could see every other Jamie in all the other universes. But she needed help to do so—a large three-way mirror set up as if it was in a department store's dressing room. I was pretty sure that she didn't need a magic mirror, but I wasn't completely confident—in my experience it didn't pay to assume.

"Yeah, you told me that when you, ah, came back. I ordered a set. Should be at the Embassy when we get home. But unless those mirrors are going to give us proof that Cliff's the Mastermind, or show us how to break the news to Chuck safely, I don't think they're what we need the most."

"Yeah. What we really need to know is if Cliff and LaRue have a death ray."

"Excuse me?"

Before I could explain what I was talking about, "Trouble" by Pink came on and we were interrupted by a voice on the intercom. "I'm sorry to wake you, Vice President and Ambassador Martini," a woman I'd never heard before who had an Australian accent said. "But we have an incoming call from a restricted number."

"Did the caller give a name, Melissa?" Jeff asked, as he sat up and turned the music off.

"No, Mister Vice President, he did not." Apparently Melissa was as big on the titles as Walter and William Ward were. Walter ran Embassy Security, and since Gladys Gower's death, his older brother William had taken over as Head of Security out of the Dulce Science Center.

"Why are we taking this call then?" I asked as I sat up as well. This was far too reminiscent of the start of Operation Confusion for my liking.

"Because the caller said it was a matter of life or death, Ambassador."

Gini Koch lives in Hell's Orientation Area (aka Phoenix, Arizona), works her butt off (sadly, not literally) by day, and writes by night with the rest of the beautiful people. She lives with her awesome husband, three dogs (aka The Canine Death Squad), and two cats (aka The Killer Kitties). She has one very wonderful and spoiled daughter, who will still tell you she's not as spoiled as the pets (and she'd be right).

When she's not writing, Gini spends her time cracking wise, staring at pictures of good looking leading men for "inspiration," teaching her pets to "bring it," and driving her husband insane asking, "Have I told you about this story idea yet?" She listens to every kind of music 24/7 (from Lifehouse to Pitbull and everything in between, particularly Aerosmith) and is a proud comics geek-girl willing to discuss at any time why Wolverine is the best superhero ever (even if Deadpool does get all the best lines).

You can reach Gini via her website (www.ginikoch.com), email (gini@ginikoch.com), Twitter (@GiniKoch), Facebook (facebook.com/Gini.Koch), Facebook Fan Page: Hairspray and Rock 'n' Roll (facebook.com/GiniKochAuthor), or her Official Fan Site, the Alien Collective Virtual HQ (http://aliencollectivehq.com/).